DAVE vs.
THE
MONSTERS
EMERGENCE

JOHN BIRMINGHAM

DAVE vs.
THE
MONSTERS
EMERGENCE

TITAN BOOKS

Dave vs. the Monsters: Emergence
Print edition ISBN: 9781781166215
E-book edition ISBN: 9781781166222

Published by Titan Books
A division of Titan Publishing Group Ltd
144 Southwark Street, London SE1 0UP

First edition: April 2015
2 4 6 8 10 9 7 5 3 1

A CIP catalogue record for this title is available
from the British Library.

Printed and bound in Great Britain by CPI Group Ltd

For SF Murphy, who is forever dragging me out of the fire.

01

A helicopter is no place for a hangover. Hooper closed his eyes and breathed carefully as the engine spooled up. His gorge rose at the toxic mix of jet fuel, stale sweat, and bile at the back of his throat. The thudding of the rotors punched deep into his chest: sickening deep-body blows that travelled up his spinal column, directly into his neck and head. He bit down hard on a gag reflex, refusing to heave up what little remained of his stomach contents, most of which he'd left in a steaming pile on the grass at the edge of the helipad.

'Oh, fuck me,' he grunted as the red and white Era Helicopter took off, driving him down into his seat. Years of ass compression had squashed the foam cushioning into a thin hard sandwich between his butt and the steel struts of the seat fitting. The chopper, a venerable old AW139, was streaked with rust and oil, the plexiglas scratched and the nonslip floor sticky with chaw tobacco and chewing gum. Like Dave, its glory days were behind it, and the air conditioning did nothing to mask the baked-in stench of sweat, cigarette smoke, and budget cologne. Dave was just glad he had the cabin to himself on this trip. The only stewed farts and bad breath he had to contend with were his own.

As they ascended, the great rusty iron lever behind his eyeballs cranked up the pressure on his headache. He squeezed his eyes shut behind wraparound Oakleys, but the bright gulf sun burned through anyway, driving a sharp spike through his eyeballs, an unpleasant contrast to the duller concussive hammering on the sides of his skull. He removed his Detroit Tigers cap and rubbed gently at the thinning hair on top of his skull in an effort to alleviate the pain – all to no avail. He kept his hair short these days. You had to when it started to fall out, and no matter how tenderly he ministered to himself, his fingertips seemed to rake deep, bloody furrows through the unprotected scalp.

'Oh, fuck me,' he grunted again, replacing the cap and making the stubbled skin disappear.

'Oh, Lord, no!' Juliette Jamieson called out from the pilot's seat. 'Bump uglies with you, Dave? I think not. I mean, y'all are purdy. In a grizzly, wore-down kinda way. But the way you tomcat around, I wouldn't let that penile biohazard of yours anywhere near my unmentionables. Probably just about ready to fall off by now, I'd reckon. I shoulda made you leave it back on the grass with your breakfast, or dinner, or whatever that nasty-lookin' mess y'all upchucked was. You know the company rules about flying with hazmats.'

Juliette added the wheezing cackle of her laughter to the rotor's roar in his headphones.

'Doritos and tequila, J2,' he said in a croaky rasp. 'Not breakfast. More of a midnight snack. To keep my strength up.'

He tried to grin, but it came out more as a grimace, and Juliette harrumphed at him, pretending to be offended. She wasn't, of course. Over the years J2 had hauled his sorry ass out to the rigs and away from whatever retarded mess he'd left back on shore so many times that he doubted there was anything he could do to lower her estimation of him as a potential husband. Men, in J2's opinion, came in two standard flavours: potential husbands and other women's husbands, and neither of them ever measured up to her exacting standards. Dave, as she never tired of pointing out, was an exemplar – she used the actual word, too, having picked it up from one of the unreadable werewolf romances she immersed herself in between flights – Dave was an exemplar extra-fucking-ordinaire of why a woman like her, a woman of independent means and good breeding hips, had to be careful. Men who weren't to be found in the blessed state of being other women's husbands were generally deserving of their wretched and benighted state by way of being . . .

'. . . unmarriageable assholes.'

'What?' croaked Dave, who'd drifted off into a hangover haze for just a moment.

'Completely unmarriageable assholes, Dave. Such as yourself. World is full of them, I said. All trying to get at my good breeding hips and my 401K.'

He did his best to zone out the lecture he knew was coming on the poor choice facing the modern marriageable lady between potential husbands who were all, without significant exception, gravely disappointing or downright dangerous.

'Or a volatile combination of both, such as you represent, Dave Hooper.'

Once they had altitude, she pushed forward on the stick and brought them around to the southeast, breaking off her lecture to check in with air traffic control. Hundreds of feet below, the trailers and demountable huts of the Baron's Petrochemical depot slipped from view as the nose dipped a little and they commenced the long haul out to Tiber Field, about 300 miles due south of New Orleans. Hooper had made this flight out to the rig so many times that he could picture the landscape without needing to look. In the sprawling dirt and gravel parking lot below were dozens of SUVs and pick-ups – way too many for the size of the depot – mostly owned by guys working a twelve-day shift out on the Longreach. They came in from all over the Gulf Coast, some even driving all the way down from Austin and Dallas, leaving their Fords, Dodges, and Chevys in the company lot to grow a second skin of red dust and oily particulates. No imports for these men, and lift kits aplenty.

In his mind's eye he could see, without looking, the taco stand where everyone stopped in for a last 'home-cooked' meal before flying out – home-cooked because Pedro, who ran the stand, lived there as well, bunking down in a sleeping bag on a pile of crushed cardboard boxes in the storeroom. With his eyes closed, Dave could see the small pound across the two lanes of unsealed road running past Pedro's taqueria. A fine example of American entrepreneurialism, the Dog House had sprung up two years ago to serve the needs of those rig workers who didn't trust their partners on shore to look after their best friends while they were out on the water. The proximity of Pedro's to the Dog House provided cheap and unlimited laughs to those who never grew tired of pondering aloud just how Pedro was able to stay in business providing, as he did, the cheapest loose meat snack anywhere on the Gulf Coast.

Hooper felt the chopper alter course and commence its run out to the Longreach. He was going out a day early but knew better than to stay on shore until the last day of his leave. He would be able to dry out and detox in his bunk on the rig, protected from his own excesses by the tyrannies of distance.

So, he calculated, six days out on the water and then back to the Baron's Death Star up in Houston, then back out to the Longreach, then . . .

He wouldn't have minded the usual routine for himself – twelve days on, ten days off – but since word had come from the company overlords that Longreach was going to test all the way down to 45,000 feet – 5000 beyond the rig's listed specs – Hooper had found himself up for months of rolling back and forth between the platform and the office in Houston. He seemed to spend most of his time in transit because, as the Longreach's boss hog of safety, his objections to the company's plan had to be 'noted' insofar as that word meant 'Fuck you, Dave, just make it happen. And while you're at it, cover our asses.'

And their asses were exposed. Highly. Fucking. Exposed. In Dave Hooper's expert opinion, at least. And on this, if not much else besides hookers and Hooters, he was an expert. Tiber Field was spread across a Rorschach inkblot of Lower Tertiary reservoirs, with multiple sweet spots of light crude hidden in among some of the oldest, gnarliest rock formations on the planet, themselves buried under thousands of feet of compressed salt.

There was a reason oil companies didn't do much drilling at those levels. There was a reason things had gone wrong for British Petroleum on the Deepwater Horizon years ago. Working a field like this was difficult and dangerous, and . . .

What the fuck, Dave, they'd roared at him in their big dumb booming voices. *Are you on board for the big win or what? There's six billion fucking barrels down there. Let's just go git 'em!*

And they had because his guys were the best and he

was pretty damn good too, and even if it meant hauling ass thousands of miles a week and banging heads with a bunch of greedy fucking suits who didn't give an actual fuck about the safety of his guys or his rig . . .

'Y'all doing all right back there, Dave?'

'Huh? Oh, sorry, J2. Talking to myself.'

He wondered how much of his rant he'd muttered angrily over the headset.

Well, tough shit, anyway. J2 knew the score. She made most of these shuttle runs with him. She flew the guys back and forth to the rig, heard them bitching about the company nickel-and-diming them to death whenever it could. The company screw only turns one way. She knew they'd done a hell of a job out there.

Thirty-five thousand feet down.

That was like drilling on the fucking moon.

Well, okay, maybe not, but it *was* a hell of a thing.

He had good reason for torching his bonus on a week-long blowout to celebrate. No matter what Annie's lawyer said. Same goddamn lawyer she was sleeping with. He was sure of that. The asshole.

J2 powered them out over the Gulf of Mexico, leaving the coast behind. Dave, who'd been trying to doze and sleep off at least some of his hangover, risked opening his eyes. He quickly squeezed them shut again. A fierce morning sun hammered down on the beaten blue metal bowl of the ocean, throwing off jagged shards of white sunlight. Each sunburst felt like a hot needle jabbed into his eyeballs. He groaned quietly, thanking the good Lord again that at least he was the only passenger this morning. The next big shift change was scheduled for tomorrow. If he'd been flying out to Longreach with Marty or

Vince, they'd have ragged his ass to bloodied shreds.

As he'd have done for them if they'd spent the last three days of their leave blowing a six-month bonus on two premium hookers flown all the way down from Nevada.

Not that they would have, of course. That sort of reprobate bullshit was strictly a Dave Hooper special. Marty Grbac might have looked like a shaved gorilla, but when he wasn't out on the rig, he was the sort of born-anew Bible-thumping bore who loved nothing more than tooling around on his old rebuilt Triumph, just like one of Steve McQueen's, taking in shows by as many revivalist tent preachers as the South had to offer.

The South, in Dave's experience, had more than enough of that Southern revivalist nonsense on offer, which was partly why he'd flown those hookers in from Nevada.

Dave had once made the mistake of teasing Marty about his faith, asking if his 'invisible friend' rode behind him on that big-ass Triumph. A permanent crook in his nose and a ghostly white scar line where Marty's fist had laid open his cheek helped Dave remember never to do that again. Pain was supposed to be an excellent teacher. Dave's own father had said as much and delivered on the principle time and again. Yet for as much pain as he had endured, he kept making the same fucking mistakes.

And Vince Martinelli?

Well, Vince came on like an enforcer for the Calabrian Mafia, but he was a true family guy. A foul-mouthed, hard-knuckled shift supervisor on the Longreach but on land the gentlest, most considerate father of three little girls and one over-indulged baby boy you could ever hope to meet.

Dave Hooper tried squinting into the sun again. Even through his shades, the bright light was painful in his eyes.

All the way down to his brainstem. He was a family guy, too.

In that he had a family.

And . . . well . . .

He shifted uncomfortably, trying to position himself in a way that didn't leave a broken seat spring sticking in his butt.

Considerate husbands and fathers didn't blow six-monthly bonus checks on top-shelf hookers from Reno, did they?

No. Considerate husbands and fathers took that sort of money and put it into college funds and made sure there was enough to cover their boys' orthodontist bills next week, and maybe they even dropped a few dollars on dragging themselves north for an access visit. They would have been there for the Cub Scouts' Pinewood Derby and done sterling duty as a scoutmaster. There would have been camping trips on which he taught the boys how to bait a fishhook and clean bass and catfish. Maybe he would have played catch with them. Sure, when he wasn't down at Joe's blowing every dime he had buying drinks for his friends and perfume and trinkets for the waitresses he'd later bang in the alley out back.

That was what considerate husbands and fathers would do: spend time with their families. His wife had tried to explain that to him many times before she packed up his boys, walked out of their company town house in Houston, and drove two thousand miles north to her dad's place in Maine. Dave risked peering out through the plexiglas again, shading his burning bloodshot eyes this time. Another man, one in less pain, might have described the water as sun-dappled. To him, this morning, the gulf looked as though it were on fire.

He blinked a few times and sucked up the pain, staring off to the northeast. Strange to think that he could follow the coastline all the way around the panhandle and up the eastern seaboard, up to Toby and Jack. This time of day they'd probably be down the foreshore with their granddad, prospecting for shellfish, maybe throwing a line out into the cold, slate-grey waters of the north Atlantic.

Same waters, he thought.

Just different.

Like a sick child fatigued by illness and empty of any real motivation, Dave toyed with the idea that he could be flying toward them right now, the earth a blur beneath him. Dave Hooper, their hero father, swooping down from the skies if J2 just pushed that stick over a ways.

But Dave Hooper the deadbeat, hungover asshole burped and tasted an acidic reduction of Jim Beam, Doritos, and top-shelf pussy-for-hire at the back of this throat. He grimaced and dry swallowed, shaking his head and throwing off any visions of imagined redemption. Time to drag his sorry ass back to the real world.

'How long, J2?'

Her voice came back through his headset.

'We got us a good two hours of flight time comin' up yet, Dave, if y'all be looking to stack some z's.'

'Yeah. I might have a nap. Late night, you know.'

'Oh, I know, Dave,' she said. 'I saw those two ladies on your Facebook page last night.'

They were flying straight and level, but his stomach dropped out through the floor of the chopper.

'Oh, man, I got on Facebook last night?'

'Yep. Pics. The images were up for hours until they got flagged. Your account got suspended for indecent use.'

He could almost hear her grinning with malice.

'Oh, for fuck's sake,' he said more to himself than to J2.

Annie had access to his page.

Even worse, Annie's lawyer had access to his page. And the boys, too, of course.

Why the hell he even had that account anymore he didn't know. He'd set it up so that Toby and Jack could stay in touch when he was out on the water. They'd begged him to when they were still of an age to innocently ask something of their dad and expect him to deliver.

Yeah. What a brilliant idea that'd been. Damn thing had fucked him up so many ways from Sunday when he got on the sauce.

A sour, shuddering breath ran out of him as he deflated at the memory of the photos he'd posted from a hot tub in Miami.

Not that he remembered much about that night.

But it didn't matter, because the woman he'd picked up in the Sheraton had kindly recorded the highlights on his brand-new iPhone – a gift from Annie and the boys, natch – and posted the all-too-admissible evidence on his Facebook page.

Not hers, even.

His.

'Ah, man,' he sighed. 'What the fuck was I thinking?'

He let his head fall into his hands. As usual, he hadn't been thinking at all.

'Whoa! Dave. Wake up. We got a problem, man.'

For one confusing moment, he was back in college and his roommate was trying to wake him up because the cops and campus security were banging on the door, looking for a missing KFC bucket.

Not a cardboard bucket full of Southern-fried awesome.

No. They wanted to ask him a few pointed questions about a giant fibreglass bucket missing from the tall pole in front of the Colonel's nearest off-campus eatery. Someone had sawed it off and . . .

Then the better part of twenty years fell away, and he came to in the cabin of the chopper hammering out toward the Longreach.

'S'up?' he asked.

His voice cracked, and he coughed until he could speak again.

'Sorry. What's up, J2?'

Her voice replied in his headset. Controlled, but only just.

'Fire on the rig, Dave. A fire and . . . something else. I don't know what.'

He was instantly awake. His fatigue and the ragged edges of the hangover sluiced away in the adrenaline surge. Dave twisted left and right in his seat, disoriented, unsure of where he might find the rig. If Dave Hooper had trouble understanding people and social graces, mechanical objects were an entirely different matter. He had a natural knack for machines, engineering, and the rigs. When he was dealing with a mechanical problem, the universe felt right, as if solving such problems was why he'd been made.

Dave knew what he had to do.

'You gotta get me down there, J2, right now.'

He waited for her to say no, to quote the company rules and federal law and common fucking sense, but after a second of silence she came back in a clipped voice.

'Yep. Okay. Gonna be a fast one, though.'

02

The column of dark oily smoke was rising high above the absurdist metalwork cube of the Longreach as J2 brought the nose of the chopper around, giving Dave a clear view forward through the plexiglas windshield. His heart seemed to stop for a second. Everything, all his organs, seemed stunned into paralysis before spasming back into life at double speed. Malevolent blooms of bright orange fire fed a dark tower of smoke as it climbed away from the platform, but within a second or two of the initial shock Hooper frowned at the . . . *wrongness* of the scene. The seat of the blaze appeared to be down in the living quarters and hadn't spread from there. The critical areas around the drill works were still clear for now. So was the helipad.

'Two minutes, Dave. I'm wheels down and gone in thirty seconds. Jonty says they got wounded. Lotsa wounded. Gonna cross-deck 'em to Thunder Horse.'

'Okay,' Hooper replied, giving her only half his attention while he leaned forward and studied the fire. It was bad. It was always gonna be bad on a rig, but it wasn't the hellstorm he'd been expecting.

'There's more, Dave,' Juliette shouted as a secondary

explosion blew out a cabin on the southern side of the platform. Dave watched as flaming debris fluttered down toward the deep blue water churning around the pylons. 'I'll patch 'em through,' she shouted. 'Put your damn cans back on, would you? And your harness.'

'Sorry,' he said, still distracted and not bothering with his safety belt. He wanted to get as far forward as he could to get a better look at the unfolding disaster. He fit the headphones back over his ears, however, even though the short cord kept him tethered in the rear of the cabin. The intercom crackled and popped just before he heard the guttural South African accent of the day shift supervisor, Jonty Ballieue, through the static. He sounded panicky, almost hysterical, and that frightened Hooper a lot more than the fire. Ballieue was one of the more unflappable yarpies he'd ever met.

'. . . attack . . . fighting them . . . coming up from the pylo . . .'

'Jonty. D'you read me? It's Hoop. I'm less than a minute out. You're breaking up, man. What the fuck is going on down there?'

'. . . ooper? . . . acking us . . . We need . . .'

But the interference washed any sense out of the few words that broke through.

'Dave?'

It was J2, jumping in on his channel, sounding even more worried than before.

'I got the navy on my case now, man. They're telling me we're in restricted airspace. They're warning us off, telling me not to land. Talking about terrorists or some garbage.'

'Bullshit!' he said in amazement. 'Are they fucking crazy? Why is it restricted to us? We gotta get casualties off. I have to get down there and get to work. Where the fuck are terrorists gonna come from out here? What'd they hijack, a submarine? Look down there, J2. There's nothing there. Fireboats haven't even made it out yet.'

'Dave . . .'

'Get me down, Juliette,' he said, talking over the top of her objections. 'You put me down and get the wounded to Thunder Horse and you'll be back at the depot before that navy asshole you're talking to has even tied a slipknot in his little pecker to stop from wetting his pants.'

She opened her mouth to try one more time, but Hooper cut her off with another harsh bark.

'Do it.'

The helicopter pilot tugged at the bill of her Era baseball cap, as though saluting him. She pushed forward on the stick and took them in.

Juliette threw them into a tight corkscrew descent that crushed him into his seat, where the broken seat spring speared into his butt like the shrimp fork of an angry little vengeance demon. The pressure on his back and neck cranked up the misery of his hangover, turning the dial to 11 on the *Spinal Tap* amp. Dave Hooper ignored it, along with the urgent need to dry-retch again and the feeling of having his eyes gouged out by the pressure of high-speed deceleration. He gritted his teeth, which were still slimy from the night before, and tried to pick out as much detail from the hellish scene as he could.

It was almost impossible. Rig monkeys and fire teams ran everywhere. Secondary explosions shook the lower levels of the structure as thick black clouds of smoke poured into the sky. He caught the briefest glimpse of a rainbow, formed in the mist drifting off a water jet, before the skids slammed down on the helipad, sending a painful jolt up his backbone.

The chopper doors flew back as evac teams wrenched the handles and wrestled wounded men into the cabin. Dave was about to start shouting directions, imposing some sense of order on the scene, when he was struck dumb by the sight of a couple of Vince Martinelli's second shift guys trying to scramble in over the top of the casualties. They looked terrified, with huge white eyes bugging out of oil-stained faces. But they didn't appear to be injured in any way. Dave shouted at them to get the hell back, but the pounding of the chopper blades, the roar of explosions, and the hoarse shouts and screams of a dozen other men drowned him out.

He tried to push the first of the interlopers out of his way and was surprised when the man suddenly flew sideways, the victim of a stiff arm jab by Martinelli himself, who followed up with a series of vicious rabbit punches to the neck of the second man. Vince wasn't fucking around, either. He really hammered the guy, forcing Dave to jump down and grab his fist as it was cocked for another strike.

'Jesus, Vince, knock it off. You're gonna kill him.'

'Sorry, boss,' yelled the shift supervisor, who looked on the edge of panic himself, 'but I figured this might happen when you showed up. Some of these fucking idiots even tried to throw themselves over the side to get away from the things. Got at least one life pod away as well.'

'Away from what?' Dave yelled as Martinelli threw the other man to the side of the helipad like a bag of dirty laundry. Dave waved his thanks at J2 as he left the helicopter behind, but she was too busy prepping to un-ass the area to pay him much heed. Martinelli grabbed his boss by the elbow and led him through the chaos on the pad. There were bodies everywhere. Burned, mangled, horribly disfigured bodies. And at least a dozen walking wounded waiting for their turn to be evacuated. Everyone looked frightened, which was only to be expected, but what Dave didn't expect was the crazed, almost animalistic terror that seemed to be driving some of them.

They had trained for this. *He* had trained them for this. They shouldn't be losing their shit.

'You gotta come, Dave, this way, quickly.' Martinelli all but dragged him along by the arm. 'Fucking things are down this way.'

Heat from the fires came at them in waves, tightening the exposed skin on Hooper's hands and face, making him wonder how long any of them could hope to survive on this gigantic ticking time bomb. He saw three kitchen hands, still wearing their stained, greasy chef's whites, fighting one another to get to the chopper.

'What the hell,' he muttered to himself as the men screamed and raged in frustration and something else, something more elemental, when the aircraft spooled up its engines and lifted off before they had a chance to board.

'This way, down this way,' Martinelli repeated. 'Come on, Dave. I don't know how long Marty and the others can hold them back.'

They cleared the area around the helipad just as the down blast of the rotors tried to push them off their feet. Dave followed Martinelli around the corner into a slightly sheltered corridor between two prefab huts. He put the brakes on, almost stumbling to his knees as Martinelli continued forward, dragging him along.

'Vince,' he shouted. 'Would you slow the fuck up and tell me what's happening? J2 said the navy was talking about terrorists. But I don't see ISIS around, do you?'

Martinelli didn't look happy to be stopping, but he looked even more unhappy at the question, as though Dave were crazy for even asking it.

'The fuck did anyone say anything about ragheads? This ain't that. It's worse. You gotta see for yourself, Dave. These things, these fucking animals, they just come out of the water. Up the fucking pylons or something.'

The space between the prefabs was narrow, and someone slammed heavily into Hooper's shoulder, pushing him into a pole as they ran past. It stunned him, and he felt an electric tingle of pins and needles run down from his shoulder to his fingertips. This seething crush of people sluicing back and forth didn't feel like his crew. It felt like a mob.

They were on a drill rig. In the middle of the gulf. Where the hell did people think they were going to escape to? Sure as shit weren't going to their emergency stations, that was a goddamn given.

Dave stood back against the wall of the small prefabricated building that housed the flight operations centre for the rig. He flicked the pins and needles out of his fingertips, or tried to, anyway.

'What, Vince? What things came up the pylons? You're not making any sense, man.'

Martinelli's face dropped.

'They didn't tell you? Jesus, I asked them to tell you. You're going to think I'm fucking crazy.'

'Try me,' Dave said.

'Monsters,' Vince Martinelli said. 'There are monsters on the rig, Dave.'

* * *

One heartbeat. Then two. Dave Hooper did not move, did not speak. It was possible he didn't breathe, either. He looked into Vince Martinelli's eyes and down into the soul of a man who was telling him the truth. Or at least the truth as he understood it. As men rushed and crowded past them, mostly headed for the helipad, Dave stared at Martinelli and saw the frightened father of four young children. In his eyes, bloodshot and gaping out from a face blackened by smoke and soot, he saw little fear of the very real danger of dying in a small supernova as the Longreach went up. Instead, he thought he saw a creeping horror of something worse.

'Vince,' he said as quietly and calmly as he could while still being heard above the crashing din and chaos. 'Tell me as quickly and as simply as you can.'

'We don't have time, Dave. We need –'

'I need to know, Vince,' Dave said in a steady voice but with great force. 'If I'm going to fight a fire, I need to know what sort of fire. If I'm going to fight . . . *things* –' He had to force himself to say it. '– I need to know . . . *fuck*, what sort of things. Or at least what they're doing.'

'*They're eating people, Dave*. For fuck's sake, there's no time for this.'

Vince Martinelli seemed to be pulled in several directions. Like the kitchen hands Hooper had seen just a minute ago, Martinelli looked like part of him just wanted to get the hell away. As far away as quickly as possible. But his shifting shoulders, the way he kept bouncing on the balls of his feet, all spoke of the need to get moving again, the way they had been going, toward the problem.

Toward the monsters, Dave thought, trying not to let incredulity run wild all over his face.

It was possible, likely even, that Vince and the others thought they had seen 'monsters' when in fact the navy might be right. Might be there were attackers dressed in scuba gear and . . . what, fright masks or something? Hooper dismissed the idea as soon as he had it. That was bullshit. Worse than Vince's monster story. He could imagine some crazy Greenpeace cocksuckers sneaking out here and scaling the rig to hang a banner or something, but a bunch of bearded fucking sand maggots like bin Laden and all of them? Forget that shit. Never gonna happen.

He gripped Vince by the bicep. Dave's large calloused hands didn't reach even halfway around the other man's upper arm. But he gave him a little push toward the stairwell.

'You can tell me on the way, then. Where are we headed?'

'Down to the first crew quarters,' Vince said, letting go of the tension that had been holding him unnaturally upright just before.

'And what are they doing down there?' Dave asked. 'These things.'

He couldn't say the word 'monster' without feeling like an idiot.

Martinelli seemed to pick up speed with every step, but he faltered momentarily, looking back over his shoulder to answer. He looked guilty.

'They're tearing shit up, Dave,' he said. He came to a complete stop again. 'And eating people.'

Not Greenpeace, then, Hooper thought. Vegetarian softcocks, the lot of them.

He had to bite down on a crazed snort of laughter. *Eating people?* If he hadn't seen the madness and horror on the helipad, he'd have bet Vince was punking him. They were in a narrow walkway between a couple of the prefab huts and were being jostled on all sides. Rig workers shouted and cried out around them, a mob scene, heavy steel-capped boots pounding on the ironwork. Martinelli gave him that same look, a furtive sort of guilty glance, before moving off again, drawing Hooper along in his considerable wake.

As they forced their way against the human tide rushing up from the lower levels, Dave tried to shake off his sense of disbelief. He was about to ask Vince if he had really said these things were eating people, but he shut his mouth as three men stumbled by. He recognised a couple of drill monkeys, Lam and Ibarra, holding up the third man, who looked like something *had* taken a huge chunk out of his left shoulder. Dave couldn't place him for a second. The stranger's face was ashen white, and his coveralls and high-visibility vest were painted in blood. With a start, he realised it was Pena, the new hydrologist. Last thing Dave had done before going on leave, he'd briefed Pena in, giving him the tour of the rig and all the emergency assembly points. The man looked very different now. It wasn't the worst injury Hooper had seen on a rig, but he couldn't help noticing that Pena had no burn marks on him. When people got hurt on oil rigs, in Dave's experience anyway, they got crushed and they got burned. He threw a quick glance back over his shoulder as the men struggled past him.

That poor bastard did look like something had taken a bite out of him, and his bright yellow vest was scored with bloodied slash marks.

Acid and bile boiled away in Dave Hooper's stomach, and his head seemed to be gripped in a tightening iron band. They hurried down three flights of steel steps and flew around one corner and then another into the densely packed grid of prefabricated living capsules that constituted the crew quarters. The smell of burning synthetics reached him just before the first tendrils of oily smoke. The crowds had thinned out, but their progress was now slowed by smoke and flame. The power had failed completely down here, and at times the two men were forced to inch along through darkness. After a while Martinelli seemed to find it all but impossible to push himself forward.

'Come on, Vince,' Hooper said, laying a hand on his back. 'I think I can hear the guys.'

And he thought that, just maybe, he could. Faint voices, shouting and screaming somewhere up ahead, the words lost in the roar of sirens, explosions, and the mad metallic clangour of a gigantic man-made structure that was violently coming apart.

Hooper found himself encouraging his friend to keep moving, to stay in contact in the darkened, increasingly claustrophobic passages. Here and there light leaked in from the outside world or small fires threw an eldritch glow on scenes of mayhem and slaughter. Dave swallowed hard as his throat locked up at the sight of a severed arm and a long, bloody smear leading away around a corner into the main lounge.

Dave bumped into Martinelli, who had come to a complete stop. The man seemed to have put down roots. A small shove failed to move him, and he pushed back against another, harder push, even reversing a few steps. Dave was stunned. Vince was straight up one of the most courageous men he'd ever met. Over the years he'd seen him run headlong into enough lethally dangerous situations and pull some poor bastard to safety to know that Martinelli was swinging a heavy pair of cast-iron testicles. But it seemed there was no way he was getting any closer to what lay at the end of that blood trail. He'd started moaning and trembling like a kid at the door of the dentist waiting for a root canal. It was like, hell, that wasn't even Vince standing there, just a tangle of fear and horror that had taken his shape.

Biting down on the anger that flared in the wake of his frustration – did he have to do *everything*? – Dave edged around the terrified man. He could still hear cries of pain and fear somewhere ahead, but here, deep down in the living quarters, the shrieking din was muffled by alarms and the roar of a nearby blaze. He could feel the air being sucked toward the conflagration and the heat radiating back at him.

'You all right, Vince?' Dave asked as he moved in front of his co-worker.

But Vince was a long way from being all right. He kept shaking his head and trying to force himself forward, but he just couldn't do it. He appeared to be stranded at a point exactly midway between his need to help and his fear of whatever was coming.

'. . . eating them . . .' he mumbled, and then stared at Dave as if he couldn't believe what he had just said.

No sense wasting time with him, Hooper thought. Whatever he'd seen when he was last down here had put the zap on his head. Dave gathered up what he thought of as his considerable reserves of patience. It really was like talking to a kid.

'Okay, then. Don't worry, buddy, I got it. Go fetch me some stretcher bearers. We're gonna need them. I think I can hear some of the guys up ahead. Injured. Go on. Can you at least do that for me?'

When Martinelli did nothing, Dave frowned and shook his head. The guy was . . . what . . . paralysed or something?

He'd have to abandon him and carry on alone.

He edged cautiously down the hallway, careful not to step in the glistening trail of blood. He told himself he simply didn't want to slip, but he also knew it was more visceral than that. Disgust and fear warding him off. Trying to make him stop, just like Martinelli. The heat grew no more intense, but he found it harder to breathe. The fire was consuming all the oxygen.

He jumped as the steel-capped toe of his boot kicked a crowbar. It was matted with blood and hair. He bent to pick it up, some ancient, deeply buried instinct making him reach for a weapon. A club. Anything. He could hear noises just ahead, around the corner in the crew lounge. A wet, crunching sound. Shudders ran up his arms and around his neck as he recognised what it was. Chewing and grunting.

Like Martinelli he suddenly found it difficult to move forward, but unlike his friend he found some reserve, somewhere, and forced himself to push one foot in front of the other, forgetting about the crowbar as he drew closer to the turn in the corridor that opened up onto the crew lounge. Light flickered from within, but it was a cold blue light, not the shifting orange-red glow of flames.

His eyes had adapted to the dark now, and in the gloom he began to pick out more details. Blood splatter. Torn clothes. A work boot with part of a leg sticking out of it, hacked off abruptly about halfway up the shin. The bone looked impossibly white, the jagged end of it sharp, like a broken branch. Hooper's gorge rose in his throat, but he had nothing left to throw up. He gagged and then spat, or tried to. His mouth was dry and sticky. An object leaning up against the wall drew his eye. He experienced a moment of recognition before understanding.

A splitting maul.

Marty Grbac's splitting maul. It lay at an odd angle against the wall, just before the corner, as though dropped there and forgotten. An oversized, inappropriate piece of equipment for an oil rig but one that Marty carried with him everywhere. A souvenir of his first time in Alaska, he'd said. And a lucky charm. It had saved his ass once, and he wouldn't give it up. The splitting maul looked like a cross between a sledgehammer and a woodcutter's axe, because that was exactly what it was. A long straight shaft of polished hickory carrying a twelve-pound head with a blunt fist-size hammer on one side and a broad, slightly convex chopping wedge on the other. The extra weight delivered a more powerful blow. Along with a giant novelty foam hand signed by Sammy Sosa it was Grbac's most prized possession.

Hooper picked it up, surprised by how heavy the thing was. You'd need the shoulders of a bull, like Marty, to swing it, and on a rig you'd rarely have the space. It belonged in a forest, a cleared forest with a whole heap of logs lying around waiting to be split for the fire.

He looked back over his shoulder at Martinelli, who was crying with the effort of forcing himself forward, his eyes pleading with Dave to forgive him. Tear tracks stood out on his filthy face. The man was such a perfect picture of misery that Dave found himself feeling more sorry for him than pissed off.

'Be cool, Vince,' he said, hefting the heavy tool. It made him feel better for some reason. 'Go get help.'

He turned away from Vince Martinelli, breathed in a draught of the thin, scorched air, and stepped around the corner into the crew lounge.

03

'Mother. Fucker.'

Dave nearly dropped the splitting maul onto his toes. He stood fixed to the floor, as incapable of moving as Vince Martinelli had been. The . . . *thing* that was eating a man looked up from its jumbo-size Happy Meal and snarled like a big cat in a zoo. Hooper didn't react immediately because the shock was so great that his body didn't know how to react. Instinctively, intellectually, he was a void.

The thing . . . the *monster* turned its eyes on him after taking one more bite out of the remains of one of Dave's best friends. Marty G. He knew it was Marty, or what was left of him, because of the tattoo just visible under the runnels of blood covering most of his one remaining arm.

'. . . *rd is my shepherd. I am his lamb.*'

The beast snarled slowly at Dave. His conscious mind lurched into action again, racing in a fever to catch up, seeking to impose some sort of meaning, however poor, on the scene before him. The first rational conclusion it reached was . . . big. This fucking thing was *big*. Marty Grbac had stood six-five in the shower, and his upper arms were the size of Dave's thighs. This thing probably stood a head taller than that.

The animal, whatever it was – it looked like some sort of hairless gorilla with a shocking case of full-body herpes – was sitting back on its haunches taking bites out of Grbac's upper body like a hungry drunk tearing chunks out of a foot-long at Subway. So yeah, it was big.

Dave's mind, still frantically cycling through possibilities, latched on to shreds of recognition or analogy. The creature's eyes were black limpid pools, like a shark's. It had no snout or nose, just two breathing slits above the open maw of a mouth filled with fangs. Not the neat, dangerous canines of a wild dog but a junkyard pile of broken tusks, jagged scythes, and barbs strung with half-chewed flesh.

An image came to him, just a flash, of sitting in a cinema with his two boys when they were much younger and he was a better father, with his arms wrapped around them as they burrowed their faces into his chest, terrified by the snarling creatures pouring out of the ground in one of those *Lord of the Rings* movies. The thing eating Marty Grbac reminded him of one of them. An orc.

An orc with nuts the size of softballs and a cock like Satan's own spitting cobra. The nasty fucking thing was fully rigid, too. Like it was getting off on eating Dave's friend.

'Fuck,' he breathed out. 'That's nasty.'

The monster snarled again, casually, regarding him with apparent indifference. A terrible sound erupted from the fetid hole of its mouth: a wet, guttural eruption, long and low, like a hippo farting in a mud bath. Dave's jaw dropped, and his face hung slack with horror as the creature . . . laughed at him. He was certain it was laughing. A snorting, sucking series of barks as it slurped up ribbons of skin like noodle strands. Dave Hooper's balls crawled up into his body. His much smaller, less scabrous balls. He shuddered with revulsion and the first stuttering paroxysm of fury.

This fucking thing was drunk on blood and bloated with hot meat. It was eating his friend, laughing at him, and waving its johnson in his face like it fully expected a free hummer. Whatever it was, wherever it had come from, nobody or nothing came onto his rig and got up in his face with that kind of shit. He shook his head almost imperceptibly, a snarl beginning to disfigure his features, answering the creature's ferocity. For the first time he took in the scene around him. Carnage illuminated by the loading screen of a game on the Xbox. Body parts were scattered about the lounge. Entrails and bloodied chunks of unidentifiable meat festooned the faded brown three-piece lounge. Blood lapped at his boots. As Dave shook his head, muttering 'No, no, no' through gritted teeth, he noticed movement to his left and then his right.

More of them.

No, that wasn't right. There were more creatures, but they were smaller than the brutish-looking thing squatting in the middle of the room. There were two, no, three of them. Demonic-looking, but lesser versions of the animal snacking on Marty's rib cage. They were monstrous baboons whereas it was a gorilla. Its jaw appeared to distend horribly wide as it crunched through bone and sinew, tearing and ripping and shaking free its meal with more snorts and grunts. And that sound, like the chuckle of a psychopathic angel. With an enormous boner.

'Fuck no,' said Dave. He tightened his grip on the splitting maul, turning left and right. The smaller creatures were definitely moving now, trying to circle around to come at him from both sides. He felt his bladder let go, and a warm rush of urine ran down his legs, the last of his big night out with the hookers from Reno. No drug tests for him, then.

He laughed.

Just one short gust of laughter teetering on the edge of psychosis. It didn't matter much now whether he'd got drunk and jumped onto Facebook last night, did it? Nothing much mattered now. Not his ex-wife. Not her carnivorous lawyer –

He snorted with laughter again. *Carnivorous. Ha. Not even close.*

Not the bosses back in Houston. Not the credit card assholes who were always chasing him. Or the IRS, which wanted to know where the hell his last two tax years might be at. Not even his own conscience about what a shitpot, worthless father he'd turned out to be. None of it mattered, because he was going to die. Eaten by monsters and quite possibly ass-fucked by their gigantic monster cocks into the bargain.

Eight or nine years of compressed frustration and rage boiled up inside Dave Hooper as he realised he was never going to get a chance to make good on any of it.

He would never see his boys again, and they would never know what happened to him. The rig would burn, and then it would blow, and all of this insanity would be incinerated, atomised. All Toby and Jack would ever know was that their dad had failed again. This time at the last thing he genuinely could have claimed to be any good at: his job. He had failed, and everyone who had relied on him had died.

The shout that welled up from deep within Dave Hooper's loneliest, most empty places was unlike anything he or these monsters had heard. It was neither fearful nor despairing. It was less a scream than a roar, a full-throated bellow of fury and outrage and a final bitter retort to every shitty deal that life had handed one poor angry man.

The biggest beast seemed startled, then amused, and finally outraged as Hooper charged across the tacky, blood-drenched carpet of the crew lounge. The thing let rip with its own war shout as it tore the remaining arm from Marty's savaged torso and waved it about like a baton, howling gibberish at the three smaller creatures. They moved quickly but clumsily, two of them crashing into each other and the third leaping for Dave but becoming entangled in a long strand of yellow-green intestines on which it had been sucking. The creature yelped like a kicked cur as it crashed to the ground.

The splitting maul described a great circular arc in Dave's hands, punching through the ceiling tiles with a burst of powder and a terrible screech of metal strips and one smashed light fitting. It was, however, unusually heavy, and driving it through the air in a short, vicious descending blur was all the strength of a man who stood two inches over six feet and had worked his whole life at hard manual labour. A man whose resentment at the world and everyone who had conspired against him was fuelled by a silent, shameful understanding that his problems were mostly his own damn fault.

The creature, which Dave would later come to understand was no ordinary monster but a BattleMaster of the Hunn, was indeed drunk on the heady nectar of fresh blood and meat. If Dave Hooper had stumbled into the lounge twenty minutes earlier, if he had been there with his friends and colleagues when the Hunn and its attendant Fangr warriors had emerged from the waters and scaled the rig like rabid monkeys, he, too, would have died. But for once in his life Dave Hooper caught a lucky break.

* * *

Urgon Htoth Ur Hunn, BattleMaster of the Fourth Legion, did not stir when the calfling appeared holding the war hammer the Hunn had so easily taken from another of the weakling foe. Indeed, from the one he was gorging himself on now. A poor adversary but a magnificent repast. Urgon Htoth Ur Hunn had never dined on man meat, although like any warrior of the Horde he had been raised on the legends of the older time when Hunn and Grymm and even Fangr had roamed at will across the surface of the world Above, hunting men for their flesh and for the pure wild joy of it.

As this new calfling stumbled upon the Hunn and his attendant Fangr, Urgon Htoth Ur Hunn lazily tore away a fresh nut of shoulder meat and chewed it slowly, enjoying the heady pleasure of the bloodwine and the satisfying crunch of bones between his teeth. It was a stirring feast. Truly. The bloodwine had engorged his loins. He was so pleased with how this adventure had gone that he had even been considering tearing off a few pieces of the kill for his Fangr leash. A rare honour to eat from their master's portion. But in the end he was enjoying the meal too much to share it. And the Fangr were already sated on calfling guts and slow with the scraps of good meat and pooled bloodwine they had scavenged from the fight, anyway.

In fact, the BattleMaster was so full of hot flesh and the just-spilled blood of his prey that he might not even finish this feast in one sitting. A great pity, because the legends had proved true and the freshest kill was the sweetest. This fine feed put to shame even the offerings of the palace blood pots, which was only to be expected, he supposed. It had been millennia since any had tasted fresh meat from the bones of men or their herds.

Urgon Htoth Ur Hunn was somewhat surprised that this last man had come to him rather than attempting to flee. The calflings he and his leash had come upon in this strange tower on stilts had made some attempt to resist him. But it was a poor and wretched display, and he knew that what little courage they showed came only from one another. When he found men on their own, or in twos and threes, they invariably fell prey to fear before the first touch of tooth or claw.

Why, he had not even drawn his blade yet.

It had not been necessary when the largest of their so-called warriors, the one on whom he was dining at this moment, had come at him with the war hammer. A valiant effort, he supposed, snorting through bubbles of blood and drool, but utterly hopeless. Urgon Htoth Ur Hunn had simply pulled the weapon from the human's hands before tossing it away and tearing off his head.

The man standing before him, reeking of fear, did not look like he would put up nearly as much of a fight. He clutched the war hammer to himself almost as a talisman. Urgon Htoth Ur Hunn doubted the calfling could lift the weapon, and almost as though the same thought had occurred to him, the puny creature nearly crushed its own hoof by fumbling the thing and all but dropping it.

The BattleMaster indulged himself in a rich, generous chuckle. He might not even kill this one. He might return with it to the UnderRealms as an offering for the palace. He had seen chain aplenty lying around this ocean keep for a proper leash. Her Majesty would surely raise him high for the prize, even higher than she would raise him in the Horde for the achievement of having breached the capstone into the Above for the first time in . . .

Well . . .

He had no idea.

The legends spoke only of the older time when the Horde was free to roam Above, defending its subject lands against rival sects, taking what cattle and territory it could from them. Urgon Htoth Ur Hunn grunted instructions to his Fangr around a mouthful of meat and bone. He told them to take the man, but carefully. Slowly. To restrain him and not to harm him too badly. He would make more than a useful prize. There would be many who would not believe that Urgon Htoth Ur Hunn had breached the capstone and walked upon the world of men, raiding one of their fortresses and feasting mightily on the occupants.

He would have just a few more bites and perhaps another draught of the bloodwine before it cooled and lost its intoxicating power. He shivered with the iron stench and thick heat pouring down his throat again. His eye membranes drooped, and he chuckled at the fierce war-face the calfling was trying to make at him. As if flaring its ugly snout and baring such dull, small teeth might undo a BattleMaster of the Hunn.

Yes, this one would make a fine gift to the palace. Her Majesty might even keep it as a pet.

It came as quite a surprise, then, to Urgon Htoth Ur Hunn, BattleMaster of the Fourth Legion, when the calfling made a sound he would have sworn was a war shout and . . . charged!

But that was not as great a surprise as finding out just how drunk on bloodwine he was when he tried to climb to his feet to meet the challenge.

* * *

The splitting maul crashed through plaster roof tiles, severed the thin aluminium strips separating them and shattered a long fluorescent light tube. Shards of glass and showers of sparks sprayed the room, and the heavy steel smashed down without slowing much or diverting from its deadly path in the slightest.

Dave had not thought to use the edged metal of the maul's axe head. Dave had not thought of much at all. The vicious heavy steel wedge was simply at the business end of the swing. He often wondered later what would have happened if the maul had been reversed in his hands and he had tried to split the creature's head open with the simple clubbing tool of the sledgehammer. Perhaps the result would have been exactly the same, if a little messier. Marty's splitting maul was an unusually heavy model, hand-tooled, as Dave recalled him saying more than once. It might have delivered enough mass with enough speed to splinter and crush the sheath of bone protecting the BattleMaster's gelatinous, chimp-sized brains. Or not. And Dave might have died there.

But that was all later.

At 11.52 am David John Hooper landed a killing blow on the poorly protected nasal cleft of a Hunn ur Horde. The axe-shaped end of the maul's twelve-pound head punched into the weaker, thinner mantle of bone just as Urgon Htoth Ur Hunn crouched and looked up toward the attacker.

The Hunn's last words were, 'You dare not do this . . .'

But Dave did, and with that one mighty blow he split the monster's skull like a rotten watermelon, and everything that had changed forever that morning changed again.

04

When Dave was nine years old, he broke his arm. Totally worth it, he told his friends at school later, when he rolled up with his arm in plaster, supported by a sling. There is no bigger celebrity on the playground than the kid who turns up with a broken bone, unless it's the kid who turns up with a bone he broke in a moment of high adventure and epic stupidity. Dave Hooper was that kid.

One day during the long, slow summer holidays that marked his ninth year, young Dave Hoover had become possessed of a plan. He would push his old trampoline, with which he was bored, up against the chain link fence at the back of the yard. The Hooper family garden faced onto an empty lot, a couple of acres of grass that grew to knee length in summer, shaded by a few stands of scraggly old trees in which crows and ill-tempered magpies cawed at one another. He would find a spare length of wood from the tree house closer to the back porch, a handy piece of gear they'd used to make his brother Andy walk the plank from six feet up when they'd been playing pirates a month or so back.

That cost him the month of June, grounded for the duration while Andy recovered from his sprained ankle. A royal ass whuppin' courtesy of the old man's leather belt, the one with the brass studs, had also been levied, in addition to the grounding. Dave had endured that without a whimper as he had learned that whimpering led to more ass whuppin'. But it certainly didn't dissuade him from his course of action with the trampoline.

He planned to lay the plank against the edge of the trampoline, and then run up it, leaping at the last moment into the centre of the stretchy canvas and launching himself into the air. Exactly like Spider-Man.

After all, the grass on the other side of the fence was long and soft and surely would cushion any impact. Especially since Dave had done those judo lessons for three weeks a couple of years ago and knew exactly how to roll out of a fall. His cousin, Darryl, who was not nearly as smart as Dave but was possessed of an admirable frontier spirit, agreed that this was an excellent plan. After ten minutes of huffing and puffing, the grunt work of moving the heavy trampoline all the way down the back garden and up against the fence was done. The plank was found, placed, and secured with a bungee strap from the back of Dave's bicycle. As the genius behind this cunning plan, Dave insisted on the privilege of the first jump.

It had been glorious.

Dave flew into the air.

He curled into a ball, fascinated by the kaleidoscopic green and blue smear of colour the world became.

It was all going according to . . .

He woke up in the hospital six hours later with a concussion and a broken forearm. When he came to in his hospital bed in New Orleans, Dave enjoyed one sweet moment of being nine years old again. Sure he hurt, and he was in a world of trouble, but it was totally worth it. The stories he'd tell when he . . .

Oh, shit.

He plummeted forward in time from that long-ago summer, free-falling through over two and a half decades to find himself, dizzy and disoriented, tucked in between cool white cotton sheets, surrounded by screens, punctured by needles from which ran tubes and wires. He was wrapped in bandages, and possibly insane.

His first thought was that he'd had some kind of breakdown out on the rig, gone crazy, ripped the place up, and now he was in a psycho ward. Drug tests. This was gonna mean drug tests. His next thought was a memory. The face of the monster.

The Hunn.

The fucking what?

The monster he had killed – he knew he had killed it – was . . .

The Hunn.

He knew that as clearly as he knew that he'd killed it. As clearly as he knew he was totally locked up in a psycho ward because he was a crazy man, thinking monster thoughts and pushing away memories of carnage and horror. For once in his mostly wasted adult life he thought maybe a little drug test wouldn't be such a bad idea. Find out what crazy shit those hookers had doped him with.

The Horde. The Hunn.

Dave started to curse. His voice was dry and rasped in his throat like gravel. He cursed anyway and pulled at the tubes running into his arms and the backs of his hands, pulling them free, becoming entangled, and freeing himself again.

He kicked off the sheets and the light cotton blanket and swung his legs down off the bed, still muttering curses. His head swam, and the edges of his vision blurred a little. He felt nauseous, but then, a 2 am breakfast of corn chips and vodka hadn't promised anything more.

A nurse appeared at his door. A big-assed black lady. He noticed then that the door was open, as was the door of the hospital room across from him. That wasn't right. He was pretty sure they locked up the psychos when they put them in the nut hatch. And that was sure as hell where he belonged. Or the drunk tank. That brought him up short and sharp. Shit. Maybe he was starting to go the way of his old man on the booze. Seeing things. Falling apart in his head.

No.

The Hunn, he knew, was called Urgon Htoth Ur Hunn, and he knew that the same way he knew his cousin's name from all those summers so long ago: Darryl Hooper. He knew these things because he had learned them a long time ago. Darryl had once nearly blown his little toe off with a firecracker. He worked for a logistics company in Norway now. Dave had fucked his first girlfriend and never told him.

That had been some sweet forbidden pussy.

And Dave had killed Urgon Htoth Ur Hunn, a BattleMaster of the Horde, in the crew lounge on the Longreach platform.

Damn. He was losing his fucking mind. Just as his old man had.

'Mr Hooper, please. Mr Hooper, you need to get yourself back into bed right now. You've been very badly hurt, sir.'

The words were caring, but the big-assed black lady nurse who said them didn't look the sort to take any guff from the likes of him. That was too bad, because Dave didn't think he'd been badly hurt. He didn't feel like he'd been hurt at all, in spite of all the bandages and the holes they'd been poking in him. Better than fine, even. As his eyesight cleared and the head spins stopped, he stretched and rolled his shoulders.

Took a deep breath and . . .

'Nurse,' he said with some difficulty. He felt dizzy again and had to sit down on the bed, which at least mollified her. 'Where am I?'

'You're safe now, Mr Hooper, but you need to stay in bed. You've been burned, and your arm is broken.'

'My arm?'

The echo of his distant past served only to confuse him. Yes, he had broken his arm a long time ago playing Spider-Man with his cousin. But he was fine now. Possibly insane but fine. The arm didn't hurt at all, and he well remembered what a broken bone felt like. It hurt for days. He lifted his arm with the moulded plastic sheath, a black armguard of sorts perforated with hundreds of tiny holes, perhaps to let the bandages breathe. He clenched his fist experimentally, waiting for the pain he remembered from that summer of his childhood, a feeling like someone had dug in under the flesh with a heavy set of pliers, latched on to the bones, and given them a vicious turn. Nothing. Not numbness. Just an absence of pain.

'Mr Hooper, sir, get back in bed. The doctor is coming. He'll be very angry to see you up like this. And I'll get in trouble; now come on, please.'

Her voice took on an almost motherly note, and it finally reached him. The nurse didn't seem to think he was crazy, just hurt. Of course that made her crazy, because he was fine. He felt like he could toss a pigskin around with this damned broken arm.

'The Longreach . . .' Dave croaked again. A bottle of water stood on the little table by the head of his bed. He used his good hand and his teeth to open it. Took a sip. It was lukewarm but beautiful. He didn't think he'd ever tasted water as clean and sweet. Before he could stop himself, he had emptied most of the bottle, although he did spill a bit down his chin. 'The Longreach,' he repeated, 'the drilling rig I was on. What's happened?'

The nurse shook her head, but in pity rather than denial. 'Oh, it's terrible. I'm sorry, Mr Hooper. So many dead and injured. I'm afraid I don't have the details, but . . .'

Dave picked up a TV remote from the bedside table and pointed it at the small flat-screen Samsung hanging from the ceiling at the end of the bed. He powered up the television, flicking through the channels looking for a news show.

Shopping Network. Some asshole televangelist. *The Golden Girls*.

'I don't think that's a good idea, Mr Hooper,' the nurse said, but he ignored her and kept flipping. He went from ancient Jerry Springer reruns, to some show about fat people, to MSNBC. Not his choice of news normally, but right now he didn't care. It was running nonstop coverage of the disaster.

Some talking head was narrating video taken from a helicopter circling a long way back from the drill rig. There wasn't much to see, just a column of smoke on the horizon. The news anchor confirmed that the chopper was being held outside a twenty-mile exclusion zone on the orders of the coast guard. Dave waited impatiently for news of casualties, but neither the anchor nor the ticker running across the bottom of the screen provided that information. After filling up minutes of airtime with speculation about a 'daring terrorist strike', the anchor threw it over to a correspondent in Washington. Dave cursed quietly again.

'You should turn that off now. It's not helping.'

The voice was male and stern. Dave looked around, expecting to see the nurse flanked by some old fart of a doctor packing the usual God complex, but was surprised to see a lean, hard-looking man in military uniform. He looked a few years younger than Dave but much fitter and somehow older in the eyes. Dave looked for stripes on his arms, which was about the only military insignia he could recognise. Three meant a sergeant and two a corporal if the movies had not lied to him. But the man's green and black speckled digicam uniform carried no stripes. Probably some sort of officer, then.

'An army guy? Son, you got the wrong oil field,' Dave said incredulously. 'Get lost on your way to Fort Polk?'

The man shook his head.

'Lieutenant Dent,' he said, introducing himself. 'United States Navy.'

That confused Dave even more. Why would a navy guy dress for the jungle? He had other issues to take up with this guy, though.

'What the fuck is this exclusion zone and terrorist crap you guys are on about?'

He jerked a thumb at the TV screen. It was the thumb on his broken hand, which didn't even give him a twinge.

'The exclusion zone was declared for a reason,' Dent said. 'Maybe you should have paid attention to it.'

'Well, I didn't see you anywhere out there lending a hand, SpongeBob, so I figured I'd just do my fucking job. I am the safety boss for that rig. It's what Baron's pays me for, and it's my cock on the block if anything goes down. So if anyone is gonna be getting excluded from the Longreach, it's not me. Got a smart-ass answer for that, Navy?'

Dent didn't respond to the challenge beyond staring impassively back, and Dave decided he didn't like this navy asshole very much. Then he decided he was leaving. After all, he had a job to do and he couldn't do it in bed. He had to see to his people.

'Are any of my guys in this hospital?' Dave asked the nurse, ignoring the navy guy. He looked around the room, trying to figure out where they'd put him. It was a standard private hospital room, well-appointed and clean. Baron's' health insurance would cover that. And there were no . . .

. . . *Hunn ur Horde* . . .

. . . monsters. There were no monsters squatting in the middle of the room, snacking down on human femurs or sporting truly terrifying boners. Dave pushed the images away. Definitely some sort of bad drug flashback, he thought, mixing poorly with shock and trauma. Those whores; they must have slipped him something sketchy.

'I was with a guy called Vince Martinelli before I, er, fell over, or passed out, or whatever. Is Vince here? Is anybody from the Longreach here?'

The nurse looked to Dent, who answered, 'That's not your concern right now, sir. All of the casualties have been evacuated, and all of the wounded are being cared for. But we need to talk to you, Mr Hooper, if you are well enough.'

Dave looked himself up and down, taking in the bandages and the hospital gown and concluding that he wasn't too badly hurt. He rolled his shoulders, patted himself down, flexed his arms. No burns, no breaks as best he could tell. The nurse had the wrong guy. Not surprising given the chaos that would have blown through this place. There were a lot of casualties off that rig. Dave started to stand up again.

On the TV screen, a spokesman from Baron's was reading a statement, declaring that it was more important to deal with the immediate crisis than to speculate about what might have caused it.

'I need to find my guys,' Dave said by way of dismissing Dent's request. 'I need to know who made it out. Whether anyone was left behind. I don't mean no offence, but you weren't there, you don't –'

'I was there,' Dent said. 'My team got you out. And we need to debrief you, right now. You're not badly hurt.'

'And I'm not hanging around to play twenty questions with you. You need to know if some jihadi nutjob swam out there and blew up my rig? No, he didn't. I don't know what the fuck happened, but this terrorism bullshit . . .' He waved one hand at the television. 'It's a crock. Briefing ended. We're done.'

As he stepped forward, aware that his tough guy routine was somewhat undercut by the sight of his ass hanging out the back of the hospital gown, Lieutenant Dent stepped in across his path and put one hand lightly on his shoulder to bar his way. 'I'm sorry, sir, but . . .'

Dave was angry, and if he cared to examine his deeper feelings, he was also frightened and confused. But he didn't care to do anything like that. He rarely did. Matter of fact, he was trying very hard *not* to think about the nightmare he'd had lying in the hospital bed. He decided that was a reasonable explanation for his memories. A nightmare while he was fucked off his nut on whatever drugs those hookers had slipped him and whatever drugs the hospital had then poured in on top to mix up a little chaos cocktail inside his head. He didn't mean to strike Dent and certainly not to hurt him. He merely wanted to brush the man's hand from his shoulder and push past him. Instead, when he attempted to palm off the sailor, his hand moved with much greater speed than he had planned, making contact with the man's forearm, which Dave distinctly heard break. A sound like the snapping of a twig in the forest, muffled by distance. And before he could stop himself, before he had time to wonder at what he'd just done and how much trouble it was about to cause, he'd already hit Dent in the centre of his chest with an open hand, again a much quicker move than he had intended, but not hard. Or at least it didn't feel hard to Dave Hooper.

Lieutenant Dent cried out and flew back across the room, crashing into a freestanding closet, which splintered under the impact.

'What the . . .'

Dave sat down on the bed, or, more accurately, he collapsed onto it butt first. In a moment that convinced him he was going insane he heard the shrill, disapproving tone of his wife berating him for setting his dirty ass down on their clean sheets. But that was just another memory. Something that had happened a long while ago. Like his cousin Darryl and the trampoline.

He was stunned. And starting to feel more than a little sickened again – hello nausea, my old friend – he knew, he just *knew* that he'd hurt the lieutenant badly. Fucked him up, even. Broken his arm at least and possibly fractured a couple of ribs. The dizzy spell he'd experienced when he awoke came swirling back up from nowhere, and he muttered an apology as he leaned back on the pillows. Blossoms of dark light blotted out half the room, and he thought he might be sick all over the floor.

The nurse – Nurse Fletcher; he had a clear memory of the name badge she was wearing without ever really attending to it – cried out in alarm. Dave lost consciousness for a moment but not for too long, because when he came to, Dent was still on the floor, moaning and clutching at his chest with his one good arm, and two hospital orderlies were standing over the bed glowering fiercely at their difficult patient.

'Fuck, I'm sorry, all right,' Dave said weakly. His head was spinning, and racking gut cramps doubled him over. The darkness reached up to him again, and this time he stayed down there for a while.

05

Over the years, Dave Hooper had come to know himself, or rather his various selves. There was Good Dave, who'd tried his honest best when he was first married to Annie and the boys were young and there wasn't much money left over when they'd divided up his pay cheque to cover all the basics. Annie had gone back to her job as an editor of technical books shortly after Toby was born, but only part time. Her pay cheques were smaller, which was a mystery to his conservative friends such as Grbac because Dubya's tax cuts should have put more money in their pockets. None of it was any sort of mystery to Dave. Politics be damned. He was just getting fucked by the infamous luck of the Hoopers.

Annie had stayed home for six months when Jack arrived, but it had not been a happy time. Later on, they both acknowledged that she'd probably been depressed. Fuck knows Dave had been.

That was when Bad Dave showed up.

Bad Dave looked a lot like his better-behaved twin, and if anything he was, at first, more charming, more helpful, more – what was the word? – ingratiating. Bad Dave was ever so supportive, offering to run down to the shops for Toby's medicine or to work an extra shift to pay for the shrink Annie had started seeing. But Bad Dave had his ways. It was amazing how much time you could cut off a run to the grocery store or the pharmacy if you really pressed the gas on your vintage 1969 Chevy Camaro with that sweet-ass 468 big block. More than enough time for a side drink at Ringo's bar and maybe even two if you took the back road on the way home to avoid the cops and explained you'd had to pull over to take a couple of work calls. It was dangerous to drive while using the phone, after all. And he was a safety guy. It said so on his name tag.

Bad Dave could be awfully convincing when he was selling a story to his wife about needing – like *really fucking needing* – to fly up to Houston over the weekend for a bunch of bullshit meetings with the suits that he agreed was a total waste of time, but what the hell, they were paying him double-time just to show up. And they could totally use a little bit more of the folding stuff.

Bad Dave could even halfway convince himself that the time he spent in Hooters while he was on the company clock in Houston was actually necessary to keep things running smoothly at home, because God knows having him around the house didn't seem to put his wife in a good mood, whereas inhaling buffalo wings and beer at America's favourite titty bar did wonders for his.

But in the end Bad Dave always had to make way for Contrite Dave, for Apology Dave, and for Dave of the Shameless Grovel and Seething Resentment. Contrite Dave had worn out the knees on more than one pair of jeans crawling back into the affections of his long-suffering wife, a painful necessity that Rational Dave, or rather the divorce lawyer Rational Dave secretly consulted once, characterised as unavoidable.

Unless he wanted to spend the next decade or so in crippling poverty after Annie's lawyer and the Internal Revenue Service were finished gouging him. Contrite Dave had more than once promised the IRS that he would get his shit together, another little secret of which Annie was unaware until her rat bastard lawyer, Vietch – an old college flame and pathetically, *obviously* desperate to rekindle the fire – somehow ferreted out the information and informed her.

Sitting up in his hospital bed, allowing the doctor to prod and probe him, Contrite Dave was feeling very, very sorry indeed. If only for himself. He was more than a little worried. The officer he'd struck – and he hadn't even tried to hurt him, not really; it was more what the old-timers called a love tap – well, he was in surgery right now, having part of a rib removed from his lung. The surgeons had also had to drill a hole into his head, according to the doctor, to relieve the pressure from all the bleeding in there.

Contrite Dave nodded quietly. Occasionally he muttered 'sorry' even though, yeah, he was mostly sorry for himself. And he let his arms hang limp while the doctor checked his dressings. Dr Pradesh, his name was. A distinguished Indian guy – a curry Indian, not a Custer Indian – and an actual professor, Nurse Fletcher had whispered to him, with a neatly trimmed silvery beard and an honest-to-God turban on his head. A duck-egg-blue turban, Dave thought. Duck-egg blue had been one of Annie's favourite colours for dinner settings and throw cushions when she still cared about such things.

Dr Pradesh looked concerned as he examined Dave's chest and abdomen. Dave wasn't sure why, because apart from feeling hungry, starving in fact, he was fine. None of the other people in the room gave him any clue about what might be wrong. The orderlies were still there and still glaring at him. Nurse Fletcher scurried about trying to anticipate the doctor's every need. And a new navy guy stood in the corner with his arms folded, regarding Dave like he was some sort of unexploded bomb. Whenever he caught the eye of this new guy, which he tried to avoid doing as much as possible, Contrite Dave could not help himself.

'Sorry,' he muttered.

The new navy guy said nothing. He leaned against the door frame, his body a huge brick of compacted muscle that somehow gave the impression of fluidity. His face was a mask behind his sunglasses, neither hard and angry nor open to debate. For all Dave knew the man could have been meditating.

Dr Pradesh finished his examination and straightened up, looking at Dave, or rather at his injuries, with obvious disdain.

'Somebody has made a very stupid mistake,' he said. Dave figured the doctor had studied and worked most of his life in England, because his accent was pure Oxford. Or what Dave assumed to be Oxford on the basis of some old movies on the TV he'd fallen asleep in front of. He was not a guy to be crossed and Dave didn't trust himself not to say something stupid and offensive. He had history against him. 'This man has not been injured at all,' the doctor said. 'I don't know how he ended up here, but he is taking up a bed that could be used for one of the other casualties. We are overwhelmed by them.'

That finally caught Dave's attention and pulled him out of his one-man pity party.

'Casualties, Doc? Or, Professor, whatever. How many casualties, how bad?'

Pradesh dismissed him with a sniff.

'A lot worse off than you, young man,' he said. It had been

a long time since anybody had called Dave Hooper 'young man'. One of the reasons he'd hired two whores from Nevada was so that one could spray a big whipped cream '37' on her chest for the other one to lick off. Man had to have something to look forward to on his birthday, after all.

'But, Doctor,' the nurse protested, 'I saw and dressed his wounds myself. He had second-degree burns to forty percent of his torso. A greenstick fracture to his right ulna. And a deep laceration running from his right armpit most of the way down to his navel. The sutures will still be in him.'

Pradesh looked at her with an expression hovering somewhere between pity and contempt.

'Then show me the stitches, nurse,' he said. 'They won't have dissolved yet. Or the burns. Either would be satisfactory. This man is fit and healthy. And from evidence of the trauma done to the naval officer, his little nap in our much-needed bed has returned to him whatever strength he lacked when carried in here. From the smell of his breath, I would imagine he was passed out drunk.'

Hooper observed the exchange between doctor and nurse as though watching a tennis match, his head turning to and fro. Nurse Fletcher was not backing down. Whatever deference she had paid to the doctor's exalted position before had been withdrawn in the face of his lack of respect for her professional judgment. If she said Hooper was burned and lacerated . . .

But he wasn't, was he? Dent had said he was fine, too. He shifted about, turning his shoulders this way and that, trying to feel the tug of fresh sutures in his skin. Or the deeply unpleasant sensation of burned meat on his own body. Second-degree burns, the nurse had said. That was gonna hurt.

But nothing. How could that be?

The last thing he remembered was . . . No, best not to go there. He was still trying to sort out his memory of landing on the rig platform from the drug-addled dream of the orcs. He didn't know what his last memory was.

You dare not do this.

He remembered swinging the splitting maul. No, he remembered *a bad dream* about swinging on something –

Urgon Htoth Ur Hunn, BattleMaster of the Fourth Legion.

What the fuck? Dave tried to shake the thought from his head. He remembered something about a TV being on in the crew quarters. A game, stalled on the Xbox. Maybe some sort of acid flashback? Man, it'd been years, but they said it could still come back at you years later.

'So he's good to go, Professor?'

It was the soldier. No, it was the new navy guy, Dave reminded himself. His voice was a strange train wreck of a Midwestern accent buried under a surfer's drawl. A voice like that, this guy got around. A replacement for the navy guy Dave had broken, he was dressed in the same digital jungle camouflage, but with a pistol strapped to his thigh. Dent hadn't been wearing no pistol. Dr Pradesh turned away from his confrontation with Nurse Fletcher, letting the new guy feel the full force of his disapproval.

'Well, he is good to get out of bed, if that's what you mean. But I don't want him leaving the hospital or even the ward until we find out who was responsible for putting him in here when he should have been sleeping off his drunkenness in a cell at the police station. You might not think it important, but I am trying to run a medical facility here, and I cannot have it descend into some sort of half-arsed pantomime of a Persian bazaar. Mr Cooper –'

'Hooper,' Contrite Dave said, getting less contrite by the minute. 'Dave Hooper.'

Pradesh carried on without missing a beat: '– will not be leaving until we find out how he made his way in here.'

And with that he turned the full force of both turban and beard on Contrite Dave.

'And rest assured your employer's health insurance will be paying for every minute you lie there wasting our precious time and resources.'

'Hey, that's cool,' said Contrite Dave, who didn't want any trouble.

The navy guy spoke up again, apparently not at all intimidated by the superior attitude of this high-talking asshole with his head in a towel. 'Doc, if he's good to go, I have orders and authorisation to take him, right now.'

Uh oh, thought Dave, his heart sinking. He'd really fucked up that other navy guy, and now he was in the shit. Not just with the government or the fucking IRS but this time with the navy. Fuck. That was probably worse than the IRS.

'Hey, I'm a civilian,' Dave said.

The navy surfer bro rotated his head a notch to the left, still leaning on the doorjamb as if they were at the bar playing pool. 'Dude, seriously? You can pretend to have a choice about this, but you will be coming with me. On foot or on your ass.'

He spoke calmly and steadily with a laid-back Californian vibe that sounded as if it had been tacked on to the Midwest inflection like a jerry-built porch. But there was no mistaking the intent behind it, as though putting a couple of rounds in some dude was no big deal. Dave didn't doubt this new guy would shoot him without a second thought. He wasn't making threats; he was just explaining how it was gonna be in his weird soft-but-hard voice.

All Dave wanted to do was get out of bed, get out of this hospital gown that left his ass hanging in the breeze, find Vince Martinelli or somebody – anybody – from the platform, and sort out exactly what had happened. But nobody was interested in what he wanted. Pradesh left off his argument with Nurse Fletcher to take up this new one with . . . Allen. The navy guy's name tag read ALLEN, and he had stripes on his collar. Dave frowned. He knew that without having to look. But he didn't remember having seen it and noted it before.

Nurse Fletcher, meanwhile increased the volume of her objections about Dave's injuries to Professor Pradesh, or rather to the back of his duck-egg-blue turban. The navy guy, Allen, glanced at the cupboard Dave had destroyed by – what? Jedi Knight Force-punching it? Allen stood with arms folded, refusing to be drawn into an argument with Pradesh. He just kept shaking his head, appearing to grow calmer the more the doctor lost it. Mr Hooper would be coming with him. End of story. The orderlies who were supposed to be watching Dave had been distracted by the three-way argument.

Dave leaned forward and glanced across the hallway into the room opposite, hoping to see someone he knew in there, possibly even Martinelli. But Nurse Fletcher's considerable bulk intervened, blocking his view. She raised her voice, trying to talk over Pradesh, who was trying to convince Allen that he was in charge. Dave was suddenly aware of just how hungry he was, ravenously so. His stomach growled and saliva jetted into his mouth as he sniffed the chemical-scented hospital air and thought he discerned a faraway hint of boiled potatoes and some sort of meat.

The thought of meat brought up memories of the

nightmare he'd rather forget, and he forced them away. The argument around him grew a touch louder and a lot more irrational. It was like listening to his two boys go at each other over some stupid and pointless playground bullshit. Nobody had answered any of his questions about the rig and what had happened. Nobody had told him who made it off and who didn't. They didn't seem to understand that he was responsible for what happened out there. He was the guy who was supposed to keep everyone safe, and he hadn't.

He had failed.

Epically.

Again.

He just wanted everyone to stop for a moment and listen to him. To answer his goddamn questions. He wanted to know why he was in hospital, apparently unharmed, when so many others were not. He wanted to know why he was having psychotic visions, even if the answer was obvious. One of those hookers had to have slipped him something last night, and he was about to fail a drug test. Probably about to be charged and prosecuted. And that wasn't even close to the worst of the shit coming down on him.

But nobody was paying the slightest bit of attention to Dave Hooper anymore. Nobody cared. Certainly not about him and probably not about any of the men and women he had failed out on the Longreach. Before he even knew what he was doing, Dave let his temper off the leash. He balled his right hand into a fist and slammed it down on the little bedside unit on which rested his empty water glass and the TV remote.

'Shut up!' he shouted, but not loudly enough to be heard over the enormous crash of the bedside table exploding under the force of his blow. He had not meant to destroy another piece of furniture. Jeez, would the insurance even cover that? All he'd wanted was to stop them from bickering and get them to pay him some attention.

Mission accomplished. Nurse Fletcher shrieked. Pradesh spun around in alarm and almost tripped over his own feet. Allen came off the wall as if roused from a nap, his hand on his weapon, ready to use it. The two orderlies didn't know what to do. Dave just stared at his fist where it hung in midair over the shattered sticks of furniture. He hadn't been looking when he'd lashed out, and his fist had come down on top of a drinking glass. It'd exploded as if dropped from a great height, and jagged shards of glass laid open the side of his hand. One long, bloodied fang of glass had penetrated the heel of his palm and emerged on the other side.

It was uncomfortable but not as painful as it should have been, Dave thought. He must be in shock. Reaching across, feeling a little queasy but fascinated at the same time, he pinched the shard between the thumb and forefinger of his uninjured hand and pulled it out. It was an unusual sensation, having something hard slide through his body like that. But again it didn't really hurt. Not like his arm had hurt all those years ago when he broke it playing on the trampoline with his cousin.

'I'm sorry,' he said in an almost childish voice. 'I hurt myself. And I broke your table.'

He held his hand up to Nurse Fletcher, who backed away from him, and then to Pradesh, whose eyes betrayed his shock. Allen also gaped at the ugly gash, but not because of any squeamishness about the blood. Presumably he'd seen plenty in his line of work. As had Fletcher and Pradesh.

What none of them had seen, however, was the way Dave Hooper's wound sealed itself and stopped bleeding within a few seconds. His hand itched terribly where he had opened it up, and he examined it with a sort of fearful curiosity, half expecting to pass out. But instead of some lipless, pulsing violation, all he saw was the blood he had spilled. He ran his fingers gently over the site of the gash.

The skin was sticky with blood but otherwise unmarked.

'Holy fuck,' Dave said.

'I told you so,' Nurse Fletcher hissed at the doctor.

06

Nurse Fletcher hurried back, wearing rubber gloves and carrying a clean-up tray. She dipped cotton balls into a bowl of warm water that was cloudy with antiseptic. After what had happened to Dent, Dave was careful not to make any sudden movements as she wiped away the blood. He was feeling dizzy again, but not because of the gore. He was certain now that he was starving. It had been a long time since he'd eaten any solid food, and that had been a bag of Doritos, and he'd tossed them up on the grass back at the depot. The hunger was becoming more than just uncomfortable. The pain in his stomach was much worse than the glass going into his hand. Or coming out.

Pradesh shooed away the orderlies when Dave agreed to behave himself on the promise of something to eat and somebody finally answering his questions. Allen, who introduced himself as a chief petty officer, some sort of navy sergeant, assured Dave he would 'brief him in' on the situation out at the Longreach, including an updated casualty list. Vince Martinelli, he said, had been taken to a military hospital with minor injuries but otherwise suffering only from shock. He would be fine.

'This is most unusual,' Pradesh muttered as the blood came off Dave's arm and hands. 'Most unsatisfactory.'

'Unsatisfactory' wasn't the word Dave would have chosen. 'Bugshit crazy' would have been his choice. Nobody had asked him about monsters or nightmares or told him to piss into a cup yet, for which he was grateful. He'd been doing pretty well convincing himself he was having some kind of acid flashback or crystal meth moment until he'd destroyed the bedside table and sliced open his hand, only to see it heal in less than a minute. That was madness enough to put a man over the edge, but at least he wasn't alone in having witnessed it. Five other responsible adults had seen it, too. And none of them had been snorting lines off some hooker's tits the previous night as far as he knew.

'There,' said Nurse Fletcher as she finished cleaning a wound that wasn't there. 'Doctor?'

Pradesh stepped forward a little cautiously and leaned over to take Dave's hand gently. He turned it this way and that, looking for any signs of the injury they'd all seen Dave inflict upon himself just a couple of minutes earlier. Again Dave was careful not to make any sudden or forceful movements. The doctor frowned and shook his head, muttering something to himself.

'We all saw what happened, did we not?' Pradesh said at last, in his snooty Oxford English.

'Yep,' noted Nurse Fletcher. 'It's just like I told you. You didn't believe me, but I told you he came in here badly wounded. And now . . .' She trailed off.

'And now,' said Dave, wincing in pain, 'I think I'm going to disappear up my own butthole if I don't get something to eat. I'm not joking, Doc. I've never felt this hungry before in my life. Feels like a fire inside me.'

'Of course, of course,' Pradesh said. 'Increased metabolism.' He spoke as though he were talking about Dave, not to him. 'Nurse, call down to the children's ward and see if they can send up a couple of packets of high-energy milk biscuits. Straight away. And talk to the canteen; have them send some of that dreadful fatty slop they served at lunch. I am sure there will be leftovers. I don't know what is wrong with Mr Hooper, but I fear his energy needs may be . . .' He paused and seemed to ponder the question. '. . . extreme,' he concluded.

'Here,' Allen said, reaching into one of the large cargo pockets of his jungle-green-coloured combat trousers and retrieving a couple of energy bars. He unwrapped them and handed both carefully to Dave, who took them with equal care. He wasn't sure what the bars were, but he could smell citrus and cocoa. Spit flooded his mouth as soon as he jammed both bars in there, working his jaws in a fury. It was as though he couldn't chew fast enough, and the pangs in his stomach sharpened while he tried to get the impromptu meal down as quickly as possible. When he was done eating a minute later, the dizziness and fatigue he had felt creeping up on him receded.

'That working for you?' the navy guy asked.

'Shit, yeah,' Dave told him. 'Man, that was bad. That really fucking hurt.'

'I'm afraid I'm going to need to schedule some tests,' said Dr Pradesh. 'Many tests. I'm sorry. This is unprecedented.'

He didn't sound as if he was afraid or even apologetic. He sounded like a guy who'd just spotted a Nobel Prize for Medicine dropping into his lap and wanted to grab it as quickly and hold on to it as hard as he could.

'Doc, there's not going to be any tests,' said Chief Petty Officer Allen. 'Not now and not here. I meant what I said before. I have orders and the authority to place Mr Hooper in protective custody and escort him from here to a secure location where he can be –'

'Absolutely not,' said Pradesh.

'Whoa, hold on there,' Dave said, adding his objections. 'You might have bought me dinner, but that doesn't mean you get to fuck me, Admiral.'

'The language is not necessary, sir,' Allen said. The words sounded weird in his oddly misplaced surfer's drawl.

It was the sort of thing Marty would have said, but Marty was dead. Eaten like a big born-again burrito. 'A sailor who doesn't swear?' Dave said, concentrating fiercely to keep his thoughts in the present. 'Seriously? Well, I'm not going anywhere and I'm not doing anyone's tests until I get some answers. You can take me to Vince Martinelli if you want, if he knows more than I do. But right now you can start by telling me what the hell happened out on the Longreach this morning. It was this morning, wasn't it? I haven't been out of it overnight?'

'No, sir, you have not,' said a new voice from over by the door.

A tall African-American man stood in the doorway. An officer by the look of him. He wore a short-sleeve khaki dress uniform, a more formal arrangement than Allen's fatigues with their pockets full of high-energy chocolate bars. A swathe of multicoloured ribbons covered a patch over his left pec, topped by a bright gold bird bearing a trident in its claws. Dave's eye was drawn to the purple ribbon. He was pretty sure his brother had been awarded one of those.

'Michael Heath, captain, United States Navy. Joint Special Operations Command,' the officer said.

Special Operations, Dave thought. Did that make the captain a Black Seal? He suppressed an embarrassed, idiotic chuckle, ashamed of himself, blaming it on feeling so dizzy and light-headed with hunger and maybe some leftover drug residue, but the captain really was *that* dark. Like he had stepped out of Africa and right into Harvard or Yale to judge by the snooty accent. Man, you could sell hundred-dollar bottles of wine with that voice.

Hooper cursed himself. *Jesus, Dave. Get a grip you redneck asshole.*

'Okay,' he said, mostly to stop himself from giggling like a stoned idiot, 'more navy guys. Awesome.'

Captain Heath considered Dave with a foreboding frown but addressed himself to Pradesh. 'Doctor, you will find papers have been served to your administrators releasing Mr Hooper into our care. We require his consultation on a matter of national security.'

Pradesh started to object loudly. His arms flew around, and he bobbed up and down on his expensive-looking loafers as he argued with, or rather at, Captain Heath.

'Well I'm afraid this will not stand, Captain Heath. It will not stand at all. This patient is under my care and will remain under my care.'

Nurse Fletcher was still invested in her issues with Pradesh, sniping at him as he railed at the iniquities of military high-handedness and fought a gallant rearguard action in defence of his Nobel.

'I told you, Doctor,' she said. 'I told you there was something wrong with this patient.'

Meanwhile the intimidating Captain Heath absorbed the doctor's attack and the general uproar with an utterly impassive face. He waited for Pradesh to take a breath, looking just like a dude with the patience of Buddha. *No*, Dave thought as his mind began to wander, *scratch that. He looks like a dude with the patience of a* statue *of Buddha*. When Pradesh paused momentarily, Heath seemed to come to life, as if he'd been in power-down. He strode into the room with a nod to Allen, and his physical presence seemed to subdue the doctor in a way no words were likely to. He limped, though, ever so slightly, and Dave's eye was drawn to the subtle imbalance in his gait. He had to make himself look away, like when you saw someone, some hot-looking piece of ass, say, with a really ugly birthmark messing up half her face. You didn't want to be caught staring. Nobody else was staring, however, or even seemed to have noticed the limp. *Probably got his Purple Heart for whatever gave him the gimpy leg*, Dave thought.

'If you'll get dressed, please, Mr Hooper,' said Heath. 'I have transport waiting for us downstairs. Time is short.'

He didn't look at his watch but gave Dave the impression he could tell the time to within thirty seconds without it.

'I must protest this,' Pradesh began.

'Of course you must,' said Heath.

'Doc, from what I've seen,' Allen said, jerking his thumb at Dave, 'we're doing you a favour. You'll thank us someday.'

'Thank you, Chief Allen,' Heath said in a tone that gave everyone to understand he didn't think the CPO was helping. Dave wondered if the captain was the senior SEAL hereabouts and quickly hid a smirk at the sound of that phrase. *Senior seal. Good one, Dave*. He couldn't shake the faint, buzzy, blurred feeling of being stoned. Not totally wasted. Just pleasantly high – say, half a joint rather than three bongs – finding everything funny and, of course . . . hungry. So hungry.

Heath produced a sheaf of paper and handed it to the doctor. 'Complaint form,' he explained. 'We'll need it in triplicate. Mr Hooper, sir. I note you are still not dressed.'

The warning tone in Heath's voice transported Dave back to his childhood. To the sound of his mom's voice warning him he'd be late for school. Again. And the fear of his father appearing from somewhere, smelling of hand-rolled cigarettes and breakfast bourbon, snarling threats and backhanding him hard enough to raise a bruise. Dave, feeling as though he'd done something wrong – you know, besides throwing that last navy guy halfway through a wall and totally smashing the crap out of a bunch of innocent hospital furniture – fumbled for an excuse until he realised he actually had one.

'I got no clothes,' he said. 'I don't know what happened to mine, and this hospital gown –'

'Chief?' Captain Heath snapped his fingers, and CPO Allen bent over and produced a sports bag, which he tossed onto the bed.

'Brought it in while you were sleeping. Had to guess at your size. Are you an Eddie Bauer man?'

'Not normally,' Dave said.

'Dude, you are today. The Original Outdoor Outpatient.'

Dave opened the bag with care, afraid that he might tear it apart, and found a pair of jeans, a T-shirt, a grey zip-up hoodie, socks, jocks, and a pair of Nikes. All new.

'Bauer's a little uptown for me,' he said.

No one smiled or reacted in any way. Pradesh was still reading the pro forma complaint letter and fuming silently. The nurse was cloaked in the armour of vindication, and the navy guys stared at him, waiting for him to do as he was told.

'Do I have to, er . . . my wallet is back on the –'

Heath cut him off.

'Contingency funds, Mr Hooper. You need to get dressed now.'

Allen herded the two civilians out of the room, with Pradesh still muttering about taking this to a higher authority.

'Section 3 of the form, sir,' said Heath.

'I told you he was burned,' Fletcher said again. 'Must have healed up just like we saw him do. Just then.'

Both military men stayed in the room. Dave climbed carefully out of bed for the first time since he'd put the unfortunate lieutenant through the cupboard door. He concentrated on the basics: removing his gown, getting dressed. He took his time with each movement, as though learning it anew. It helped keep his mind off things.

'How many dead and injured?' he asked as he dressed. Better to think about other people's problems than the pile of shit he seemed to have his face planted in. 'You never told me.'

Chief Allen didn't hesitate. The surfer dude aura faded as he relayed the bad news. 'Last figures I had were twelve dead, including one woman from your catering staff. Eighteen missing. Twenty-six injured, nineteen of them critical. I'm sorry; I don't have any individual details. But your colleague Mr Martinelli did make it out.'

Dave got his leg through jeans that were just a little big for him. He was glad of that. If he had to pull them on with any sort of effort, he feared tearing them like tissue paper. He felt awkward dressing in front of Heath and Allen like this. It was stupid, because he was used to showering with dozens of naked rig monkeys. But Heath in particular seemed to emanate censorious judgment. He hadn't mentioned the other officer Dave had put into surgery, but you could tell he was pissed about it.

What's wrong with me?

An image of the thing from his nightmare forced itself into his thoughts. He pushed it away and cursed instead at the butcher's bill from the rig. That was what he should have been worrying about. Not bullshit drug flashbacks. He was responsible. No matter what had gone down out there, he, Dave Hooper, was the guy paid to make sure shit didn't go down on the platform. And he'd failed. He wanted to climb back into bed and pull the covers over his head.

It was a miserable feeling. The last couple of years, as everything else in his life turned to shit, he'd at least been able to hang on to the idea that no matter what else might happen, whether he was hungover or reeking of paid-for-pussy, Dave Hooper turned up and got the job done. Dave sat down heavily on the hospital bed, all the giggles gone now. He pulled on the shoes and did up the laces. Tied them as carefully as a first-grader.

'Hello?'

A candy stripper stood at the door, bearing a paper bag. From the smell of them, the promised cookies. Saliva jetted into Dave's mouth again. Captain Heath thanked her with more grace than Dave would have thought possible given his uptight personality, but his smile vanished when he turned away from the girl. 'We good to go?'

'I think so,' Allen said as Dave shrugged on the blue US Navy hoodie.

'I got some questions,' Dave said.

'So do we,' Heath said. 'So that's a win-win situation. We can talk in the car. You can eat your cookies if you behave yourself.'

Dave opened his mouth to ask what they were gonna do if he didn't behave himself, but the exaggerated head shake from Chief Allen prompted him to stow that particular line of inquiry.

It was dark outside and felt like mid-evening to Hooper. As they strode through the crowded lobby of the hospital – he still had no idea which one, adding to his deepening sense of being lost – he looked around for a clock, not wanting to ask the military guys. He didn't want to feel like he was dependent on them or owed them anything. An old-fashioned analogue clock like you sometimes saw at railway stations hung on the wall over the main entrance.

9.25 pm.

Holy shit, he'd been out all day.

The foyer served as an anteroom to the ER, and business was brisk. Three flat-screen televisions hung from the ceiling, two of them turned to the Shopping Network but one running coverage of the Longreach disaster from CNN Hong Kong of all places. A small group of people were gathered beneath that screen, but it wasn't the centre of most people's attention, most likely because none of the news channels had anything new to report. Like Dave, they were out of the loop. Heath kept them moving, not giving Dave a chance to stop and take in the report. As they approached the exit, two other men, both of them bearded and tattooed, both wearing fatigues like Allen, fell in alongside the party, sketching salutes.

'Rest of the team is outside,' one of the beards told Chief Allen. He regarded Dave with all the respect due a small dog turd on a cocktail fork. 'A little much for one guy, isn't it?'

Allen shook his head. 'Nope. Trust me, or you can ask Lieutenant Dent if and when he wakes up.'

Dave didn't like the sound of that. Neither did the beards by the way their expressions darkened. He looked up at the clock again just to escape the judgment in their eyes.

Shit.

'I need a phone,' he said, slowing down, causing the SEALs to bunch up around him. 'I need to call my wife. Or, you know, ex-wife soon enough. This thing's been all over the news. She'll worry. She does that. And my boys . . .' He trailed off.

Chief Allen raised an eyebrow at Heath, asking a question silently, and the captain nodded but checked his wristwatch. Just letting Dave know they were still on the clock. Allen reached into another one of his cargo pockets and fished out a cell phone. It looked cheap but new.

'It's a burner,' he explained. 'All set up. With Sprint, sorry. Reception will probably be lousy. But it's got twenty bucks on it. Good enough?'

Dave thanked him and took the candy bar phone as they got moving again. It had been a few years since he'd used one, and he remembered how awkward he'd found them. The buttons were so small, and this cheap piece of Chinese crap felt breakable. He was extra careful, but before he could finish entering the number, Captain Heath reached over and laid a hand on his healed forearm. The guy might dress like a desk jockey, but his hands were as hard as any rig monkey's.

'You only need to tell her that you are alive and well,' he said. 'Tell her you're going to be busy helping out. It won't be a lie.'

Dave bristled at being told what to do, but he reminded

himself that these guys had sprung him out of the hospital, promised to answer his questions, and bought him some new threads. Plus, he'd put their friend, that Dent guy, on the operating table. Still, Dave Hooper did not like being told what to do. He resisted the urge to give this asshole the brush-off, worried he might send him flying through a plate glass window.

He didn't need to go breaking any more navy guys if he could help it.

'I just want to let my boys know I'm all right,' he said. 'I should have done it before now. Soon as I woke up. I'm not much of a dad, I know that. But I'm the only one they've got, the poor little bastards.'

'Fine,' Heath said as though conceding a minor debating point. 'But keep it brief. And simple.'

The sliding doors rumbled apart as they approached the exit, and for the first time in many hours Dave caught a breath of fresh air. Or at least of outside air. The parking lot smelled of exhaust, oil, decaying rubber, discarded junk food, the sickly sweet syrup of an abandoned Coke . . .

He stopped breathing and gagged.

When he was an undergrad many years ago, he'd dropped acid before going to a party just off campus. When the tab came on, he experienced a few minutes of sensory crossover, seeing sounds and hearing colours. There was a word for that, he knew, but he'd forgotten it. The sensation had passed, leaving him with the raw certainty that he'd been inhabited by the spirit of a wild dog, and he had been able to smell even the most faintly detectable whiff of a scent drifting by on the breeze.

This was what an acid flashback really felt like, he thought as he stood on the steps of the hospital, aware of hundreds of different odours, each of them separate and unique. It was strangely reassuring, providing an explanation for the psychotic visions he'd been having. One of the whores had totally slipped him something. Had to have. If he ever found his wallet again, it was sure to be light a couple of credit cards and most of his cash. And fuck them in the neck, anyway. He'd maxed out that plastic a long time ago.

'Are you all right?' Allen asked without sounding as if he gave an actual shit. He was just checking on his package. Heath was staring at him, too, concern creasing his brow and altering the planes of his face, which had been such an unreadable mask until then. The escort reached carefully for sidearms, not sure what to believe or expect.

Dave took a few breaths through his mouth, trying not to smell anything, and closed his eyes until the world stopped spinning. He gradually regained his sense of balance. 'I'm fine,' he said. 'I just had . . . I dunno. I just felt a bit weird.'

Heath watched him as though he were standing on a land mine and any movement might kill them all. Satisfied that they could move safely again, he said, 'Let's get in the car.'

07

One of the pirates drove the Ford Expedition while the other one took the shotgun seat.

Dave had taken to thinking of them as the pirates, since nobody had introduced the two bearded and tattooed bodyguards. Or guards, or whatever they were. Hairy fucking SEALs, he supposed.

Heath and Allen rode in the back with him. They were all big men, and it was crowded back there. Also, although he could totally imagine Heath being driven to a meeting or cocktail party or torture session in some undeclared black ops detention facility, Dave Hooper was a working man and usually rode up front.

Not this time.

A second identical vehicle followed them, presumably with more navy guys.

Bad weather was closing in, blowing grit and drifts of rubbish, loose paper and plastic bags, across the road. Every now and then an unusually strong gust would buffet the car. He felt like an old man because of all the extra care he was taking not to break anything. The seat belt he pulled on slowly and clicked into place as though the clunky metal fittings were made of brittle plastic. He used his little finger to pick out Annie's phone number on the burner again.

The pirate with the black beard concentrated on the drive as Dave waited for his ex-wife to pick up the phone. Then, as he had so many times before, he corrected himself. She wasn't officially, *legally*, his ex yet. But that happy day was coming soon. Heath didn't even pretend to look out the window on Dave's left. He kept his eyes on his primary mission, Mr David Hooper.

They rolled down cracked asphalt streets that had last been resurfaced long before Katrina. Passed another hospital parking lot where hospital workers in scrubs moved about, perhaps coming on shift, perhaps taking five for a smoke. The New Orleans skyline was difficult to pick out at street level, but at one point he thought he recognised the Louisiana Superdome and wondered if they ever got that place cleaned up.

Before long, they climbed a ramp onto westbound US 90.

The phone rang and rang. Dave was aware of his heart rate increasing as he waited for the connection. It was like he was back in those days when Annie was just starting to lose faith in him. He was Contrite Dave all over again. This time he was ringing up to apologise for not telling her earlier that he hadn't been incinerated in the blaze on the platform. Or shot by terrorists or eaten by monsters.

He shook his head and let that last thought fly past. The only reliable memory he could count on was stepping off the chopper and waving to J2. Everything from that point on had a bad, dreamlike quality. In spite of his disgruntlement at being ordered by Heath to keep it short and simple, Dave was planning to do just that anyway. He didn't have the words to explain what had happened and what was still going on. All he knew was that he was deep in the shit, and in a strange way that made this call easier. If there was one thing Annie O'Halloran was used to, it was taking phone calls from Dave Hooper apologising from somewhere deep down in the shit. She answered after another five or six rings.

'It's me, babe. I'm sorry I –'

She cut him off. Of course.

'Oh, my God! You are in *so* much trouble. Do you have any idea what we've been through today. You . . . you . . . inconsiderate jerk. I . . . I . . .'

Her anger stumbled and tripped over into something more confused. An emotion with less clarity than her habitual bad temper. She started to cry, explaining that she'd had to pick the boys up early from school to whisk them away before they heard something on the playground about what was happening down on the Longreach.

'I had to give them sedatives, Dave. I had to take them to the doctor and give them drugs because they were both hysterical.'

He mumbled his apologies. It was such a routine exchange for them, as familiar as slipping on a comfortable pair of shoes. His wife – no, his ex-wife-to-be, crying and shouting, barely able to keep a rein on her feelings. And him, face hot with shame and not a little resentment that yet again circumstances beyond his control or even imagining had brought them to this.

'Look, Annie. I'm sorry, I'm so sorry, babe.'

He jerked the phone away from his ear as she suddenly shrieked at him, 'Don't you *babe* me, David Hooper. Not now, not ever again. Oh, my God, what you put those boys through today, and all because . . . What, why did you do it? Were you in some bar somewhere? With one of your *ladies*?'

Annie loaded up the word 'ladies' with enough venom that he could taste it at the back of his mouth. She had the timing wrong, but she knew him well enough.

'No,' he said. 'I've been in the hospital. I just got out.'

An immature, unworthy part of him enjoyed being able to say that. It was wrong, and he knew he was hooked up all wrong because he enjoyed it, but that was just how it had gone between them. Annie O'Halloran might have been a lapsed Catholic, but although she'd given up the church-going, there was no letting go of the old Catholic guilt, and there was no way Dave Hooper was ever going to let go of using it against her.

'I'm sorry, Annie,' he continued, 'and I'm really sorry about the boys. I know it's late, I know I should have called earlier, but I just got discharged, and I've been under most of the day.'

That broke the free-running torrent of her anger and grief like a boulder tossed into a stream in flood. 'Oh . . . damn, look, I'm sorry, Dave, it's just that we've been so worried, the boys, you know, and . . .'

'It's okay,' he said, making it sound like he was the one making a big concession. 'You're right. I'm sorry the boys had to go through that. Are they okay now?'

Her voice cracked back like a whip. 'I told you, Dave. They're sedated.'

'Oh,' he said in a small voice. 'Right.'

This was a hell of a thing to have to discuss in front of strangers. He was able to catch himself before he added 'I forgot'. Forgetting about the sorts of things that other, better parents seemed to remember without effort had been another issue between them.

'Is it true what they're saying?' Annie asked. 'Some sort of terror thing.'

'Who's saying that?' Dave asked, fending off the question. 'The media?'

He felt Heath go ever so slightly taut in the seat beside him and experienced the narrowing of the man's focus on him as something distinct and uncomfortable.

Annie was sobbing now, her voice hitching and difficult to follow.

'Oh, I don't know,' she said between her tears and gulping for air. 'The company isn't saying anything. I tried to call them, but they brushed me off. Obama's not saying anything. Nobody knows what's happening. We don't even know how many people di . . . died. How many, Dave? How many?'

'A dozen or so dead,' he answered in a flat voice. 'About twice that missing. Probably dead, I reckon, from what I saw out there. Lots of injuries. Annie, you probably know more about it than me. I've been under sedation as well. I don't know jack shit about what's happening out there now.' He stared pointedly at Captain Heath, a challenge of sorts. The navy officer just twirled his finger to signal him to wrap it up.

'But I'm all right,' he said. 'Hardly even scratched. I just got knocked out, is all. And I have to get back to Houston to help out. So I have to go now, honey. This isn't even my phone. I had to borrow it.'

Instantly, Annie was alert, her suspicions tripped by the admission, so late in the conversation, that he was with someone.

'Who are you with, Dave? And where are you? You haven't even told me.'

He looked at Heath as he answered her.

'I'm in New Orleans,' he said. 'And I'm not with anyone special. Just some guy. From the coast guard.'

He wasn't sure why he lied. It just came naturally. Dave could have sworn he detected the ghost of a smile on Heath in the dark of the car.

'I gotta go, Annie, really. Tell Toby and Jack that their old man came through. Tell them I'll see if I can get home soon as –'

He was looking at Heath as he said that, too, but the man was unreadable. Annie apologised a few more times for being such a bitch to him, and he let her apologise because it made him feel better. Dave said goodbye and cut the connection, offering the cell to Heath, who merely indicated that Dave should throw it into the cup holder up front.

'Ex-wives,' the driving pirate said. 'Can't live with them, and you can't drop them into an extraordinary rendition program. Not without answering a lot of questions.'

His bearded buddy laughed, and they exchanged a fist bump.

The car left the built-up area of the city behind. Rain spotted the windshield, and Blackbeard, who smelled powerfully of chewing tobacco and Old Spice, flipped on the wipers.

'So where are we headed?' Dave asked.

'An airfield,' said Heath, 'restricted.'

Before Dave could ask another question, like which goddamn airfield and why, they reached the Mississippi River. Dave could see what looked like a power plant out the window. Hundreds of lights burned and twinkled in the darkness, their hard glow softened by the constant drizzle, and Heath spoke again.

'What did you kill out on the Longreach, Mr Hooper? And how?'

His stomach flipped over. All the half-remembered terrors from his nightmare came flooding back in behind his eyeballs, and Dave had to face the possibility that they weren't half remembered at all.

'What do you mean?'

It wasn't a serious question. He just didn't know how to answer the navy man, didn't know how he could even begin to answer honestly. Heath seemed to understand that Dave wouldn't be able to respond right away.

'We've reviewed all of the CCTV coverage that we could recover,' he said. 'And we've conducted after-action interviews with survivors. Mr Martinelli was very helpful. He saw what you did, and the teams we put in confirmed the details. It's important that we know what happened. We need to know what you killed, Mr Hooper – and how. Because nobody else on that platform survived an encounter with these hostiles.'

Dave shuddered with deep-body revulsion. His gorge rose as he remembered the thing . . .

Urgon Htoth Ur Hunn.

. . . sinking its fangs into Marty Grbac.

Urgon Htoth Ur Hunn, BattleMaster of the Fourth Legion.

'What are you? From *The X-Files* or something?' he asked weakly.

'I work for JSOC, Mr Hooper,' Heath said. 'Joint Special Operations Command, just like I told the doctor back at the hospital. We responded to the emergency on the Longreach because local emergency services called it in as a potential terrorist strike. That's a scenario we have prepared for, but it was not a terrorist strike, Mr Hooper. We need you to tell us what it was.'

Dave's hands were shaking as he rubbed his eyes. He swore softly.

'I'm sorry, Captain, but I got no fucking idea what

happened out there. I thought it was a nightmare. Just a bad dream or some drug fuck-up at the hospital.'

He didn't feel the need to come clean about the pharmacological lucky dip he'd been into the night before he flew back to the Longreach. As far as drugs went, Heath seemed likely to be one of those zero-tolerance types. He'd probably just bite down on a piece of rawhide if you had to dig a bullet out of him.

'I was really hoping you'd tell me something,' Dave added.

They rode on in silence, the rhythmic thumping of the tyres rolling over joins in the freeway surface the only sound in the car. Sodium globes in the overhead lights poured sick yellow light into the cabin through the rain-slicked windows. With the Mississippi River behind them, they continued down US 90.

'Dude, why don't you start by telling us what you remember?' Chief Allen suggested. 'Don't try to explain what happened or why. Just tell us what you recall from the moment you landed on the helipad. Even if it sounds crazy to you. We hear crazy stuff all the time. Seriously. We don't judge.'

Torn between not wanting to sound like a maniac and not wanting to have his worst fears confirmed – that he had suffered some kind of psychotic break – but desperately needing to confide in somebody, Dave rubbed his eyes and told his story in a monotone, embellishing it as little as possible. Quite the opposite in fact. He made no mention of the name Urgon Htoth Ur Hunn, whoever or whatever the hell it was. He'd squirm like a worm on hot barbecue coals before he'd say anything about any damned BattleMaster of some bullshit monster legion to these guys. They'd probably kick him out the door while the car was still moving. And to be truthful about it, he had trouble getting the details straight in his head, anyway. Seemed that when he thought about it, he had no idea what the gorilla-orc or the ape-demon had snarled at him. Yet at the same time, he remembered exactly what the fucking thing had meant.

How was that even possible?

'They were, I don't know, animals or something,' he said, knowing that they weren't.

Hunn. This is their name, and even the dead shall fear them.

'Describe them,' said Heath. He didn't sound even the least bit dubious.

Dave shifted uncomfortably in his seat. He was aware of the attention of the two pirates turning back on him. 'I thought they looked like, I dunno, giant baboons or something. Hairless, though. Or the big one, anyway. A bald-ass monster baboon with leprosy or some shit. It was covered in all these sores and scabs. But it had, I dunno, kind of a tough-looking hide. Like a rhino.' He didn't mention the enormous monster testicles and raging schlong. How could he? 'And it was tattooed,' he added, as though that made up for it.

'Monsters Ink,' the pirate driving the Expedition deadpanned.

'Ha, gold.' His colleague nodded, sharing another fist bump to pay him for the quip. Blackbeard flicked on the indicator and powered into the left-hand lane to pass a pick-up loaded down with farm tools. Heath just nodded. He didn't look sceptical or surprised. His dark face remained blank, awaiting more information. Allen, on the other side of Dave, had leaned forward and turned toward him, but as promised, he gave no impression of judging the crazy story to be, well, crazy.

'How many of these tattooed creatures do you recall seeing, Mr Hooper?'

Dave didn't care to recall the scene at all. He knew it would be a long time before he didn't close his eyes and see what was left of Marty Grbac.

'One big fella and a couple of smaller ones. Different species maybe.'

He said nothing else as the vehicle descended down a long curving ramp before merging onto Louisiana 428. Taking a moment to sort his thoughts out, he watched the perfectly normal highway at night become a perfectly normal four-lane road split by an unremarkable green strip drinking up the rain. The scent of the rain was there, too. Powerful. Coming in through the air vents, cleansing the nasty scent of the hospital parking lot from his sinuses.

And then Dave knew that the smaller ones were called Fangr. He knew it the same way he knew that the vehicle they were riding in was a Ford Expedition. He'd never owned one. Never driven an Expedition or even caught a ride in one. It was just something he had learned at some time. From an ad, probably. This was a Ford Expedition. The scabby hairless gorilla that had bitten Marty's head off was a Hunn ur Horde. The smaller, thinner creatures with claws like Wolverine were Fangr, and they belonged to the Hunn. Like slaves or something. Captain Heath didn't seem to suspect he was holding anything back. Not on purpose at least.

'Different species, you think?'

Dave shrugged. 'I dunno. I'm not a biologist. Are gorillas and chimps different species? Not that these . . . other things –' He almost called them Fangr. '– were like chimps. You couldn't dress 'em up in butler clothes and make a movie with 'em or anything. Unless it was a fucking horror movie, I suppose.'

'How'd you kill them, Dave?' Chief Allen asked.

Dave shook his head as if denying what he had done.

'I'm sorry, but I really have to eat,' he said, becoming contrite again and hating the whiny tone in his voice. 'I can't think straight, I'm so fucking hungry, I'm dizzy with it. No joke, hombre.'

Heath tapped two fingers on the back of the driver's seat.

'Do we have any of the milk biscuits from the hospital left?' he asked.

Blackbeard fussed about with one hand on the wheel before throwing Heath the paper bag and giving Dave the impression he'd been meaning to scoff them himself.

They had to detour through a local chain, Raising Cane's Chicken Fingers, when Dave's appetite came roaring back again soon after he'd finished the dry, crumbly hospital snacks. The navy guys had hustled him out of the hospital so quickly that he'd left without getting any of the canteen slop Pradesh had promised. The hunger wasn't just a matter of discomfort or inconvenience. He wasn't being a little bitch. The pain in his guts was a huge and terrifying thing that came on like a killing fever. He was worried the SEALs would laugh at him, but he had no choice, and he all but begged them to stop for some real food this time.

They didn't laugh. Heath thought it serious enough to warrant immediate action, hauling out an iPhone, one of those new big-ass models Dave had been coveting, and searching up the nearest food source. He used Google, not Siri, and found a Cane's drive-through on a tributary road that took them five minutes out of their way. It was tucked between a pool supply store and a shuttered business that had sold rubber stamps.

Dave gagged again when Blackbeard rolled down his window to order and the pungent smells of grease and oil, rubber and rotting food scraps poured in. Nobody else seemed to notice, and with the smell of fried chicken being the strongest odour of all, Dave's hunger won out over his nausea.

The dead-eyed teen working the window delivered their order in less than a minute, and Dave was ploughing through four Caniac Combos before they were out of the drive-through. Each combo consisted of a half-dozen chicken fingers, crinkle-cut fries, coleslaw, slabs of Texas toast, and sauce. For good measure the SEALs threw in two chicken sandwiches and four extra-large cups of chocolate milk. Before ordering, some consideration was given to getting a Tailgate Box of 100 chicken fingers, but Dave waved that away.

'Been watching my waistline,' he said.

'Wow,' Chief Allen said as he searched through the pile of junk food. 'There's nothing healthy at all here. Fat, fried salt, fried sugar. No lean protein. No clean carbs. It's all garbage.'

'Prayer and meditation will only get you so far,' one of the pirates said.

'But that is still some considerable distance on you infidels,' Allen replied without discernible malice. He had settled for a plain chicken salad sandwich, had even asked for whole wheat and been disappointed. The captain went hungry. Assuming he ever got hungry. Heath looked like he took his daily fill from bad vibes and rainwater. Dave choked his food down as quickly as he could, and only the black-bearded SEAL took to the food with a level of gusto approaching his. Blackbeard chewed and swallowed methodically while Dave struggled to shove every spare calorie into the burning hole of his hunger as quickly as possible.

'Dave,' Allen said. 'We're not in boot camp, dude. You can slow down. Nobody's gonna steal your feed bag.'

'No.' Dave shovelled another handful of chicken fingers into his mouth. 'Can't.'

The pirate grunted beneath his Amish-thick beard in a way that might be thought of as laughter. He settled in to drive one-handed while clutching a sandwich. A steady rain beat against the Expedition's windows and windshield, forcing him to slow down a little, but never once did his other hand put the sandwich aside to grip the wheel.

'You see this Prius in your blind spot, right?' Chief Allen asked.

'Don't care much for backseat driving when my wife does it, Chief,' the pirate said. 'And yeah. They've been back there since we left the chicken shack.'

'Chief, let him drive the vehicle,' the captain said.

'I'm just trying to get us there in one piece,' Allen said.

Dave leaned forward to spy a Prius keeping a steady pace right alongside the rear door. A thin, sallow-skinned driver was having an animated conversation with someone in the front passenger seat. Behind them a trio of children screamed, bounced, and threw things at one another. Pandemonium in the land of the Birkenstocks while the Prius driver remained oblivious to the second Ford Expedition closing on the rear.

'Lead, this is Tail,' a radio crackled. 'Sure those aren't your kids?'

The pirate shook his head. 'Negative. Last I heard, my old lady was bangin' some biker dude.'

Dave recognised the look on Allen's face right then. It was the same expression Marty wore at times: tolerant disapproval. Dave couldn't help liking this guy. Maybe it was just that he reminded him of Marty, who could be a censorious, judgmental asshole, too.

'Decorum, gentlemen,' the captain said. 'We have a guest. Let's not trash the reputation of the United States Navy in one outing.'

'Right,' the pirate said. 'Tail, this is Lead. Gonna brake and drop in behind the Prius.'

'Tail copies.'

The Expedition slowed down only to find the Prius stubbornly maintaining its position. Blackbeard slowed down to thirty-five, hit the blinker, and began to merge toward the Prius. Then and only then did the driver notice, get the hint, and get out of the way.

'The stubborn was strong with that one,' said the beard in the shotgun seat.

'You got kids?' Dave asked him.

He nodded. 'Four. I like to keep busy between deployments.'

'And those are only the ones he knows about,' Allen said.

Dave pushed another fistful of chicken strips into his mouth and swallowed them after a few bites for the sake of form, all the time wondering if it was possible for him to detach his jaws now. Didn't seem to matter how much he ate; he remained ravenous. Through the window he saw the oldest boy in the civilian car, maybe five or six years old, dark brown curly hair with skin that didn't match the driver's. Maybe they were a mixed couple, then. He couldn't see the woman in the dark.

The boy didn't smile or wave at Dave. In fact, the boy didn't take any notice of Dave at all. Instead, he was pointing at something off the side of the road.

'Yeah, four kids,' the beard repeated.

The Expedition's windshield shattered, the view of the hood suddenly obscured by a dense latticework of fine white cracks.

'Whatthefuck . . .'

The safety glass exploded inward with a hollow boom, showering them with thousands of tiny jagged chips. Everything slowed down just as it had when Dave had broken his arm as a kid. No, in fact, it was even slower than that, time's arrow suddenly arrested in flight by some weird super slo-mo effect that the special effects guys at ESPN would have paid good folding money for. Dave had plenty of time to watch the small galaxy of safety glass stars rushing toward him. Rushing slowly.

Slowly.

S-l-o-w-l-y.

He dodged smoothly to one side, taking cover behind the headrest of the front seat as the silvery storm swept into the rear of the SUV's cabin. He distinctly saw four separate pieces rake long bloody furrows in Captain Heath's face, one of them just below his left eye. The skin there bunched up as the shrapnel ploughed a rough trench through his flesh. Dave looked on, horrified, unable to turn away, as the man's cheeks seemed to dimple under the impact.

Another dull, heavy thud. A second impact, followed by a tearing sound and Blackbeard's strangled cry.

Dave saw Chief Allen lean forward, still gaping at the driver, who slumped forward in the seat with what appeared to be a one-inch-thick dowel rod pinning him to the seat. A dark arrowhead the size of Dave's clenched fist protruded from the back of the driver's seat just a fraction of an inch away from Captain Heath's kneecap. Scraps of meat and leather swayed from the vicious-looking stone triangle. In a weirdly detached moment, Dave seemed to have all the time in the world to ponder the oversized arrowhead. It was barbed and fashioned from some sort of glassy, volcanic stone, he thought, something like Apache Glass or Pele's Tears.

'Shit,' Allen said and time sped up again. The SEAL in the front passenger seat reached across, put the vehicle in neutral, and grabbed the wheel, leaning over the gearshift column when another arrow punched through the windshield. Although he was curled up around his pile of food, the arrow passed close enough for Dave to feel its passage over the back of his head. It speared into the seat behind him, preventing him from sitting up straight again.

Heath had a radio out. Dave had no idea where he'd been hiding it.

'Contact, contact, contact.'

The radio responded. 'Copy. Contact at eleven, engaging.'

The Expedition rammed into the back of the slowly rolling white Prius, spinning it 180 degrees. Dave caught sight of the oldest boy's horrified face as the vehicle flipped and rolled. Safety glass disintegrated and a little body flew out through a broken window in time for physics to bring the metal Prius frame back into contact with the asphalt, crushing the child in the process.

'No,' Dave mouthed helplessly, feeling paralysed by horror in a way he hadn't been back on the rig.

Metal crumpled around him and crunched, more glass shattered, and Dave felt the world slip sideways. Air bags exploded into the cabin, knocking Allen back. He cried out in surprise. They should have stunned Dave, but everything had slowed down again. Physics and consequence moved so impossibly slowly in his world that he was able to watch each of the safety bags fill up the interior of the vehicle as if they were party balloons being blown up by children. A fine white dust drifted off them with a dry, acrid chemical smell. He watched, fascinated, as the faces of the other men flinched involuntarily. The implacable Heath scrunched up his eyes and gritted his bright, perfectly straight teeth as his head turned away from the billowing white walls that came at him from all sides. It was as though he were watching it all happen on a small screen somewhere. The SUV started to tilt, and for half a second, stretching out over a small eternity, he was certain they were going over. Then the vehicle shuddered and bounced back to earth and stopped moving in any direction. As though hitting the play button on his phone or TV, the natural second-by-second progression of time resumed.

'Cut him out,' Heath yelled as the air bags deflated.

'He's pinned to the seat,' Allen said. 'No time for that.'

Dave heard another sick wet thud, and the other SEAL up front screamed before slumping forward, his skull split by a huge, ugly-looking throwing star.

Still bent over by the arrow shaft, Dave reached across Allen and tried the door, but it wouldn't open. In a fit of frustration, he lashed out with a cramped side kick. The door buckled and boomed. 'Watch your legs,' he said, and Allen tucked them as far out of the way as he could. Another kick, harder this time, and the whole door flew off with a sound like a shotgun discharge, flying across the street, skimming the tarmac, and sending up a brief shower of sparks. He heard someone curse behind him. Heath. Dave stumbled out into the rain, climbing over Allen, disoriented and unbalanced. Tried to get his bearings when a fast, black blur slammed him back into the side of the Expedition.

He grunted as the impact drove the air out of him but he shook it off with surprising ease. It felt no worse than a heavy hit on the training bag back in his college football days.

A radio crackled somewhere, but Dave heard it as though the speaker were standing next to him.

'Can't get a clear line of fire.'

It was an unsettling auditory illusion.

Dave took in the dent he'd left in the side of the Expedition. The car looked as if it had come off a lot worse than he had. The side panel at the rear had buckled like a crushed beer can. But that might have been the original crash.

And then he saw it.

Another monster, similar in basic form to the Hunn and its leashed Fangr, but even taller, with an almost insectile appearance, recalling a giant mantis. It had a quiver full of javelin-sized arrows slung across its back, worn over a leather scale shirt that hung down to its knees. Presumably protecting its junk. A brace of axes and strings of iron throwing stars hung from the monster's hips, held in place by a belt of leather discs embossed with metal studs. With its long-limbed gait, Dave could imagine it leaping at him like a demonic grasshopper.

'I will feast on your loins,' it said.

'Wow, that's not gay at all,' Dave said, although mostly to himself.

Sliveen, he thought. This thing is called a Sliveen. Or maybe *the* Sliveen, and the surprise of knowing what it was followed close on the heels of his surprise at realising it had not spoken in English but he'd still understood it.

Dave put aside any disorientation, pushed off the side of the wrecked automobile and took up a fighting stance with his fists bunched in front of him, feeling completely ridiculous. Like he was shaping up to some drunk in the back bar at an Irish funeral. He had not been in a for-real, no-bullshit fight since college and his football days. A few push and shove bar-room confrontations for sure. But Dave was much more of a sucker punch 'em and run type.

The Sliveen hefted a throwing axe, twirling it in his hand. *Uh oh.*

Gunfire struck the creature from Dave's left: a burst from a machine gun of some sort. Chief Allen, still in the Expedition, was hosing the ugly fucker down with a short, stubby-looking weapon and yelling at Dave to stay the hell out of the way. It wasn't nearly as loud as Dave would have expected, and there wasn't much of a muzzle flash. As he stood there, feeling like an idiot with his fists bunched in front of him, he had time to wonder if that fat black nozzle was some kind of attachment, a suppressor or silencer or whatever they called them. Whatever it was, it didn't cut the . . . the Sliveen . . . in half, but it did have an effect of sorts. Thick blood spurted and bubbled from the creature's flanks where the bullets chewed through leather armour and . . . what?

Was that chain mail? It sparked and flashed as the bullets hit, and Dave knew, he just *knew*, that yes, the Sliveen scout was outfitted in boiled leather and light chain mail.

It shrieked as though stung by a swarm of hornets, staggered backward, and turned toward Allen.

Heath appeared at the rear of the vehicle and opened fire with a pistol. A big fucking hand cannon, a .45 by the look and sound of it. The gun roared with every shot, and fire leaped from the muzzle. No suppressor there. The rounds hit the Sliveen in its centre mass as the soldier would have been trained to do. It dropped the tomahawk and staggered back under the impact.

'Shoot it in the head,' Dave cried. 'It's wearing armour. Shoot it in the fucking face.'

But Heath had already emptied a whole clip into the monster's upper body.

'Chief, get out of there,' Heath yelled.

'No good,' Allen cried. 'I'm pinned.'

The creature looked like it was in real trouble. It struggled to reach back over its shoulder, producing a bow and arrow. Dave spluttered at the incongruity of it all. The bizarre old-time weapons put the zap on his head even worse than the rabid monster wielding them.

The burning pyre of the Prius caught his eye. The boy stared sightlessly back at Dave, pinned under the wreckage, all life long gone.

The family members in the Prius were all dead.

Fuck this, Dave thought.

Drawing on his linebacker days, he launched himself across the short distance separating the Sliveen from them. He dropped his shoulder and pitched into the creature, driving the thing to the ground.

It screeched in rage – and in pain, he hoped.

'You dare touch me, calfling?' the creature said, baring its teeth. 'You dare –'

Dave had straddled the Sliveen, but it was strong even with a clip or two of lead inside it. Taking a pointer from all the Ultimate Fighting Championship vids he'd watched out on the rig, he kept its long arms pinned with his knees and drove his fists into its face, shattering nostrils, cracking the long, distended jaw, pulverising the eyes, the cheeks, the mouth, everything.

'*Fuck you,*' he shouted into the disintegrating face, and then he lost himself in a tightening, accelerating spiral of rage and bloodlust. This was for Blackbeard. This was for the Birkenstocks in the Prius. The little boy easily coulda been Toby or Jack. This was for Marty and Vince and everyone on the rig. But mostly it was for Dave, who was heartily pissed at how much trouble and grief these fucking things seemed set on causing him.

His blows rained down faster and faster, mechanically, methodically, but it seemed as though they landed at half speed, then quarter speed, then in the same super slo-mo he recalled from the car crash. He dismantled the skull of the Sliveen in much the same way a meth head might pull apart a rotisserie chicken, punching and tearing and ripping until all the skin and flesh and greasy meat and giblets and stuffing were just an oily slick on the road surface, and he suddenly had to stop because he was punching the asphalt and it was hurting his knuckles.

'Towel,' Chief Allen offered. His hand was shaking. Not so much the Midwestern surfer bro now, eh, Chief?

'What?' Dave asked, still disoriented. The scent of burning flesh from the Prius had his stomach churning and turning. Wasn't Allen pinned in the car? How long ago was that?

'You need a towel,' Allen said unsteadily. 'You're covered in . . .'

'Chitlins, I believe,' Captain Heath said. 'In the local vernacular.'

Dave stared at him. Heath made a joke? Now?

He addressed the quartet of men from the second Ford

Expedition. They stood around the Sliveen, weapons trained on the corpse, faces slack with shock or something like it. 'Stay here to manage containment with local law enforcement,' Heath said. 'We need to get this thing out of here.'

'Sir,' Chief Allen said, 'we can't just mount that thing on the hood like a deer. People will stare.'

'Gator,' Dave said in a tired voice. 'Wrap it up in something. Tell anyone who asks it's a gator. Tell 'em the head got chewed up in the prop. Hide's still worth hauling somewhere.'

He examined his hands. The knuckles he'd skinned raw had healed already. Bright pink skin had closed over the exposed bone he'd opened up pounding the bitumen. They itched like a bitch.

'Casevac?' one of the new arrivals asked, taking in the wrecked Expedition and the corpses in the totalled Prius. Allen walked over there. He knelt down on one knee in front of each body and closed the eyes. After he closed the last child's eyes, he bowed his head for a moment.

No one said a word, bowing heads themselves, even Heath.

Prayers, Dave thought. He bowed his head, but he wasn't a praying man and he felt awkward doing it, like he was pretending and they would soon catch on to him. When Allen rose from his devotions, he returned with a pair of dog tags in his hands that he put deep in his pocket. The rain had matted his beach boy hair.

'Casevac, Captain?' the SEAL from the second car asked again.

'They're gone,' Heath said. 'It's too late for that. A gator carcass?' he said to Dave. 'I can work with that. Let's get rolling.'

* * *

They tied down the Sliveen while Heath checked the bodies of his men. Dave examined the shattered Expedition to push back at the useless feeling that had come over him.

Chief Allen came up alongside him. 'He wasn't really divorced.'

'What?'

'Divorced,' Allen said. 'It was just a joke. An old one. Fratelli. Dude with four kids. Linda, his wife, she's strong but . . .'

Allen seemed to give up on the thought, turned his back to the scene of the ambush, and checked the tie-downs. Dave wandered over to join Captain Heath, who was now poking around in the Prius. He felt guilty, as though all of this were somehow his fault. That, at least, was a sensation he knew. Almost reassuring in its familiarity. He imagined Annie's voice in the back of his head. *Happy now?*

'I'm about done here,' Heath said, emerging from the wrecked vehicle. The four nameless operators from the second Expedition had sealed off the site with hazard tape and conjured up an old tarpaulin to wrap the Sliveen carcass. Traffic was starting to bank up beyond the makeshift roadblock. The squad leader seemed to be on the radio with the local first responders. He looked grim.

'Our lift is about an hour away,' he said.

Heath nodded.

'Fine. Keep the lid on here. And be ready for any follow-up attacks. We'll take your car to the station.'

'Aye, Captain.'

Without another word, Dave, Heath, and CPO Allen got back on the road.

* * *

Nobody spoke until Allen had them back up to cruising speed. The silence weighed on Dave, a feeling as real as the extra weight they were carrying on the roof of the SUV.

'So, Mr Hooper. What is that?' Heath finally asked, pointing one finger straight up.

'A scout,' Dave said, as though admitting his own guilt. There didn't seem much point denying the weirdness of the situation anymore. 'I think they're called Sliveen. There'll be more of them spooking around. Doing your job,' he said, tapping the back of Chief Allen's headrest.

'How many?'

Dave shook his head. 'I dunno.'

'And you called it a Sliveen. Why? How do you know that?' Heath went on.

Dave had cleaned himself up as best he could, but he still felt tacky with dried blood and gore. Allen was behind the wheel, keeping a close watch on the road. Dave and Heath were in the back. Heath wasn't glaring at Dave or showing much in the way of emotion at all. His face was spotted with blood and badly scratched. He had bandages over the two worst cuts. The others he'd let scab over. It lent him a morbid aspect in the jaundiced glow of the highway sodium globes. This didn't seem to be the moment to bug him about personal grooming.

'Captain, would you believe me if I said I got no idea how I know? Just like I don't know how I killed that thing back on the rig. Or the ugly cocksucker we got tied down on the roof. *I just don't know.'*

Heath stared at him for a second, weighing the answer. 'Let's rewind,' he said at last, and Dave marvelled at the guy's capacity for absorbing madness and bullshit. You had to wonder where he'd been to find that level of Zen cool.

'You were telling us what you remembered about the attack on the rig.'

You dare not do this . . .

Dave nodded as he gathered his thoughts. The crash and the slaughter they'd just left behind already seemed distant and unreal.

'I picked up Marty Grbac's splitting maul. It's a wood-cutting tool. Shouldn't even be on a platform,' he said, relieved to be talking about something other than monster orcs with giant balls, leprosy, and a taste for ribs, or strange ninja demons with bows and arrows. 'He picked it up in Alaska coupla years ago. Carried it with him everywhere. It was –'

'I know what a splitting maul is, Mr Hooper,' Heath interrupted, but gently. 'And that's what you used to kill it?'

When Dave spoke, it was without conviction. He was worn down flat. 'Guess so,' he said. 'I sort of remember stepping up to this thing and swinging on it, but after that I got nothing. I woke up in the hospital, and your guy was there. No,' he corrected himself. 'The nurse was there. Nurse Fletcher.'

He caught himself before he added 'the fat black chick'. Then he silently cursed himself for even needing to. He'd learned that sort of shit from his old man and it was a lifetime's work unlearning it.

'Your lieutenant came later. I'm sorry about that, by the way,' he said.

Heath inclined his head, reminding Dave of a priest accepting a confession. Another childhood moment. 'Lieutenant Dent will recover,' he said. 'He's had worse injuries.'

'Like you?' Dave asked, looking at the man's leg again. He could see now that the limb he had thought was injured was in fact missing. Heath was rocking a bionic leg.

'Roadside bomb,' the captain said in a way that ended the discussion. 'Are you sure you don't remember anything after hitting the largest of the creatures? Do you remember what you just did to the . . . gator?'

'The Sliveen? Yeah. I remember,' Dave said, shifting in his seat. 'Mostly. I guess I might have gone a little elsewhere at the end.'

Heath made a noncommittal noise.

'Yes, we noticed.'

There wasn't much to look at outside the car, just blurring scrubland. He trusted Chief Allen to keep his eyes peeled for another ambush. Dude had to have more practice at that than Dave did, after all.

'But the hostile back on the Longreach?'

'The Hunn,' Dave said, feeling as though he were jumping off the end of a pier into ice-cold water. 'I'm pretty sure it calls itself a Hunn.'

That got Heath's attention and Allen's, too, Dave could tell from the way the captain's shoulders tensed and he turned his head just a little toward the rear of the SUV. It was as though Dave had finally told Heath something he didn't know.

'A Hun, you say. Like a German?'

He shook his head.

'No, a Hunn,' he said, pronouncing the 'u' at the back of his throat and drawing it out just a little. Once he had said the word, it was as though the spell was broken. He didn't care what these guys thought. If he was nuts, he needed treatment. 'A Hunn,' he continued. 'A BattleMaster of the Legion.'

'A what?' Allen asked.

Dave Hooper released a long, stale breath tainted with cheap chicken and old cooking fat. He tried to lean back and close his eyes, but the headrest got in the way.

'I could tell you,' he said, 'but then you'd have to lock me up for a crazy man.'

'We are very accepting of eccentricity, Mr Hooper,' Heath said. 'Try us.'

Well, that seemed true enough, so he tried. As they passed through a light industrial area, Dave searched memories that until today he had not known he possessed. Perhaps because until today he had not. He tried his best to explain as they passed a U-Store-It.

'I don't know why I know this, or think I know it, and you're not going to believe me, but you asked. So I'll tell you what I know,' he said, 'without having one fucking clue why I know it.'

Remembering what happened on the platform, recalling what he had seen, was like thinking about the years of his life he had long ago left behind. His marriage, college, his childhood. It was all there. He just needed to focus and recall.

'Its name was Urgon Htoth Ur Hunn.'

He wasn't sure how he even knew how to pronounce the name properly. He usually had trouble ordering Italian takeaway.

'It was . . . He was a BattleMaster of the Fourth Legion,' Dave said, feeling embarrassed as he did so and without really knowing what the hell he was talking about until he slowed down and really thought it through. It was like recognising every word in a book he did not recall reading.

'That's a bit like you, Captain,' he said. 'An officer. It sounds impressive, doesn't it? BattleMaster of a whole legion, but there's . . . let's see . . . only about two and a half thousand Hunn to a legion, four or five legions to a regiment, ten regiments to a Horde, and hundreds of regiments to a Grande Horde. No. To *the* Grande Horde.'

Heath didn't exactly lose his shit, but his expression was obviously shaken as he examined Dave's face for signs that he was lying or had gone insane.

'The creature told you this?'

'Fuck no, as if. It just sort of sat there making a meal of Marty Grbac and snorting at me until I caved its fucking skull in.'

'And that's when you were able to understand it? To know what it was?'

Dave shook his head.

'No. That's when I took a little nap and woke up in the hospital. The next thing I know, I'm throwing guys through cupboard doors and I've picked up some sort of postgraduate degree in Monster Studies. Tell you the truth, Heath, I'm really hoping to wake up on the floor of my motel in an hour or so with a couple of hookers from Reno sitting on my face having a pillow fight while I vomit up whatever prohibited monkey gland extract they slipped me to bring on this bullshit hallucination.'

The Ford took a right turn past a Blue Angels jet raised on a pole for display. They'd arrived. Somewhere. Tall trees loomed over them, creating a dark tunnel through which they rolled at something just over a walking pace. Allen turned the wheel to steer the Expedition through a set of concrete barriers, pulling up at a guardhouse where a sailor in a black rain slicker asked for his ID. The sign above the gate informed Dave that they were at NAS JRB New Orleans.

'This your secret base?' Dave asked.

'No,' Heath said.

The sailor waved them through the gate. Heath pulled out his phone, punched in a number, and said, 'This is Heath. Get the helo ready; we leave in ten,' before expanding on his answer to Dave. 'No, this is not the restricted area. We're going somewhere more secure.'

Dave took in the perfectly manicured grass and the well-maintained lamplit streets. It all seemed so normal even if it was a military base late at night.

'It's not a hallucination, is it?' Dave asked at last.

'No, Mr Hooper,' said Captain Heath. 'I'm afraid not.'

08

They flew for an hour or more. Midnight found them far beyond any stretch of country with which Dave was familiar. He peered out at the ground below them every now and then. Sometimes he saw the fat snaking lanes of a well-lit freeway cutting through the primordial dark. More often, they flew over poorly lit one- or two-lane blacktop roads. Once or twice he picked out small freestanding buildings, sometimes lit with neon. Gas stations or general stores. He'd grown tired after eating, tired to the point of slurring his words and struggling to keep his eyes open. Heath had decided that Hooper needed to be 'properly debriefed', and he didn't want to 'contaminate' that process in the helicopter, so he let his man catch a little shut-eye.

Dave fought to stay awake, mostly because he dreaded falling asleep, fearful of what might chase him through his dreams, but he needn't have worried. The food brought on a warm and heavy lassitude, and despite his best efforts and the roar of the engine and rotors, the motion of the helicopter periodically put him under. When he passed out, he slept heavily, without nightmares or waking terrors. It was just like flying out to the rig, sleeping off a party. He did experience a moment of profound disorientation upon being jolted awake as they touched down on the tarmac in the darkness. The hookers, the chopper flight out to the platform, everything – the memories all came at him too fast, and he had trouble placing himself in time and space. He rubbed the stubble on his face as the pilot shut down the engine. It felt like the only real thing in the world.

'Where are we?' he asked, feeling dizzy. He also was thirsty from the chocolate milk. Dairy did that to him, and he regretted not sticking to Coke.

'A training area,' Heath said. 'Off the books. You can't find it on Google if you try. At least not for now. If you come with me, Mr Hooper, I will get you bedded down for a few hours. You need some real rest. You have a busy day tomorrow, and I have reports to file. Many reports and a few letters to write, I'm afraid.'

Dave didn't like the sound of that. He'd had to write a couple of those letters. They sucked.

'Hey, good luck, man,' Allen said, taking Dave's hand in a firm grip. The chief's eyes looked troubled by the earlier violent insanity, but it was the first genuine goodwill Dave had felt from anybody all day, and he appreciated the gesture.

'Thanks for the chocolate bars,' he said, yawning and feeling a little embarrassed by it. 'I think you might have saved my life, Chief. Seriously.'

'That was some nasty business tonight, man,' Allen said. 'That thing had us dead. You totally saved our hides.'

Not everyone's, Dave thought before stumbling as he increased his pace to catch up with Heath, who had forged ahead. He left Chief Allen looking a little bereft and lonesome in the deep gloom of the night. For some sort of secret military base – that was what a restricted facility was, wasn't it? – his surroundings looked like any number of mining camps or depots he'd been through over the years: prefab huts, shipping containers, warehouses, vehicle parking lots, and security fencing. A light drizzle fell from low clouds, probably the far edge of the storm that had been closing in on New Orleans when they'd left.

There didn't appear to be much activity in this part of the base, but then, it was late at night and Dave had no idea how big the place was. Captain Heath led him up a muddy path to a demountable hut in which Dave could see lights burning. The guy moved well for a cripple. You wouldn't have known from the way he carried himself that he was part cyborg down there. Heath had said something about an airfield, but aside from the helicopter pad there was no sign of a runway anywhere nearby. By then, however, Dave was too tired and out of it to care. The exhaustion that had nailed him in the car had rolled back in like a very high tide. The lunacy of the day felt long distant, unreal. He wanted a hot shower and a soft bed. Or even an army cot. And what would be best of all would be crawling into that cot and waking up in the morning to discover he really was in some motel somewhere, fucked off his skull on drugs.

He knew that wasn't going to happen, though. As much as he felt like he was sleepwalking, this was real. He'd seen two men die a few hours ago. Then he'd killed whatever had killed them. The Longreach – that was real, too. As distant and abstract as it felt. All of it. He stifled a yawn and nearly tripped himself dragging his feet up the stairs. His head was reeling.

Heath pulled back a screen door, and thumbed a combination into the keypad of the sturdier metal door behind it. The lock disengaged, and light spilled out as he pushed on the handle.

'Through here,' he said.

Dave wasn't expecting what he found inside. A nurse was sitting at a desk doing paperwork under a hooded lamp; behind her half a dozen or so beds were occupied by men and women Dave recognised as his co-workers from the Longreach. Well, one woman, anyway: Charlene Disch from the flight ops centre. She was asleep, probably sedated given the way her face was twitching and small moans were escaping from between her lips. Every once in a while she'd start kicking and shivering before settling back down again to a low-level snore.

In the cot next to hers lay Vince Martinelli, so big that he spilled over the sides and his feet dangled in space off the end. And in the cot after Vince, Dave thought he recognised J2. His spirits lifted a little.

'Try not to wake them,' said the nurse. 'They've had a tough time of it. The last of the debriefs wrapped up only two hours ago. I had to fill them full of Ambien to get them all down.'

'Who you got here?' Dave asked, keeping his voice low, fighting back exhaustion but needing to know. He'd been trying to get a line on his guys all day, and this was the first real proof he had that any of them had made it out in one piece. It was also the first evidence he had of him not being an A-Class fuck-up. His people got out alive. These ones anyway.

Nurse Hubbard wore the same digital jungle camouflage fatigues as Allen. A cup of coffee steamed under her desk lamp, illuminating a blizzard of forms, records, and notes. She searched around in the confusion of papers for a moment, the bags under her eyes showing the weight of her day at Camp Mysteryland. She found what she was looking for, a clipboard, and with a glance to Captain Heath for the okay, she handed it to Dave.

There was a list of names on it, all of them people Dave knew.

'What? So these are the ones you said were missing?' Dave asked as he read the names, blinking once or twice to clear his vision, which was still blurred with weariness.

'They're not missing anymore,' Captain Heath said. 'I apologise for the confusion. We've had our own troubles trying to sort things out in the chaos. In any case, here they are.'

Dave's temper flared at the obvious attempt to wave away the deception.

Heath put his hand on Dave's shoulder, almost a fatherly gesture, which was odd, since Dave was sure he had a couple of years on the captain, but it was the most human thing he had seen the guy do since they'd met.

'I need you to know that we are trying to be forthright and completely up front with you. I am pathologically honest by nature,' Heath said. 'It's a weakness of mine.'

'It doesn't seem to have hurt your career.'

'It has, more than you would know.' Heath let that sit between them for a moment, without elaborating. 'When we have information we can share with you, we will do so. I hope you will do the same with us.'

He means it, Dave thought. But meaning something and making it happen? Two different things. Especially with the fucking warheads. His brother had taught him that. In a way, Heath reminded him of Marty Grbac. Just as Allen had. Or maybe he was looking for reminders of his friend when there were none to be found. Physically Marty and Heath couldn't have been more different: a huge Polack meat locker and an

African-American whipcord pulled tight enough to snap if you plucked him the wrong way. But Marty had been a perpetually earnest born-again boy scout, and Dave suspected that Heath might be a member of that happy-clapping congregation, too.

He tried to call up a memory of Marty offering a prayer before every meal. Marty making the sign of the cross every time he climbed into a helicopter. Marty boring everyone senseless with exciting new engine parts for his motorcycle that he'd scored on eBay. Anything to drive away the image of the Hunn sucking on him as if he were an oversized frozen tequila popsicle. The image, the fatigue, and the stress of the day finally pulled Dave's plug. He staggered forward, crashing into Hubbard's desk, nearly knocking over her mug of coffee. The room swirled and swam around him, and he felt Captain Heath grab him by the elbow, half carrying and half pushing him toward one of the cots. The scuffed linoleum floor pitched and yawed underfoot as though they were at sea. He felt himself falling down the face of a great black wave. Crying out. But the wave closed over him before he knew what he was trying to say.

Someone was shaking his shoulder. It wasn't the first time Dave had experienced that sensation of rocking back and forth in his flesh while dope and booze sloshed around in his head. So deep was his slumber that the sounds that reached him were akin to someone shouting at him from above the water. It sort of reminded him of someone's wife screaming at the top of her lungs while he went down on her in a hot tub. That had been in a company compound in Saudi Arabia. She wasn't *his* wife, of course.

The rocking continued, back and forth. For once, blessedly, there was no tightening band of iron wrapped around his poor skull, no asshole pounding away to a bass beat with a sledge inside his brain. He felt remarkably clean, disgustingly healthy, and even a little blissed out.

'Dave!'

It must be important. The rig is on fire, or is it the roof? We don't need no water, Mom; let the motherfucker burn.

'What?' the muffled man's voice said. 'Wake up, Dave.'

He recognised the voice as Vince Martinelli's, and he came awake as abruptly as light flooding a darkened bedroom when you flicked the switch. There was no grogginess or confused dislocation. The transition from deep sleep to wakefulness was instant. He remembered all but falling into the hut some time ago – he had no idea how many hours, or minutes, had passed – and then Vince was shaking him and saying his name. There was nothing in between. Just a void.

He opened his eyes and blinked the crust of sleep from them. It was morning. He could tell by the quality of the light in the room. It was different, natural. He was still dressed in the Eddie Bauer gear Allen had given him back at the hospital, but somebody had undone his belt and taken off his shoes. The ever-thoughtful Heath, perhaps, or maybe that nurse. She'd been a little bit into him, he thought.

'Vince, hey, you okay?'

Vince was leaning right over Dave's cot. He looked terrible, with raccoon eyes and pouchy, sagging flesh hanging from his face. Juliette Jamieson hovered behind him, regarding Dave with a deeply anxious expression. He knew that look. That was the look people gave him when they expected him to Sort This Shit Out.

Dave was tempted to run for the door.

'Oh, thank God,' Vince said in a voice that seemed to have lost most of its power. 'I thought you were gone, man. I've been trying to wake you, but you wouldn't wake up. Like you was in some sorta coma or something.'

'I'm fine,' Dave assured him, sitting up and swinging his feet over the side of the camp bed. In fact, he felt better than fine. He felt as though he'd just smashed out the most awesome gym session of his life, as though he could walk out into the street and bench-press a few cars. And then he remembered Lieutenant Dent flying across the room yesterday. He stood up, carefully, making sure not to lay even a finger on his friend.

His pants were loose. He took the belt in one, two more notches, gently. A quick glance around the room told him they were alone.

J2 edged around Vince. She looked as though she didn't want to be overheard.

'Dave,' she said in a stage whisper. 'I think we're prisoners here. They're not letting us go. My ma will be havin' kittens by now.'

'Be cool, J2,' he said in as reassuring a voice as he could. 'I came in last night under my own steam. Guy brought me in, Captain Heath, he was kind of a puckered ass, but he was okay. They got their reasons for all the security, I guess. Where are the others?' Dave asked when he noticed that the rest of the cots were empty. 'I thought I saw Charlene in here last night. And a couple of other guys from the Longreach. But I crashed out.'

Vince looked over his shoulder as though he feared he, too, was being watched. 'I know. I've been trying to wake you for half an hour. I coulda lit a fire under your ass, Dave, and you'da slept through it.'

'So where are they? Did Heath take them?'

Vince Martinelli nodded gravely. 'The scary black dude? Him and some other guys. They were all armed, Dave. Not rough with it or anything but acting like they'd shoot us if we gave them any trouble.'

J2 nodded in agreement, her eyes wide and fearful. She hadn't been out on the rig long enough to see what was happening down on the lower decks, but she'd probably heard plenty about it while she shuttled the casualties to the other platforms and back to shore. After last night Dave wasn't surprised that they'd put a bag on her and any other firsthand witnesses. Made denying the truth and the madness of it a little easier, he supposed. Funny. On TV when the secret government conspiracy spooled up, you were always rooting for the rogue agent or the investigative reporter or whoever to bust the thing wide open. But having seen what he'd seen in the last twenty-four hours, Dave wasn't convinced he was with Mulder and Scully on this. Annie, he knew, would freak the fuck out. Multiply her reaction about 350-million-fold and you'd have the likely response of the American populace.

'Yeah,' he said slowly. 'Look. There's some weird shit going down. Out on the platform . . .' He paused, looking at his knuckles, which had healed so perfectly that you never would have imagined he'd taken all the skin off them pounding a monster's skull into street pizza late last night. 'Here as well.'

Dave struggled to push down the feeling of vertigo that wanted to seize him.

Vince Martinelli heaved himself up slowly from where he was crouched at the edge of the bed. He stood a few inches taller than Dave and had to lean forward to speak to him when he lowered his voice. 'You're fuckin' telling me, Dave? I was there. I saw it all. I was there before you got to the platform. I saw what happened to Marty and the others. And then you . . . I mean, what the fuck, man? What was that thing? And those other things? With the claws? And you? Everyone else who went up against those things is dead or busy dying right now. But you . . .'

'Vince told me, Dave. He told me what you did out there,' said J2. 'You're a hero.'

No. Dave was a freak and an accident and maybe contaminated with some sort of toxic monster goo that was fucking his shit right up; that was what Dave was. He wanted to wave her away, but Vince had taken hold of his arms and dug his fingers in, shaking him a little, as if the truth might fall out.

Recalling what had happened at the hospital, Dave gently placed a hand on one of Vince's thick forearms and eased it away.

'I don't know, guys,' he said. 'I remember everything pretty well, up until the moment I hit that thing with Marty's splitting maul. After that, it's all a blank till I woke in the hospital.'

He didn't share with J2 and Vince his strange, newly acquired knowledge of the Hunn and its Fangr attendants. The navy guys had let him tell his insane story. And they'd dealt with one of those things up close and nasty personal. It had killed two of them, and they'd driven through the night with the corpse of the splatter-headed fucker roped down to the roof of their SUV. That was the sort of thing that had to make a guy receptive to a little weirder than usual storytelling. But he didn't think Vince was ready to roll with that level of crazy. Because truth to tell and sure as hell, Dave Hooper wasn't.

'You saw what happened, Vince,' he said, leaning forward and joining their conspiratorial circle. 'You tell me what the fuck that was about. Last thing I remember from the Longreach is swinging on that . . . animal, whatever. And then I wake up in the hospital. A couple of hours later I'm here. I haven't even checked in with the office yet. They probably think I'm still out on the rig.'

Martinelli eased himself down onto the cot, which creaked under his heavy frame. He moved like an old man with ground glass in his joints. J2 took up a perch on the cot across from them.

'I'm sorry, Dave, I'm really sorry, man,' Vince said, shaking his head in distress. 'I tried to follow you in there. I really tried . . . But . . .'

Juliette patted him on the arm. 'You did fine, Vince. You got us off the rig. That was better than most of them. You helped get Dave out.'

Dave gave him a very light fist bump on the shoulder.

'My man! There you go.'

But Vince wasn't about to shake off his blue funk.

'I fucking wimped it, man. You . . . you rocked those fucking freaks. I just –'

Dave cut him off as gently as he could.

'Hey, be cool, Vince. I was there, remember? You don't have to apologise to me. Most of the guys on that rig were clawing each other's eyes out to get away from those things. I saw you stiff-arm a couple of them off J2's chopper, remember? But you manned up and did the job, buddy.'

Vince had his head in his hands and looked as though he was trying to fold himself into a small ball of grief. An impossible task, given his size. Dave laid a hand on his shoulder again and squeezed, but very, very gently. J2 patted his arm and cooed meaningless nothings like a mother soothing the many hurts of a small boy. When Vince Martinelli looked up, his eyes were red-rimmed and watery.

Dave paid him off with a level stare.

'Tell me what happened, Vince. I need to know. Come on.'

Vince took in a deep breath and gathered himself. He tried to speak, but instead he choked up a little, coughing to cover it. Another breath, and he sat up straight. J2 patted him on the back. It really did remind Dave of dealing with a child.

'I could hear that thing in there with you. In the lounge. I could hear it . . . eating and, I dunno . . . laughing?'

Hooper confirmed that with a sombre nod.

'Yeah, I thought so too. Go on.'

'I knew . . . I knew what was around that corner, Dave. And I let you go, 'cause I just, I couldn't.'

He appeared to slump forward a little again and lifted his head only when J2 patted his enormous suntanned neck and said quietly, 'Come on, Vince.'

'It's all right, man,' Dave added. 'We're out of it now. Keep going. The navy guy, Heath, he told me you saw it all.'

Vince shook his head. Emphatically.

'No. Not all of it. It took me a while to get my shit together. But I did. When I heard you cussing the thing out. You called it a motherfucker. Do you remember?'

Dave didn't and shook his head.

'I'd seen you pick up Marty's splitting maul. Not that I thought it'd do much good against those fucking devil things. But I knew you had it. And I could hear you cursing out that thing. And it was sort of laughing or chuckling, and anyway, I got moving again. I picked up some crowbar that was lying there. Thought maybe if I got a lucky hit in, you know? Or maybe I could just swing it and drag you back out.'

Dave encouraged him to keep going. The Hunn would have killed Vince just as surely as it had killed Marty. He knew that but kept it to himself. Let Vince keep a shred of dignity to himself. Probably wouldn't do to let him know just how close he'd come to being devil food, too.

'Anyways, I come around the corner just as you charged at the big one. It was sitting there. Honest to fucking God, Dave, I'd swear that thing was laughing at you. Like when Marty laughed at that college boy who called him out in Houston that time. You remember that. Fucking Marty.'

Dave remembered. Bible thumper or not, it wasn't a good idea to upset Marty Grbac. 'Sure. Go on.'

'So you started swinging that thing, and there's not much headroom in there, so you took out some roof tiles and an aluminium strut. Fucking plaster dust and shit everywhere. But that big ape's not laughing no more. It's looking sorta shocked and then really fuckin' pissed at you and . . .'

A spasm passed across Vince's face. Like he needed to throw up.

'It took off Marty's arm then. You remember that?'

J2 was looking a little the worse for the telling of it, too.

Dave remembered the moment. An unpleasant memory he'd be a long time leaving behind.

'And it's waving Marty's arm around like one of them conductors at the opera.'

Vince was caught up in the telling of it now. And the more he spoke, the more came back to Dave.

'Those nasty little scissor-hand fuckers that come up the rig first; they were starting to move then, but they were too late.'

He smiled, but without any joy.

'You got that thing right in the snout. Or that hole where

it shoulda had a snout. It was looking up at you, fucking fangs everywhere, but it was too slow. Like you get late on Thanksgiving, you know . . . when you've eaten and drunk too much.'

'Yeah. I know that one,' Dave said, and as he said it he knew it to be true in this case, too.

Urgon Htoth Ur Hunn had feasted well. Too well. The Hunn had found himself bloated and blood drunk just when he encountered a calfling with the horns to glory itself in . . .

Dave shook his head, trying to throw off the . . . *memory* . . . someone or something else's memory, like a spider that had crawled into his hair.

He was convinced now that he was not just recalling the encounter as he remembered but as . . .

Urgon Htoth Ur Hunn . . .

. . . as this fucking *Urgon* thing did.

'What happened?' he asked, not really wanting to know but needing to.

'You killed it, Dave. Smashed its fucking coconut. And there was this . . . I dunno . . . like a flash or something. And I went down. Man, I was vomiting and spinning out, and . . . and it was like the worst fucking hangover I ever had, back in the day. But it passed quick. I got up.'

Vince looked him in the eye as though seeing Dave for the first time. J2 was staring at him in the same way. Perhaps she was scratching him off her long list of totally un-wedding-worthy assholes.

'You were down, man. I thought you were dead.' Vince shook his head slowly. 'But it was dead. The monster. And all its little monster friends, too. They got a few licks on you, but they were gone too. Like they died of shock or some shit.'

09

Heath came into the room so soon after Vince Martinelli finished telling his story that Dave wondered if he'd been eavesdropping. He looked for a one-way mirror or something like it but found nothing. The barracks hut was as spare and utilitarian as he remembered it, with tube lighting running through the rafters. The roof, he realised, was just heavy canvas. There were eight camp beds, six of them rumpled and vacant at this point. A series of cabinets and shelves ran along the back tent wall, probably stocked with medical supplies. A pair of oxygen tanks plus a quartet of what looked like military trauma bags also were stowed back there.

Captain Heath looked fresh and crisp, the same as Dave, which wasn't natural for Hooper at all. Two men in a different type of camouflage, with name tags that clearly marked them as marines, flanked Heath left and right. Dave would have guessed they were jarheads even without the USMC tags. They were both huge and intimidatingly fit, with shaved skulls that for some reason made him think of monks from the Middle Ages. Or kung-fu movies. Yeah, definitely kung-fu movies with fighting monks. It unsettled him a little that their eyes seemed lit with the same type of crazy as the Hunn back on the rig. They were also armed, with pistols strapped to their thighs. Captain Heath apparently felt no need for a weapon.

Both Juliette and Vince appeared wary, even anxious, as the military men approached. Dave just wished he were wearing shoes. Standing there in his socks seemed to put him at a disadvantage.

'Good morning, Ms Jamieson, gentlemen,' Heath said. 'You still have forty minutes to eat if you wish.' He seemed to measure Dave's reaction to that announcement, but the maddening hunger of the previous evening had passed.

'You hungry, you guys? You want to eat?' Dave asked.

'What about the others?' Vince asked in a subdued mutter that wasn't like him at all.

'Fair question,' Dave said directly to Heath a little too loudly, overcompensating for his friend and maybe for himself. 'Where are my other guys?'

The soldiers, or troops . . . was that what you called marines? He wondered about that and discovered he didn't give a fuck. Whatever they were, Dave put them on edge. Heath had come the length of the barracks with the two guards – they were definitely guards – keeping a few feet back. The captain bent over and retrieved Martinelli's shoes from under a camp bed. He passed them to the larger man without comment.

'Mess hall,' he said simply. 'You should join them now. We have a busy day. More debriefs, tests to run. You need to get going.'

'Tests?' Dave asked. He hated tests.

'Mr Hooper, you've all been exposed to some sort of hostile organism. You may be contaminated or infected with bacteria or viruses or some form of non-obvious toxin. We cannot safely release you back into the community, to your families, until we are sure you're clean.'

Heath looked at Martinelli when he mentioned their families.

'I wasn't exposed to anything,' J2 said defiantly. 'All I did was fly wounded men off the rig. But you grabbed me anyway and hauled me out here in the middle of nowhere for no good reason I can think of.'

Heath inclined his head toward her, almost conceding the point.

'Ms Jamieson, it's true you weren't directly exposed, but you carried casualties who were. Until we know what we're dealing with, what transmission vectors –'

'Transmission what?' Vince asked in an angry tone that flared out of nowhere, causing the two marine guards to turn their cold eyes on him. It made no difference. He just pushed on.

'This wasn't no bug or virus. These things stood taller than me and had teeth like feral hogs. Unless one got a bite of J2's ass, there's no transmission vectors to be talking about.'

He turned to J2.

'You felt anything bite you in the ass yesterday, darlin'?'

'Not a thing,' she replied, jutting her chin at the navy guy. 'So I guess I can go. I got three cats to feed at home, you know.'

Dave rubbed his scalp. He was gonna need a haircut soon. That had crept up on him too.

'Look, Heath, can you give us a second? Vince, you spoken to Gina yet?' Dave asked.

Vince nodded. 'They let me call her yesterday. She was a mess. And they wouldn't let me say a fucking word about what really happened.' He glared at the navy officer.

'Then that's why you're here, J2,' Dave said. 'They want

to keep you from going on TV and blabbing about what happened. Right?'

Heath looked unimpressed. Dave turned back to the chopper pilot, who was even more worried now.

'But don't you worry none, J2. There's hundreds of people know what happened out there. Maybe they got a lid on this today, but by tomorrow it'll be off. There'll be no lying about what happened. I figure Captain Heath here, or rather his bosses way up the fucking food chain, are just trying to figure out what Obama is gonna say when he faces the press corps to explain how a bunch of devil-orcs just chewed up one of Baron's' platforms and how they've got it under control and there's nothing to worry about and everyone should just turn back to the Shopping Network. Right? Ah, there they are.'

Dave spied his own shoes and pulled them on, not waiting for a reply from Heath. He took his sweet time easing his foot into each new Nike and then methodically tying the laces, partly to exert some control over the situation but mainly so that he didn't have to ask for a new pair of laces.

'Infected, bullshit. So much for pathological honesty, Heath. If we were infected,' he said, looking up from his shoes to frown at the officer, 'you wouldn't be taking us to your mess hall or standing there without even a face mask. You'd be all tricked up in one of those biohazard suits, like in some virus movie. So yeah, we'll come and get some breakfast. But you can stop bullshitting us right now, too. Why are we being held here, and what is happening out on the rig?'

The two guards stiffened almost imperceptibly behind the one-legged captain, but Dave found he had no trouble discerning the tension that tightened their shoulders just a notch. Heath smiled.

'You're not just a dumb cracker, are you, Mr Hooper?'

'If by that you mean a rednecked moron, no,' Dave answered. 'So you can lay off treating me like one or like one of your toy soldiers there. And J2 and Vince as well. All of us. Just 'cause we get our hands dirty at work doesn't mean we're shitkickers or shit-eaters. We work hard, and some of us party hard, and we make good money. But the company as a rule doesn't hire morons. Not below C-level executives, anyway.'

'Yeah, what he said,' J2 added with as much wounded dignity as she could muster in her bright pink training pants.

Vince couldn't help grinning just a little.

Heath nodded. 'I have my orders to follow, Mr Hooper. But I prefer honesty. It is refreshing. Corporal, you are dismissed. Why don't we talk things over on the way to the mess?'

The marines didn't argue; they just barked an acknowledgement and stomped out of the room in perfect time. *Man*, Dave thought, *if only I could get those assholes on the rig to obey me like that.* Then he remembered that a lot of those assholes were dead, and he felt bad about thinking it.

They followed Heath out of the medical tent, stepping into the humid morning, a thin fog hovering over the campsite. Dave idly wondered if they were still in Louisiana. They were definitely in the South. The campsite appeared to be fairly basic, with a Hummer here, a truck there. Generators ran in the distance, and there was the faint, oily metallic bite of diesel exhaust in the air. No one went running by in formation shouting songs or screaming for blood. Instead, they went about in groups of two and three, talking as calmly as if they were at a corporate retreat.

There were salutes, though, which the captain kept up without even pausing when those who passed him said, 'Good morning, sir.'

Strange, Dave thought. So unlike his world. But this was where his little brother had chosen to live. And it had killed him.

'Ms Jamieson, Mr Hooper, Mr Martinelli,' Heath said, 'we still have no idea what happened out on the Longreach yesterday. I told you that already, and it was no lie. The only way we're going to find out is with your cooperation. But whatever happened out there, I'm sure you'll agree, does not come within the acceptable definition of normality.'

Vince Martinelli stepped sideways to avoid a mud puddle and then spat into it.

'It doesn't come within a thousand fucking miles of normality, Commander,' Vince said. Dave was certain Vince took some pleasure in purposely getting the rank wrong, but he also noticed that Heath didn't seem to care.

He made a note of that.

Vince, however, had recovered some of his balance and was warming up to half power with his rant. 'Something out of *Hellraiser* comes up on the rig without us even knowing and gets to chowing down on half the crew. Dave here, yes, this man right here, opens a can of whup-ass even I didn't know he had, makes out like fucking Thor on their asses, and next thing we got Agent Nick fucking Fury spooking us away to his top-secret HQ fuck knows where. Only thing we're missing is the Helicarrier. Are we going to see one of those pop over the trees in a bit? 'Cause that'd be cool. What do you say, Admiral?'

'I see,' said Heath, stepping around another, larger puddle near another khaki-coloured frame tent, 'that you're quite an Avengers fan.'

'My oldest girl,' Vince said, easing off the throttle some. 'She's got all the comic books. Real paper ones too. Not some fucking app crap. But they're just comic books. This is real. What are you? Really? You're not navy or even Special Forces, I bet. You CIA or something like those *Men in Black* guys? But you know, for real?'

Captain Heath stopped just outside the door to the mess hall. Dave had to admit he was interested in the answer, too, and happy to let Vince have his head. Heath didn't seem in the least bit fazed. If anything, he was amused.

'I'd very much like to have a Helicarrier, Mr Martinelli; that would be outstanding, but I suspect Congress would balk at the cost. Besides, something about them strikes me as impracticable. But that doesn't really apply to your question, so I'll answer it as honestly as I can.'

He took a deep breath and adopted a measured, serious tone. 'As I explained to both you and Ms Jamieson yesterday, I work for JSOC: the Joint Special Operations Command. There is no X-Files unit. Agent Fury does not work here. It's like Secretary Rumsfeld once said: "You go to war with what you have." And right now JSOC is what we have in theatre, and even then only by accident.'

'Bullshit,' Vince said.

'Hollywood is half a continent away, Mr Martinelli,' Captain Heath said. 'Langley is half a continent in the other direction. The navy doesn't do accidents on purpose. We try to prevent them or fix them. We don't use them as excuses.'

'Gulf of Tonkin notwithstanding,' Vince said.

Dave scratched his head. 'I think that was LBJ.'

'Gentlemen,' Heath said.

'Well, you've used this one as an excuse to keep me from my kittens,' protested J2.

'Ma'am, if it please you, I will assign a lieutenant junior

grade to go straight to your apartment and feed your kittens for as long as the United States Navy has need of your cooperation.'

'Really?' said J2. 'I could get me a handsome lieutenant that easy?'

'Easy, tiger,' Dave said before addressing Heath. He couldn't keep the scepticism out of his voice, but he made a point of getting the rank right. 'Captain, my business is oil. Your business is war. You think we're at war now?'

It was Vince who spoke first, who said what Dave wanted to say. 'But those things weren't soldiers. They were . . . monsters.'

Heath didn't answer; instead he merely raised an eyebrow at Dave who shifted uncomfortably as he pushed away thoughts of legions and Hordes and the BattleMaster calling itself Urgon Htoth Ur Hunn. Vince had seen the thing, but he hadn't talked about *any* of that stuff. But Vince hadn't killed the thing, either. Vince hadn't thrown a guy across the room with a flick of his wrist or punched another monster to jelly on the road last night. Vince didn't have a head full of insane monster stories . . .

'Mr Hooper?'

Captain Heath interrupted Dave's fugue state. Martinelli was looking at him as well.

'You all right, buddy?' Vince asked. 'You sort of checked out on us there for a minute.'

'Sorry,' Dave mumbled. 'Guess I'm still a bit out of it.'

'Maybe some waffles,' said J2, who seemed much happier at the idea that she might soon trap a handsome young naval lieutenant within the confines of her apartment.

Dave chanced a look at the navy man, getting nothing but a hard, searching stare in return. He agreed he was feeling pretty hungry and some waffles would be a good idea. 'I should also check in on the others,' he said to Vince. 'They're going to want to know that the company's got their back.'

'Does it?' Vince asked pointedly.

Captain Heath turned and opened the door to the mess hall for them. 'We have contacted both Baron's and the nominated family members for each of your colleagues. Some have spoken to their families already. Baron's is cooperating with our investigations and with operations on the platform. As of this morning all the crew who could be accounted for are listed as being on duty. You're still drawing a pay cheque, Mr Martinelli. You, too, ma'am.'

'Better not be coming out of my vacation pay,' J2 said.

They stepped into the mess, a larger frame tent on a permanent foundation, similar to the one they had slept in overnight. The room was full of uniforms and a few civilians, though none from his rig. Everyone stopped talking and looked at them.

No, correct that, Dave thought.

They were all staring at him.

He tried to ignore it and asked Captain Heath what he meant by 'operations'. Heath answered directly, or at least appeared to.

'FEMA has now declared a ten-nautical-mile exclusion zone around the platform, enforced by the coast guard and navy. The fires on the rig have been put out, and after-action teams are doing the SSE.'

'The what?' Dave and J2 said at the same time.

'Sensitive Site Exploitation,' said Heath. 'Collecting the data.'

'The data?' Vince said, still not getting it.

'Bodies,' Dave said, guessing.

'And parts of bodies,' Captain Heath added.

'Oh, damn.' J2 grimaced.

Heath said they could eat in a connected tent for the officers, away from curious stares and awkward silences. Dave supposed news of their arrival would be all over the 'restricted facility'. All closed shops were the same. Gossip was a highly tradeable commodity, and half a dozen survivors of the Longreach fire – it now was being sold as some sort of conventional explosion, much to Dave's chagrin – would shine like newly minted coins.

Two TV sets were on in the mess hall as Heath took them through. Both were tuned to news channels, but only one was showing visuals of the platform at that moment. Smoke and fire poured out of the crew quarters. It must have been a replay of yesterday's video. Dave would have liked to have stopped and listened for a few minutes, even though he knew it was all going to be bullshit. If the talking heads had been fed a line that it was some sort of fuck-up that'd caused the explosion, he knew that his cock was on the chopping block for it.

But that story could never stand up, could it? Just as he'd told J2, way too many people had seen the Hunn and the Fangr. The truth, bugshit crazy as it was, was going to spill, and very soon. Maybe even today. The terrorist story already seemed to have collapsed if they were now running with this accident line. Again he bristled at the unfairness of it. There had been no goddamn accident on his rig. But how long would it be before somebody tipped a bucket of shit on him anyway? Hell, if he ran to the press with stories about demon hordes, he'd do the job for them.

'Baron's appoints lunatic as safety boss on rig. Rig blows up.'

End of story.

He was turning away from the screen when the hunger pangs took him again, stronger than last night. More painful. He folded up like a cheap Chinese umbrella, dropping to the floor and knocking over a couple of plastic chairs as he fell. He cried out in shock and pain as something like a cold iron fist closed around his intestines and squeezed.

'Oh, God . . .' he gasped. Sweat broke out on his forehead, and within seconds his armpits were soaked. He shivered and drew his knees up to his chest. He was dimly aware of chaos breaking out around him, of raised voices calling for help. J2 was shrieking. He even heard the word 'corpsman', just like in a war movie. He felt himself lifted up and carried somewhere. Fluorescent tubes burned his eyes with harsh white light. He tried to speak, but the pain was too great.

Heath's face was in his, shouting at him.

'Can you hear me? Can you tell me what's wrong?'

Dave's teeth chattered as he tried to force them apart. His tongue seemed swollen.

'Hnn . . . hunn . . .' he managed before another wave of racking gut cramps doubled him over.

'Did you say something about the Hunn?' someone asked.

'No, here, let me through.'

It was a familiar voice, but in his distress and discomfort Dave could not recall why. He felt a new presence looming over him but was unable to open his eyes. It felt as though the Silveen's chain-mail fist had ripped out his insides.

'Here. Get this into him.'

'Are you crazy?'

Dave was vaguely aware of an argument breaking out around him, and he wanted to scream in frustration. He managed to prise his jaw apart just wide enough to say something when somebody shoved something between his lips.

Chocolate.

Saliva jetted into his mouth so quickly that he felt himself gagging on it. He bit down on the chocolate, thankfully only chocolate. Whoever had saved him with a chunk of Hershey Bar got his or her fingers out from between his teeth pronto. He pushed himself up onto his elbows, gesturing frantically for more chocolate, anything anybody could give him. He recognised Allen at last as the navy SEAL handed him the rest of the Hershey's Bar.

'That's three you owe me,' he said.

Dave was too busy eating to reply. They'd thrown him onto a spare table. He saw his friends and co-workers from the Longreach looking on in a mixture of horror and concern.

'You all right, Dave?' J2 asked.

'You may not believe me, Ms Juliette,' he said through gritted teeth, 'but I'm really fucking hungry.'

Heath barked out orders, and men and women disappeared, only to reappear a few moments later bearing trays of food. Dave's hands were shaking as he snatched at the greasy breakfast offerings. Strips of bacon. Pork sausages. Hash browns. Scrambled eggs scooped up in his bare hands and half smeared over his unshaven face. He didn't care. The more he ate, the faster the terrible pain in his stomach subsided. Heath's marines cleared the anteroom of onlookers as Dave slowly recovered. Only the rig workers, Heath, and Allen remained.

'Oh, my God, Dave,' J2 said in awe when he was finished. 'You could go pro with an appetite like that.' He had consumed enough food for five men. Maybe more. The pain was gone, and he patted his stomach gingerly, expecting to find his belly grossly swollen. But he felt neither heavy nor bloated. It was as though he had already digested the food, as though he'd burned it up while he was eating it.

'Got to eat a good breakfast, J2,' he said, finally realising that most of his rig crew was in the officers' mess with him. They looked down on him with a mixture of concern, fear, and awe. 'Most important meal of the day. Hi, everybody, by the way.'

A few of them laughed, but nervously. The other workers from the rig crowded in around him, eager for news from the outside world and wanting to know how he had survived. Alberto Santini, a geologist, had seen the creatures coming up the drill bit and run to raise the alarm. Henry Blucas, one of Vince's second shift rig monkeys, had been in the crew lounge when they broke in and had seen Marty try to fight them off. He'd taken an ineffectual swing at one of the 'little fuckers' – the Fangr – before abandoning the idea as hopeless and running, screaming, for the flight deck. Clay Toltz, a large-bellied African-American who was new to the rig and had been supervising the drill crew far away from the action, had been one of the first down into the lounge after Dave had killed the Hunn. He was still making the sign of the cross every time he spoke of it.

'Damnedest thing I've ever seen,' he said again and again. 'And I grew up in Baltimore.'

The last survivor was Terry Higgins, an Englishman, an instrument and control engineer of about fifty years of age who looked like he'd put on another decade overnight. He had been hiding in the showers across the hall from the crew lounge and had emerged in his underpants and a towel just as Dave swung the hammer. He confirmed Vince Martinelli's story about what had happened next.

'It was like cutting the strings to a bunch of puppets when you hit that big bastard,' he said. 'They all went down.'

'What's up with you, Dave?' J2 asked. 'You looked mighty sick just then.'

He knew she was probably paying a little more heed to Heath's stories about infections and transmission vectors now.

'It's like I told you, J2,' he said. 'Shit's been weird all over. Not just on the rig. I ain't been myself. Not bad. But not myself.'

'Honey, bad is yourself,' she said, and a few weak chuckles eased the tension.

Surrounded by people he knew and felt he could trust for the first time in a while, Dave almost threw his hands up in defeat and told them everything. About the strange things he just seemed to know about the creatures that had attacked them. About his weird superhero strength that seemed to cost him terribly, if these recurring spasms of violent hunger were somehow connected to it. But he needed no warning look from Captain Heath to shut the hell up. He knew it as a righteous certainty that if he told them everything, they'd think him crazy or cursed. They would back right off of him. And the last thing he wanted at the moment was to be left alone.

'I don't know, J2,' he said. 'I guess we all had a bad day yesterday. And I didn't eat. It catches up with you. I just got dizzy. Sorry for freaking you out. Been more'n enough of that to go around. What about you guys? How you all doing? You being looked after?'

They were subdued in their responses. Higgins complained about not being able to get a decent cup of tea, and Toltz worried that he hadn't been able to reach his daughter on the phone.

'Is that going to be a problem?' Dave asked Heath. 'This man needs his kid to know he's all right.'

Heath showed them his open hands. 'If you need to reach out to your families or your employer, that's fine. We'd ask . . .' He paused. 'The president would ask that you don't go talking to anybody about the details of what you saw yesterday. We don't know if this was a one-time event or if you guys cracked open some sort of chamber with your drill and let these things out. We just don't know enough to be able to tell people anything yet without scaring the hell out of them. And that includes your families. So no, you didn't wake up in North Korea. You can call your daughter, Mr Toltz. But please, let's not make things worse.'

It was hard to imagine how they could be worse for Dave, but J2 was babbling by then, asking Heath about whether the president really had asked after them.

'He may even want to talk to you later,' said the officer, eliciting great excitement, except from Higgins, who muttered something about celebrity politicians jacking up his tax rate.

'When can we go home?' asked Clayton Toltz, damping down the buzz of conversation. They all wanted to know the answer to that.

'You'll appreciate that we need to interview you, examine you, make sure we know as much about what happened as possible. As soon as that's done, you're out of here. We don't really have the facilities on this base to cater to houseguests. And as soon as we know what we're dealing with, we can get on and do our jobs. And hopefully you can go back to yours.'

'Is the government gonna stop us from telling our stories?' Blucas asked. 'Because we could get some good money for these stories. From the real news, too. Not just cable.'

Dave was alarmed by the idea and surprised when Heath brushed off the rig monkey's concerns. 'We can't stop you saying or doing anything, Mr Blucas. It's not like in the movies. We're not going to disappear you. There were 143 people on the Longreach yesterday. Our latest figures list thirty-seven of them as dead. Twenty-four are in the hospital with very serious injuries. And the remainder are scattered around the gulf on a variety of ships and onshore facilities. Not all of them know what happened. As I keep saying, *we* don't know what happened. That's why we need your help. The initial reports yesterday, that terrorists had attacked the platform, came from your own people. Some of them are still insisting on that today. But eventually the truth will out. And probably pretty quickly. We need to get in front of that. Do you think you can help us?'

They were subdued, but nobody pushed back.

'Can you tell us one thing?' Vince asked.

'If I can,' Heath answered.

'Are there more of these things?'

'And can you kill them?' Santini tossed in from over in the corner.

'There could well be more,' Heath told them, not exactly lying, but not being pathologically honest about things either, Dave thought. 'And yes,' he added to Santini, but in such a way that he addressed all of them. 'We can kill them. Just ask Dave.'

For the first time in days, Dave grinned and nodded.

'Oh, shit, yeah,' Dave said. 'We can kill 'em good.'

What he didn't say was, *And there'll be lots to kill. Armies of them. Legions.*

10

The navy split them up after breakfast, sending each of the survivors off to be examined by teams of doctors, psychologists, and otherwise anonymous personnel with no specific job description who interviewed them about the events of the previous day until they had all talked themselves out. As they rotated from one folding table to the next in a couple of large tin sheds, it was pretty boring for the most part, featuring plenty of 'hurry up and wait' according to one army guy in Dave's entourage. They all had an entourage, just like that TV show. But his was the largest and included Heath and Allen, who remained with him throughout the morning. They seemed to have no function other than to be there as familiar faces. Maybe to stop him going all snarly Hulk and smashing the place up, he thought with a wry grin that he quickly hid. It still didn't spare him from hours of tedium, though, while laptop keyboards got hammered and Surface tablets were stroked. Mystery guys in white coats checked and signed printouts and transcripts while more mystery guys with no specific job description consulted one another in low voices as all the information they gathered was sucked off to Christ knew where. Dave wasn't actively separated from his co-workers, but the military kept them tumbling through the morning like lotto balls, and he had no real chance to check up on any of them.

He supposed it wasn't much different from what he would be doing if he were back in Houston trying to get to the bottom of what had happened out on the rig. Lots of interviews. Lots of cross-checking.

There'd be less of this secret squirrel bullshit, though.

The procedure was the same for everyone until about eleven in the morning, when Dave was herded away from the others. His little entourage, grown to seven strong, trudged through rain that was pouring hard now, turning the compound into a muddy quagmire. After a few miserable minutes in which the rain eased off a little, they arrived at what looked like an exercise station, where a marine sergeant with a name tag that read SWINDT waited for Dave with a face nearly as foreboding as the tattoos on his oversized biceps. Until yesterday he would have been an intimidating sight, but Marty Grbac had been possessed of a set of guns every bit as impressive as Sergeant Swindt's, and the last Dave recalled of them, some blood-drunk super-orc was using the bones of those big ol' ham hocks to pick his teeth. Swindt stood next to a chinning bar, and standing next to him, looking less impressive as he tried to keep the rain from his glasses, was a navy officer who introduced himself as Lieutenant Johnson. He had to juggle a clipboard and an iPad in a heavy LifeProof case to shake hands.

'We're going to do a physical fitness test,' Johnson said.

'A what?' Dave asked. 'Seriously? I'm back in gym class? Do we have time for this?'

'Yes,' Captain Heath said. 'We do. Sergeant Swindt will explain what you need to do.'

Sergeant Swindt explained the marine version of pull-ups in granular detail, taking care to point out all the thou-shalt and shalt-nots of what would and would not constitute 'a proper pull-up for the purpose of this test'. Apparently the marines had very particular ideas about that sort of thing. Swindt certainly did.

'The chin-up has a variety of different forms, all of them wrong, except for the form I shall now demonstrate,' he barked.

He leaped a few inches into the air, grasping a bar that was beaded with rain. The giant marine used a closed grip with his thumbs tucked in on the opposite side of the thick iron bar from his fingers, but he did not use the momentum of the jump to complete the first pull-up, instead fully extending his arms while tucking his feet up behind his knees.

'The body is pulled up until the bar touches the upper chest,' he said without any apparent difficulty or discomfort. He might as well have been leaning against a bar as hanging from one. 'One repetition will consist of raising the individual's body with the arms until the chin is above the bar before lowering it until the arms are fully extended again. The individual will repeat this as many times as possible. Kicking motions are permitted as long as the chin-up remains a vertical movement and the feet and/ or knees do not rise above the waist level. I will prevent the individual's body from swinging by extending my arm across the front of his knees while the individual remains on the bar. The individual may change hand position during the exercise providing he does not dismount the bar or receive assistance. The individual may rest in the up or down position, but resting with the chin supported by the bar is prohibited. Are you ready?' Sergeant Swindt asked.

'Fuck,' Dave sighed. 'Did the individual mention that he fucking hates pull-ups?'

Swindt genuinely seemed not to care about that information.

Dave shook his head at the waste of time and effort and in his frustration leaped up a notch too hard. His eyes bulged as he suddenly found the bar below him at waist level before he dropped effortlessly back down to the ground with a splash.

The military observers all took a step back from the spray of mud while Lieutenant Johnson began scribbling notes into an iPad with a stylus.

'Well, that was weird,' Dave said.

'Please complete the exercise as instructed,' Swindt said as though he hadn't just witnessed a middle-aged man break the surly bonds of gravity as if they were made of rainbow ribbons. Not feeling entirely sure about what might happen next, Dave looked to Allen, who shrugged and smiled at the bar.

'Remember, it's a pull-up, not the high jump, dude.'

Dave adjusted his take-off for a little less spring and found the bar height easily this time.

'Begin,' Swindt said.

Dave could feel his weight hanging from the bar, but it was merely an awareness of the mass rather than any sort of difficulty. It no more strained his arms than picking up a magazine would.

'Hmph.'

He adjusted and held on to the bar with just one hand. It was no more of an inconvenience. Not really.

'Both hands on the bar, please, sir,' Swindt growled.

But Dave didn't need both hands on the bar. He ripped

off ten or eleven chin-ups using only one arm, a wide grin cracking his face. Raising a beer to his lips might have taxed his strength more than this.

'You want me to start over? Do it the marine way?' he asked, hanging from one hand, dropping in a couple more chin-ups just to show off. He was almost laughing.

Allen rubbed the bridge of his nose and groaned. 'This is going to be a long day.'

But it wasn't. Not at the base, anyway. Swindt gave up trying to instruct Dave in the correct form for a sit-up somewhere around the hundred mark. The Marine Corps non-com refused to count any rep without the proper form, which confused Dave at first when he was happily grinding out what he estimated to be his thirtieth or fortieth sit-up while Swindt leaned over him grunting, 'Six, six, six . . . seven, seven . . .'

Dave ignored him, fascinated by the change in his body. He had tried to get into the small, basic gym on the Longreach a couple of times a week, and the physical demands of rig work were a good way to keep up a constant calorie burn. But the food out there was all high-fat and high-carb stuff, energy-dense eating, a bit like the navy mess, and although he liked to think of himself as being in pretty good shape for a guy his age, there was no denying the baby blubber eel that had taken up residence around his midriff the last few years.

Or there had been no denying it.

The blubber eel was gone now. In spite of Swindt's annoying inability to count past a number bigger than all of his fingers and toes combined, Dave kept on at the sit-ups, poor form or not.

'Thirteen, thirteen, thirteen . . . fourteen . . . fourteen . . .'

He couldn't help looking at where his stomach normally would roll over the top of his jeans. You couldn't always see it when he was standing up straight. Sucking things in a bit. Wearing a loose shirt. But here he was laid down on a muddy rubber mat, wearing jeans and a T-shirt, folding himself in half as he rolled through a hundred-plus sit-ups without breaking a sweat or even losing his wind. And the eel was definitely gone.

'I think that's probably enough, sir,' Lieutenant Johnson said. 'Sir?'

Allen's voice cut through the dull patter of rain. 'Hey, Dave. That's enough, man. You're just showing off now.'

He came out of his private thoughts, shaking his head to throw off the raindrops that wanted to run down into his eyes. 'Sorry,' he said, abandoning the exercise and climbing to his feet, noticing that his knees gave him no trouble when he did so. They'd started to stiffen up in the last couple of years, making him less enthusiastic about jogging up and down the multiple flights of steel steps on the rigs and probably opening another door for the eel to slither in and take up residence, too. He patted his stomach now. It was flat and hard. It didn't feel like his body anymore. Or maybe . . . no . . . it did feel like his body, but back when he was young and still playing football.

'Got something else?' he asked Swindt, who regarded him with a neutral expression.

'You deadlift?' the marine asked.

Dave shrugged. 'Not much. Half my body weight usually. It's my back and knees . . .' He trailed off. 'I guess I should give it a try, though.'

Swindt nodded once. Lieutenant Johnson, who was trying to get a final count for the sit-ups from Swindt, followed them over to a bench and a rack of weights and plates that Dave was thankful to see was partly covered by a canvas tarpaulin.

'You want to start with your body weight?' asked Swindt, who now seemed more curious than threatening. 'What are you, 180-something?'

Dave sucked air in through his teeth, admitting he hadn't hopped on the scales for a while. 'Wasn't sure I'd like what I found,' he said, and thought he might have topped out at over 220 in the winter months.

'My guess, 205,' said Swindt.

'I got ten bucks on 210,' Allen chipped in.

'You'll lose your dough, Chief,' said the marine. 'Lieutenant?'

Lieutenant Johnson seemed surprised to be consulted. He'd been busy wiping mud splatter from the case of his iPad.

'How much did Mr Hooper weigh in at this morning, sir?' Swindt asked with exaggerated patience.

'Oh,' said Johnson, checking both his iPad and the papers on his clipboard. 'That was . . . er . . . 207 pounds . . . which would . . . er . . . give Mr Hooper a BMI of twenty-six for his height, which is overweight . . . and . . .'

'Hey,' Dave said. 'I had that big breakfast, you know. You gotta spot me a couple of pounds for all the good navy grub.'

Two-oh-five, though? That was a lot better than he'd been expecting.

'I say 205,' Swindt insisted, ignoring the evidence of Johnson's iPad. 'We'll start with that.'

Allen and Swindt loaded up a long bar with more weight plates than Dave had ever imagined lifting in his life. Even with all the freaky shit that was going down, he was nervous.

'Did I mention my bad back?' he asked without much confidence.

'The effective range of an excuse is zero, Mr Hooper,' Heath said. Dave couldn't tell if he was joking.

'This is just for your warm-up set,' Swindt said without looking at him. The plates kept clanging together on the bar, sinking lower and lower into the rubber matting under the tarp. The observers in his entourage crowded in under the canvas to get out of the rain, which had thickened again.

'Two-zero-five,' Swindt announced. 'We'll call it there.'

And then the instructions began again.

'The individual will stand with his toes just under the bar, feet slightly wider than his shoulders . . .'

Dave listened this time, because although he had done some deadlifting – you had to in his industry; it was one of the basic strength builders, and at his age he needed to at least make a token effort – he knew his form wasn't good. He tended to bend his back and his knees when they should have been straight, which he could get away with at low weights, but at this level . . .

He balefully examined the Olympic-sized bar with a heavy mass of dead iron clamped on to each end. That was his body weight there, or as close enough as made no difference. And, as more than one woman had complained over the years, having one whole Dave Hooper land on top of you wasn't the most comfortable experience.

'You will pull back your shoulders and push out your chest . . .' Swindt continued.

Dave wondered how much the marine could deadlift. Or bench. Or twirl around over his head. At least one soaking wet Dave Hooper, he'd bet.

'I'm not really dressed for this,' said Dave, who was still in the clothes Allen had provided him with yesterday.

'Just do one,' Captain Heath said. 'See what happens.'

He took up his position at the bar, allowing Swindt to adjust his foot placement and grip.

'Bend your knees, not your back,' said the marine, and Dave lowered himself to make the first lift. He squeezed the bar, as someone had told him to or he'd read in some fitness magazine or seen on *Biggest Loser* or something years ago, took a deep breath, exhaled, and lifted.

At the last moment he checked himself. Memories of the last day, of Lieutenant Dent flying through the air, of the bedside unit splintering under his fist, of the chin-ups, caused him to dial it back just a little.

It was a good thing he did.

The 200-plus pounds of metal flew up off the rubber mat, slipped out of his fists at the top of the lift, and tore through the canvas tarpaulin with a dull, wet roar.

'Move!' Swindt roared, charging at the assembled officers, his arms wide as if to gather them up. Allen swore and dived out the side of the makeshift tent. Dave was aware of everything slowing down. Everything but his thoughts. The physical world, the world of real things, seemed to move in super slo-mo, and when he focused, he could pull in tight on all the little details: the individual threads of the tarpaulin stretching and snapping and coming asunder; the first drops of rain tumbling in through the rent in the cover; the muddy fantails thrown up by the shoes of the officers as they ran; the way Allen turned his body in midair when he dived, tucking in his chin and making a circle of his arms as he dropped one shoulder and transitioned from a horizontal dive into a falling shoulder roll. But most of all he could see the giant weight set climb into the leaden sky like a bottle rocket. The tarp, torn free of its moorings and shredded by the passage of the weight bar, flapped gamely after it, but rain and aerodynamics conspired to drag it back. All this Dave observed as if sitting in his favourite armchair in his apartment back in Houston, watching a replay on ESPN.

But that was out in the world. Inside Dave's point of view, everything sped up. He found he was able to calculate the exact trajectory the lethally tumbling deadweight would take. Equations he hadn't thought of since his undergrad engineering days spilled across his conscious mind, providing vectors and angles of escape and acceleration. He was able to imagine the flight of the slowly spinning weight bar as it reached its apogee high above the camp and began a long, chaotic tumble back to earth. He could see from the paths they had all taken in their escape that Johnson had chosen poorly, and long before the weight crashed down on the lieutenant's right shoulder, Dave was able to 'see' the outcome in all its unpleasant detail. Shattered bones, rendered flesh, a skull crushed and split open, spilling its grey, steaming contents into the mud.

He pushed away the images of yesterday's slaughter on the rig that wanted to come flooding back in behind his eyeballs. They were replaced by even more upsetting images of that little boy in the Prius. An unpleasant electric tingle ran over his skin, and he snarled in a strangely animalistic fashion. That kid wasn't much younger than his own youngest, Jack. And then he couldn't help imagining the Hunn and Fangr fighting over Toby and Jack, tearing them apart . . .

But even as he saw all those things in slow motion, he was already moving at such speed that the others would later say that it was as though he winked out of existence for a second until they picked him up again as a blur of fluid motion threading through their stationary forms.

He cleared the tent just before it collapsed in on itself, and using the edge of the rubber mat, the last firm foothold he knew he would enjoy, Dave Hooper launched himself skyward. Whereas he had surprised himself before by nearly jumping over the chinning bar, there was no surprise this time. He knew that he was about to leap sixty-three feet and four inches into the air, where he would intercept the weight bar at the zenith of its flight, grasping it firmly with both hands, his left hand nine inches from the weight plates at one end and his right hand a little closer, at seven.

Dave made the intercept exactly as envisioned, pulling the weight bar out of its flight path and down onto a new and safer course.

He landed in the clear, between two sheds, holding the bar as though it were no heavier than a pool cue. The sound of impact as his feet punched into the sodden earth rolled away from the explosion of mud like the fart of an elephant god.

Dave tossed the weighted bar to one side. He was standing in a crater at least a foot deep.

Captain Heath cancelled the rest of Dave's physical, including a three-mile run in the rain that Dave was more than happy to miss. He hated running even though he *felt* as though he could cover three miles in a couple of minutes. Thinking about that only led him to thoughts of the Hunn, however, and he shied away.

The entourage broke up, and Dave found himself herded into an aid station by Allen and Heath. He looked around for his crewmates from the rig but saw no sign of them.

'Debriefing,' said Heath.

'Please roll up your sleeve, sir,' a nurse said. Concentrating fiercely, she took samples of his blood, filling seven tubes from each arm. When she whisked the needle away and swabbed the puncture wound, a cloud crossed over her face.

'There's no . . .'

'Don't worry about it,' Allen said. 'Dude here's like a self-sealing tyre.'

'Next station,' Heath said. 'Let's go. We're on the clock now.'

And so it went for the next half hour as they fairly ran from one station to the next.

'Turn your head and cough, please.'

'Childhood disabilities?'

'Any broken bones?'

'Allergies?'

'Do you feel abnormal in any way? If so, could you please describe it?'

Dave answered that one with a snort. 'You're shitting me, right?'

'Do you have a history of mental disturbances?' a navy shrink asked.

'Where did you say you broke your arm when you were a kid?' the X-ray tech asked.

Standing before one of the navy doctors, Dave pointed at his right arm.

The X-ray showed no evidence of the fracture.

'Could you fill this cup, please?' a nurse from earlier in the morning asked. She was a smokin' hot blonde with lips that were all lurid promise. Best thing he'd seen on this miserable base so far.

Bad Dave came roaring back in the worst way.

'I could fill more than that if you like, honey,' he said.

'Just the cup, sir,' she said, blushing.

Don't blow hot, he thought, filling the cup in a bathroom while Allen looked vaguely in his direction. *Just don't blow hot.*

It was a legit concern. His cock had stiffened like a length of rebar when he started to imagine the sorts of things he could get up to, or down to, with a woman like that, and his balls were humming like a coal miners' choir. Dave feared that once he let the old persuader out of its cage, there'd be no getting it back in without some sort of action.

He also didn't want these navy guys ratting him out to Baron's. If he'd taken his usual drug test out on the rig, he would have had a small bottle of baby piss to swap for his own sample, courtesy of Vince Martinelli's youngest. Here, however, he was probably going to start alarms ringing in about three seconds. He forced his mind to settle down, forced it away from thoughts of the nurse and onto the thick pile of unopened letters he knew was sitting on his kitchen table back in Houston. Correspondence from the IRS.

His dick deflated like an old inner tube, and within a minute he'd managed to fill the specimen jar with a full measure of Dave's Golden Ale. He finished up, washed his hands as his mother had taught him, and returned to the nurse's station, where she waited with Allen, her face unreadably neutral except for the high colour in her cheeks, which had not faded.

Ha, still got it, Dave thought.

Blondie took the cup, gloves in place, and pulled a tab on the side that showed her the results.

Here we go, Dave thought.

'Good to go,' she said.

No. Fucking. Way.

He couldn't believe it. No way had he just passed a drug test. Most of the bonus he hadn't spent on pussy he'd blown on top-shelf coke a week earlier. There had to be snowdrifts of the stuff still blowing around in his system.

'You are my new best friend,' he told her, almost sighing with relief.

'I already have enough *friends*,' she said.

Whoa. Dave was certain *that* was a come-on. No way he could have misinterpreted that, and he was about to reply in kind when he felt the first familiar pang in his stomach again. This time he knew what was coming.

'Hey, Allen,' he called out.

'Yeah?'

'You think there'll be any waffles left at the mess tent?'

He fed. Half an hour of relentless two-fisted piggery that accounted for all of the leftover bacon and biscuits in the camp kitchen. Allen shooed away most of the onlookers, but there was no getting rid of the personnel detailed to KP for the morning. They watched in awe as Dave did his trick, making enough food for three grown men disappear inside one. Chief Allen excused himself for a few minutes while Dave was fuelling up and then returned with an armful of new clothes, fatigues similar to those the SEALs wore, which looked a shade different from the jarheads' preferred patterns. Although, Dave corrected himself as he sucked up another rasher of bacon, preference probably had nothing to do with it. He'd never understood the way the uniforms kept changing on *Stargate*, which he used to enjoy watching with his boys, and to his civilian eye there seemed to be no rhyme or reason to people's fashion choices on this base, either. Some were tricked out in what looked like quite formal attire. Some got around in gym gear. Others wore what he assumed were combat fatigues like the ones he climbed into after his second breakfast. He'd never asked his brother about it and never would now, of course. A terrible sadness washed over him, as bad as any of the animal grief he'd felt when they told him Andy was dead. It was so unexpected, and so fucking bad that he had to hold his breath lest it come out in a sob. And then, just as abruptly, it was gone and he was delighted to find that the cargo pockets of his pants were filled with CLIF protein bars and energy gels.

What the fuck?

His emotions were everywhere and for a second he was struck by the image of himself as a spinning top just about to wobble out of control.

Enough of this teen girl bullshit. Get a grip, idiot.

He checked his new wardrobe again. It was something to do. Something to distract his thoughts. He had a pair of tan combat boots and a black T-shirt. Good. Allen also set body armour down in front of him with ammo pouches filled with yet more food.

'You can change back at your tent,' Allen said. 'When you're done here.'

'I'm not enlisting, you know,' Dave said, forcing himself into the moment. Into this moment.

'We wouldn't have you,' Allen shot back. He attempted a lopsided grin, but to Hooper the stress lines around his eyes looked every bit as deep as they had after the ambush last night. 'We still have some standards,' the chief petty officer said. 'But everyone wears a plate carrier to the site. It's just the rules. Also, I got you a CamelBak. Filled it with Gatorade. Might help.'

'Plate carrier?' Dave asked.

Allen held up the body armour, which looked like a pair of bib overalls with the bottoms cut off. 'A lot of guys leave the plates behind, don't like the weight. I'd prefer you left yours in. The captain will have my ass if you get killed and you aren't wearing this.'

'Okay.'

His hunger abated after another half a loaf of white bread smeared with grape jelly, and he followed Allen back to the medical tent where the rig survivors had bunked down last night. There was no sign of his crew.

'They're doing psych evals about now,' Allen said. 'See if they're crazy enough to let loose in the real world again.'

'So they're going home today?'

'Or tomorrow.'

'After the story breaks for real?'

Allen rewarded him with a half smile.

'Now you're learning.'

Once dressed, Dave looked like a street person who'd lucked out in the garbage cans behind a surplus warehouse. The T-shirt was a size too big, at least across the stomach, although the sleeves and shoulders were a little tight. He adjusted the straps and Velcro on the body armour, which felt like a life jacket to him, familiar from drills out on the platforms, light and not particularly burdensome.

'Thanks for these,' he said, holding up a peanut butter and caramel-flavoured OhYeah! bar.

'Thank the long-suffering taxpayers of these United States,' Allen said, reminding Dave of the unopened letters from Uncle Sam's shakedown man back on the kitchen table in his apartment. He dreaded to think what might be waiting for him in such a heavy-looking pile of envelopes. The thought occurred to him as he laced up his new boots that he might be able to cut a deal with the IRS, some sort of contribution in kind where they gave him a tax credit for killing those things out on the Longreach and last night on the way here. After all, you could totally look at that as a community service in a way.

It was a selfish thought, he knew, unworthy of the current circumstances and disrespectful of the losses and suffering others had endured yadda yadda yadda.

And yet . . .

The same way he'd been meaning to sit his ass down and do his taxes, he'd also been meaning to get an accountant. Someone he could just give those unfiled returns to. Somebody who could get him out of the hole he'd dug himself the last couple of years. As he fitted and straightened the government-issued clothes and pondered just how much the military at least seemed to want and *need* his help, Dave Hooper had to ask himself if maybe an accountant wasn't the right call to make here. Maybe a lawyer would be better. Or an agent who could find the right sorts of lawyers and accountants. He was gonna be a celebrity after all, one way or another, and celebrities all had agents to take care of their business, didn't they?

He stomped the boots into place and stood up, noticing the huge old blank Sony TV in the corner of the room. It looked like one of the last WEGA models, as big as the moving van that delivered it, thought Dave, who'd paid cash for the latest Samsung flat-screen with his bonus before this last one. The one he'd spent on hookers and blow. The cash transaction brought down the price – the TV was probably, no, almost *certainly*, stolen – and left no trail for Annie's douche bag lawyer to follow.

He wondered when, or if, he might ever get home to enjoy firing up Ol' Sammy again.

'We good to go?' the chief asked.

Allen had changed his outfit, too, and it didn't look like a change for the better. He wore digital jungle fatigues and boots, with pads on his elbows and knees. His helmet, which rested on a table on a stack of auto mags and old copies of *Sports Illustrated*, bristled with all sorts of attachments on a complicated rail system. He seemed to be carrying half his body weight in weapons and ammo. Dave wasn't a gun nut. Never had been, and he took a powerful dislike to them after his brother was killed, but he knew enough to be able to recognise a shotgun, some sort of assault rifle, two pistols, a bunch of grenades, and a long, wicked-looking fighting knife. He wasn't sure he'd want to go up against any of the . . .

Dar Hunn. Dur Fangr.

. . . the creatures he'd encountered on the rig with a little bitty pig-sticker like that, but a snout full of buckshot or a burst of armour-piercing ammo would probably do the job.

'Go where?' Dave asked.

Allen answered with one word: 'Longreach.'

His heart sank, but he had known it was coming. They were always going to take him back out there, make him walk through everything again.

'Sure, let's rock,' he said without enthusiasm as he stripped the wrapper from an OhYeah! bar. He chewed mechanically, eating for fuel, as he recalled the feeling of the splitting maul smashing through the thick mantle of the Hunn's facial bone and gristle. He could remember a lot more of the encounter the farther he was from it, and that was a problem. Because he'd like to get as far away as possible from that day as well as forgetting all about it. At first it had seemed like a barely remembered dream. Now the moment of impact was a muscle memory as tactile as if he had swung the heavy sledge just a second ago.

'What happened to the one we killed last night?' he asked as Allen gathered up his kit and they headed toward the exit. He didn't feel comfortable calling the Sliveen by its name. It sounded like madness in his head when he formed the words.

Allen shrugged.

'No idea. That's way above my pay grade, Dave. It could be a thousand miles from here by now on a slab at the Smithsonian or Area 51.'

'Really?' Dave asked, his interest piqued. 'There's an Area 51 for real?'

'No. But maybe there should be.'

'Oh, okay.'

He finished the peanut and caramel snack, no longer hungry. He was learning to recognise the signs of the weird, almost instant starvation now and thought perhaps he could keep the pain at bay with smaller but regular deposits of energy-dense food. Dr Pradesh had been right, he thought. His metabolism was running at white heat. It had burned off his love handles and blubber eel, and given him a stripped down, almost Spartan look that he thought of as gaunt rather than healthy. It had been so long since Dave Hooper had gone without a cushioning layer of fat under his skin that he'd forgotten what being fit looked like.

Like CPO Allen, for instance. The SEAL was all hard lines and angles not because he worked for it but because he worked hard at his job, and the physique just came as part of that deal. He looked like a clenched fist.

'What d'you think's up with me?' Dave asked him as they emerged into waning afternoon light and waited, presumably, for Heath to return. 'You must have seen some shit out in the tropics and such. Weird diseases and stuff. Anything like this?'

Dave plucked at his fatigues, indicating that he meant the radically transformed body within them.

'Superhero syndrome?' Allen asked. 'Sorry. Nope. I've

seen dudes stoned off their gourds on khat and bennies and weird cocktails of third world hooch. Seen them do stuff, running around full of bullet holes when they should rightly be lying down and dying quietly. But no, Dave,' he said quietly. 'I haven't seen anything like whatever aids or ails you.'

Allen, who'd struck him initially as a laid-back surfer archetype, at least once upon a time, in his pre-SEAL days perhaps, had come over kind of gloomy and reserved since the ambush, despite a few jokes from the gallows. He didn't mention the men who'd died or the family in the Prius, and Dave wasn't inclined to bring it up. He figured a guy would talk about that stuff when he wanted to, and probably not with the asshole who might be responsible for it in some way.

'You scared?' Allen asked.

'Guess I might have reason,' Hooper admitted. 'The whole circus act this morning with your man Swindt. That was cool, but no way was it right. Kinda freaks me even more than what happened on the Longreach.'

Allen was surprised. 'Why?'

Dave shrugged, stood up, and walked a small circle on the gravel path in front of the medical tent. They were tucked away in a quiet corner of the base. He could see personnel moving about here and there but still no sign of his fellow civilians.

'We were drilling down deep, Chief. Really deep. A record, in fact. Did they tell you that? We'd just drilled the deepest hole any motherfucker drilled anywhere on this planet. Ever.'

Allen nodded.

'Yeah. I read that in the briefing note. So?'

'You ever seen photos of the things live down at those depths?' Dave asked. 'It's a horror movie down there, man. Pressure means they stay down deep, but we see things sometimes. Shadows on the edge of the cams and stuff. Not just giant squids and sea snakes with teeth like fucking kris daggers. Worse than that.'

Allen smiled, a weak effort but genuinely made.

'Yeah, I got Discovery Channel, man. I've seen that stuff, too. Monster fish. About this big.'

He held up one hand with the thumb and forefinger extended, their tips an inch or so apart. 'And if they come up off the sea floor, they explode, though, don't they? Can't handle the lower pressure, like you said.'

'Yeah,' Dave said. 'But the fact stuff lives down there, it just proves stuff lives down there, and it's like nothing we're used to seeing up on the surface. So those things yesterday . . .'

Urgon Htoth Ur Hunn . . .

You dare not do this!

'. . . I guess we could have broken into a cave system or something, like a sealed ecosphere, something old and, I dunno, different. Some place evolution went bad. Like the jungle that Ebola virus came out of.'

'Maybe,' said Allen, but he didn't sound as though he was buying it. Dave didn't really believe it, either, because part of him knew different.

'Anyway,' he went on, staring into the grey drizzle with his back turned to the SEAL, 'I'm just saying, as bad as that was yesterday, shit happens in my world. Just like yours. I knew a guy got eaten by a tiger once. A fucking tiger, seriously. Another drill site, over on one of the Indonesian islands, we had to bring these guys in to catch a whole bunch of gators, or crocs I suppose, after they ate some of the locals we'd hired.'

'So dudes get eaten all the time in your line of work?' Allen asked, sounding amused in an abstract way.

'Not all the time, no. And not on the rigs. But stuff happens. You know . . .'

He tried to blow it off.

'But that deal with the weights and the chin-ups this morning? That's not some insane *Twilight Zone* bullshit. That was *me*, Allen. I threw 200 pounds of heavy metal through the tent and way up into low orbit. And then I jumped up there like Keanu fucking Reeves doing his Matrix thing and I plucked it out of the sky before it fell on Lieutenant Johnson.'

'Johnson? Really?'

'Yeah. I didn't tell you that. I could see it happening before it happened. Not looking into the future like down a time tunnel or anything. Just looking at what was happening and *knowing* how it was going to turn out. Like when you see some guy walking through the park and a kid hits a fly ball, and you just *know* it's gonna brain this dude. And it does.'

'Yeah,' Allen said, nodding his head. 'Been there more times than I can count.'

'Well, that ain't right, is it? None of it. Not my physical this morning. Not the way I've turned into a human garbage disposal. Not the twenty or thirty pounds of gut flab I've dropped doing it. None of this shit.'

He waved his arms around, taking in the wet compound, the leaves blowing across the muddy ground, the forest closing in on them at the edge of the camp, the whole world. The two men fell silent for a while.

'And it all changed after you killed the orc?'

'The Hunn,' Dave offered. 'It was a Hunn. Some sort of soldier beast or demon or something. Orc's close enough, I guess, if you really want to get sued by the Tolkien estate. I thought the same thing when I saw it. Humanoid, or maybe primate enough to make you think in those terms. Been a long time since high school Biology for me.'

'So how do you know it's one of these Hunn?' Allen asked, pronouncing the word correctly.

Dave returned to his perch on the small wooden set of steps leading up the tented medical station.

'Same way I knew exactly where that weight bar was gonna fall. I just knew . . . The thing was a Hunn, called itself Urgon Htoth.'

'The hell is that? Old German or something?'

'No idea. But my head is full of this crap now if I want to open Pandora's box and look in there. I could tell you Grymm fairy tales about the Hunn and the Fangr and Sliveen and Gnarrl. About the Grande Horde and the Threshrend and the UnderRealms. The banishing. The long dark . . .'

He stopped himself because Allen was staring at him with frank disbelief and not a little alarm.

'Have you told Captain Heath about this?'

Dave shook his head.

'Not all of it. Just a little about the Hunn. And the little butt buddies it had along. The Fangr. And the Sliveen scout last night. Didn't want him thinking I was bugshit crazy. Like you do now.'

'No, man, no . . . I . . .'

Allen tried to sell his denial, but Dave had seen the look on his face when he'd revealed just a little of what was running through the back of his mind, just below the level of consciousness.

'And these things you, er, you know? They came on after you killed the thing? The Hunn.'

'Urgon Htoth Ur Hunn.'

'Yeah, that guy. You got, what, his memories and your

Avenger mojo at the same time? When you brained him?'

Dave said nothing, but the fear in his eyes confirmed everything.

'Sounds like one of those Native American myths,' said Allen. 'You know, where you eat your enemy's heart to consume his strength and courage. 'Cept in your case you just splashed his brains on the wall and put the zap on his groupies.'

'The Fangr?'

'The walkin' dead with the stupid long talons, yeah. Both of your friends said that. When you dropped the Hunn, the others went down with it. Dude, we're a long way through the lookin' glass here. You have to tell Heath. He needs to know *all* this stuff.'

Dave raised a hand in front of his face, turned it around, and looked at the veins under his suntanned skin and the fine blond hairs on the back of the hand. It was recognisably him. Maybe a little thinner. But him. This was the hand that had scooped a million peanuts out of a thousand bowls in God only knew how many bars over the years. The hand that had smacked the fine tattooed ass of that top-shelf hooker he'd flown down from Nevada and ridden like a bouncy toy less than two days ago. The hand that had stroked his wife's hair in long-ago and happier days. He placed the tips of his fingers gently on his eyelids and rubbed at them. He was tired and very worried.

'I really don't want that thing in my head,' he said. 'I don't want any of it.'

Allen stood up at the sound of someone coming down the path.

'Didn't say it was in your head, Dave. I don't believe in old Indian tales about eating a dude's heart to harvest his mojo. I believe in Colt automatics and well-managed supply chains, planning, prep, and the application of measured force to defeat superstitious crap like that or bin Laden's beardy nutters.'

'And you believe in God, too, don't you? You're a Christian. Like a real one.'

'I try,' Allen said.

'Yeah, my friend Marty, too,' Dave said, but more to himself. Captain Heath appeared, striding around the corner of the big tented building, crunching up the muddy gravel path as though having only one leg to get through the day was no problem at all. Like Chief Allen he was dressed in fatigues and body armour, but he carried only a pistol on his thigh. The same one he'd shot at the Sliveen, Dave supposed. Had Heath lain awake last night replaying the crash and killings over and over again? Or had he just written up his reports and taken to his cot for a couple of hours of shut-eye?

'Are you well rested, well fed, Mr Hooper?'

'Sure,' said Dave. 'Why? We going on an adventure?'

'We're going back out to the Longreach, sir. I want you to take me through exactly what happened and have a look at the SSE data. It might shake free a few memories. Or some intelligence we can use.'

'SSE? Back to the rig? Is Vince coming? Or any of the others?'

Heath held up his hands. 'One question at a time. Yes, we're going to review the sensitive site data. As for your friends, including Mr Martinelli, they'll be released later today. They've signed non-disclosure agreements about their time on this base, and we'll be returning them first to Baron's for whatever debriefing your company deems necessary and then on to their families.'

Dave frowned.

'But not me?'

'No, Mr Hooper, not after this morning. I'm afraid you still have much you can help us with. Plus your family is some distance away and you are estranged from them as I understand.'

Dave frowned, 'Well, not estranged . . .'

Captain Heath continued. 'The rig is still classified as a high-risk area, Mr Hooper. Nobody from Baron's has been allowed inside the exclusion zone. It's too dangerous. But I don't imagine the same is true for you.'

Dave didn't know what to say to that.

'No,' he admitted at last. 'Probably not.' He stood up at the same time as Allen, who made remarkably little noise for a man so loaded down with equipment. 'Any other reason?'

'As I expected, the real story is beginning to form up in the real world. The mainstream press isn't touching it yet, but some of your colleagues are leaking to the blogs and the gossip sites. Some went straight to Facebook. A couple have been tweeting their versions of events.'

'Versions?' Dave asked. 'Leaking? Heath, they're just people. Talking about what happened. Not like that supernerd who pissed off to Russia after he ratted out the fucking NSA.'

'Mr Snowden,' said Heath, saying the name as though it hurt him to pronounce it.

'Whatever the case, I give it another day before the president has to start answering questions about an attack from Middle Earth. So you'll appreciate that he would like as much information as quickly as he can get it.'

'Fair enough,' Dave said. 'If I'd been sober on election day, I'd have voted for him. First time, anyway. Suppose it's the least I can do.'

'Nah,' Allen said, giving Dave a nudge with one padded elbow. 'There's plenty more.'

12

There was no long, fraught car ride back to New Orleans. They boarded a grey chopper at the base in a clearing that looked to have been hacked out of the wilderness in the last week. It was obvious that the trunks of the saplings at the edge of the clearing were freshly sheared off. A driver shuttled them by Hummer from the compound over to the helipad, a ten-minute drive on an unpaved road through thick forest. Rain fell heavily enough to obscure the track here and there, but the driver didn't slow down. He seemed to know the way, and Heath ordered him to go as quickly as he thought was safe and then some.

'The story is coming out,' he said as the Humvee slid around a long bend in the road. Allen, meanwhile, kept nudging Dave to spill the crazy beans. 'Bill O'Reilly was mouthing off about Greenpeace a little earlier. Calling them whack jobs because one of their kids got on Facebook with a story about a military cover-up out on your rig. A bioweapon gone wrong. O'Reilly smacked them hard. He's gonna look pretty foolish by the end of today.'

'Yeah, but Greenpeace doesn't need Bill O'Reilly to help them look foolish,' Dave said.

'My daughter's in Greenpeace,' Heath said without elaborating, and that shut the conversation down for a while.

Dave could hear the engine and the rotor thump well before they entered the clearing. Another half-dozen or more SEALs were already embarked, seated in the rear cabin. Allen greeted them all with his middle finger and a boyish grin. He didn't bother introducing Dave over the roar of the engines, directing him to a berth at the back of the cabin. Heath took a seat up front with the pilot. Maybe he was even qualified to fly this thing. That tin leg didn't seem to hold him back otherwise.

When they were securely buckled in, Dave asked Allen how he had gotten into the SEAL business. It was a thin effort at diverting the chief from the course he seemed set on of getting Dave to come clean to Heath about the full extent of his craziness. Surprisingly, it worked, giving Dave time to think about how he was going to explain to the navy officer what a fucking nut bag he'd thrown his lot in with. Well, it worked for now, at least. Even Allen didn't expect him to shout over the roar of the chopper.

'Dude,' Allen said, looking almost wistful even as he raised his voice. 'I was a lifeguard in high school. Surf patrol, you know. I volunteered for that – it was an awesome way to meet babes – but I picked up some paid work at a community centre pool, too. Some old dude there talked me into competing in the Lifeguard Olympics. Our company did that every year, you know, for morale and so on. Anyway, my senior year we won. I wasn't doing much else with myself. Steve, the same dude, talked me into going to see a recruiter. The army guys treated me like dirt but the navy was cool, showed me some videos, and I was hooked. Went on to SEAL training, and here I am.'

'Lifeguard Olympics?' Dave asked, nearly shouting now. 'You mean like *Baywatch*?'

'Sorta.' Allen grinned, the first time he'd done so all day. 'It was cake compared to SEAL training.'

The take-off put Dave back in the moment just a day earlier, an eternity ago, when J2 had tormented him about his hangover. No trace of the headache or nausea remained, and he realised for the first time that it, too, had vanished when he'd clubbed the Hunn to death. There was a chance he'd slept it off at the hospital and woken up groggy with sedatives. But probably not. He'd probably burned every molecule of alcohol in his body the same way he'd torched an inhuman amount of cooked meat and chocolate bars since. Be interesting to get his hands on a bottle and see whether he could neck it without any ill effect. Or a doobie.

Or even a line.

Oh, yeah. The chance would be a fine thing.

The grim faces of the men around him, all of them hidden behind combat goggles, did not inspire any confidence that he had fallen in among wayward party animals. Not when they were on the government's clock, anyway. Some of them hadn't shaved in weeks, a stark contrast to the marines and regular sailors he'd seen on the base. In fact, Dave thought they were a pretty rank-looking bunch, but in the way that you might expect an Old Testament prophet to be all rank and stringy and totally uptight about his very particular brand of shit.

Then he looked at his own camouflage trousers and oddly fitting T-shirt and figured he'd keep his fashion tips to himself. A few of these characters looked like they wouldn't be opposed to the idea of shooting old Dave in the head and tossing him out of the chopper. How many of them knew what had happened to their pirate buddies? How many blamed him? Probably all of them from the vibe he was getting.

Really not feeling the love for our man Dave from this crowd.

The roar of the engines and the thump of the rotors made any prolonged conversation pointless, and he got to wondering what these guys had been told about the situation they were flying into. The captain had surprised him so far with his no-bullshit policy. Most likely Heath had given them *all* the information he could gather, including the results of the morning's 'tests' on Dave. A couple of the SEALs were checking him out, obviously unimpressed and deeply sceptical. Also, there was the media. Without a phone – his old iPhone had gone astray – or ready access to a working screen of any kind, Dave hadn't caught up with the outside world since catching a glimpse of the cable news at the start of the day. Apart from the Greenpeace kid Heath had mentioned, maybe, and some public relations douche bag at Baron's hinting human error might be to blame for the disaster – Dave's error, let's be clear – there had been no indication of the Longreach story taking any weird detours away from agreed realities. How long could it be, though? Not soon enough for Dave. He really didn't want to be the one standing next to Heath or Obama or whoever when they did their 'Orcs Attack!' press conference.

It was too loud in the helicopter to ask Allen about any of it or to tell Heath anything about his earlier discussion with the chief and the uncharted depths of knowledge about the Horde that he seemed to possess now. The SEALs were plugged into some sort of tactical network through complicated headsets. Allen would occasionally push a button on his earpiece and talk into the tiny boom mike just off to the side of his mouth. But nobody had offered Dave anything like that, and when he'd asked, Allen had shouted back that there was no point.

'You're not trained for it, man. We got troop net and command net on this. We can't have anyone getting on yapping away. Bad enough when you get the wrong brass on the net. It'll mess everything up; trust me.'

Okay. That was cool. Dave wouldn't allow an outsider to come onto his rig and start dicking around, either. But it meant that for the moment he was cut off, cocooned within the early evening darkness and the roar of the helicopter. There was little room to spare in the cabin because of the SEALs' equipment and in one or two cases the sheer size of the men. Two door gunners manned a couple of Gatling guns. Dave was totally sure they were Gatling guns, like right out of the movies. He kept himself tucked up tightly on his little fold-down seat, looking out of the open door as the forest slipped under their wheels.

The stormy weather had cleared as the sun set, and only a few thin strands of cloud obscured the first gleaming stars and a bright three-quarter moon that glistened on the rivers and streams and the bayou below. Lights stood out here and there, singly and clustered in small settlements. The towns grew larger as they flew south, and New Orleans loomed on the horizon as a dome of light. The chopper swung around to the southeast, just perceptibly, to avoid overflying the city. Dave could see flashes of sheet lightning out over the water, and then he realised that some of the flashes were on the ground inside the city. As they drew closer, he was certain he could see fires within the greater metro area.

'What's that?' he shouted to Allen, pointing at the flickering light source.

The SEAL consulted his comm gear and called back,

'Nothing. Just a little riot. Gang fight or something. There's been some gunfire, so we're jagging east to avoid it. Be embarrassing getting shot in the tush over our own turf.'

'Yo,' said one of the SEALs, pointing at the tiny light show. 'Murder city nights.'

It was an in-joke or reference worth a few appreciative nods and fist bumps from his friends but lost on Dave.

He gave Allen a thumbs-up to signal that he understood before fetching another protein bar from one of the cargo pockets of his pants. He could sense himself getting peckish again and wanted to eat something, anything, before the racking gut cramps doubled him over. *Ha! Scored*, he thought as he recognised an Eat Smart Choc Peanut Caramel Crunch. He knew this one from the vending machines at the depot. As far as tasteless protein slabs went, it wasn't too shabby. Not as gooey and sticky on the teeth as some other bars and sporting just the right amount of crunch. Like a chocolate Rice Krispie, he thought as he reduced it to a memory in a couple of bites, following up with a gel tube that he found he could easily read in the dark. A PowerBar Gel Double Latte, it tasted no worse than the instant coffee at work, and with the Eat Smart bar it eased his emerging hunger pangs, tamping them down nicely.

The SEALs were all packing four-eyed night vision goggles, which again he had not been given, but again he didn't much care. As Dave took the time to look around the cabin, he found that deepening nightfall didn't really handicap him. The colour was washed out of his surroundings, but he was able to make out even fine details in a clear monochrome grey. Something new, he thought. He'd been putting off seeing an eye doctor about his worsening eyesight, an inability to refocus from long to short distances. Hadn't even been able to admit to himself his eyes were going after he bought a magnifying glass to keep at his apartment. It wasn't for reading small print, of course. No. It was for burning bugs and toy soldiers when the boys came for an access visit. Which, of course, they never did. Now he could read the small print on the gel tube in the dark of the chopper cabin.

In normal circumstances Dave would have been bringing the awesome since the rig attack. He'd kicked some ass, dodged a hangover, destroyed the buffet, dropped a little weight, and gotten in an epic gym session. He was by any measure fucking crushing it. But his stomach fluttered with nerves as he read the label on the gel packet:

110 CALORIES

TOTAL CARB 27 G

SUGARS 10 G

SODIUM 200 MG

All in tiny little letters he'd have been unable to read not long ago even at high noon in direct sunlight. The hammering thud of the rotors fed vibrations up through the soles of his boots into his butt and guts. He absentmindedly ate another bar, mostly for something to occupy him.

He'd had a couple of skin cancers off last year. Side of his neck and just behind one ear. More occupational hazards given how much time he spent in the sun. His barber spotted the small lesions on the back of his head. Dave had been watching the sore on his neck that never went away, just under his left ear, watching it the way you would watch a strange dog standing astride your path with its hackles up. He knew it was probably bad, but if he didn't go to the doctor and the doctor didn't confirm that . . . well, he was sweet.

The basal cell carcinoma had been diagnosed during his annual physical, and the doctor at Baron's had cut it out in the surgery that day, all the while cursing him for an idiot for letting it go so long.

The sense of creeping dread that he'd swallowed hard every time he woke up and looked at that small red sore that never healed? Yeah. That. Right now. Raised to the power of *what the fuck was happening to him*?

'Damn.'

The unfamiliar voice of one of Allen's comrades shook him out of the reverie. One of the SEALs was pointing off toward where a genuine light and magic show flared and sputtered in a blacked-out section of the outer burbs.

'What's that?' someone asked.

'Looks like the Central City projects,' replied a voice with a distinct Cajun lilt. 'Mebbe Calliope or Magnolia. Same old same old.'

'Looks like fucking Helmand at that time of the month,' said a monster of a man called Igor. Sporting an Amish-style beard on steroids, the man had biceps the size of bowling balls. Of all the men on the chopper, Dave figured this guy was the one who could give him a run for his money on the weight bench.

'Damn. That's tracer fire,' he heard Allen call out.

A couple of voices chorused together:

'For illuminating targets. And destroying personnel.'

Another in-joke, he gathered.

Before he could crane around far enough to see, the chopper's flight path took them beyond the point where he could get a good angle. He sat back, cupped his hands over his mouth, and called out to Allen, 'What was all that? Sounded serious.'

The SEAL didn't seem to think so.

'Drugs, for sure. Seen worse in Florida. Flown over honest to God street wars in Mexico that'd put that side show out of business,' he said, jerking his thumb back in the direction of the city.

The cabin settled down again, and soon enough they'd crossed the coast and were flying out over the barrier islands, heading south for the Longreach.

Some of the SEALs dozed on the flight out, but unlike his last trip to the platform, Dave stayed awake the whole way. He topped up the tank with another protein bar and sipped some Gatorade from his CamelBak, but otherwise he was alone with his thoughts.

They weren't pleasant.

He thought that if all that had happened had been a garden-variety fire and explosion on the rig, he'd have been better off. He'd have dealt. He told himself that if there had been some extreme but rational explanation for the things that had crawled up the pylons or the drill, something like his theory about cracking open an ancient ecosphere, he could have dealt with that, too. In good time.

But there was nothing on God's green earth that explained what had happened to him personally. Not the sudden *Super Friends* status update or the utterly alien memories that seemed to come with them. Memories of long eons lived . . .

In the UnderRealms.

Yeah. That shit. Knowledge of a world he'd never even imagined before. A world of Hunn and Gnarrl. Of minions and Thresh. Of the Grande Horde and the Low Queens and . . .

He shook his head.

It did not help to think about that stuff. About what it might mean. It was like stories of murdered kids, paedophiles, people with basketball-size tumours growing out of their nut sacks, and those special kinds of retards who liked to run lawn mowers over puppies.

You might see that sort of thing in the paper, but if you were smart, you let your eyes move quickly over it to the nearest convenient sports story. You didn't want that poison inside your skull. It was like the images of that poor little bastard in the Prius. The look in his eyes just before all that fast-moving metal fell on him.

Better to look away.

Dave stretched back as best he could and ignored the vibration of the airframe as he leaned his head against the thin cushioning. He thought about his own boys, Toby and Jack. He still hadn't had a chance to catch up with them yet, and he was starting to feel guilty about that. That was a bad sign. He knew from experience that he was a slow starter on guilt trips, and if he was feeling it only now, he was probably too late. Annie would have them out of school for a few days. He knew how that went, too. She'd cut them off sugar and gluten. Not that they'd ever tested positive for a gluten allergy. She just thought everyone should eat less gluten. She'd shut down the TV set and unplug the net and take the boys completely offline, reading bedtime stories to them about how everyone was different and that was okay. Making them watch the gay episodes of *Glee*, which seemed to be all of them as best Dave could tell. Oh, and there'd be no adventures with trampolines and tree houses for his boys, either, not so long as Anxious

Annie had them in lockdown. And lockdown was her usual response to any Dave-related problems, even though this one totally wasn't his fault. But he wasn't there to explain that to them, was he? And for once, maybe, he had to admit, she might be right to pack them in Nerf.

'Whatcha thinkin', Dave?' Allen shouted over the rotor noise.

'I'm thinking my ex-wife has told my kids that I probably blew up the Longreach by drunk-driving a train into it.'

Allen mocked up a look of profound disbelief. 'Yeah? Looked to me like you were thinking about the very serious talk you'll be having with Captain Heath just as soon as we land.'

'Oh, yeah. That, too,' he shouted back.

He'd be on the platform tonight and most of tomorrow, at a guess, but he was sure Heath would let him get in touch with the boys when they'd done whatever it was that needed doing out there. Fucked if he knew what he was gonna tell them, though.

Lies, probably. He was good at that.

13

'Two minutes.'

Allen kicked the toe of his boot and relayed the message from the pilot. The SEAL team, or whatever they called themselves, appeared to power up around him, with men checking their own load-outs before cross-checking one another's. With nothing to check, Dave contented himself with scanning the ocean for familiar sights. He could make out Thunder Horse on the horizon. The red and white structure was the largest rig in the Gulf of Mexico. It had survived stormy weather and hurricanes. Would it survive an invasion from Dungeons & Dragons as well? A pair of ships from the navy sketched a lazy patrol around the massive facility. Destroyers, he supposed. Bigger than coast guard cutters, smaller than an aircraft carrier. He'd seen other ships on the way out to Longreach, including something that might have been an aircraft carrier.

Were any of his people still over at Thunder Horse? He hoped not. The casualties should have been evacuated to shore by now, and anyone who was good to go should be long gone.

What could the crew of that platform be thinking, though? Had Thunder Horse played host to a couple of survivors babbling gibberish about monsters and demons boiling up out of the water? Were they watching satellite news, scoffing at the ignorant crap the media always said about the industry, or talking quietly, fearfully, among themselves as the first hints of the truth leaked out in the wider world?

'Yeah, Ortiz, he said something like that when we got him in off the Longreach. Poor bastard was burned up pretty bad, but he was talking some crazy shit about monsters, not fire.'

Allen held up his index finger: 'One minute!'

Dave expected the SEALs to start cocking weapons, but nobody did. Allen appeared to check the safety on his M4, but that was all. Then he could see the Longreach as the Seahawk swung around on the final approach, and he knew they weren't going in guns blazing.

The rig was lit up from top to bottom, with unfamiliar emergency lighting strung up around the most heavily damaged sections. The helipad was brightly illuminated and busy with military personnel, including a guy with bright paddles who waved them in.

As the big bird flared, Dave suffered a few flashes of recall from the last time he'd set down here.

Vince stiff-arming guys out of the way as they scrambled to get on the evac flight.

The burns. The open wounds.

You dare not you dare not you dare not . . .

The chopper settled down with a dainty one-two step, and rather than rappelling down ropes or diving for cover, everyone exited as though climbing off a bus. The feel of the deck under his new boots was strange, familiar yet wrong. He stayed bent over for a little longer as he cleared the rotor blades. The Seahawk felt much bigger and more dangerous than the civilian models he was used to shuttling around on. He joined Allen and his guys off to the side of the helipad, waiting to be introduced, but Captain Heath had other plans.

'If you'll follow me, Mr Hooper,' he shouted over the noise of the chopper lifting off. Allen gave him a brief wave before leading his men off toward the far side of the pad, where the SEALs appeared to have set up some kind of temporary command post in one of the converted shipping containers given over to the platform's admin section. Heath, who seemed to have no trouble finding his way around the unfamiliar structure, led Hooper down the same path he had taken when following Vince Martinelli. They passed marines geared up for *Call of Duty*, more guys who looked like carbon copies of the SEALs, and a lot of support folks, both men and women. He had no idea what any of them were doing. That was the reason this place felt wrong. Or one of the reasons. He had exactly zero clues about what was happening here now. But at least nobody was running around screaming and dying, so that was a good start.

Captain Heath turned left instead of right after passing the small flight operations shack and took the steps down to the main canteen rather than the smaller crew lounge where Dave had found Marty Grbac. A couple of marines stood guard outside the heavy plastic swinging doors. They wore rubber gloves and masks. Heath collected his own protective gear and passed some back to Hooper. Dave thought the paper mask wasn't necessary, but he put it on anyway. The smell coming out of the canteen was foul. It clashed with the odour of cooking food in the nearby kitchen. He could see marines moving in and out of the kitchen service doors with boxes of food from the freezers. Probably a good idea to get them away.

'Excuse me.' A young girl in a lab coat pirouetted past him

carrying a tray full of what might have been liver. It looked and smelled wrong. The space where he'd eaten so many meals was unrecognisable. Heavy plastic sheeting covered all the walls and the floor. Temporary lighting burned harsh and white, throwing everything into hard relief. Seven or eight people in biohazard suits ghosted around four stainless steel trolley tables on which lay the remains of the Hunn and its acolyte Fangr. The science types had all pulled back the hoods of their white coveralls, and like Dave and Heath they wore only paper face masks.

'We've tested for airborne contaminants,' the officer said, as if reading Dave's mind. 'Nothing. A bad smell, but that's what rotting flesh smells like.'

Dave knew the stench, but this was not just the foul smell of dead meat gone bad. He could stick his head into his refrigerator back in Houston for that experience. No, he recognised the stink of decaying demon flesh. A rank odour as old as the sediment through which they'd been drilling these last months. He had always known it.

Just as he'd always known these creatures. That was why Heath had brought him out here. He'd been worried that the navy guys would think him mad when he let them know a little bit of what was happening inside his head.

It was worse than that. Now they thought he was useful.

His feet seemed to be stuck to the floor, making it impossible to move toward the trolleys. The medical staff, or researchers, or whatever they were, had ceased their endeavours one by one as they took in his arrival. They were all staring at him.

More fans.

He felt Heath's hand on his arm, urging him forward, but gently.

'Come on. Tell me what you can.'

The human contact was enough to get him going again. He approached the largest trolley, on which lay the corpse of the Hunn. It was odd. He'd only had a few seconds when he'd first encountered the beast, and then he'd been in a hospital bed and everything had changed. So there hadn't been time to note any details beyond the gross and obvious ones such as its size and inhuman features. Yet when he let his eyes travel up and down the corpse, from the massive horned feet to the crushed ruin of the face, he saw particulars that were entirely new to him, details he hadn't had time to attend to before, such as the extent and meaning of the vivid artwork tattooed all over the Hunn's putrefying hide.

He stared at the swirls and loops of black ink.

They told a story.

Yet in really seeing these things for the first time he also recalled them from a sink so deep and vast that it triggered an association from his own past, from some bullshit class in undergrad psych he'd crashed once because he was chasing some girl who was enrolled in it.

Race memory.

Dave shuddered and tried to step back, but Heath was there with his hand on Dave's shoulder now. It wasn't a physical barrier, not really, but it was enough to block his retreat.

'What's up, Dave?' he asked with surprising care. 'Tell me what's happening.'

Hooper felt sick and dizzy with hot flushes.

'I need to sit down,' he said.

A woman in a biohazard suit dropped what she was doing to the creature. She bustled her assistants aside and pushed a stool underneath Dave.

Dave dropped onto the stool, letting his head fall between his knees and trying to control his breathing. He took long, slow breaths, ignoring the foul miasma of rotten meat. A few more of the researchers gathered around him, and one fanned his face with a manila folder.

'Get him some water,' the women in the biohaz suit said, perhaps a bit more loudly than she needed to. Her accent was very British. 'Maybe a bucket as well. We do not need any additional contamination in here.'

'English,' Dave said, trying to distract himself from the nausea.

'Once upon a time,' she said. 'Don't make a mess.'

'Are you hungry?' Heath asked, ignoring the interchange. 'Do you need to eat?'

'No,' Dave said, managing a grim chuckle. 'For once I am completely off my feed, but thank you. Ma'am, I won't need that bucket. Thank you.'

'Doctor,' she said without turning to face Dave. She was really into her autopsy or whatever she was doing. 'Or Professor, not ma'am. Professor Emmeline Ashbury, Office of Science and Technology Policy. You may call me Professor Ashbury.'

'Okay,' Dave said, a bit taken aback. 'Ah, sorry.'

'Apologies are unnecessary, and they do grow tiresome. That's why I left England,' she said, poking at something deep within the creature's chest. 'Sorry, sorry, sorry. Ooh, this looks interesting.'

And with that she lost interest in Dave.

'Don't know how anyone could think of eating after seeing that thing,' one of the techs said as he laid an unidentifiable green organ on an exam tray.

They were probably going to be skipping meals until they got the stench of death out of their nostrils and clothes. And skin. Dave drew in a deeper breath and rubbed his forehead, gratefully accepting the proffered bottle of water. It was cool and possibly the most delicious drink he'd ever tasted. Pure, clean spring water.

'Sorry,' he said in a cracked voice. 'I just . . . It just got to be a bit much, is all.'

'Take your time,' Heath said.

'Perhaps a medic,' Professor Ashbury said over her shoulder, briefly taking her eyes off the body cavity. 'He looks rather wobbly, don't you think?'

'No,' Dave answered. 'Seriously, I'll be right. I just need a minute.'

'Really?' Ashbury said. 'That long? I heard you killed it a lot quicker than that.'

He closed his eyes and concentrated on his heartbeat, slowing it down. It had been pounding away like a trip-hammer in his chest. He imagined himself on a beach in Bali, a nice spliff in one hand, a disgracefully cheap cocktail in the other. A day of fishing leaving a nice patina of relaxed exhaustion over him after a fine meal. Perhaps a couple of adventurous Swedish backpackers with giant Nordic breasts and . . .

No, that was enough. He could feel the rebar coming back. He opened his eyes.

'I'm good. Let's do it.'

And he was ready this time as he approached the remains of Urgon Htoth Ur Hunn.

You dare not do this!

'Slavaattun mal shastarr,' he said to the corpse with a sneering leer.

'What?' Heath frowned at him.

Whoa. Where the fuck did that come from?

Dave repeated the phrase to himself, but slowly.

'Roughly translated?' he said to Heath. 'I guess I do dare, bitch.'

The captain kept his expression neutral.

'Yeah, sometimes I surprise myself, too,' Dave said. He took his time circling the stainless steel trolley, and the researchers all moved aside for him. Along with the killing stroke he had delivered to the Hunn, Heath's people had been nickel-and-diming it to pieces as well. An incision sliced here. A plug taken there. And in the centre of its massive chest an equally massive Y-cut scar where they'd opened old Urgon up, all the better to empty him out. Dave had no interest in what they found in there. Three stomachs, two hearts – a primary and a secondary – some really nasty digestive juices, and a long intestinal tract that pooped tiny little rock-hard marbles of demon guano when the monster was done digesting his meal.

A cloud passed over his face. The Hunn's last meal had been a friend of his. He pushed the thought away. He was becoming practised at that.

'This ugly-ass motherfucker,' Dave said, 'is a Hunn.'

The simple declaration seemed to cast a spell over the room, suspending everything. He gathered his thoughts from wherever they came and pressed on.

'One of the six clans of the Horde. The Hunn are the largest, most savage of them. They are the shock troops of the Horde,' he said, looking directly at Heath. 'The heavy infantry, I guess you'd call them. And this one here, he was a BattleMaster of Hunn. They're born, not made. Your average vanilla-flavoured Hunn Dominant, which is just a gay monster way of saying 'warrior', will run to about seven foot tall and weigh in at maybe 300, 350 pounds. Most of it, as you've probably seen, is pretty densely packed muscle. They probably have the strength of about a dozen men. Or maybe half a dozen Sergeant Swindts,' he conceded. 'I guess you've run your tape measure over this bad boy, so you already know that a Master of Hunn can top out at over eight foot and weigh another sixty or seventy pounds. Without armour.'

One of the researchers raised a hand and opened his mouth to speak, but Dave waved him off. 'I'll get back to the armour,' he promised.

'So. The really big, dumb bastards like to call themselves BattleMasters. They're like you, Heath. Officers.' Dave tapped the side of his head. 'Sorry. Can't Google up a direct comparison, but if you want to imagine them being about eighteen, maybe *nineteen* times stronger than a grown man, you wouldn't be far off. They're pretty fast and nimble – given they got all that mass to move around – and when they take a swing at you, holy shit, they do throw out the hurt bombs. Their bones are dense . . .'

He looked around at the white suits for confirmation. A couple of them nodded, including Ashbury, who had abandoned her autopsy to take in his lecture.

'That rhino hide they're covered in is thick but strangely sensitive to UV damage. It picks up a lot of infections. The infections suppurate and rupture. It can make them vulnerable. Their hide is normally as tough as boiled leather, but when it ruptures . . . not so much. That's why they wear armour. It's also why they have tattoos in a dumbass sort of way. The ink our boy here got himself would have hurt like a bastard when it went on.'

He paused for a second, closing his eyes and searching for the knowledge.

'They use bone needles and the ink of this sort of squid. Urmin. Rhymes with vermin. But lives on land. And the suckers on its arms all have little razor teeth around them.'

He checked to see if everyone was still following him. They were with rapt, horrified attention.

'Anyway, a dude with a lot of tats, he has sucked up some real pain to get them. The design tells a story, but you know, blah blah blah. I'm a badass from a line of badasses. We're all considered very macho.' He grinned. 'Anyway. Game stats. The fastest of them can run at about . . .' He closed his eyes again and did a quick calculation. 'About forty miles an hour for short distances. But they get puffed quickly. Like I said, that's a lot of weight to go hauling around at high speed. Mostly they like to jog around at a slow lope, accelerating when they close with an enemy, or prey. Which to a Hunn is pretty much the same thing anyway.'

He had circled around the top of the dissection table until he stood next to the half-crushed head of the corpse. He wrinkled his nose in distaste.

'He's no oil painting, is he? Anyway, more fascinating factoids: they have very poor eyesight, especially in bright sunshine, but their sense of smell is about as good as a hunting dog's. They can sleep standing up. They can hold their breath for a loooong time. Can go four or five days without water. Ten if they can get some blood to drink. Yeah, I know. Gross. The hide can be up to two inches thick in places.'

He looked up at Heath again. Unlike the brainiacs who seemed happy to defer to his superior knowledge, Heath looked as if Dave had just dropped his pants and mooned the lot of them. Allen was right. He should have found the time to give the captain a heads-up about this.

'But the hide's not impenetrable,' he said, pressing on regardless. 'These things fight with edged weapons, up close and very personal. When they want to reach out and touch someone at a distance, they'll throw a spear, or if you're dealing with the Sliveen, they'll notch an arrow.'

'The Sliveen?' Heath asked. 'The scout?' His face was a mask of deep concern, but Dave didn't care anymore. They had asked him here to do his party trick, and he was going to do it. It felt good to let go of this stuff. A blessed fucking relief. As though giving it up made it somebody else's problem.

'One of the six clans,' he explained. 'You ever watch those *Lord of the Rings* movies?'

'Fuck yeah!' said one of the younger male researchers before blushing with embarrassment.

'Well, just imagine that movie with orcs pretending to be ninjas.'

'Awesome,' the same guy said in a quiet voice.

'Yeah, the Sliveen think they are. The Hunn disagree. A Sliveen is what hit us on the road last night.'

'These things have already made it to the mainland?' someone asked.

'Not now,' Heath said. 'Continue, please, Mr Hooper.'

'The Sliveen also like to think of themselves as being very sophisticated,' Dave said, then stopped. 'Hey. Did this asshole come packing a sword? A really big sucker?'

'It did,' a bald man said. He'd just come into the room with the air of someone who liked to make a big entrance. 'I've done some preliminary investigations, but we lack the facilities for metallurgical or linguistic analysis. Aside from the basic facts we could ascertain here – it was made by a tool-using, tool-making culture, designed primarily for combat, with some symbology indicating that it may also demonstrate rank and achievement – we have not been able to learn much about the material culture of this or the other creatures.'

No one said a word. The bald man, who sported a shocking red neckbeard, was a bit short and a bit wide. He looked less of a pirate than he did a pirate's fat cook. He seemed to waddle when he shuffled about in his biohazard suit. The arms and legs had been taped up to take up some of the slack. A pair of wire-framed glasses sat over the paper mask; behind them lurked a pair of sharp small brown eyes. He could just as easily have been an accountant at Baron's rattling off numbers concerning dividend payments. Except for the beard, of course. The bean counters always looked about twelve years old to Dave.

'I think I understood some of that,' he said to the new guy.

'Dr Raymond Compton,' Heath said. 'Director, Office of Science and Technology Policy. Also, academic resources and special projects chief.'

'Or to put it another way,' Dr Compton said, 'I'm in charge.'

Dave didn't buy it. The little man didn't look like he could manage a classroom of frat boys, let alone the military types answering to Heath.

'No, I take it back,' Dave said, biting down on a number of possible retorts. 'I'm confused again. Anyway, it's a pity the sword was sent away. The swords have stories on them, too.' He looked directly at Heath, 'Good intel.'

'I believe I told you that, did I not, Captain?' Dr Compton said with a look on his face that Dave recognised. The look of a man whom no one ever listened to and who resented the hell out of it. Of course, Dave had his own experience in that area. Without a PhD he'd made do with boyish charm and bull-shitting. Compton, having a PhD and that big important title, looked as if he hadn't learned the trick. Oh, yeah. Dave knew this sort. He had to be right, and he had to have the last word.

Always.

The less I have to deal with this asshole, Dave thought, *the better*.

A few steps carried him down the table to where the Hunn's massive arm lay. He picked it up. It had three . . . fingers, he guessed you could call them. And a thumb. He remembered opposable thumbs from school. They were important. 'What do you call those animals with these kind of fingers and toes, like horns?' he asked nobody in particular, assuming that a roomful of pointy heads would be able to provide the answer.

'Ungulates,' Ashbury said. She appeared to be in her late thirties with a look that used to be described as handsome on the ladies of a bygone age. She was pretty, he supposed, but strong-featured. Dave could see two spots of high colour on her cheeks over the top of the paper mask.

'So what are you guys, the monster squad or something?'

'I'm an MD with supplementary degrees in anthropology and forensics,' Professor Ashbury said. 'I have also published several papers on exobiology. Dr Compton's speciality is –'

'Anthropology,' he said, as if that trumped exobiology with maximum prejudice. 'During the war I did a lot of work on the US Army's Human Terrain System. Before that I had some passing contact with the exobiologist community and their love of imaginary xenomorphs.'

He said that as if it should mean something to Dave.

'Xenu the alien? Like Tom Cruise worships?' Dave said, genuinely confused.

'No,' Ashbury said, not amused. 'Exobiologists study extreme habitats and the life-forms that occupy them here on earth, and we make educated guesses about the way xeno-morphs – aliens – might evolve on other planets.'

'These things aren't aliens,' Dave said, flicking Urgon on the side of the skull. 'Well, I guess they're not from this world, strictly speaking. But they're definitely not from Klingon, either. Although, looking at him . . .'

Heath stepped in to bring him back on topic.

'Professor Ashbury and her staff are all security cleared for government work at the highest level,' he said. 'Nobody thinks these things arrived here from outer space.'

'But unless you want to bring in Buffy the Vampire Slayer as a consultant,' Ashbury said, 'then exobiology is your go-to reference group.'

Compton had traded his poker face for a much more dissatisfied expression. He was a barrel-shaped man who didn't seem to have much actual strength to him. Dave wondered what his hands were like, probably smooth, soft, without a day's worth of honest work on them. All his achievements came through teaching instead of doing.

'How is it you came into possession of this knowledge, Mr . . . Cooper?' he asked, stumbling slightly over Dave's last name.

'That's Hooper to you, Grizzly Adams.'

'How, Mr *Hooper*, did you come to know all this?' Compton repeated. 'It seems a preposterous suggestion that you have taken it in by osmosis.'

'I'd like to know that, too, Dave,' Heath said quietly. 'You said you knew a bit about these things, but nothing like that.'

'Better explain yourself, Hooper,' Ashbury said with a

twinkle in her eye. 'These guys are such uptight arses at the best of times that I don't even notice it. But I'm sensing a lot of extra pucker in the room right now.'

Some of the scientists tensed. The *Lord of the Rings* kid, who appeared to be in his early twenties and way too young to be doing secret government experiments on alien life-forms, looked like he might wet himself.

Dave folded his arms and fought the old familiar urge to lie and distract.

'Look. I'll be fucked if I know,' he said to Heath. 'A couple of days ago I couldn't have told you any of this stuff. But a couple of days ago this ugly motherfucker –' He smacked the Hunn with the back of his hand. '– hadn't crawled onto my rig and bitten the head off one of my best friends. There's a fuckin' preposterous suggestion for you right there, Doc. I hadn't discovered my previously unknown ability to juggle refrigerators and small cars at the same time. Another preposterous suggestion. And I hadn't put a hammer through old Urgon's skull here and apparently downloaded all of his nasty fucking hopes and dreams.'

His voice grew louder as his temper got the better of him, and he finished by slapping an open palm down on the chest of the dead demon. It sounded like a rifle shot and brought the two marine guards running in from outside with their weapons up. It also collapsed the monster's chest cavity like an old paper light shade.

Ashbury jumped back a little in fright. Somebody swore.

'Easy, Marines,' Heath said, calm and cool, without raising his voice. He put his hand on the top of the closer marine's rifle and lowered it back to the floor. 'We're fine. Stand down.'

Everyone was looking at the body and at Dave.

'Sorry,' he said at last. 'Still don't know my own strength.'

'Okay,' Heath said in a soothing tone. 'Let's get back on track, shall we? And, you remind me, Mr Hooper, I want to talk to you about that hammer later.'

He sounded like Dave's old man right then, making an appointment to take him out to the woodshed.

14

The impromptu lecture wrapped up after two hours. Once Dave started talking, there seemed to be no obvious place to stop. Heath's expression went from surprised to incredulous to angry before settling back into his usual blank mask. As much as Heath and the scientists were unbalanced by the performance, their surprise was mild next to Dave's own. In the end he kept talking because it was easier than stopping to consider the implications of what he'd already said.

'The Horde are like an army,' he explained as his voice grew hoarse. 'No, scratch that. They *are* an army. But we're not their enemy. We're their food. Their rations. There are other armies. Real enemies. More like them,' he frowned.

'Noted,' said Heath. 'But let's stay on topic for now. The Horde.'

There was so much more he could have told them. He'd barely started in on the Fangr, but it was getting very late and the researchers had been working all day. Dave felt himself getting hungry, too, and rather than run down his store of energy bars, Captain Heath, looking hollow-eyed and subdued, decided after consulting with Compton that they could reconvene at 0600. He suggested that the doctors and professors and their assistants might like to consider some questions to ask Dave rather than having him simply ramble on with whatever came to mind.

That would be better, Dave thought as they moved outside onto the deck of the platform. A fresh southerly breeze blew across the rig, giving him a chance to clear his mind a bit. He found that he didn't know what he knew until he decided to think about it. It would be a whole hell of a lot easier to just answer whatever questions they fired at him, although he'd already disappointed Professor Ashbury with his inability to get into any physiological detail beyond the obvious. As he tried to explain, he didn't much understand human anatomy beyond the basics, either, but he left the makeshift morgue with the impression that Compton thought he was some sort of bullshit artist.

He'd add it to the long list of things he didn't give a fuck about.

Dave had flown out to the platform with Allen's SEALs, but the other military personnel on the rig seemed to be mostly marines. Some of them had set up guard posts equipped with machine guns. When he gave some thought to it, he realised that these guys seemed to understand the rig nearly as well as he did. They'd put those meat grinders exactly where you would expect trouble to rear its ugly, snarling head if it came up from below looking for a snack. Other marines were at work patrolling the Longreach. Still more were busy clearing away the debris and damage and getting some basic systems running again. They were all armed and wearing vests that made them look like his boys' Teenage Mutant Ninja Turtle figures. Heath had told him how many marines and SEALs and sailors were on the rig and how they were organised, but that military stuff about platoons and squads and whatnot went in one ear and out the other. More important than how many platoons went into a company and how many companies could sink a battleship, they were changing shift – or 'watch', Dave supposed – when he finished telling his monster stories and went looking for a feed.

Although the crew lounge where Marty had died was still sealed off, Longreach's kitchen was undamaged. A few sailors from a nearby ship had cross-decked to cook some chow, using the platform's own stores. Heath said something about the corps eventually getting their own cooks in, which was neither here nor there to Dave. He was just looking to get fed. A temporary mess station sat up near the helipad in a windbreak created by two shipping containers converted to offices. A heavy tarpaulin offered some overhead protection, and four long folding tables provided a makeshift serving space. Marines and sailors lined up to get their trays filled with whatever came out of a series of heavy green plastic cases.

Dave stepped up and looked inside one, finding a stainless steel tray full of food.

'Dave?' Heath gestured him over to a spot, pointing to a stack of similar containers each marked with his name. 'I have yours over here. And I got you this.'

Heath produced a large metal spoon from his pocket.

'And we need to talk,' he said.

'You're breaking up with me?' Dave asked as he sat down in front of the first food container and waited for Heath to do the same.

'That little tutorial you gave back there, Dave; you surprised me.'

'Me too, man,' he said, distracted by the smell of hot food

as he opened the first meal case. Ignoring Heath, he removed the lid and used the overlarge spoon to work his way through the warm fried chicken and rice inside, stripping the meat and sucking the juice out of each bone before opening a second case to attack the mashed potatoes. A quick glance into the third revealed mac and cheese, or whatever the navy used for cheese. It was agreeably thick and gooey. The navy officer frowned and contented himself with a hard-boiled egg.

'Living large there, Cap'n,' Dave said, happy to be eating again with no sign of the buffet running low.

Heath peeled the egg and ate it, washing it down with a metal mug of black sugarless coffee.

'I don't eat a large meal in the evening,' he said. 'I have to watch my calories very closely.'

'No five-mile runs anymore, eh?' Dave said without thinking. 'D'oh. Sorry,' he added quickly. 'That was my inner asshole talking. It's gotta be hard, your line of work with that injury.'

He waved his spoon at the artificial leg.

Heath shrugged.

'There's many with worse. Much worse. I'm lucky.' Heath fixed him with a level stare, like a butterfly chaser pinning a new catch to a board. 'You weren't exactly square with me, were you, Dave? About how much you knew, or know, about these creatures. You seem to know a hell of a lot more than you let on at first.'

A dozen marines gathered nearby with their trays. A few of them pointed and gawked as Dave put away thousands of calories without stopping to draw breath. Some looked envious, some horrified.

Dave shovelled the food into his mouth partly to fuel up

but also to give himself time to think.

'Look, I'm sorry about that,' he said at last after cleaning out another meal case of mac and cheese. 'But you gotta cut me some slack, man. I'm just getting used to all this. Between you and me, I wasn't in the best of shape when I choppered back out here. You know, before it all went down. I woke up in that hospital thinking I was having some kind of bad acid flashback.'

'You took acid?'

Heath sounded as horrified as a man with his emotional distance could be. Dave laughed out loud and almost lost a mouthful of macaroni.

'Nah, not for years.'

And thanks for not asking about all the lines of blow I vacuumed up back in that motel.

'But yeah, when I get off the platform, I like to play hard. I'm not gonna apologise for that. I spent most of my marriage apologising for shit I really shouldn'ta had to. At least, not at first. But I got to admit there was a part of me thought I was fucked up on something or having some kind of breakdown. You know, like having bugs coming out from under your skin, 'cept these critters were seven foot high.'

He stopped talking to shotgun a bottle of water down, then opened another foil-covered food tray. Pineapple and pork with some sort of thick yellow noodles.

'I thought I was going nuts,' he said as he looked around for a fork to wind up the noodles. His spoon wasn't going to be much use. Heath produced a plastic fork from the discarded food packages. 'And if you heard some of the shit running through my head when we first met,' he said, 'you'd have thought the same thing.'

'What shit, Dave?'

Heath was remarkably patient.

Hooper shrugged.

'All that stuff I was telling the eggheads. I didn't even know it was there until I started looking for it. I mean, what sort of things do you know, Heath?'

He waved his cheap plastic fork at the man's head. A strand of noodle flew off and landed on Heath's arm.

'Shit. My bad.'

Heath flicked the sticky yellow strand onto the metal grillwork of the deck.

He didn't seem inclined to make anything of it, so Dave carried on.

'You think about it. You got a lifetime worth of learning up there in your head. But a lot of it, most of it, is filed away. You couldn't get through the day if it wasn't.'

'True,' Heath said. 'But you could have told me. Command is going to want to debrief you properly. They'll want to know everything.'

He emphasised the last word.

'And they're going to blame you for not letting them in on it earlier?' Dave asked.

Heath frowned.

'I don't care about that. I care about knowing as much as possible about any potential hostile. That knowledge could save lives. Like the ones we lost on the road,' he added pointedly.

Hooper stopped eating and put down his meal case of pork and noodles.

'Dude, you gotta believe me: that was as big a surprise to me as it was to you. There's nothing I could have done to warn you about that. I didn't know the Sliveen was out there.'

'But you knew the Sliveen existed. And that they're scouts. You even said as much to Chief Allen. You said they do his job.'

Dave stopped for a moment to ponder that. He resented the implication that the ambush was somehow his fault. But he resented even more the idea that Heath might be right.

'But I didn't know,' he protested, not liking the whiny tone creeping into his voice.

Heath didn't escalate the issue. He merely fixed Dave with the same level stare.

'But if I knew that you had much greater knowledge of these things, I could have asked you the questions that needed to be asked. There's no avoiding it, Dave. The ambush wasn't your fault, but you had a responsibility to tell me what you knew, or at least to tell me that you possibly knew something about this enemy that I could have used.'

'But I didn't know about the ambush, or about the Sliveen . . .'

'You didn't know about the ambush or about that particular scout. But what can you tell me about the Sliveen now?'

Dave tamped down his frustration and mounting anger and took a moment to focus on the question. What did he know about the Sliveen?

A lot, as it happened.

He sighed and started to talk.

'The Sliveen are like, I dunno, the ninjas of the Horde. Or the SEALs, or whatever. They're a small clan, and they consider themselves superior in skills to even the Grymm.'

'The Grim?' Heath frowned.

Dave sighed.

'See. This is a fucking rabbit hole, man. Or you know, what do they call those things, those patterns? A fractal. Does that sound right? It just goes on and on, deeper and more fucking complicated the more I look into it.'

Heath shook his head. 'It's not exactly right, but go on. Skip the Grim. We can come back to them later. We'll come back to all of this later. Just tell me what you know about the Sliveen, off the top of your head. Right now, without thinking too much about it.'

Dave swapped his small plastic fork for the spoon he'd been using and chased the last pieces of pork and pineapple.

'The Sliveen are the scouts,' he said. 'They cover long distances, alone or in small groups. They're not brawlers like the Hunn, but they're savage in a stand-up fight. Prefer to snipe at you from a distance with a . . . a war bow. Like our boy last night. Or a sort of crossbow thing. Smaller, but easier to carry.'

'Do you think there'll be more of them spooking about back on the mainland?'

'No idea. Honest Injun.' Dave held up one hand.

'Please don't be needlessly offensive,' Heath said before putting his coffee mug down, empty. 'Nobody has asked you the obvious question,' he added before Dave could be offended by the implied criticism.

'Which is?'

'What are they doing here?'

Alternating between multiple trays, Dave shovelled another spoonful of mac and cheese into his mouth and thought about it for a moment or two as he chewed. He couldn't remember enjoying the taste of a meal so much as he did this one. 'They had no fucking idea what they were doing here,' he said at last, staring into the distance, out across the darkened sea. 'Besides feeding.'

Another spoonful of mashed potatoes. He closed his eyes and thought about it some more as he swallowed the creamy, buttery spuds. They were surprisingly good. Much better than the lumpy, watery mess he was used to on the rig. It reminded him of some of the epic pig-outs he'd indulged in at college many years ago, after a couple of bongs brought on the munchies.

'They've been down there, in the UnderRealms they call it, for a long time. Long enough that they remember us as nothing more than cattle, wandering the fields, you know, grazing, waiting to be eaten. They call us . . . calflings, I guess would be closest. Like veal. Extra tender 'n' tasty,' he said, scraping the last bits of mac and cheese out of the tray.

Dave focused again, following what he now thought of as the Hunn's race memory back through the millennia.

'I don't know that they even think of us as being civilised. It's possible they disappeared before civilisation got going.'

'Disappeared?'

'You seen any around before yesterday?' He paused to follow the thought wherever it might go.

'They were driven into the UnderRealms,' he said. 'Or their myths tell them so.'

He carefully set the first three cases aside and dragged over the second round. Inspecting the contents, he placed the pulled pork in front of him, more mashed potatoes to his right, and the green beans to his left. The lack of a fresh crusty bread roll for the pork was a bummer, but he pitched in anyway, grinning in spite of it all. It was a hell of a thing, being able to eat whatever the hell he felt like without guilt or consequence.

'A bit like us being driven from the Garden of Eden,' he said around a mouthful of pork. 'Everything's hookers and blow, and then you've been kicked out on your bleeding ass in the dark and the rain.'

'By whom?'

Another pause.

'The Sky Lords.'

'Oh, come on, no.'

Dave threw his hands up, sending a dollop of potatoes at Heath. Thankfully it missed the captain's ear by a few inches and plopped harmlessly onto the deck.

'Shit, sorry. But yeah. See, that's what I mean about you taking me for a crazy man. The Sky Lords. Sounds kind of faggy, but that's what the Hunn call them. I dunno who or what the fuck they were. But they ruined the party for everyone. Well, for everyone whose idea of a party was biting the heads off screaming village folk.'

'Village . . .?'

Dave took a bottle of water from a pack of twelve, drained it in one shot, and shook his head.

'Don't suppose you got beer? No, forget it. Anyway, long story short, these things gotta predate what we think of as civilisation. You know, ancient cities, Roman roads, microwave mac and cheese. I can't tell you by how much.'

He gave it another few moments of thought.

'They don't think about time like we do. There's no calendars or alarm clocks down there.'

He stopped talking with a spoon full of macaroni halfway to his open mouth. When Heath made as if to ask him a question, Dave held up one hand. He concentrated, and Heath let him be, waiting him out.

'They don't have any technology as we'd understand it,' Dave said after a pause. 'No . . . machinery as such. Some forging and smithing, you know; Dark Ages stuff. But even Roman engineering would have been beyond them.'

'You studied history?' Heath asked.

Dave shrugged, scooping up some pulled pork from the bottom of the can. He chewed, swallowed, and slid the empty case aside. He was inhaling this stuff. He really ought to slow down and just enjoy it. 'The history of engineering. For my undergrad, the usual requirements. I think Western Civ was one of the few bullshit courses I enjoyed. Anyway, you asked about them disappearing. I reckon they were gone, banished, before human civilisation really got going.'

'Maybe it couldn't get going while they were around,' Heath thought out aloud. 'Professor Compton might have an opinion on that.'

Dave couldn't give two shits about Compton's opinion on anything. He leaned forward to check another case that held greenish scrambled eggs, ham slices, and hash. He pitched into the eggs, not really caring about the colour. It was probably a herb, and he was still peckish. When he was done searching 'his' memory and ready for some hash, he answered Heath.

'Urgon doesn't have an opinion on that,' he said.

'Urgon? He's your man now?'

'My bitch.' Dave smiled. 'I made Urgon my monster bitch. Now he has to step and fetch it for me.'

'So what do they want?'

He didn't even have to think about that one. It was a question that answered itself. Dave was famous in the crew lounge for his Schwarzenegger, and he drew on it now. 'Vat is der greatest pleasure? To vanquish your enemies and chase dem before you, to eat der horses and ride der vimmin.'

Heath observed him for a full second.

'Was that a joke?'

'No, that was Conan. But it's not a thousand miles removed from the way our boy Urgon does business. Or did. It's been a long time since they've walked the OverRealms. The Above.'

'The over . . .?'

'This,' said Dave, waving his spoon around a little more carefully this time. 'Our turf. And no, I don't know how they got here. Neither did he. He was just out hunting.' Dave turned his head to one side as he pulled out the memory. 'Hunting minion. A lesser demon. Tough meat but good for smoking. If you're a Hunn. Anyway, he was tracking a nest of them; next thing he knows, he's swimming up toward the light, which he's never seen, he's only ever heard about it. And then he's climbing the rig, and . . .'

Dave put his spoon aside for a moment and shut down the recall.

'And then it was feeding time,' he said quietly.

'I'm sorry,' Heath said. 'You can . . . remember that? As he did?'

'Yeah,' Dave said. 'But I'd prefer to not have the replay running behind my eyeballs if that's cool with you.'

Heath agreed. He looked about five years older than when Dave first had seen him.

'This is what the instructors used to call an out-of-context problem,' said the naval officer, sounding very tired. Dave started in on the ham slices and hash browns. His appetite remained unaffected.

He looked on as a couple of marines who had located the supply room and found a batch of brand-new galvanised-tin mop buckets scooped ice cream and cookies into them. They churned up the mix with a beater fitted to a scavenged power drill. There were excited grins all around as they doled the results into Styrofoam cups. Dave thought maybe a bucket full of that might not be a bad idea. The dairy would make him sleepy.

'The marines don't normally get to eat this well,' Heath said by way of explaining the ice cream. He seemed almost embarrassed. 'Not in the field. It would be MREs until they got the kitchen going.'

'You don't have to explain. Rig monkeys are animals. You got choir boys there.'

'The food on your rig was going to waste,' Heath said, as if it was important. 'And I don't think MREs are going to do it for you in the long run. I want to see what the docs have to say about your metabolism.'

That dampened Dave's enthusiasm for the cookout.

'Yeah. I been wondering about that. Whether it's always gonna be like this. I might have to live in a fucking food court.'

He was just about to pitch into his mop-bucket-sized chocolate shake when he was interrupted.

'Do you mind if I join you, gentlemen? I couldn't sleep.'

Heath stood up as Professor Ashbury approached their patch of deck, forcing Dave to remember his manners as well. Grunts of exertion surrounded them as the marines chose that moment to wind up their meal break and head out on patrol. Once upon a time Dave Hooper might have waddled off in a food coma after them, but now he bounced up onto his feet with no effort at all. Neither bloated nor heavy, he did at last feel as though he could stop shovelling food into his head hole.

He was thirsty, however, and fetched himself a Coke from an ice-filled cooler.

He could hear the marines joking about him as they left on their patrol.

It was odd to think of armed soldiers heading out on patrol when all they were doing was walking around his platform. Heath picked up a folding chair newly vacated by one of the jarheads and twirled it around for the professor to sit on. She thanked him and carefully placed a mug of something hot on the fold-up mess table.

'Doc.' Dave nodded.

She fixed him with an unreadable expression. Freed of her biohazard suit, she was, he found, quite striking. Not a chick who'd be posing for *Sports Illustrated* anytime soon, but he could see how some men would find her easy on the eyes. Men like Dave, say.

'You really should refer to me as Professor Ashbury,' she said. 'Or Dr Ashbury; either is applicable. My friends call me Emma, but I do not think we will be on a first-name basis.'

'Wow,' Dave said, a bit put off. 'Okay, Professor. Have it your way.'

'Anything you can tell us?' Heath asked.

'Not without lab work, which will have to wait until we get back to the mainland,' she said, stifling a yawn.

'Coffee won't help you sleep, Doc,' Dave informed her helpfully. 'Sorry. I meant Prof.'

'Cocoa,' she explained. 'With a nip of rum. Not enough alcohol to disturb my sleep patterns but enough to relax after a hell of a day.'

'Hey, no need to explain. That's my type of bedtime drink.'

She sketched a smile but purely for the sake of form,

rearranging her features because it was required. Like Heath, she must have been tired and, at a deeper level, unbalanced by the way the rational world had totally tipped off its axis. The three of them found themselves alone. It was a familiar but unsettling scene to Dave Hooper, who could feel the rig around him, the miles of pipes and tons of metal and concrete, floating, creaking, shifting here and there in ways it never had before. The feel of it was wrong. He could hear the dull clang of boots ringing on steel stairways as squads of marines stomped off on patrol. The usual hum and rumble of the drilling machinery was silent, but he could hear generators and even, if he strained, conversations to which both he and the Longreach were unaccustomed. For one disorienting second he managed to filter out a whole snatch of dialogue from an unfamiliar voice somewhere nearby.

'. . . some shit right out of King Arthur, dude.'

'. . . fuck you, you're full of it . . .'

'. . . not lovin' this freak show . . .'

'. . . like a fucking slaughterhouse, man. Worse than fucking Baghdad. Way Karsoe tells it . . .'

He pulled away from it, slightly disturbed at the fidelity of the sound. It was as though he'd dialled in on the conversation the way he might focus on a line of text in a book. But there was nobody nearby to account for the dialogue.

'Mr Hooper?'

It was Professor Ashbury.

'Dave,' he said, coming back to them. 'Call me Dave.'

'All right, then; I will call you Dave. Are you okay, Dave? You looked somewhat woebegone.'

He snorted in between gulps of the chocolate thickshake.

'Woebegone? My grandma used to say that.'

'Mr Hooper . . . Dave . . . is having a few adjustment issues,' Heath explained. 'We all are.'

Ashbury raised an eyebrow. 'Indeed.'

She wrapped both hands around the chipped enamel mug and took a pull on her cocoa. When the mug came away, it left a small frothy moustache that she licked at like a child. Dave found himself smiling at the sight. And then he found himself having to adjust his posture because of the erection that started to strain at his pants.

Oh, for fuck's sake.

There had been a bad time a year back when he'd seriously thought about seeing his doctor about getting a script for some Viagra. Then he'd thought about just ordering some on the net. Then that crisis had passed thanks to a Waffle House waitress. She'd smothered, covered, and chunked him all the way to recovery. But this . . . He shifted uncomfortably in his seat. This fucking rail spike in the pants was new and not entirely welcome. He tried to hide it behind the ice cream bucket in his lap.

The prof was a good-looking lady but not his type, and he knew for a certainty that he wasn't hers. She was too smart.

Annie had taught him the dangers of smart women. Annie and her goddamned college crush lawyer, Vietch.

'Thirsty,' he said, draining the bottom half of the Coke he'd fetched. It was icy cold, and he was hoping it might put out the fire or at least give him a cold spike headache to chill things down a little. He kept hold of the makeshift ice cream bucket.

It didn't help. He was uncomfortably aware of Ashbury's scent and the bow of her lips and . . .

'Dave?'

Annoyed, he slammed the galvanised-tin mop bucket

down with a sound like a gunshot. Everyone jumped, including him, and the big can tipped over, spilling the last of its contents. It was crushed in the middle, the way he'd crush an empty can of Bud during the Super Bowl.

'Oh, man . . . sorry . . .'

Heath mopped up the spill with a napkin, which made Dave feel bad because the captain had to get down on his robot leg to do it, and Ashbury offered rote assurance that he had nothing for which to apologise, which was demonstrably fucking untrue given the one-legged man swabbing the deck in front of him. Heath finished and dropped the sodden napkin into the ruined bucket.

'You've been through an extraordinary ordeal, Dave,' Ashbury said. 'Quite literally. People use "literally" nowadays as an inappropriate modifier. But in your case it is apt. Your experience was outside the ordinary realm. You're still going through it. It's natural that it would unsettle you.'

He thanked her and shifted his position again, finding that by throwing one leg over the other, ankle on his knee, he could open up a little wiggle room for the old persuader. He sighed audibly with the relief.

'Thanks, Prof,' he said. 'I shouldn't complain. This is just . . .' He threw a look across at Captain Heath. 'What was that you called it all? Out of context?'

Heath nodded, and Dave waved one hand around to take in the rig. Then he gently picked up the crushed bucket. 'There is no context for any of this. Not outside of the SyFy Channel. I mean, you guys? Maybe you've dealt with this sort of thing before?'

His look was hopeful, but Heath gave him nothing.

'I was the available JSOC asset in theatre, Mr Hooper. I was down here supervising a completely routine training exercise.'

Professor Ashbury looked like she was searching for something encouraging to say. In the end all she could come up with was vague conversational filler.

'I suppose we shouldn't be surprised, by which I mean we, not you, Dave. We spend our professional lives imaging the extreme. Trying to quantify it. Establish parameters. We –'

'So you haven't been to Area 51? Either of you?'

No, they hadn't.

'Captain Heath has been very good about all this, you know,' she said, throwing the officer an encouraging glance. 'He's been very good about you.'

'*Professor*,' Heath said in a warning tone.

'Oh, come on. The man has been to hell and back. And he obviously doesn't have the emotional or intellectual skills with which to cope.'

'Hey!'

'Captain Heath,' she continued, favouring Dave with a significant glance, 'has probably saved you from extraordinary rendition . . .'

'Professor!'

'No. It's important he understands. There was a chance, Dave, that you could have ended up in a cell somewhere, sedated and chained down. I know Captain Heath argued very strongly against that, and to be honest, I think he saved a few lives doing so. I've only skimmed the briefing on the changes you've undergone since first contact, but it's enough to know that containment would have been the wrong option. Practically and morally.'

Dave's thoughts were shooting about like a pinball getting flipped hard.

'Rendition. Like a terrorist?'

'No,' Heath said. 'More like witness protection. And it was only one option. Quickly rejected.'

'And what were the others?' Dave demanded to know, fighting his temper again. 'Snipers? Air strikes? Grabbing my family? My boys?' He knew that nobody would think of trying to pressure him through Annie.

Heath looked pissed, mostly with the professor, who for her part was entirely unrepentant.

'We've never dealt with something like this,' she said in a calming tone, deflecting his last question by answering the original one. 'But we have protocols. All of them untried. Untested. You came out of a violent first contact that no other subjects survived.'

'Vince did.'

'No. Mr Martinelli observed the contact from close quarters,' Ashbury corrected him. 'He did not take part in it directly. You survived a hostile contact, but the protocols defined you as compromised.'

'Because I survived?'

'Because you survived.'

'*Oh, bullshit.*' Dave's anger finally broke out, but only in verbal form. He was careful to keep his hands, which had balled up into fists all by themselves, deep inside the pockets of his cargo pants. He squeezed his eyes shut so hard that stars and roses the colour of dark blood bloomed behind them. When he opened them again, with his fury contained and slowly abating, he spoke though gritted teeth.

'I had a brother. *Had* one. My baby brother. Went off and joined the army after 9/11. Thought he was gonna chase bin Laden down himself. Instead he got blown up and shot to pieces in a fucking soft-ass Humvee in some Baghdad shithole because of fucking protocols and parameters and metrics and all of that shit you people go on with. I know the fucking ragheads who set off the bomb and pulled the triggers killed Andy. But your man Rumsfeld? And his fucking known unknowns? *His* protocols? He put him there to be killed. For no good reason.'

He blazed defiance at Heath.

His brother.

His fucking brother.

'I am sorry, Dave,' Emmeline Ashbury said in a very quiet voice.

A tightness had closed up Captain Heath's face, but when he spoke, his voice was also quiet.

'I am sorry about your brother,' he said. 'Your loss. I didn't know. It wasn't –'

'It wasn't in the file?' Dave snapped, already feeling guilty but not willing to let Contrite Dave back in yet. Angry, Ugly, Asshole Dave would have his moment of glory. 'There was no protocol?'

Heath looked embarrassed. Dave let go of the anger with one hot, ragged breath.

'You wouldn't,' he said. 'There were a lot of things people didn't know about Andy. One thing, he signed up under Mom's name. They changed their names when my old man ran out. I thought, fuck that old prick. It's my name. He can't have that, too. So I kept it.'

An awkward silence enveloped them. And with it came the embarrassment, the hot shame that rose up from his neck and burned his cheeks.

'I'm sorry,' he said in a small voice, feeling like a very small man. 'I shouldn't have said all that shit. I admit I got issues with the government, the military. But you're just people. Not the thing itself.'

Dave could hear a rhythmic tapping and realised to his shame that it was Heath, nervously jiggling his artificial leg. The titanium limb knocked against the leg of his chair.

'I apologise,' Dave said roughly. 'I run off at the mouth sometimes. Like a fucking idiot, and yeah, like a bigot sometimes. Like my old man. I didn't mean any disrespect to you or your service, Heath. Andy, he was proud of serving.'

The tightness around Heath's eyes remained, his jaws clenched, and when he spoke, he also obviously had to force himself to dial it back.

'I accept your apology, Dave.'

For one mad and dangerous second Bad Dave almost flared up again, *because who was this asshole to judge him?* But he stamped down on that shit. Hard.

Heath appeared to force himself to speak quietly. 'Everyone loses something in war. Even when you win, you lose something.'

'Yeah,' Dave agreed.

He'd lost something, too.

His Superman boner.

15

The minion had no name of its own. A lowly creature, it knew what it was and what it served: its hunger and its queen. It snarled at the wretched thresh circling its kill, perhaps looking to rush in while it was distracted by feeding. Oh, and it was so easy to be distracted by this fine meal. Exactly how long had it been since any had tasted the meat of the frail two-legged creatures that screamed so sweetly when you bit into them?

The minion knew not.

Just that it had been too long. So many turnings trapped in the UnderRealms, forced to hunt and feed on the creeping urmin and inferior thresh such as the two that bumbled through darkness behind it, splashing and grunting in the brackish brown waters that flooded the ruined village. The minion kept one eye trained on them but knew itself to be safe from attack while it remained in the pool of light where it had dragged the carcasses to feed in peace. Thresh did not stray into the light. It would burn the hide from their backs.

The minion grunted in good humour as it tore off a limb and stripped the meat from the bone by pulling the tasty treat out through three layers of fangs. So sweet and soft, not at all like the meat all minion recalled from the ancestor memories of long ago, when their kind moved upon the upper world with freedom. Legend dimly recalled these creatures as being much tougher and stringier on the fang. They often tasted sour, it was said, and it wasn't unknown to have to spend a good long time chewing on their gristle and bones.

It pulled off a leg and crunched happily through the thick upper thigh, almost giddy with pleasure at the warm juices that still squirted and the rich, heady marrow that lay inside the bones. The meat was well marbled with fat, lots of gorgeous yellow fat.

Oh, Her Majesty was going to be pleased when the minion reported back to her that the path to the upper realm was clear again.

As long as it could remember to save some of the feast for the offertory. It would not do to come before the throne with a full belly and empty claws. It had seen even daemonum superiorae go into the blood pot for less.

The minion snarled a warning into the dark as it sensed the thresh working up the nerve to charge, perhaps imagining that if they were quick enough, they might get in and out of the light without being too badly burned. It could understand that. The smell of fresh meat must be driving them to madness. The minion knew it was having trouble restraining itself as it drove a snout deep into the steaming, still quivering viscera of one of the prey.

It just tasted so goooooooood.

So good indeed that the minion, never really known for intelligence and restraint, did not pause to wonder from where the light in which it squatted and ate was shining. It had imagined at first that the great golden armoured beast on which the prey was riding would flee when the minion attacked. But no, it sat, seemingly uncaring of the fate of its masters, howling with a rhythmic thumping sound that reminded the minion of mating season. Perhaps the chariot beast was in season, and if that was the case, waiting to see what the male of the species was like might be foolhardy on the minion's part. Its bright eyes shone forth, illuminating the remains of the meal. But no warmth shone from them. Not like the dangerous heat that pulsed off the fires this prey was known to carry through the night sometimes. Fire that could consume vampyri and Hunn and Fangr and even Grymm in a twinkling. Fire that could harm and even kill a whole rank of minion were they foolish enough to remain exposed to it for too long.

The meat, however, was . . . distracting. It melted in the mouth and sat warm and heavy and pleasing in all of the minion's stomachs. If only the prey had not died so quickly, the minion might even have had the pleasure of a live meal and bloodwine, a delicacy so rare even in the older times that it was spoken of as myth. There were ancient minion that claimed to have eaten so and spoke of a special tincture that infused the prey meat when they were allowed to baste in the juices of their own terror during a meal.

The minion doubted those stories now.

How anything could contain the hunger long enough to bother, it did not know.

This meat was just so sweet.

16

It was the chocolate thickshake that did it for Dave in the end. He felt uncomfortably full for the first time in days. There was a peculiar pleasure to be had in sitting back and lightly drumming his greasy fingertips on that tight, distended belly. A pleasure that lasted for all of ten minutes, and then the tiny bulge above his belt buckle marking the final resting place of so many chickens and pigs and their friend the thickshake was gone, and he was back to his new, sleek swimwear model profile.

'Damn. I'm getting a cover of *Sports Illustrated* out of this,' he said.

Professor Ashbury marvelled as though he'd just shown her a particularly intriguing card trick.

'I've seen some odd things today, very odd, but watching you consume a trailer park's worth of garbage food and then do your miracle weight loss thing, I will concede that was a rather special moment, Dave.'

Heath, who had seen it all before, checked his wristwatch and announced himself ready for the rack.

'But there's one last thing you could do for me,' he said to Dave.

'Sure, name it,' Hooper replied, still feeling the need to atone for being a dickhead earlier.

'Professor, would you like to come along?' Heath asked. 'It won't take long, and this has been bugging me since I found out.'

Dave was more than just intrigued now. Heath was not the sort of guy to let anything bug him for very long. He was more the sort of guy to call in a strike from an orbital platform or perhaps file the problem to death. In triplicate. The more time Dave spent around him, the more he came to see Heath as an uptight but potentially violent bureaucrat.

'We're headed to the crew lounge,' the captain explained. 'Where you encountered the Hunn.'

Before Dave could object, Heath hurried to explain himself. 'The site's been cleaned out. Sensitive Site Exploitation was thorough and used a standard decon protocol.'

'Go on,' Dave told him.

'But there was one thing left,' Heath said. 'We couldn't move it.'

Professor Ashbury seemed to know what he was talking about. She regarded Dave with a carefully composed expression, giving nothing away.

'What?' he asked.

'The hammer. Mr Grbac's splitting maul. We can't move it.'

Now Dave was confused rather than intrigued.

'Why? I buried it in Urgon's melon, not the steelwork.'

'Probably better you just come along and see for yourself. You might "remember" something more.'

Whatever the problem was, Heath seemed at a loss. Contrite Dave had no objections. He had his atonement to be getting on with, and he wasn't at all sleepy. Matter of fact, he had no idea how he was going to get his head down and was worried about being out of it tomorrow, with Professor Compton shooting him the stink eye and loading him up with questions he couldn't hope to answer. Just to make him look like some sort of idiot rube in front of Emmeline.

Or Emma. He wondered if she liked to be called Emma in bed.

Then he stopped thinking about that because it was becoming obvious. Again.

He turned his thoughts back to Compton. That served to soften the rail spike. Dave Hooper had met plenty of guys like Compton before. They saw the dirt under his fingernails and the grime worked into his old shirt collar, and they thought *redneck*. Didn't matter that he had a couple of bachelor's degrees and a master's in engineering and knew enough about academia to know that he could go play their reindeer games as a teacher if he wanted to. But then he remembered what his dad had always said.

Those that can't do, teach.

These pricks, Dave had decided long ago, just couldn't see past a bit of oil and grease.

'Let's go, then,' he said. 'And I'll consult the ol' monsterpedia for the splitting maul of the gods,' he said, tapping the side of his head.

Turned out his Rolodex was possessed of a bottomless trove of lore concerning legendary weapons. That was how he thought of it, too: 'lore'. Despite being pretty sure he'd never had reason to utter the word before. What was he, the Nerdlinger General? As they wound through the maze of flame-scored corridors, working their way around restricted and unsafe areas, up and down stairs that were sometimes internal, sometimes external, and sometimes a hybrid of both, he worried that the answer to that might be yes. Dave apparently now knew more about legendary swords and celebrated battleaxes than the world's geekiest tabletop game geek. He'd known a couple of champions at college; engineering schools seemed to attract the type. But he doubted they could match his arcane expertise in edged weapons of storied and gore-splattered renown. All of them with names like BoneCleaver and DragonRend. All of them with their own 'souls'.

'Oh, for fuck's sake,' he muttered.

'Is there an issue?' Professor Ashbury asked.

'Giant man-eating nerds. Really, you don't want to know,' Dave said, and went back to pondering Marty's splitting maul. But apart from nearly falling into a dark, bottomless well of memory where hundreds of legendary war hammers lived – *'Tremble before Mighty Trhondor's Hammer of Flattening'* – he came up empty-handed.

As they weaved past a patrol just before the turn to the crew lounge, Heath stopped and asked the sergeant in charge if he could borrow one of his marines.

'Sure, Captain. Take your pick.'

'Private, you'll do,' he said, pointing to the largest man in the unit, a slab-shouldered brute whose assault rifle looked comically small in his hands.

'Sir?'

Heath asked the giant marine to follow them into the lounge. He hadn't been lying about the clean-up job. Dave's mild apprehension about returning to the slaughterhouse was unfounded. The room was empty. It had been stripped and sanitised. The smell of bleach was strong enough to bring tears to the eyes. The tiles he'd knocked out of the ceiling had even been replaced from somewhere. No bloodstains marked the floor or walls. He could hear cooks and other personnel preparing the rig's kitchen for breakfast. Swap the civilians for cooks in camouflage and it was possible to convince yourself that nothing had happened. No evidence of any kind remained of the terrible violence done here. Except for one thing.

Marty Grbac's splitting maul.

It lay on the tiled floor. Still matted with dried blood, bone chips, shards of broken fang, and a few strands of coarse hair that looked like they'd come off the back of a feral hog. The straight hardwood stock still bore a bloodied imprint of his fingers. Or maybe Marty's. Dave couldn't say.

The sergeant, whose name tag identified him as McInerney, ordered his men to keep watch in the hallway outside while he took up station by the door, as curious as anyone about what Heath was up to. Private Everding stood at ease, waiting to be given another order but not looking much at ease to Dave's eye.

Hooper made to reach for the splitting maul, but Heath held up a hand.

'Just a moment. Everding? Could you try to pick up the hammer for me?'

'But sir . . .' the marine started to protest.

'Just indulge me, son. I said *try*.'

The marine threw a pleading look at his sergeant, who merely gestured at the splitting maul with his free hand. 'You heard the captain. Give it your best.'

Private Everding didn't look happy, but he did as he was told.

Handing his rifle to Sergeant McInerney, he approached the heavy tool reluctantly. Dave could understand that. It was filthy with blood and worse. Professor Ashbury circled the room for a better vantage point.

'What's going on here?'

Compton. Was he stalking them? It was the second time he'd walked in on a show-and-tell.

He waddled into the room, clad in khaki trousers and a rumpled dress shirt. Ashbury gave Compton a brusque nod of professional acknowledgement.

'Captain Heath thought to bring Hooper in on this,' she said, waving one hand at the splitting maul.

'I see,' Compton said. 'You should have called me.'

'My apologies, Professor,' Heath said. 'I am used to operating in the field without direct supervision.'

Dave, who had no idea what was up, just watched from where he stood on a light patch of tiles where the TV once had lived. Where had that gone? he wondered. After another fruitless appeal to his sergeant, Everding dropped into a squat over the long hickory shaft. He looked like a man about to attempt an Olympic lift. Rather than picking up the hammer, as Dave had expected, with his dominant hand, just under the heavy steel head, Everding placed both hands about equally distant from each end of the shaft. Then he tried to hoist the weight. He looked ridiculous, as if he were goofing around. And then . . .

Everding tried to lift the hammer.

'What the fuck?'

Dave's eyes went a little wider, then narrowed as the enormous marine heaved and strained. Cords stood out on his neck, his face turned dark red, and he grunted with the effort.

The handle moved maybe an inch before he gave up and let go, stumbling back across the room, where Heath had some difficulty preventing him from crashing to the floor.

Everding had failed.

In Dave's mind, a monologue on the event sank into the trove of lore.

'Many from the village had tried their hand to shift Maul the Suresplitter. All who made the attempt failed, for the Suresplitter awaited . . .'

Okay, enough. Dave willed himself out of that particular nerdspace in his brain.

'Thank you, Marine,' Heath said. 'Care to try, Sergeant?'

McInerney's grin widened.

'I watched Joey Cuomo try the same thing this morning, Captain. He didn't do much better. Reckon I'll treat my hernia to the day off if you don't mind.'

Heath grinned back at him. A small thing, but it was a warm, genuine smile, one of the few Dave had seen from him. In contrast, the captain's glance at Compton revealed little but impatience.

'Fair enough. I don't imagine the professor or I would even move it the inch Private Everding achieved.'

They all looked at Dave.

'So, what?' Dave said. 'You just sort of pulled Urgon's head away from it?'

'After a fashion,' Ashbury said. 'It made the most awful mess.'

Dave bent forward to pick the maul up or at least to try. Heath warned him to be careful.

'Remember what happened to the weight bar. Take it easy, Dave.'

Good point, he thought without saying anything.

'This will be interesting,' said Compton, as though Dave

were a labrador trying to play the piano.

Dave stood over the end of the shaft and looked at Emmeline Ashbury.

'See what happens,' she said. 'Please, however, do exercise some care.'

He stood up straight again, examined the problem, and cautiously toed the handle with his boot. The end of the shaft moved about six inches when he pushed it. It felt no heavier than it had the last time he'd touched it, which was to say heavy but manageable. He gave it another small nudge with the same result.

'Oh good grief,' Professor Compton said.

'You want to try again?' Dave asked Everding, who was staring at him as if he'd grown another head. 'Might've just been gummed up with monster blood. That stuff's like superglue.'

'No, sir,' said Everding.

'Alrighty, then.'

Dave leaned down and picked up the hammer, grimacing a little at the sticky filth encrusting the handle. Unlike the weight bar, which had felt as though it was made of foam, this felt pretty much as he remembered it. In fact, *exactly* as he remembered it. Heavy but usable. He hefted the piece and gave it an experimental twirl. It swung around in a tight figure eight at such speed that the air whooshed.

'Holy shit,' Everding exclaimed. Then, 'Er, excuse me, ma'am.'

But Ashbury wasn't interested in his apologies. She was staring at Dave as he twirled the heavy maul like a conductor's baton. It blurred with the speed of the movement, and Heath finally called out, 'Dave! That's probably enough.'

'Oh, sorry,' said Dave, who'd forgotten himself, lost in the strange simple joy of playing with Maul the Hunnsplitter. Or maybe Sledge the Melon Smasher. Or . . .

He was gonna need a name for this thing. He knew that the way he knew burgers needed beer.

The stiff breeze coming off the improvised fan blade was ruffling Emmeline Ashbury's dark hair, and the sound of the hammer's passage was a deep thrumming hum. A little like a chopper blade without the percussive note. He had to remind himself that a day ago he'd used it to put down a monster that was sitting right here, snacking on his friend like a piece of beef jerky.

He swung the top of the handle into his palm with a meaty crack. The steel head glistened dully where it wasn't covered in dried gore.

'Thank you,' Heath said, obviously relieved. 'I could see that thing flying through a wall and taking out half the rig.'

'I think she could probably do that,' Dave said with a trace of awe. 'Would you mind if I cleaned her up? She's kind of gross.'

'I got it,' said Sergeant McInerney before ducking out the door.

'You're assigning this object a gender role?' Professor Compton asked. 'It is just an artifact.'

'No, she's more than that,' Dave said, looking anew at the splitting maul. 'She has . . . I dunno, something. Why not give her a name? You never named a car, Doc?'

Compton said nothing.

The remaining marine nodded with apparent understanding.

'Maybe I should name her Annie. A steel tornado of unholy destruction? Or not. We'll see.'

'There has to be a rational explanation,' Professor Ashbury said. 'For all of this.'

'I agree with my subordinate,' Professor Compton said, ignoring the death glare his subordinate sent his way. 'Extraordinary as events may seem, I doubt we are dealing with magic here. Some arcane technological event, perhaps.'

In spite of the caked-on bloody gruel, Dave found that he wanted to hold on to the splitting maul. It felt natural, the way a really beautifully crafted baseball bat did. Or a pool cue. Or a fine piece of ass . . . or anything, really. Any tool that had been carefully crafted by a skilled maker with one purpose in mind. The wood grain meshed and melded with his calloused hands, generating a soothing warmth of reassurance.

He hefted her again, examining the crusted wedge of the axe head.

She had . . . potential.

'Professor Ashbury?' Heath asked. 'You got anything?'

She shook her head.

'I'm at a complete loss, Michael. I think you might need to get some more professors out here. Scholars of old Icelandic legend perhaps. Or some Beowulf nerds. I'm sure you can find some starving adjuncts who would be willing to take the government's coin for this project.'

Professor Compton gave Ashbury a look of disapproval before adding his own thoughts. 'I have some cross-disciplinary experience in anthropology and English mythology.'

'Okay,' Heath said. 'Your theory?'

'Not so much a theory,' Compton said. 'If we were a pre-technological, prescientific culture and we bore witness to this act, we would describe the moment as magical. We would lack any other rational explanation.'

'Why don't you just go ahead and quote Arthur C Clarke?' Ashbury said. 'You're most of the way there.'

Compton pushed on, ignoring her. 'Mr Hooper is in possession of what seems a charmed weapon. The act of killing the creature appears to have given him special powers and privileges. In mythology there would be rituals to attend to. But step back from the process and imagine giving a caveman a handgun. He would feel the same confusion and awe and imagine the need to reach for a magical explanation. Simply because he didn't understand the process and the technology. He would shroud any understanding in worship and ritual.'

Heath looked at Professor Ashbury.

'Probably,' she conceded.

'Well, the first ritual ought to be to clean her up,' Dave said.

McInerney reappeared right on cue with a wet cloth that he handed to Dave. 'Spoken like a marine.'

'Thanks, man,' he said before slowly wiping down the length of the dark wood shaft, folding the cloth over, and cleaning the head. It was an imperfect job, but he found that he didn't mind a few blood spots and impurities. They, too, seemed right. As if they also had potential.

'So? Can I keep it?' he asked. It seemed that he should ask permission even though it was Marty's. Or perhaps because it was Marty's. There were undoubtedly protocols for dealing with the personal effects of the dead.

'I don't know what else we'd do with it,' Heath admitted. 'If you dropped it here and walked away, I don't think it would ever leave the room. I suspect it would be here until the rig rusted and fell apart and it dropped down to the seabed.'

'We should get back to work, sir,' McInerney said.

'Of course, Sergeant. Thank you for your help. I'm sorry to

keep you. And you, too, Everding. Thank you.'

'Wouldn't have missed it, sir,' McInerney replied. 'C'mon, let's go start some more rumours.'

The marines departed, leaving Dave and the others in the bare, sanitised surrounds of the empty room.

17

The thresh remained in darkness while the filthy minion gorged itself on meat that rightly belonged in their gullets. They had been the ones to lay the fear on the prey as the calflings rode along so proudly on their captured beast of burden. Did the minion think it was easy reaching out to the mind of such creatures, travelling at great speed, fast enough by their reckoning to outpace a full grown wulfin?

Short answer, no.

Because minion didn't think at all. Thinking and minion were as inimical to each other as vampyri and the dawn. Minion were best at charging and biting and tearing the limbs from enemies and prey, none of which required a great deal of thought. Just lots of teeth and claws and fast springy haunches, of which minion had an elegant sufficiency.

They were also, the thresh admitted, not so bad at biting and tearing considerable chunks of hide from unwary thresh that strayed too close to them, especially in the first moments of a feeding frenzy.

Thresh, however, prided themselves on their thinkings and ponderings. And right now these two were pondering how to distract a stupid, puckering sphincter of a minion from its dinner long enough that they might enjoy a nibble of their own. A while longer and this one would be slow and even stupider than normal with the carnage coma their gluttonous kind always suffered. But likewise, in a little while longer that greedy bastard was going to scarf the whole thing! They cautiously scouted the scene, looking for a way in.

The great armoured chariot whence the prey had been pulled looked to be the possession of a mad wizard of immense wealth and power. A throbbing, thumping sound whumped methodically at the humid air around them, a mourning cry for the half-consumed master who lay on the ground in a strange, ceremonial robe thrown asunder. The magick chariot itself was a blaze of gold and sparkles with luscious hide seats of blood red on the inside. Many a magnificent beast must have been slaughtered and drained to provide the opulence for this mode of conveyance that the queen herself would be proud to rest in. Even the wheels were fashioned of pristine silver that reflected the light from a thousand unseen candles.

The thresh knew the minion could hear them as they manoeuvred through the ruins of the calfling village, around the edge of the kill, careful never to stray into the burning light of the carrier beast's enormous eyes. But the minion could not hear them as they conversed and plotted, for thresh made no noise at all when doing that. Instead, the thresh remained within the shelter of a brick structure possessed of a red metal roof that held the distant memory of meat, spice, and calfling musk. A fallen temple, perhaps, given its size and complexity. They stayed away from the glaring yellow light of another calfling temple where dead flesh was burning, filling the air with a stale, nasty, oily odour that clashed violently with the sweet, delicate scent of the fresh kill.

They spoke into one another's minds with nary a whisper on the cool night air to give away their communication. Indeed, that was how they had brought down the prey in the first place. Forcing, with great difficulty, a mirage into the mind of the rider who held the odd reins of the golden chariot. The constant drumbeat – *whumpety-whump-whump-whump* – pounding from the chariot made it difficult to penetrate the comparatively feeble mind of the wagon's driver.

Surely not a wizard or sorcerer; this mind had been cluttered, addled with drunkenness and some toxin the thresh could not quite puzzle out for they were both immature and lacked the thinkings of a full grown Thresh or Threshrend. Nonetheless, little did it matter as they shivered and hopped in hungry frustration while other calflings stayed under the protection of great candle lights that burned everywhere. Those calflings screamed in fear and anger while holding up charms and glowing amulets as if to ward away thresh and minion alike.

Futile, of course.

So no, it had not been at all easy reaching out into the mind of the chariot master, and the effort had left them exhausted, which was why that minion really was drinking the *urmin* piss, slouching out there in plain view, gobbling down their dinner. After a good while circling and stalking about in the dark, the same thought occurred to both thresh at the same time, as such things often did.

Why did they not flinch from the light of the carrier beast's eyes? So bright was it that their own eyestalks should have shrivelled and burned black from the intense glare. The two shadow creatures exchanged a significant look. Slowly, and as quietly as possible, they crept upon the feeding scene. They could sense the fevered terror of nearby calflings, but they paid them no further heed. For one, the filthy minion was dining magnificently on the repast that was rightly theirs. And for two, there was the troubling truth of the second minion, or rather its carcass, brought down by some dark magick a calfling wizard had unleashed before the minion overwhelmed the cattle.

They remembered and looked at the crowd of calflings as they emerged slowly, cautiously into the light, all the while keeping an eye on the remaining minion. One calfling wizard-warrior, braver than the rest, stood a little forward of the mewling pack. He had long locks of dark hair and wore white robes cut to display his own tattoos. That gold chain might mean something. The strange headdress with a flat, tongue-like protrusion was surely significant. A strange, indecipherable rune stood out on it, a sign of the human wizard's magickal order. In consulting the memory of the thresh, they found nothing to aid in their considerations. None of the magick amulets or boxes the calflings held spoke the word of death or gave the sign of flame that attended it. That was a relief. Wizards and amulets seemed in copious abundance in this realm.

That, the thresh agreed, was the only explanation for the vexing problem of how calfling prey had brought down a single minion at all. Best to ponder such things at leisure, however, after eating.

The thresh hopped out of the shadows and onto the road. They stalked around the wreck of another magick chariot, fearful that at any moment a stray shaft of light might fall upon their oozing hides and flay them off in a bright phosphorescent burst of white fire and pain. But even as they crept closer and felt the familiar and disagreeable tingle of strong moonlight on their backs, they sensed no threat from the blazing eyes of the carrier beast or the tall candle pyres that threw their own weak glow over the village ruins. It was as though the chariot beast's eyes were alight and yet dead at the same time, possessed of none of the malevolent puissance that attended illuminations here in the Above.

Perhaps the stories were wrong, they exchanged in silence. Perhaps it had been so long since anything had hunted in the realm of men that myth and legend had replaced true thinkings and ponderings about the Above.

The thresh crouched closest to the greedy minion suddenly started in a panic when an eyestalk dipped and noticed a thin red point of light lying across its forearm. The opalescent pus that ran from its pores should have ignited. But instead it merely glistened in the cold, harmless fire of the light. The thresh skinned back their thin lipless mouths, exposing rows of serrated teeth as a scheme passed between them in a glimmering of quickthinkings.

One hungry, surly minion might well pull the big thinking head of an unwary thresh clean off. Well, maybe not so clean. But one bloated, blood-drunk fool of a minion, engorged with man meat and dizzy with the marrow spins, was almost certainly not a match for two of the quickest, thinkingest thresh the nest of il-Aron had ever hatched.

Their fangs, glinting in the harmless light, began to move along the gum track in their distended mouths, building up such speed that they soon blurred into a single cutting edge, super-hard, razor-sharp, and positively humming as they burst from concealment and fell upon the hapless minion.

In the distance, a strange howling sound filled the air, rushing toward them. Perhaps another creature was feeding tonight.

18

Neither Dave nor Professor Ashbury was tired, but Captain Heath was as good as his word and took himself off to his cot, with Professor Compton worrying at his heels the whole way. Once they dropped out of sight, Dave turned to Ashbury and sketched a formal bow.

'Walk you around the grounds, Prof?' he asked in his best imitation of Good Dave. 'A stroll can sometimes clear the head and put a fella in the mood for bed.'

'That sounds like a well-worn family aphorism,' she said.

'A what?'

'A saying.'

'Ah, then you're right. My grandma used to say it all the time. Believed it, too. She came to live with us after the old man took off. To help out, you know.'

He took the splitting maul along with him, not because he expected any trouble on a platform full of marines and navy SEALs but because it felt like he should. Like it was his responsibility.

'Lucille,' he said.

'I'm sorry.'

'BB King named all of his guitars Lucille. I'm thinking of

naming this baby here. Lucille would work.'

'Why, if you don't mind my asking?'

'I like BB King.'

'No, why must you name it?'

Dave paused for a moment. The storms of the last few days had broken up, and out here, where they walked around the southern terrace, the sky was densely speckled with twinkling points of light. A day of rain and wind had sucked most of the warmth from the air, and he was glad of the new hoodie he wore, this one a thick grey woollen number from the Naval Academy. The prof was buttoned up inside a Burton ski jacket.

'Would you believe me if I said I had to? That I didn't have a choice? Just like when I get hungry.'

He held the maul up between them, gripping it with one hand just below the head. Moonlight glinted on the axe blade.

'It's like . . . I dunno . . .'

'You birthed it?'

Dave searched her expression for a sign that she was being sarcastic, but the professor seemed more intrigued than anything.

'No. Not birthed it.'

God, that sounded like something Annie would say: 'I birthed these children for you, Dave. I birthed them.'

'No,' he said, starting to walk again. 'But it feels like I have to. Like leaving it nameless would be wrong.'

'Okay, then. I suppose you had best name her. Lucille is good. I have an aunt by that name. A genuine 1960s hippie. She was groovy, in the dictionary definition of the word. Beads and everything.'

Dave held the head of Marty's splitting maul up at eye level. He spoke to it as though it were a child.

'Lucille, I'm glad to make your acquaintance.'

He meant it playfully, but as he addressed the maul, it seemed to grow lighter in his hand. His grip became surer, and a strange, not entirely pleasant shiver ran down his arm and through his body, into the deck beneath his feet.

'Whoa.'

'Is there a problem?' Professor Ashbury asked. She had stopped walking, and her eyes were alive with concern. 'Are you okay, Dave? You look like you just got a shock. An actual shock.'

She was right. He was covered in goose bumps. They faded quickly, but he hefted the maul, examining it closely.

Lucille did feel lighter. A hell of a lot lighter.

'Well, that was strange,' he said. 'Not the strangest thing to happen today but weird enough.' He let the hammer drop, careful not to hit or even touch Emma with it. 'I think she likes her name.'

These are their names, and the dead shall know them well.

He shivered and stepped off, eager to be on the way again.

'Come on,' he said. 'There's a nice terrace out of the wind on the far side of the rig.' They walked in silence for a few minutes, exchanging a few 'good evenings' with a squad of marines they passed under the communications shack. Marines, Dave had been surprised to discover, were all about good manners. Clouds passed over the moon at one point when they were traversing an unlit walkway. Professor Ashbury found herself unable to proceed in the darkness, but Dave's night vision adjusted without his even being aware of the change. He noticed her difficulty and reached out a hand, gently taking her by the arm. She gasped.

'It's cool. I got you,' he said. 'Just walk forward.'

He led her across the gantry. Small, shuffling baby steps

for her and longer, more confident strides for him. But slowly, like a dancer, so she could keep up.

When they reached the other side, a Coleman lamp spilled a wedge of light onto the deck from around the corner of a prefab unit that had housed crew before it had been burned.

'Thanks,' she said, genuinely shaken. 'I don't like heights or the dark.'

Dave waited a beat before laughing.

'And so you thought you'd seek your career in outer space?'

'Not exactly. No. It's just . . . oh, shut up, you.'

She backhanded him, which didn't hurt at all. The moon came back out, and they made it to the terrace without any further problems.

'You think there's anything up there? Really?' Dave asked, pointing at the sky with the maul. The dense steel head blotted out some of the star field. When she answered, her voice was tired. She still sounded a little nervous.

'My scientific scepticism took a beating today. I don't feel like I know much of anything anymore.'

The boots of a marine patrol clanged on the metal runway above them, fading as the men tromped around to the western side of the platform. The running lights of a couple of USN destroyers blinked in the haze to the south, enforcing the exclusion zone around the Longreach. They bobbed and ducked on the swell churned up by the earlier storms, a chaotic drumbeat that sent waves crashing against the pylons below in an unpredictable, arrhythmic dance.

The pylons and the drill shaft were all being monitored by newly emplaced security cams. Infrared and something called 'lamps', according to Heath, which apparently weren't lamps at all.

Emmeline, who confessed herself too wired and anxious to sleep, let Dave lead on their stroll around the platform. He was familiar with late nights spent walking off his worries. On any given night this last month he could have chosen to lose sleep to worry about his mounting stack of credit card bills; his unfiled tax returns; how to pay for the boys' school fees, which were about to double when his wife enrolled them in some new joint – *not flying in a couple of top-shelf hookers might have helped with that*; how to keep a little back for himself so that Annie's lawyer boyfriend didn't get everything; the drill of course, which was operating way outside its specs; the bosses in Houston who'd forced that situation on him; the way his car guzzled coolant at about a hundred times the rate it should have; the way he seemed to really *need* a drink these days instead of just wanting one; a new sore, which looked just like the old ones, which he'd finally decided to pay attention to about a month after it had appeared on his chest and refused to heal – to all of these worries and more he could add his new ones.

And take at least one away.

The small red sore on his chest, which had almost certainly been another basal cell carcinoma, was gone.

Woo fucking hoo.

'Something funny, Dave?'

'Just trying to get some perspective,' he said as they climbed the stairwell on the southwestern corner, stopping on the platform just below the helipad, which afforded them a view all the way over to Thunder Horse. The Longreach's sister platform had its own small flotilla of coast guard vessels and warships, four of them that he could make out, dancing a complicated waltz with the destroyers currently guarding the

Longreach, although how exactly a guided missile destroyer was supposed to guard against something like Urgon Htoth Ur Hunn turning up in your media lounge he wasn't sure.

Emmeline Ashbury leaned against the safety rail protecting her from a long fall to the waters swirling against the massive concrete pylons beneath them and rubbed her hands together. 'Cold,' she said.

Dave could feel the chill in the air right enough, but tonight it wasn't cutting into him the way it might normally.

'Seriously,' he said, looking up at the stars again. 'Did you ever expect to find anything up there?'

'Expect? No. A good scholar never expects or anticipates anything. You theorise. You test. You wait for the results. But it's poor form to expect anything. Publicly at least.'

'So why do it?'

Her eyes lit up with a smile that started at the corner of her mouth, highlighted her cheekbones, and crinkled the corners of her eyes.

'You got me.' She put up her hands in mock surrender. 'Guilty of expectations.'

Dave's return smile was queered by the effort of ignoring the rush of sexual imagery that flowed into his mind's eye when he saw her impossibly white teeth in the moonlight. Annoyed with himself now, he kept a pleasant expression on his face as he jammed one hand into his pocket, pretending to warm it when he actually was trying to disguise the return of his boner.

Despite what Annie thought, he wasn't seventeen years old. He knew the difference between appropriate and inappropriate boners. Turning at an angle to shield himself further, he pretended to be fascinated by the flight of a chopper from the rear deck of one of the destroyers.

'You think they'll keep you on this gig, Prof? Seeing as how it's not aliens or anything?'

'For a while. We're here, we're cleared, the president will want his own eyes on this. That makes us more useful than someone who might have a clue.'

He snorted at that, the weary response of a guy worn down by years of having other people's idea of compromise forced on him.

'Yeah. I can see that. All the baby scientists and your guy Compton, are they all likely to stay on? I don't think he's a fan of old Dave.'

It was her turn to snort.

'It's not you, it's him. He really didn't want to come down here. On the other hand, when you are partly responsible for the creation of the Human Terrain Team program, your prospects for giving TED talks in Seattle are slim indeed. He has a knack for organising and running things.'

'A bureaucrat,' Dave said.

'By necessity,' she said.

'So he's the boss?'

'He oversees the office. Micromanages quite a bit when he's not talking at people. He wouldn't appreciate being lectured about your monsters.'

Dave almost protested that they weren't his, but of course they were. Neither of them would be standing here if he hadn't lost his shit and brained the Hunn when it was plastered on . . . His train of thought nearly jumped the tracks at that point.

When it was drunk on Marty's blood.

'But isn't this like the discovery of a lifetime? Monsters among us?' Dave asked. 'Plenty of juicy research grants out of this. Better than the global warming scam.'

'Don't be a fucking idiot,' she said quite severely to that. 'It's unbecoming and unnecessary.' Ashbury seemed to gather herself with a deep breath, which she let out in a heavy sigh. 'We're cleared because we're locked down by non-disclosure agreements. The whole world could be talking about this tomorrow, but we won't be allowed to. Not in public.'

The navy chopper passed out of view around the bulk of Thunderhorse at the same moment the faint sound of its rotor chop reached them on a vagary of the breeze. A commercial airliner passed high above, away to the south, probably headed for Little Rock or Memphis. He'd had an app on his iPhone that could have told him just by pointing it at the lights in the sky, but of course that was gone now, too. He hadn't had a chance to get online and check if it was still alive somewhere. The freshening wind carried the scent of the platform away, replacing the industrial smells of oil and chemicals with clean salt air and brine and traces of rainwater.

None of which Dave cared about.

He just wanted to find a way to either hide or get rid of a large, inconvenient erection that was jutting halfway out to Cuba. He found that by placing one foot on the guardrail, he could more easily cover up. It wasn't funny. If anything, it was kind of painful, and he wondered if he'd actually gotten his money's worth from the Nevada hookers because at his age he should have been good for a few more days.

'What do you think's gonna happen, Doc?' he asked, hoping to distract himself.

'You're not going to stop calling me that, are you?'

She was leaning back against the safety rail now, which only served to emphasise the line of her breasts, even through the heavy ski jacket.

'I forget things,' he said. 'But come on. Seriously. You're the expert. What's gonna happen?'

'To you? I don't know. But I was not feeding you a line before. There were people higher up the food chain than Heath who wanted to drop you in a hole until they were sure you weren't dangerous. You'll want to keep that in mind, no matter what happens.'

He frowned.

'And they gave you a security clearance?'

'I see you know how this works,' she said. 'Yes. They did. But I like to think that was for the autopsy on ET and keeping quiet about how the pod people took over the Republicans. For stuff I have issues with, I keep my fingers crossed. And throwing honest citizens in a hole for no good reason, that I don't agree with.'

She jutted her chin at Hooper, as if challenging him to come back at her. But he didn't.

'Wait,' he said as if he meant to challenge her. 'ET's dead?'

'Deader than disco.'

She smiled and reached into her jacket and produced a fifth of Pendleton whiskey.

'You take a shot, Dave? You look the kind of man, if you don't mind me saying so. And I think we earned it today.'

She unscrewed the cap and downed a slug before passing over the bottle. He got a strong scent of whatever perfume she wore as she handed him the whiskey. When he put the glass to his mouth, the taste of her lipstick was strong. It didn't help much with his boner problem, which was made worse yet by how different she seemed now from the ball-buster he'd met earlier. What the fuck had gotten into this woman?

He passed back the bottle.

'Thanks. Heath's okay, I guess. But he doesn't seem the type to run an open bar on board.'

'Oh, don't be so hard on him, Dave. He's not so bad. You were a bit of a jerk tonight, and he let you slide on that.'

'He did,' Dave conceded. 'And I was.'

Another drink burned down even more smoothly than the first.

'I'm sorry about your brother. Iraq, wasn't it? I thought that was a bullshit war.'

'They're all bullshit. But yeah, you and me both. Thanks. So,' he said, wanting to get away from the topic of his brother. He never really wanted to talk about Andy. 'You know him well? Heath, I mean.'

'Well enough.'

He filed that away next to Heath having told him that he was just an asset in place. That there was nothing special about his being here. The doc, he was glad to see, was a lady who could handle her liquor. There was no dainty sipping for her. She took a man's measure from the bottle before recapping it and stashing the fifth back in her ski jacket. Wisps of cloud drifted across the face of the moon, but his eyes adjusted again. He could see well enough in the dark to make out the tiniest blemish where the bottle had smudged her lipstick.

'I didn't just mean about me before,' he said. 'When I asked what you thought was going to happen, I meant, you know, generally.'

She turned around from where she'd been leaning back on the rail, which put her a little closer to him. Close enough that their elbows touched. She didn't move away, but after a while he did. It was just too awkward to be that close to her. To any woman, he suspected. Not that he wasn't interested. Obviously.

A woody reaching halfway to next week testified to just how interested. But Dave knew all about getting himself out of trouble and trying to tumble this woman into the sack was a gold medal start on getting himself *in* trouble. For one thing, she might be his only ally in this whole miraculous clusterfuck. Chief Allen didn't count; he was more of a friendly snack machine.

If Ashbury noticed him distancing himself, she gave no sign of it.

'It depends, Dave,' she said. 'Is this story going to break? Certainly. There's just too many people who know, people outside their chain of command. The contact was too remote for them to shut down the site quickly but close enough to a major transmission vector that there was no chance of controlling the . . .'

She stopped.

'Damn. Look at me. Two drinks and I reveal my secret identity. Jargon Lady. But I guess you were asking whether it's over. You know, besides your couch session with Ellen, and the *60 Minutes* special, and the whole upcoming Festival of Dave, and the overexposure of Dave and the inevitable vicious backlash against Dave, leading to the second coming of Dave, most likely on *Dancing with the Stars*. Can you dance, by the way?'

'Sure. I'm a middle-aged white man. I got the moves.'

It was her turn to laugh out loud. It was a light, bright sound on the darkened mausoleum of the Longreach. When she was done, she said, 'But I guess you mean is it over with those creatures?'

He didn't speak. He didn't need to.

'You'd know better than me,' she said. 'What's your best guess? Are we done with them?'

Dave really wished he could have another shot.

'Nope,' he said. 'I doubt it. I don't like thinking much about it. Whenever I spend any time doing that, you know, going down the . . . memory hole . . . that thing opened up in my head, it feels like I might not come out.'

'It's amazing, isn't it?' she said. 'If we didn't have those ugly bastards on the slab downstairs, brains in a bucket, just like ET, you'd probably be locked up as a lunatic. But we do have them.'

She shivered and moved in close to him.

'Anyway, I'm cold,' she said. 'And tired now. And a little scared. Walk me back to my cabin, would you? That's not a come-on, by the way. I'm genuinely scared. And cold. And if I wanted to fuck you, I would tell you. I have Asperger's Syndrome.'

Dave stopped mid-stride.

'Shit? Really? I . . . thought . . .'

'What? That I wanted to fuck you? Or that I'm retarded now?'

Dave tugged his Annapolis hoodie down to conceal the raging hard-on as best he could, but he was pretty sure she spotted it. And every time she dropped an F-bomb it got worse.

'No,' he said, struggling. 'I just thought . . . I thought. Okay. Yeah, I thought Asperger's meant retarded. You sort of threw me with that.'

'Well, it doesn't. So fuck off with that idea. But walk me home anyway.'

She looped her arm through his and pulled him forward.

'It's dark,' she added. 'I don't want to fall off this fucking oil rig. You're the safety chap. It's your job.'

He caught up with her, almost stumbling over his own feet.

'So, since I'm doing you a favour here, you can do me one,' Dave said.

She gave him a look.

'Not like that,' he added quickly. 'Just what the fuck is wrong with your friend Compton?'

She shook her head. 'He is not my friend. He is my boss at OSTP. When they need additional knowledge or help with a particular field, Compton is the one who contacts the best and brightest. As for what is wrong with him, that would be the US Army Human Terrain System.'

'Again with that terrain thing? What is it?'

'Using the tools of anthropology to understand the enemy in Afghanistan and Iraq,' she said. 'A big no-no in the discipline. He's pretty much blacklisted from any academic position, tenure track or part time, forever. The non-disclosure agreement prevents him from writing a book on his work, so that avenue is closed to him as well.'

'Don't you have the same problem?' Dave asked.

'No,' she said. 'I never went to Iraq or Afghanistan, and I don't use my skill set in support of programs like Human Terrain. There's always a berth for me somewhere. The space program is a lot more militarised than you'd imagine.'

'I doubt that. I got a pretty lurid imagination.'

'Besides, between guest speaking, medical research, and this job I get by quite well.'

'So he's frustrated?' he asked.

'Very much so,' she said. 'These days he couldn't get hired as an adjunct if his life depended on it. The government pretty much owns him so long as he doesn't piss too many more people off.'

They reached the bottom of the stairs and turned down a corridor.

'They're going to want to know everything, you know,' she said as they left the mezzanine level of the stairwell. As soon as they were out in the breeze, the unseasonably biting cold became much more unpleasant.

'Who? The media?'

'No. Jesus for an engineer, you can be dense, can't you?' She punched him playfully on the arm again. 'The government. Heath is a believer in you, Hooper. For a born again, he's quite the empiricist, you know.'

'I *think* I know what you mean by that,' Dave said. 'And Heath's a God botherer, eh? Figures.'

'No, it doesn't. And I mean that the evidence out here, the accounts he's gathered from other witnesses, and the time he's spent with you, it's all convinced him we're in a genuine first contact situation. Just not one covered by the protocols. He's feeling his way through, and one of the things he feels is that you're telling it straight. Especially about downloading the creatures' memories, or mind state, or whatever.'

Dave could smell meat cooking slowly down in the kitchen, but for once he wasn't hungry. Not for food, anyway.

'Really?' he said. 'Because I'm not sure I trust it or even believe it.'

She stopped, forcing him to pull up, too.

'Why not? Memory is just encoded electrical signals. It's a phase state, a hypercomplicated one but describable if you have the language, replicable if you have the technology.'

'Which we don't. Do we?'

'No,' she agreed. 'But last time I checked, 38-year-old men didn't go leaping a hundred feet into the air, either.'

'Thirty-seven. I'm not that old.'

'Congratulations. But back on topic. Last I checked, monsters didn't chew up oil rigs. And magical hammers didn't . . . Hey. That's warm.'

She'd touched the head of the splitting maul and pulled her hand away quickly. Dave hadn't noticed anything usual about . . . Lucille. Not since she'd given him that mild buzz a little earlier.

'Do you mind?'

The prof carefully reached out and touched the brutal-looking axe head, running her hand over it and caressing the sledgehammer. It didn't help Dave's little problem.

Not so little, he corrected silently.

Emmeline put her hand on his arm. 'It's like you've got your own hot water bottle there. No wonder you don't feel the cold. Just one more thing to add to the list of inexplicable curiosities.'

She let her hand fall away.

'I wouldn't call what happened to you a gift, Dave. It feels like a burden. It's not just about the miracle weight loss cure or cartoon superpowers. You have all this knowledge, too. What you don't have is the knowledge *of* that knowledge, if that makes sense. You don't know what you know. How far down it goes. How wide. How to catalogue it all. In the end, even if no more of these things come up, the government is going to want to make sure they know exactly what you know.'

Dave didn't reply. He heard Allen approach long before the chief petty officer appeared, boots ringing on the steel decking. He looked agitated.

'Found you,' he said. 'Hope you weren't planning on going to bed,' he said, oblivious to any double meaning. 'We have to get back on shore now. Orders from JSOC.'

'What's happened, Zach?' Ashbury asked.

'More of Dave's monsters. A heap of them, coming up out of the sewers in New Orleans. We're taking half the marines we got here with us. There's a big firefight under way. It's confused. Cops. Gangbangers. Some crazy fucker with a crossbow, they say, like the one you killed after Raising Cane's. And monster –'

'Wait,' Dave interrupted him. 'Did you say a crossbow?'

'Or a bow and arrow. One of the cops took a shot in the head.'

'*Sliveen*,' Dave said. 'You want me along, don't you?'

Allen's eyes slipped to the splitting maul Dave carried on his shoulder.

'Captain Heath insists. You, too, ma'am. And Professor Compton.'

'He will be less than thrilled, but I'll get him,' Ashbury said, excusing herself to run back to her room to grab a backpack and 'some things'.

'Borrow a gun if you can,' Dave called after her. 'A big one.'

'Come on,' Allen said, tugging at his elbow. 'Heath wants to talk to you before we fly out. And, hey, you know, sorry, dude.'

'Sorry? Why?'

Allen smiled at him.

'The doctor lady is kinda hot.'

19

The thresh ate well.

As large and powerful as the minion had been, it indeed had been slow and stupid after gorging greedily on its meal. It had grunted once as they flew out of the darkness and clamped their jaws onto the exposed nerve ganglion bulging at the rear of its neck. It was a heavy brute, and it had taken their combined strength to drag it back out of the uncomfortable light and into the familiar, reassuring darkness of the red-roofed stone temple. Oh, but it had been worth the effort. When they tore open the belly of the beast and ripped into its two stomachs, they were rewarded with a feast of pre-chewed, partly digested man meat. Their eyestalks were rigid with the pleasure of it. How smart they had been, they assured each other by quickthinkings, to have allowed the minion to bring down their prey and prepare it so well for them. Such a sufficiency of the achingly sweet delicacy did they recover from the minion's digestive tract that they themselves were quite stupid and slow with feasting when yet another of the timid, slow-moving calflings arrived barking, holding some sort of black tool in its hand.

The thresh laughed. What a pathetic little thing. Oh, they

would surely eat this one next or even keep it alive for the journey back to the UnderRealms.

This one, too, rode in some form of chariot that howled through the night, flashing cold blue and red fire that they now knew to be entirely harmless. Clad in a skin of white and painted in blue clan livery; the thresh had never seen such a thing. A strange scent was in the air, twice-burned flesh, perhaps. Having been hatched long after their kind had been banished from the Above, they supposed there were many things they had never seen. But race memories lived on long after those who had first known them were gone. Great was their pride in thinking out such a difficult and confusing think as the memory of the beast-drawn carts that Man had been known to ride. Try as they might, however, the related memory of how such a chariot might move without the power of a beast to pull it was beyond them. Such thinking was probably the preserve of a Master Scolari or maybe even the queen. It was possible, they supposed, that the creatures that powered it were inside the chariot, armoured and protected from thresh and minion alike.

The thresh wondered what these chariot beasts might taste like and whether it might be possible to crack open the shell in much the same way a swarm of thresh could strip the armoured skin from an old fallen Drakon.

Giddy with thoughts of carrying their news back down below where it might be thought on by intellects far greater than theirs and, it had to be admitted, a little slow-witted and drowsy because of the huge meal they had just gobbled down, the thresh did not react with any great speed or efficiency to the arrival of yet more food in yet another beastless chariot possessing the same howling call. This one also threw out great fans of light from its eyes without any of the telltale flicker of fire that men were known to use for their invidious purposes. With mouths so full of sticky shredded meat that their teeth could barely move along their jaw tracks, the thresh exchanged a few torpid thoughts on the matter without concluding anything.

Their own bellies were just as full as the minion's had been, and so no hunger frenzy drove them, but they could not help idly speculating on what a fine meal this prey would have made had it arrived before the others. It couldn't be a calfling. No, this prey was easily twice their size and wrapped in the most fetchingly dark hide, which must surely be all the sweeter to the fang. They could smell and even sense its fearful thinkings over the considerable distance that separated it from them, and they languidly attempted to grow that fear in the hope that it might paralyse the creature, thus keeping it for later consideration. The old memories spoke of men who neither fought nor ran when confronted, instead soiling themselves most deliciously with their own juices and pastes. What rewards might await them, they thought to each other, were they able to make this one baste itself thus before taking it below to the nest.

When it evacuated the contents of its stomach, the rich smell of fermenting bile, burned meat, and some unknown but powerful sweetness reached their scent receptors almost immediately. The man was joined by a second one, this one pale in the forearms and face yet wearing a black robe of sorts as well.

The thresh's forest of eyestalks, which had been drooping, went rigid again.

Oh, we must have them now, they decided.

The thresh launched themselves at the prey. There could be no question of leaving these creatures to wander off of their own accord. They had no idea how that unique combination of scents and tastes had arisen, but it was imperative that the meal not be allowed to escape. Why, it was even possible they might present the repast directly to the queen herself without the usual pre-chewing and digesting customary for tribute feasts. She would want to taste this meat in its natural state, they thought. To allow the flesh to speak for itself without a lot of unnecessary tearing and rending and cooking in the acids of the blood pot.

Unfortunately, they were no more able to move with the speed and agility of a freshly hatched carver daemon than the minion had been when it was full of tasty man meat. No sooner had the thresh determined to charge back into the strange, cold, harmless light to disable the large man with the pleasingly dark hide than one of them tripped on the ruined masonry that lined the red-roofed building, falling face-first to the ground. This village seemed large for one that had fallen to ruin. There were snares and pitfalls all around, large holes filled with brackish water, and a veritable blizzard of fragile containers, skins, and pouches was strewn about.

The blow all but rendered the stricken thresh unconscious, and its nest mate tumbled over as it attempted to arrest its own flight forward lest the quickthinking link between them be severed by distance. How fortunate that no other nest mates or minion were around to witness their embarrassment. The thresh that had not been knocked nearly insensible reached out with its thoughts to soothe and revive its mate and had only just regained a proper bond when the most awful, unthinkable thing happened.

A flash of light.

A thunderclap.

As the grumbling, injured thresh put one claw to its head to rub at the spot where a large bump was already rising, its skull burst apart in a shower of gore. It dropped dead amid the rubble and detritus of the ruined village.

The surviving thresh stood frozen in place, its jaw hanging open with long tendrils of man meat and minion innards still swinging from its fangs. And then it screamed. A long, hideous psychic scream that was completely inaudible to anything but a fellow dweller in the UnderRealms.

20

The SEALs were much twitchier on the flight back to the mainland. There was none of the lazy grace and relaxed camaraderie Dave recalled from the earlier ride out to the rig. Allen's crew – his chalk, he called them – had known what they were flying into then: a secured landing, with ice cream. Nobody had any idea what awaited them now. The cabin of the Seahawk was crowded with the original SEALs plus another three or four spares they'd picked up, the two academics, and Dave. He was carrying something this time, too.

Lucille.

The navy commandos had eyed him warily when Allen escorted him onto the helipad, but they had all heard about the weird 'magic' hammer, and they seemed to regard it with even more suspicion than they did Dave. None of them, except for Zach Allen, had seen him with Swindt at the base. But Professor Ashbury told him that half the men on the platform had tried to move the hammer at some point yesterday.

'And Excalibur kicked all of their arses,' she said.

He held the maul between his legs, which were closely pressed together in the crush, with the oversized steel head on the metal plating underfoot. Some of the SEALs muttered that they'd never take off with that thing on board, but they did, and now the Seahawk pounded north across the gulf waters, clearing the outer islands of the barrier as Dave wondered what lay ahead.

It was impossible. Urgon had nothing to tell him. As well as Dave could work it out, the Hunn had blundered into the human world by accident. He'd been on a hunting trip that unexpectedly had turned into a much grander adventure. Try as he might, Dave found that he knew nothing about what was happening in New Orleans. All he knew of the city was whatever he'd known two days earlier. The Hunn was ignorant not just of that particular city but of all cities, even ancient ones. When last they had seen humans, they were draped in animal skins, shivering and starving in the clammy depths of caves or the meanest little clutches of mud daub huts.

Lucille seemed to hum in his hands. Maybe it was just vibrations coming up through the deck, but it sent a wave of unease through Dave that grew with each passing minute. He was still getting used to the idea that Marty's old maul had somehow changed, just as he had. She felt . . . eager. And hungry in the same way he had been forever hungry since taking down the BattleMaster. But Dave also felt like he was forgetting something, and that bugged the hell out of him.

The SEALs talked quietly among themselves on their private net, linked together by the headsets they wore. You could almost work out the command structure of the squad, or chalk or whatever, by the flow of information from Heath to Allen and out via two other SEALs, one of whom was that huge bastard with biceps like bowling balls. Igor. Or maybe that was a nickname; Igor was a pretty stupid thing to call a kid. A shaved head taller than Dave, the man eyed him with open suspicion and contempt from behind his thick, bushy beard.

Not a new best friend, then, Dave decided.

Both Ashbury and Compton were plugged into that net too, but not Dave, of course. He sat nursing Lucille and watching the reflection of the moon on the surface of the waters below, a mad diffracted shower of silver on the choppy water. Another helicopter, this one a big twin-bladed model, also carried marines from the platform. Dave could see it to his left, trailing below and behind the Seahawk; other marine helicopters followed out of sight, part of an aerial armada.

There should have been some sense of reassurance with so many tooled-up, well-trained killers around him. But the electric itch of the splitting maul's wood handle against Dave's palms continued to bug him as they approached New Orleans. It was becoming uncomfortable. The sensation mingled with his annoyance at being excluded. It wasn't because they didn't trust him. Not exactly. He was pretty sure Heath and probably Allen had his back, but he remembered the chief petty officer telling him there was no way they could plug him into their combat net because he wasn't trained for it. He'd just get in everyone's shit and mess with it. But Compton and Emmeline Ashbury, he could see, seemed comfortably nestled within the group's command structure.

Heath or Allen would ask some question of the professors, who would consult each other before answering. The information then propagated quickly through the unit. It was hard to hear over the uproar of the engine and the rotors, but they seemed to be talking mostly about anatomy. They could have asked him, of course. He knew more about Hunn and Fangr anatomy than any of them. But he wasn't a professor, and so he wasn't qualified to wear the headset, apparently.

Dave was so lost in his resentment at the perceived slight that he missed the first time Ashbury asked him a question. He felt her kicking his leg. She had changed out of the Skechers she'd been wearing and into heavy work boots.

'What?' he called over the noise.

'The crossbow orcs,' she shouted, covering her mike. 'What did you call them?'

'Could be Grymm,' he shouted back. 'Or Sliveen. And they're not orcs. But they do use war bows. The Sliveen, that is . . .'

He trailed off when he saw Compton rolling his eyes.

'And they're akin to scouts or skirmishers?' Ashbury asked.

He was aware that everyone in the rear cabin was watching him now.

'Think of the Sliveen as stealth fighters,' he replied. 'Like special forces. They're a smaller clan than the Hunn, but they reckon they're way more badass in war craft than all the rest of the Horde. Didn't you dissect the one we killed on the way to the base?'

Ashbury threw a glance over at Heath, who answered for her.

'We didn't retain control of that specimen,' he said loudly enough to be heard over the rotors. 'Another agency has it.'

Dave frowned.

'The CIA stole your monster? Dude, that's not cool.'

Some of the SEALs shifted in their seats, turning toward the exchange.

'Another agency,' Heath repeated.

'Not our office,' Compton barked at him over the roar. 'Not the only people qualified to do this work.'

The professor seemed to blame Dave for this.

'What did you just say about the Grim?' Heath asked. 'You

mentioned them earlier, too. Do they use crossbows?'

'The Grymm,' Dave said, unconsciously rolling the 'r' and drawing out the 'm', which he punctuated with a slight, guttural 'ugh'. 'They got a lot of religious hang-ups,' he added for no reason he particularly understood.

'The Grim? Dave?'

He admonished himself silently. He was concentrating so fiercely on trying to extract something useful from his monsterpedia that he didn't notice how intently everybody was looking at him, including the academics and Allen.

'Sorry,' he said aloud. 'I forget. Yeah, the Grymm. Another smaller clan, much smaller than the Hunn and Fangr in numbers but much better trained. Well, okay, they train, which sets them apart. Makes them unique, actually. They might use crossbows; I'm not sure when. I didn't exactly get the Einstein of the UnderRealms here.'

He closed his hands over the end of Lucille's shaft and rested his chin on them, allowing his mind to wander where it might tell him something about this new class of horrors he hadn't thought much about before.

'They're the palace guard too. Of the queen.'

Ashbury stared at him.

'There's a queen?'

He nodded.

Professor Compton spoke up. Unsurprisingly, he seemed even more pissed with Dave.

'And you didn't think to provide us with this information earlier?' Compton snapped. 'Do you have any idea what the existence of that sort of hierarchical authority implies, of the societal complexity needed to evolve such a structure? Quite likely this entity is broken into factions that can be exploited if we can properly understand them, much in the same way we're able to understand different tribes in Iraq. You should have told us this information sooner.'

'You didn't ask!' Dave shouted back. 'Listen, I'm not a fucking soldier or a professor; I work on the rigs. I got the *Encyclopedia Satanica* jammed into my fucking head. How am I supposed to know what you think you need out of it? Do you shout at your textbooks when they don't volunteer information for you?'

'Secondary source material yields answers with ease to those who are functionally literate,' Compton shot back.

'With that charm I'll bet you were able to get all sorts of firsthand information from folks in Iraq,' Dave shouted back, using the uproar of engines and rotors as an excuse to yell into Compton's face. 'I know I sure want to tell you everything I know.'

'This isn't helping, Professor Compton,' Ashbury said.

Compton was sitting against the rear bulkhead, like Dave, but Ashbury had placed herself between them before take off. The anthropologist leaned forward to eyeball Dave, who didn't bother moving his unfocused gaze from where it had settled in the middle distance.

'Hooper. Listen to me. This is important. We're flying into a hostile contact with these things, and you're holding back information.'

'I'm not holding back anything,' he said. 'If you want to know, you have to ask the right question. Engineers understand that basic concept, but apparently they don't teach that in remedial anthropology. It isn't like quoting game day stats for the Dallas Cowboys.'

Dave could feel the tension rising in the cabin.

'What do you want to know?' he asked finally. 'I answered all your stupid questions and you didn't ask anything about queens or social complexes or anything. You asked about the Fangr's toilet habits, Professor, not their royal fucking family.'

A couple of the SEALs turned their hard eyes on Compton but then divided their hostility to include Dave as well. They looked unimpressed with all the civilians on their helicopter.

Compton continued, undeterred by Dave's anger or the SEALs' disapproval.

'That sort of information can tell us how they organise themselves, you idiot. About whether they need to organise themselves. Do they live in cities? Do they self-organise like a hive, or have they evolved more complicated systems of consent and control? What about logistics – how do they feed and supply themselves? What about their political structures? Their economy? It's important if we have to fight them, and we almost certainly will, in a very short time. We need a deep understanding of them or we're going to have an Iraqi quagmire in our own backyard.'

'Oh, really? I thought you solved Iraq.'

It was assholes like this who had gotten his brother killed. Before he could stop himself, Dave made to reach for Compton with half a mind to fling him out the open door of the Seahawk, but Ashbury's hand reached his and short-circuited the thought process. He shook off the impulse, but it left him feeling sick and hollow. And weird. It felt as though Lucille wanted Dave to snatch the man out of his harness and throw him out into clear space.

Twelve or thirteen magic pounds of hardwood and cold steel with a personality. A psychopathic personality.

Awesome.

Although he could hardly blame her in this case. Compton was a dick.

He shook his head again, rejecting the crazy idea of Lucille the splitting maul as someone real.

'Jesus, just stop it, would you,' Ashbury said in a tight voice, 'You're behaving like a couple of jerks, which I totally understand because you *are* a couple of fucking jerks, but –'

'I think, Emmeline, that this fellow is leading us into more trouble than you can imagine,' Compton shouted back at her.

'I'm not leading you anywhere,' Dave said. 'I haven't even got one of your stupid Xbox headsets.'

But Compton was working himself into a state and wasn't interested in being talked down.

'And we don't know what's inside your head, Hooper. Or how or why it got in there. We don't know whether we can trust you. There's nothing, absolutely *nothing* to say you haven't been assimilated or co-opted by these things. You say yourself they're in your head. If so, why are we even listening to you?' he asked.

Dave's anger might have returned, but the guy was so obviously shitting himself under all the bluster that it was hard not to feel some pity for him. Hard but not impossible.

'This is not what I signed on for,' Compton protested loudly into his headset. Dave had no idea who he was talking to, or yelling at, really.

Igor the giant extended his forefinger at the end of a long, meaty arm straight into Compton's face, forcing the smaller man back and leaning forward as the academic gave ground.

'Compton, this is exactly what you signed on for. You tucked Uncle Sam's greasy dollar into your G-string, and now you're gonna do a little pole dance for him. So unless you got something useful to add, I'd suggest you close your pie hole and let us get into character. We've had no chance to prep beyond a five-minute brief that sounded like an elevator pitch for the fucking *Evil Dead*. Nobody needs your hysterical pre-game bullshit. So I will ask you: Do you have anything useful to add to our brief, Professor?'

'How dare you? I'm in charge here!'

'Of nothing,' Igor replied. 'Captain Heath is in operational command, so sit your candyass back and shut the fuck up before I shut you up.'

The professor leaned back against the bulkhead, folded his arms across his chest, and went quiet, staring out the open hatch into the night sky.

Zach Allen shook his head at Igor. 'Little harsh, dude.'

'Don't tell me you weren't thinking the same thing,' Igor, unrepentant, said.

Zach turned to Professor Ashbury. 'Do you have anything for us?'

To Dave it looked just like the better half of a good-cop, bad-cop routine. And he'd been on the business end of a couple.

'Dave is your best source of ready information,' Ashbury said. 'I can give you better answers if we have enough time, but it appears we do not.'

'You mind if I ask if you have a plan?' Dave said.

'We're going to deploy about a mile out from the incident. At Touro Infirmary,' Allen said, making eye contact with Compton while he explained things to Dave. 'We'll patrol in. Aggressively. State police and NOPD SWAT will guide us there.'

Igor spoke up again. 'Hey, Compton, you won't be coming with us. So feel free not to piss your pants now.'

Allen's intervention restored some calm to the cabin. Not

that the SEALs had been in open rebellion. Nobody besides Igor had even spoken during the set-to between Dave and the academic, which he found amazing. If he'd been flying into a shit fight with a dozen or so of his guys from the rig, they'd have landed the chopper surrounded by a little cartoon storm cloud with lightning bolts and fists and the occasional comic *BIFF!* coming out of it.

The SEALs checked their gear, pointedly ignoring the fracas. For his part, Compton folded back in on himself, muttering something of no consequence.

'Ten minutes,' said the pilot, Dave guessed, the voice crackling over the intercom.

Dave could see the coastline. New Orleans was a smear of light through the bubble canopy at the front of the chopper. The Mississippi River curled around the city, bringing to mind the childish notion of a castle protected by a moat. Barges and other vessels made their way up and down the river, oblivious to any peril that might befall them. Water was no barrier to the creatures of the UnderRealms.

The city of Mardi Gras and spring break hotties seemed remarkably tame and quiet from the open door of the Seahawk. No explosions lit up the night. No jets flew in low to attack swarms of Sliveen or Grymm, Fangr or Hunn. No flaming pyres were in evidence, no blood pots overflowing with tribute for the Low Queen.

Blood.

Tribute.

Dave was positive he was forgetting something important. Or worse, as Emmeline had said earlier, he needed to know something but didn't know what to ask himself. Lucille was definitely humming now. Singing to him. The vibrations thrumming up his arms and into his neck were starting to give him a low-grade headache, a bit like a six-beer hangover.

'Hey, Dave.'

He dropped back into reality, such as it was. Allen leaned forward to talk to him. If possible, he looked like he was carrying even more weapons than on the trip out to the Longreach.

'S'up, Chief?'

'The profs gave us a pretty basic briefing package about the likely vulnerabilities of those things you killed. But a few of us were wondering if you had any advice. You know, where to aim. That sort of thing. They've got more than one heart, right? Will they keep going if we put a round through the big ticker but not the backup?'

Compton looked as though he wanted to answer, but Allen turned a shoulder to shut him out. Even in the darkness of the cabin, with the chief's face blackened by camouflage paint, Dave could see the concern in his eyes.

'And like, how fast are these things?' Igor asked. 'I heard they're like fucking cheetahs over open ground.'

Dave really was the centre of attention now.

Compton was ticked off but quiet. Ashbury licked her lips and seemed nervous on Dave's behalf. The fighting men in the chopper all hung on his response.

'Just gimme a moment, would you?' he asked.

Dave Hooper closed his eyes and breathed out slowly. Then in. Slowly. It was some bullshit yoga thing Annie had tried to teach him years ago. When she decided he needed to find an alternative to calming himself down with a couple of fingers of Jack Daniel's every night.

He hadn't stuck with it, of course. It made him feel like a dick. The yoga, not the Jack. But he had to find a way to clear his thoughts so that he could concentrate, and there was no bar service on the Seahawk. He was still just learning to search the Hunn memory. It didn't come with an index. But he found it did come easier if he didn't force things. Pushing too hard could lead him down any number of blind alleys.

What would Urgon do? He tried to imagine fighting the Hunn as a Hunn. As a member of the Horde. What would he do? Where would he strike?

. . .

. . .

. . .

He opened his eyes.

'Unless you got a clear shot at the face or you're packing armour-piercing rounds, the head isn't such a great target,' he said. 'Not on the Hunn, the big ones, and definitely not on a BattleMaster Hunn, who you won't miss because they're even bigger. But the nasal cavity is a weak spot. And the throat. And there's a bunch of vital organs down the lower left of the torso. If I was gonna hit one of them, that's where I'd aim. The hide is thinner, and the bone cage around the body mass sort of peters out above that. They'll be armoured there because of it. But it'll be boiled leather and maybe some mail or plating.'

'Armour?' one of the SEALs asked with real doubt in his voice. He seemed very young.

'It's not like a vest, son,' Dave explained. 'It's not meant to stop penetrating strikes, more to deflect slashes and swipes with edged weapons. So don't go getting into any knife fights with them.'

He was serious, but it brought forth a few appreciative grins from the commandos who sported their fair share of cutlery on their vests and belts. Gallows humour, he supposed.

'So, if you got armour-piercing rounds, that's good. And tracers, too. They hate fire.'

'Way ahead of you,' Allen said. He tapped his ammo pouches. 'Prof's orders. Got us some tungsten polycarbonate rounds mixed in with tracer. That ought to do it.'

'And Willy Peter,' Igor said, fingering something shaped like a soda can on his equipment vest.

'Make you a believer!' chorused a couple of his squad mates.

'Willy who?'

'White phosphorous,' Allen explained. 'Burns like the devil's own curried egg farts.'

'What about the smaller ones?' somebody asked. 'The fangers?'

'*Fangr,*' said Dave, drawing out the second syllable. 'They're faster than Hunn. But easier to kill. Smaller, weaker. But there's more of them, and they run in packs. Three or four, controlled by a Hunn dominant. Hose 'em down if you got the time and distance.'

Professor Ashbury nodded. 'We examined one of them first. They are definitely vulnerable to small arms fire: multiple redundant organs but none of them well protected. No evidence of armour or tools among them. Dave, they tend to rely on their claws and their fangs, correct?'

'Definitely.' Dave nodded, happy for some useful assistance while Compton sat with his arms crossed. If he didn't know better, he'd have sworn the professor was pouting.

He had a sudden moment of recall from his own life for once.

'You remember that dinosaur movie. *Jurassic Park*? You remember the sneaky little dinosaurs?'

'Raptors,' Ashbury supplied.

'Yeah, them,' Dave agreed. 'The Fangr are just like them. They'll tag-team you and try to flank you. One suddenly pops on your left, shoot right first. Cover each other.'

'Then they'll rely on speed and their strength?' she asked.

'Yes. Don't try going to a hand-to-hand brawl with them,' Dave said. 'They'll pull you apart like a Tyson chicken.'

He could see a few of them repeating the advice to themselves over and over.

'Five minutes to the X.'

They were over the city now, just under the few remaining storm clouds and thunderheads. It was a terrible night to be flying. A section of the metro area was blacked out and emergency vehicles seemed to be speeding everywhere, but that might have been normal for New Orleans.

'Thanks,' Allen said, tapping the side of his boot against Dave's.

Hooper leaned forward to ask him a question. With the change in angle he saw just how much air traffic seemed to be up tonight.

'What's the X?' he called out. 'Is that like on a map?'

Compton closed his eyes and shook his head.

'Like on a map,' Allen agreed. 'The X is the target. Used to be we'd assault there, on top of the enemy. Vertical envelopment. Kick down the door, go in hard.'

'Like in that movie about the army guys in Africa, right?' Dave asked.

'Rangers, yeah. Right,' Allen said in a way that sounded a lot like 'Rangers, no, fuck off'. 'Anyway, Iraq taught us differently. Now we like to insert farther away and walk in. Quietly. Sometimes so quiet that we'd be standing over their beds before they knew it.'

'But we're not doing that tonight?'

Allen smiled. 'I'm not sure what we're doing tonight. Other than what you've given us, we can't get clear intelligence. We've got reports of everything from rabid animals to escaped apes eating people in Central City. We don't have a clear picture of what is happening at all,' he said. 'Fog of war.'

'It is like they're beaming down from the fucking *Enterprise*,' Igor said. 'They could turn up anywhere, right?'

Dave shrugged. 'I'm sorry, man. That I don't know. Until today they were trapped underground. Or, in a different, sort of lower dimension, or something. I dunno. And I don't know if that barrier is completely gone or if there are just holes in it.'

At that moment, Dave saw the first explosion.

21

The solitary thresh had never known solitude. From the earliest sentient moments of clawing its way out of the egg into the seething tangle of its newly hatched nest mates, it had always known their thinkings and they had known its. The mind of the nest was as much a part of its existence as the dark ichor running through its body or the pus oozing from its hide. To be without the thinkings of its nest mates, even just the one with whom it had squeezed through the rent in the barrier to the Above, was as painful as a shaft of daylight falling across its face.

Not that the thresh had ever seen daylight, of course, but the nest legends spoke of it in tones of awe and horror. And the thresh could understand why. Even the bright moonlight that had kissed its hide shortly after it emerged from the ooze at the bottom of the flooded caves had set its bright opalescent pus tingling. And from what it remembered of legend, moonlight was nothing more than the merest reflection of sunlight. Oh, what horrors must await the thresh caught on its own and staked out by men to meet the dawn as told of in the tales whispered to newly hatched nestlings.

No errant beam of moonlight had shattered the skull of

its nest mate, however. That had been some arcane magick of the Above. It remembered the nest mate rubbing its forehead, disgruntled and snarling from tripping over the ruined masonry. It remembered.

A flash of lightning.

A thunderclap.

A searing white, hot spike of pain that ended abruptly with the very sinews of sentience shredded into bloody mush.

The solitary thresh felt its ichor run cold at the memory.

No matter what thinkings the thresh thought of, it could not reconcile the fate of the slaughtered nest mate with what it knew of Above. No myth or legend spoke of magick that tore thresh apart with the violence of sunbursts. It was certainly not the lesser hazard of falling moonlight that had taken its mate, for what little moonlight there had been had most agreeably disappeared shortly after they'd arrived. The work of Sky Lords, no less.

The floor of the flooded cave system under the calfling settlement was a treacherous place, rotten with a maze of tree roots and sucking ooze and hard rocks that banged and scraped the hide as the thresh fumbled about under the surface of water that ran thick with human waste. With a gut full of fermenting Man blood it could stay submerged for very long periods, but even so the creature was beginning to feel the burn in its lungs as it searched anxiously for the passage below. The torment of solitude was greater, however, calling it back to the nest, where it no longer would be alone with its own thinkings.

A splash a short distance away startled the thresh and almost drew it back to the surface for an unnecessary breath of air. Forcing itself to swim lower, the thresh might have cursed the fickle nature of the Sky Lords had it not immediately swum under a smooth arch of rock and found itself at the site of the breach. The thresh praised the Sky Lords for leading it there and offered abject grovelling thinkings in recompense for having doubted them. When it kicked down for the floor of the cavern, its claws soon found the thick, gluey mud littered with the bodies and bones of small surface-dwelling creatures that sank down to decay in the ooze.

With a silent cry of triumph it drove its claws in deep and pulled itself down. The mud closed around its head, and for the briefest moment panic threatened to overwhelm the daemon inferiorae, but the choking claustrophobic feeling quickly cleared as the thresh found itself emerging up through the floor of one of the sulphur pools in a cavern a short scuttle away from the nest it had left earlier.

Instantly the soothing balm of the nest mind spread over it. The chattering, skittering thinkings of its nest mates, the slower more considered ponderings of Threshrendum superiorae and nest elders, and beneath them all the slow hot beat of the infinitely vaster and all but imponderable mind of the Low Queen. She of the Horde.

The thresh let go of all the pent-up fears and questions and shock and horror and awe and delight and wonder at everything it had experienced with its slain nest mate since they had stalked the minion all the way into the Above. This unexpected outburst of thinkings and feelings spread out through the nest in a wave of propagating shock. Hatchlings, newly broken through the shells of their eggs, ceased to tear and rake at one another, winnowing out the weakest of their litter. Nest elders stood staring at one another in blank disbelief at the thresh's memory of the Above, a place none but the queen herself had seen. Hunn dominants murmured darkly at each other, skinning back thin lips from fangs and flexing long talons at the whispers of the minion that had stolen into their realm before somehow finding its way Above.

Shame upon unutterable shame suffused the collective mind of the warrior class that they should have been so humbled. First by a minion that avoided their watch and then by a thresh of so few years that had stalked the minion into the very Above, slaughtered the filth, and returned with a belly full of tribute. Returned also with a worrying memory of inexplicable and hostile magick.

The nest in its entirety released a silent gasp at the memory of the thresh that had died Above for no apparent reason. The survivor hurried down and down through the honeycombed tunnels toward the heart of the nest, encountering more of its kind the closer it got. Talons clacked and scratched at dripping walls as Threshrendum hissed and snarled quickthinking praise on the young adventurer for its triumphant return. Beneath their thoughts, however, the thresh also knew their hunger for the meat fermenting in its belly, jealousy that one so low might now be raised higher in the thinkings of the queen, and fear and even disbelief at the recall of that moment when the other thresh had died. The prodigal daemon increased its speed, not conscious of any plans but driven by a need to return to the deepest, safest part of its nest, where it might sit and share its thinkings with those who might just understand them. Just outside the central chamber, where tunnels from all over the Horde realms converged, its progress was stopped by a short, simple command that landed in its mind like the hammer blow of a BattleMaster of Hunn.

Attend to your queen, now, thresh. Guardians Grymm! Bear forward my tribute and attend.

The thresh staggered under the force of its monarch's will. The press of daemonum that had been gathering around it, slowing its approach to the heart of the nest, all but dissolved as two Grymm warriors, standing at least thrice as tall and noticeably thicker in limb and longer of fang and talon, appeared beside it. They did not restrain the thresh, did not even seize it, in fact. They may well have snapped off a limb had they done so. Instead, the two formidable killers took up an escort position on either side and began to move forward, carrying the thresh along with them and parting the crowd by force of will.

They passed into and through a grand chamber of the nest, where a host of curious daemonum sniffed the air and observed the returning hero with shining black eyes and jaws agape. The small party hastened on through the crowd, past the communal blood pots, and on into a wide channel at the rear of the chamber that climbed away to one of the queen's private parlours.

Fear licked like flames at the edge of the thresh's thinkings as the small party approached their ruler and progenitor. The thresh was aware of an uneasy silence falling over the nest behind it as it climbed into the small winding tunnel leading to her chambers. All would be aware of what had happened, of where it had been, and none could understand. The Above had been barred to their kind for so long that some even doubted its existence. Not individually, of course. To question the memory of the nest and, more important, the queen would never do. Such insolence could only end in the blood pot. But if one sat in one's cave very quietly and opened one's thinkings as wide as possible, one could just detect a faint stirring of doubt, almost beyond perception. Doubt, perhaps, in the idea of ever returning to the Above rather than doubt in its existence at all.

Yes, thought the thresh. That was how it would prefer to imagine any such lack of faith should the queen question it on the matter.

The queen's thoughts grew oppressively strong as they approached some of the innermost chambers. The thinkings and feelings of its nest mates, all of them, seemed to be crushed out of its mind by her presence. As though she filled the thresh completely with her power and her knowing. By instinct, the thresh dipped its head and fell to the floor in supplication as they entered. On either side of it the Praetorian Grymm likewise went down, retracting fang and talon and dipping their heads, baring their necks for a killing stroke.

– *You have tribute.*

The queen's voice rumbled in the thresh's mind like the grinding of tectonic plates. The thresh abased itself, sliding even closer to the hard rock floor of the chamber.

– *Attend me, thresh, and allow me to sup of this tribute that I might judge its worth and your fate.*

The thresh cautiously inched forward, a little too cautiously, earning it a kick in the rear from one of the warrior attendants. That was enough to send it scuttling forward until a thought from the queen brought it to a halt. The thresh concentrated and heaved, regurgitating the better part of the meal it was carrying in both of its stomachs. It retched and retched, emptying its guts lest there be any question that it had not rendered full tribute. So fulsomely did it vomit up the fermenting remains that its vision blurred and the room began to spin.

It felt the presence of the queen in its mind, stroking it and calming its fears as only a mother could.

– *You have done well, nestling. I can smell the rotting hide of the minion you defeated. Praise be to you for your victory. And praise, too, for this gift of sweetmeat. It has been an age since we last fed on this delicacy.*

The thresh was aware of movement in the dim red-lit cavern as something immense and powerful shifted in the gloom and dragged itself forward. It felt vibrations in the bedrock as the queen pulled herself toward the steaming pile of human offal. It could sense fear leaking out of the closely guarded minds of the Grymm on either side of it and wondered how much of its own abject awe and terror they sensed by mere observation. Possibly none. The Grymm remained kneeling with heads bowed down. The queen alone knew its thinking now. Jaws distended with a wet creaking sound, and one of her tongues shot out with a rasp, scooping up the pile of remains in one motion. The thresh felt her satisfaction, indeed her pleasure, at the meal as its own. It sensed regret at the meagre provisions but excitement at the prospect that she might feast properly soon.

– *There were others, you said.*

The thresh was almost paralysed by the majesty of her presence, but she insinuated soothing feelings into its mind and the small daemon was seized by a new and unexpected confidence.

– *Yes, Majesty. Another of the Men. Larger and darker of flesh. We attempted to take it, but my nest mate was destroyed by strange magicks.*

It felt the queen's scepticism at its thinking but knew that she could not deny the clarity of its memories. She knew its thinkings and feelings as though they were her own, and she could see in her own mind how the other thresh had been destroyed as they moved forward to seize the prey. The thresh had the unprecedented and wholly unsettling experience of examining the memory with the queen, pondering it with some of her reflected intelligence and her vast accumulated store of knowledge and lore. It learned more of men in that brief moment than it would have learned in a lifetime of listening to stories around the blood pot.

Men, it learned, had pleaded with their gods to spare them. From all the sects daemonum. And most especially from the blood pots of the Horde, the mighty Hunn and leashed Fang and the heavy claw of the Grymm. For whatever reasons the gods had seen fit to separate the realms, turning daemon on daemon for millennia. Of men's world now, the queen knew nothing. But she well remembered them as feeble creatures. Not enemies, just food. They had no magicks. They cowered in caves and behind trees waiting to be eaten. They lashed together thin branches to shelter them from the sky and beat useless implements out of soft metals. Iron was unknown to them. Pushed to extremes, they might fight to preserve their young. But nowhere in her memory, which stretched back across oceans of time, had any men ever conjured up magick enough to reach out and slay a daemon in such fashion.

The thresh had the merest idea that the Sky Lords may have separated the realms for that very reason: lest men and their beasts be hunted out. It also knew the contempt of Her Majesty for such thinkings. Who were the Sky Lords to banish them? But just as important, where were these gods now that the barrier between the realms had been breached? The thresh was just beginning to get an inkling of its monarch's thinkings on the matter when she withdrew from its mind and it found itself prostrated on the stone floor with only its thin and meagre thinkings and the silence of the Grymm guardians for company.

As it lay exhausted and sickened, it retained but one clear memory of the privileged violation.

It had not been her only servant to pass through the barrier. Her Majesty knew of others. Some great change was upon the world.

When next it heard Her Majesty's thoughts, they came at a remove, not arising within the thresh's own mind as before but arriving within it as she spoke to all of them.

– This shall not stand. We shall not be mocked thus. Not by the likes of men. My captains ur Hunn and ur Grymm, you shall gather the necessary forces and return to the Above with this thresh if the path lies open still. You shall secure our passage there. You shall learn the nature of these magicks that destroyed our nestling, and you shall lay our vengeance on those responsible. Come hence to me when these things are done and I shall make due preparations for my return to the world of men.

22

The Seahawk put down on the hospital helipad, and the SEALs poured out of the cabin to ring the aircraft. Christ knew what they were expecting to fight off, but they were all ready for it. Down on one knee, lying prone on the concrete, scanning left and right, the sky, the small structure where the local police officers waited. Compton, Ashbury, and Dave followed them.

As the big bird took off, Dave watched four more aircraft, weird airplane-helicopter-looking hybrids, orbiting the hospital. 'Ospreys,' Ashbury said when he asked what the double-bladed machines were. A couple of faster-looking helicopters had joined the transports, bedecked with an assortment of weapons.

Gunships, Dave thought. For sure.

Captain Heath keyed his mike and ordered the marines to await further instructions. The noise from so many aircraft was enormous. Louder than anything Dave had ever heard on a rig.

Dave felt as anxious and unsettled as he had when each of his sons was born. He'd known the world was changing then, too, the world of Dave at least. And it was one of those things he'd never told anyone, certainly not Annie, but he didn't expect the change to be all for the better.

He felt the same worry gnawing at him now. He wanted to call it free-floating anxiety because a hot psych major he'd balled in college had said that once and he'd liked the sound of it. It seemed to explain a lot of shit, especially about the hot psych major. But when he examined the feeling, there was nothing free-floating about it at all. Nor was it a sensible reaction to the circumstances.

He looked at Marty's splitting maul, which he held with both hands.

Lucille.

It was this fucking thing; he was sure of it. Lucille ached to be buried deep in the broken bone and flesh of the Horde.

'Not going to land them?' Dave asked, nodding at the choppers, as much to distract himself as anything.

'Can't land them on this.' Captain Heath gestured at the pad. It was way too small. 'No sense putting them here when they're faster in the air. I'll keep them as a reserve until I know what's going on. I've got so many conflicting reports, it's hard to know what we're dealing with.'

Bent over, with the ferocious downdraught trying to knock them off their feet, the odd, disparate group shuffled over to meet the locals. The police captain gave Dave and Lucille a doubtful once-over but said nothing.

'You Captain Heath?' the man shouted. He looked to be in his fifties, with a small potbelly and thinning silver hair. He'd taken off his NOPD baseball cap to avoid losing it to the rotor wash.

Heath introduced himself and the two professors but not Dave. Or Lucille.

'Captain Eichel,' the cop yelled over the roar of the choppers. 'Len Eichel, Sixth District, NOPD. We're glad to have you boys with us, sir.' Eichel couldn't help taking another glance at Dave. Though Dave was dressed in camouflage trousers and body armour, his grey hoodie and the growing tufts of decidedly unmilitary hair on his head marked him out as different even among the SEALs, who took a relaxed approach to their appearance. The splitting maul didn't help matters, either. The two eggheads didn't draw the police officer's attention in the same way.

'What is the situation, Captain?' Heath shouted. 'My briefing was pretty spare about details on the ground.'

'On the ground, under it. All over,' said Eichel. '911 is jammed with calls, and my people are having trouble sorting them all out. I'm getting reports of these things between Toledano and Martin Luther King Jr Boulevard. So far, aside from prank calls, there's nothing outside of Sixth District that I know of.'

'Describe them,' Heath said.

'They're like rabid people-eating dinosaur apes or something,' Eichel said. He consulted a notebook for a moment. 'Hairless gorillas. The pig monsters from *Star Wars*. The bad guy from *Galaxy Quest* –'

Heath cut Eichel off. 'Okay. Do you have firm numbers?'

'No, I haven't been able to get that yet,' Eichel said. 'What the fuck are they? Some sort of experiment gone wrong? Is that why you're here? 'Cause those Greenpeace guys been saying on the news that this –'

'They're dangerous. But we can take them,' Heath said, cutting him off. 'Is that good enough for you?'

'It'll have to do for now, won't it?' Eichel said with a sour expression that sort of impressed Dave. This guy was pissed, but he wasn't going to dick around. He just wanted to deal with the problem. Understanding what the problem was could wait.

'I can brief you on the way down,' Eichel said. 'We've got armoured transport can take you right into Central. Roads are lousy with traffic coming out. Vehicles. People on foot. It's a damned mess. There's a lot of armed civilians down there, too. Most of the fire you can hear is from them, not my teams.'

As the choppers departed, Dave was able to hear the crackle of gunfire that had been masked by their presence. A lot of gunfire.

Heath pushed a button on his headset and issued orders to get off the roof. A moment later Allen and the monster SEAL called Igor began moving among the SEALs, not shouting, just quietly directing them away from the roofline and toward the little concrete structure housing the stairwell that would take them down.

'Captain Eichel, we will need a firm estimate of how many hostiles we're dealing with. Not an exact number. Just a good estimate.' It was Ashbury, with her finger poised over a small, glowing iPad in a ruggedised case.

'Hostiles? Is that what we're calling them?'

'Well, they're pretty bloody hostile, I think you'd agree.'

Eichel nearly stumbled on his feet as they rushed down the stairs. 'That they are, Ms. And no, as I told your captain, we have no idea. It's an unholy bedlam down Central. I got four officers down already. Hospital here's overwhelmed with civilian casualties, mostly gunshot wounds. But there are some bad ones, too, people with animal bites on them. And there's thousands more on the streets, heading out across the rest of the city.'

'Dave?' Professor Ashbury said. 'You got anything?'

'Nada,' he answered quickly before thinking of something.

'Captain . . . er, Eichel. How long since your first calls came in? How long these things been running around, you think?'

The SEALs' boots hammered on the concrete below.

'Who are you?' the cop asked, eyeing the big maul Dave carried over his shoulder.

'Consultant engineer,' Heath said before Dave could say anything.

Eichel wasn't convinced, but he had to take Heath's word for it.

'We had initial reports of a vehicular accident on Toledano, possible driver under the influence. That became a report of a rabid animal eating the driver and an escaped ape killing a bystander.'

Eichel shook his head. He'd obviously seen a lot in his years, but this . . .

'And it's not even a full moon. When our officers arrived, they found two of these . . . things eating someone in front of a McDonald's. Shots fired, which bagged one of the bastards. The other ran off,' Eichel said, half out of breath, sweating with stress and exertion.

They stopped on a landing for just a moment lest the overweight policeman had a heart attack. He caught his breath and motioned for them to move on. Dave recognised Eichel's distress. It had been all too familiar to him until a day or so back. He was a big man, once powerful and still strong, but too many hours behind a desk sucking down bad coffee and free doughnuts had done its worst. The wheezing pant as Eichel sucked in breath, the high colour on his cheeks – yeah, Dave Hooper recognised all that. One hand went down to his own stomach. Flat and hard.

As they started moving again, though, Dave felt just a

touch weaker. Maybe a little light in the head and shaky on his feet. He pulled out an energy bar and chewed without joy or even much relief.

Eichel continued between breaths: 'That was hours ago. Everything was starting to calm down. We had someone from the university coming out to look at the thing we shot down. Then a bunch of these medievalist-type bow and arrow bastards come boiling up out of the ground.'

'I need firm numbers on how many we're dealing with. What you thinking, Dave?' Heath asked.

Hooper answered that by asking Eichel another question.

'Central City? Is it crowded? I don't know New Orleans that well. Central City sounds like an office park. Did it flood in Katrina? Is it, you know, abandoned?'

Another flight of steps.

'Oh, hell, no,' Eichel told him. 'No offices there. It's residential. Must be 20,000-plus live down there. A busy part of town for us most nights. Although a lot of the locals seem to be getting the hell out now. Why?'

Dave shifted Lucille from one shoulder to the other as he rounded another landing. She was starting to get heavier, and even though it was bullshit crazy, he'd have sworn she felt sullen or even despondent. Not that he'd be saying anything like that right now. Not to this police captain. He directed his answer at Heath and Ashbury.

'It's just a guess,' he said, 'but I don't think they'll have spread out too far yet. With that much prey packed in so tightly, the Hunn will feed. They won't be able to help themselves. It'll be like sharks in a frenzy. If there's any Sliveen, they'll be more disciplined, spread out individually in a loose circle around the raiding party. You'll have to watch for them.'

Captain Eichel regarded him with frank disbelief.

'Son, what flavour of crazy are you?'

'Minty fresh,' Dave said as he rummaged through his memories again. 'Of course, it could be a small hunting party, like back at Longreach. There might only be a few of them.'

'A suggestion,' Professor Ashbury spoke up. 'Dave, you said they last recalled us as being pre-technological, correct?'

'Yeah, they were the ones with the technology,' Dave said. 'Such as it was. They haven't changed much.'

Ashbury nodded. 'They'll be experiencing their own culture shock at the changes that have occurred since their last encounters with humanity. That may give us an edge.'

'They could be off balance.' Heath nodded, then raised his voice just a notch without yelling. 'We have an opportunity here. Let's expedite, gentlemen!'

The tightly packed pod of military personnel increased its speed down the steps, all but carrying Eichel along with them. Dave had to marvel at Heath's agility on that robot leg. It must have been hell where the metal joined the flesh. Compton, he noted as he turned on a landing, had drifted to the rear of the pack, where he didn't have to move as quickly.

'Captain Eichel, can you get your patrol officers to disengage from any contact with the hostiles?' Heath asked. 'Get them to work clearing civilians from the area. You got a SWAT team out there?'

Eichel nodded and puffed. 'I've got two tactical platoons. One is at Sixth District station waiting for instructions. Other platoon's with me, here. Also got Louisiana state police SWAT in by helicopter.'

'If you would, detach them to us,' Heath said. 'I don't have formal authority, but it would be best if we worked together.'

'Done,' Eichel said. 'We can argue about the posse comitatus and invoicing later.'

That sounded like a joke, but it probably wasn't, thought Dave, who was a veteran of many small but vicious bureaucratic wars with both the feds and his own head office.

They arrived at a ground floor parking garage. Hundreds of people were crammed into the space, which had been transformed into a triage centre. Two armoured vehicles waited on the street outside. A quartet of Crown Victoria police cruisers were parked at odd angles to the stairwell with their doors open, officers standing outside or opening trunks to gather up body armour and weapons. Dave smelled blood and fear and a rich stink of human waste thick on the air. It was chaos. There was no order to the mob scene. Men and women with terrible wounds bled out, screaming on the tiles. Children in hysterics ran around or simply rolled themselves into tiny balls and hid wherever they might. Medical personnel in bloody scrubs, and in some cases street clothes, moved around, trying to bring order to the mess.

Dave almost barrelled into Emmeline Ashbury, who was brought up short by the spectacle.

'Watch where you're going, Thor,' she said.

He experienced the strange warping and stretching of time he recalled from the morning he'd thrown the weight bar into the air. Everyone around him was moving as though caught in taffy. He adroitly stepped around her to avoid a collision, and the world suddenly sped up again.

Ashbury jumped as though he'd popped into existence in front of her. She uttered a little cry of surprise, but the momentum of the SEALs pouring out of the stairwell and making for the nearest exit at a jog carried them along. Heath stepped over to the hood of the nearest cruiser and unfolded a map, scrutinised it for a moment, found what he was looking for, and gave orders to the helicopters above.

'Captain Eichel,' Heath said. 'I've got two Marine Corps Cobras in the air now. They'll scout the area for us and see if we can get eyes on the hostiles. In the meantime, I want your patrol officers, street cops, and any other non-SWAT assets to fall back and form a defensive perimeter.'

'Where?' Eichel asked. 'These things could be anywhere.'

Eichel took the map and quickly sketched out a ragged rectangle with his pen. 'Here's where we had our initial incident call. I haven't had any reports of these things west of Toledano or east of MLK Boulevard. South of Magnolia it gets hazy. Radio is spotty there. Always has been.'

'I'd say use those streets as your perimeter, then. That sound right, Dave?' he asked, turning to Hooper.

'If they stop to eat, yeah,' he said. 'And if they have limited access to the Above.'

'We'll have to plan on limited access by virtue of the fact that I don't have the resources to deal with them popping up everywhere. We'll work with what we have.' Heath turned back to Eichel. 'You decide where to bunker up. Let me know soonest.' Heath started to move his hands over the map, indicating where he wanted to deploy the human forces. Dave pulled up a little at that thought. Human forces? How the fuck had it come to this?

'Eichel, if you can assist in evacuating the civilians from this area,' Heath said, circling a four- or five-block diamond shape south of Claiborne. 'Meantime, my team will move north with your SWAT platoon. Hold the other platoon in reserve at the station until we have the hostiles spotted. Understand?'

'You got it,' Eichel said. 'You gonna call in the army? There's national guard here, too.'

'We're mobilising every available asset,' Heath said. 'But how many of your officers are also reservists and guardsmen?'

Eichel nodded. 'Point taken.'

'Yep,' Heath said. 'This will be over before the guard gets up on deck. As it stands, I have additional marines inbound from the *Bataan*, but their ETA is three hours at best. JSOC latest is that rangers and elements of the 82nd are en route, but that'll be even longer; twelve to eighteen hours is their best estimate.'

Oh, man, Dave thought. *You are going to need all of them and more before this is over. Small scouting parties lead to war bands which lead to Cohorts which form Talons and . . .*

Eichel took a deep breath. 'We're on our own, then.'

'For now,' Heath said. 'But we've got your back. It won't be like Katrina, I promise you.'

Allen came back from the street. 'Sir, it is pure chaos out there. We could take the vehicles, but it'd probably be quicker to move up on foot.'

'Fair enough,' Heath said, scrutinising the map again. 'Emma, what do you have on your feeds?'

Professor Ashbury set her tablet down on the hood of the car. A green-lit video stream from an airborne source highlighted a small party of creatures moving across an open lot. She brought the image out wide to show the surrounding roads.

'Louisiana Avenue is jammed with refugee traffic. But Toledano looks passable on foot,' she said.

'Let's move north quickly and in force,' Heath said, wrapping up the map. 'When we make contact, we'll try to fix them in place. Any questions?'

Dave found Heath at his side, a hand on his elbow.

'I need you to stick close to me, Dave. Don't go getting any ideas about charging off. I need you to tell me, as best you can, what's happening.'

'I got no fucking idea what's happening,' he said, trying to throw off the gathering depression that wanted to envelop him. He could feel every pound of Lucille on his shoulders now. They began to ache with the effort needed to carry her.

'But, er . . . Captain, if this is a scouting party, it'll just be like an advance group. You get that, right?' he said.

'Yeah. Come on,' Heath said. 'I'm sure as soon we make contact with the enemy, everything will become crystal clear. Let's go.'

Now, *that* was a joke, Dave knew.

They cleared the hospital with its scenes of Dark Ages horror and misery, emerging into a cool night in which the SEALs awaited them, arrayed in a large semicircle, weapons out. Two armoured personnel carriers, big eight-wheeled numbers in the white livery that made them look like ice cream trucks of the Apocalypse, stood growling and coughing diesel fumes around a crowd of police cruisers and civilian vehicles. Some of the SWAT officers worked with the regular cops to maintain some measure of control.

Allen nodded toward the traffic jam. 'See what I mean?'

If anything, the scene outside the hospital was worse than it had been inside. The crowd was thousands strong out there. Some streamed into the hospital grounds. Many were passing through and moving on. Still others looked to have set up camp with whatever they'd carried from home or possibly looted along the way. Music pounded from dozens of cars' sound systems. A couple of flares burned bright pink and green. Dave counted at least four separate brawls. He heard more gunfire, much closer this time, but it had no effect on the crowds.

The rear hatch of the nearest armoured car swung open, and a man in black coveralls hopped down to run over to them. He sought out Heath, introducing himself as Lieutenant Ostermann, NOPD SWAT.

'Sorry, sir,' Ostermann said. 'Road net is jammed up. It's a mile and a half from here.'

'Fine,' Heath said. 'We're good to leg it. Can you get your men disengaged?'

Ostermann nodded. 'Definitely; we're with you.'

Dave chewed on another energy bar and sucked a mouthful of Gatorade out of his CamelBak, trying to sift some useful advice from the trove of race memory and lore stored within his head. It was still hard to know what to look for when you didn't know what to look for. And it didn't help that Ashbury and Compton were deeply invested in their own distracting argument.

'They will need us,' she insisted.

'They'll have him,' Compton shot back, jerking a thumb in Dave's direction. 'You know the rules. We establish a reference point as far forward as possible but *not* in the combat operating post. We stay in contact –' He tapped a finger against his headset. '– but we don't *make* contact. We . . .'

She looked ready to slap him when Dave intervened.

'He's right, Prof. You don't want to be getting snuggly with these things.'

'I followed your advice,' she said defiantly, quickly drawing a pistol from a concealed carry holster at the small of her back. 'See?'

'What I see,' said Dave, 'is someone who is gonna get bitten in two. Listen to Professor Compton, would you? He's a professor and he has a neckbeard. You don't so he wins this round. Establish whatever it is you're establishing as far back from the Hunn as you can. And be ready to get the hell out of there, too.'

'Dave. These men haven't had a chance to study this problem at all. Five minutes. That's all the time we had to brief them back on the rig. And what you said on the flight in. Shoot here, here, and here,' she said, summarising the advice and pointing at her face, neck, and lower abdomen.

'I'll go with them,' Dave said. 'Whatever they need to know, I probably know already. But you don't. Unless one of these things wants to explain the role of plumbing in the social hierarchies of the Grande Horde,' he said, winking at Compton.

Heath cut the argument short by returning from his conference with Ostermann.

'Got a contact report from the local PD that's been verified by our Cobras,' Heath said. 'We're moving north to Magnolia Street.'

Heath looked to Dave then.

'Problems?'

Dave shook his head.

'I dunno, Heath. You know your own business. Your plan sounded all plausible and shit before. But you don't have a lot of guys, even with the marines and the SWAT dudes. You gonna be able to deal?'

'What will the Hunn do when they find out they're surrounded?' Heath asked.

He knew the answer to that without even having to reach for it.

'They attack. Everywhere. All at once,' he said, leaning against Lucille as if she were a gentleman's walking stick. 'They don't like being hemmed in. Drives them nuts.'

Heath thought it over.

'Actually, that is sort of what we would do; not so different from us, then. But we'd probe for a weakness and then concentrate. Let's at least go measure their strength,' he said. 'If it's a company of sword-wielding orcs, no problem. A battalion or more, well, I got some air support en route or on station.'

'Those choppers you had,' said Dave. 'Those big fucking Gatling guns could be handy. Leather armour ain't gonna help when those things open up.'

'They're refuelling,' Heath said. 'They'll be back. But I have Cobras and more assets inbound.'

He turned to the professors.

'If the two of you would set up here at Touro, I think that would be best,' he said. 'Any insights you can glean from the video feeds would be welcome. You can come up when NOPD has the resources to get you closer. Requisition a command truck or one of those armoured units if you have to. But get everything shipshape here first, because we'll fall back in this direction if we have to. If we don't have an engagement first.'

Neither of the academics looked happy, but for different reasons, Dave thought.

More gunfire erupted nearby, this time eliciting screams and drawing the attention of a couple of SEALs. Ostermann joined them after briefing his own people.

'We need to get going,' he said. 'T-Qube Suarez's crew just rolled on Magnolia.'

'Who? What?'

'T-Qube. Local notable. That's his turf down that way,'

Ostermann explained. 'Patrol says they're rolling in force.'

'Gangsters?' Heath asked.

'New Orleans' finest.'

'Great,' said the navy officer. 'That won't complicate things at all.'

He keyed his throat mike and sent orders out to both SEALs and marines on the command net.

Ashbury looked fit to be tied. Dave reached out to her, but she turned and stomped away, refusing to talk to anyone. He shrugged it off.

'Sure you don't want to come with us, Prof?' he asked Compton. 'You might get lucky. Catch one of these things taking a dump.'

23

A vanguard of Sliveen insisted on the honour of the First, as they always did. Pathfinders, they had forged past the thresh, confident about what they would find on the surface: prey. A pair of Hunn with their leashes of Fangr followed to provide support should the unexpected magicks of the prey prove difficult.

Thinkings and feelings, a slithering knotted mess of them, fought for the thresh's attention as it led the main body of the Queen's Vengeance through the honeycombed maze of tunnels and warrens back to the point where the barrier between the realms had come apart. It felt pride that the queen should have entrusted it to lead the warriors Above. Well, not that it was leading, of course.

The BattleMaster Urspite Scaroth Ur Hunn would lead the Dread Company of two augmented talons with the thresh to guide him. But one could not take from the thresh the fact that it took the field at the head of the Vengeance. So yes, pride was appropriate. And some fear, as it was surrounded and carried along by those very same warriors, any one of which could cleave the thresh in two with a single slash of talon or blade. Fear, too, that the passage Above might have collapsed, leaving it to look foolish as it scratched and skittered about in an increasingly desperate search for the breach. The warriors almost certainly would strike it down if it had misled them.

Two full Talon of Hunn and their attendant Fangr escorted the thresh, with the Queen's Choice of Grymm to represent her personal will. The thresh tried to think just how many they might number in total, but the thinking of a number increased by another number and then another was beyond it.

The thresh could see that there were many more warriors hurrying toward the breach. A formidable force indeed. Not a legion of course. Or a regiment. But neither were they as few as a simple cohort. And with the royal warrant to search out and fall upon the men of this village to exact Her Majesty's vengeance for the killing of a nest mate, they had, the thresh was sure, a sufficiency of talon and tooth and blade.

The warriors hunched over as the tunnel roof dipped lower, but the thresh, being considerably smaller, was able to remain erect while Urspite Scaroth Ur Hunn was all but doubled over. The thresh could see the subtle trail left by the scouting party of Sliveen and Hunn.

Urspite Scaroth Ur Hunn held up one clawed fist.

'Hold and prepare. We await the clawhold. We have not long to wait.'

The thresh tested the breach in the barrier and found it to still be there. It could sense the passage of the Sliveen and the Hunn through the opening. They were too distant for it to sense their thinkings, but they had found the breach with no trouble at all.

Just before they had reached the small, dank alcove where the thresh had earlier followed the minion through the rent in the barrier, a difficult and worrying thinking had arisen in the small mind of the creature. So much seemed different from what little it knew about men even as it retained some dim recall of Her Majesty's far greater knowledge and memories of them. The queen knew of men as feedstock. None had ever slain a daemon of the UnderRealms in open combat.

But the thresh had seen its companion destroyed before its very eyes. And the realms had been separated for so long. Was it possible that men had been gifted by their gods with new and powerful magicks? After all, the same gods had chosen to interfere with the natural order of things when they banished thresh and all the other clans and sects to the UnderRealms. Was the outrage done to its nest mate beyond even the thinking of She of the Horde . . . The thresh banished the thinking before it formed. That way lay the blood pot.

Still, it was worrying indeed and the thresh felt a great strain inside its skull when it tried to think of such things. Time passed without notice to the thresh as it struggled to control its dangerous ponderings.

It was all taking too long.

Urspite Scaroth Ur Hunn grew impatient. Glory was within reach Above, and surely his scouts would not linger beyond the time necessary to bring back a simple report of what lay ahead. The dominants gripped their spears and blades tightly, snarling and grunting as they waited for orders. They had been waiting for quite some time, in fact.

'Bring me the thresh.'

Hunn and attendant Fangr stood aside as one of the queen's own Lieutenants Grymm motioned the creature forward. The thresh cowered at the side of Scaroth, sensing the black mood falling across the commander's mind, as he saw the great taloned fists cracking and flexing with frustration.

'We wait no longer. You will lead, little one.'

The lieutenant pointed at the scummy, sulphurous pond. The thresh showed its fang tracks, and without so much as a grunt of warning it pitched forward.

Praise be to the Sky Lords, it seemed even darker than it had been the last time the thresh had emerged in this realm. The Above was unpleasantly cold.

With traces of the bloodwine still coursing through its veins, the thresh had no trouble staying submerged in the frigid waters of the flooded tunnel while it waited for the warriors to follow it through. One of Her Majesty's Lieutenants Grymm appeared first, shaking its snout vigorously as it pushed up through the mud. The thresh could not be certain, but it suspected that the Grymm was more than a little disoriented at the transition. It snarled, and the thresh hurried to abase its thoughts before the superior daemon.

The rent in the barrier was not large, and it took about as long for all of the members of the Dread Company to pass through as it might to pluck the spines from an urmin. As more of the host passed through, however, the tear appeared to grow wider so that the last revengers were able to pass through as a group rather than singly. That bore thinking about, the thresh decided. But later.

The tunnels under the village were not large, and all the Hunn were forced to stoop over. The shorter, thicker Lieutenants Grymm, too. Only the thresh and the Fangr could stand upright.

As the last of the warriors fought their way up through the mud, BattleMaster Urspite Scaroth Ur Hunn cast a single thought into the mind of the thresh.

'Lead on.'

Following the scent of the minion it had tracked on its last visit, the thresh pointed a talon up at the ceiling above, which was dripping with mud and wet where the sky above it could be seen through a crack. A great hammering noise could be heard, along with the wails of the creatureless chariots. The scent of slain calflings reached them all.

Urspite Scaroth Ur Hunn took a whiff of the air from Above, rage boiling from his thinkings. A light played over the hole to the Above that caused some of the host to scatter.

'Deprived of the first kill. There will be a reckoning.' Enraged, Urspite Scaroth Ur Hunn roared. 'Forward!'

24

The police got no respect in New Orleans. They frequently had to brandish their weapons at the very people they were trying to help. As Dave kept an easy pace with the trotting SEALs, he could hear the choppers whirling overhead. Not just police and military, either. There were at least three news channels up there, shining powerful searchlights down over Central City, as if to light their way. Heath and Ostermann cursed them.

'That's supposed to be a no-fly zone,' the SWAT leader complained.

Heath talked into his radio from time to time, giving brief instructions while keeping up a fast trot, his own rifle now to hand. Allen's four men were to the right of Toledano, and Igor the Giant's men were to the left. SWAT, for better or worse, had to stop and deal with one problem after another, then run to catch up with the SEALs.

'Captain?' Dave asked the naval officer.

'Yes?'

'You watch horror movies?'

'No,' Heath said with a visible effort to control his impatience. 'If you've got a point, Dave, I'd appreciate your getting to it.'

'Just seems to me that splitting up like this is a bad idea,' Dave said. 'In the movies it always goes badly.'

'This isn't a horror movie,' Heath said.

'Says you,' Dave scoffed.

'Look,' Heath explained. 'I'm not dividing my forces without reason. We have reserves. I can deploy them when I know where they'll do the most good. I have air assets I can call down if we get surrounded, cut off. Believe me, we've been doing this shit for years. And I need to leave some forces back at that hospital because if the Hunn roll over us anyway, they'll head straight there, won't they?'

'The all-you-can-eat buffet?' Dave said. 'For sure.'

'So we need some assets there to maintain a semblance of order and to rearguard the next evacuation if necessary.'

The crowds were thinning now, pushed south by police cruisers flashing their lights and using bullhorns to hurry everyone along as quickly as possible. This was a poor district. The SEALs and SWAT team jogged down long stretches of narrow one- and two-storey homes broken up by a surprising number of churches. Many of them, Dave was disturbed to see, were full of parishioners. Lights burned brightly, and hymns drifted out on the autumnal air. A good number of the homes, too, were alive and alight. Many seemed to be hosting impromptu parties. Ostermann peeled off to remonstrate with a couple of patrolmen who had demonstrably failed to convince the locals of the imminent danger they faced.

Another news chopper hammered low overhead.

'Flying to the X,' Allen called back over his shoulder.

Their journey north proceeded in fits and starts as the SEALs paused whenever they came to an intersection, with Allen or Igor holding up his fist to bring them to a halt. They would do a quick survey of the danger area, followed by the all clear and a resumption of the run. The pauses often allowed the SWAT team to catch up after dealing with its own unavoidable delays. Ostermann clearly didn't like stopping to defuse confrontations between gangs of young men or to get thick knots of dawdling civilians on the move again, but he had no choice. The gang brawls could quickly turn to shootings, and the slow shuffling mobs that stopped to watch them were forever threatening to block traffic or, Dave knew, attract a feeding frenzy.

He motored along at a steady trot, feeling as though he could keep up this pace all night, and he didn't doubt that Allen and the others could match his every step. It was Heath who impressed him the most, however. He could tell the man was favouring his good leg now, starting to drag the artificial limb a little, but he never slackened in his pace. Dave made a face at the idea of how uncomfortable it must be for him. That tender nub of flesh and bone pounding into whatever arrangement of steel, plastic, and padding marked the point where the body met the prosthesis.

They came across their first body lying in a pool of blood at Loyola and Toledano. An African-American male. As Allen's chalk established security around the intersection, guns out, backed up by SWAT, one of the SEALs approached the body cautiously, covering it with his weapon. He used a boot to roll the corpse over. There were three gunshot wounds to the chest.

Ostermann arrived at a trot, sweating heavily. He shook his head and flicked off some of the perspiration with one hand. Around them civilians stood on porches, sporting an assortment of weapons ranging from baseball bats and kitchen knives to double-barrelled shotguns and pistols. Dave took it all in, tasting the rain soon to come in the air, the fear and mistrust of the locals, and the waste of a life on the street. Nobody made a move to approach them, to explain what had happened. He wondered if one of the rubber neckers had cut the man down.

'Not our problem,' said Heath as the sound of distant gunfire echoed across the cityscape. 'Let's keep moving north.'

They resumed the long run, pushing on to Magnolia and turning east. Here the houses were even meaner and more dilapidated, often leaning over, surrounded by tall weeds. Small factories and warehouses, their functions often a mystery, took up double and sometimes triple allotments between the shotgun shacks. Dogs barked, sounding utterly feral.

The street was dark, illuminated by a burning car that had run into a power pole and the blue-white sparks of the fizzing, crackling power line that now snaked across the crumbling tarmac. Ostermann ordered one of his men to call it in to the power company. To get the grid shut down on this block.

Chief Allen appeared beside Dave as they gave the downed line a wide berth.

'How you doing, Dave? Hungry?'

'Not yet, Zach.'

'You'll want to keep your nutrition up, dude,' Allen warned. 'Metabolism will be running hot now. Keep it stoked.'

The SEAL passed him a couple of gel packs that Dave sucked down gratefully even though they were unpleasantly warm.

As Dave finished the second gel pack, he could hear the sounds of battle. Or slaughter. The screams of people being eaten alive. Animal cries as tooth and claw tore open flesh and shattered bone. He didn't want to, but he concentrated, homing in on one particular channel the way you might try to follow a single instrument in a song. He teased out something like the slurping sounds you heard in an Asian food court.

Noodles. Thick, wet noodles.

'Better hurry,' he told Heath. 'It sounds like a lot of critters ahead.'

'How many?'

Dave concentrated his hearing, trying to filter out the arguments, the sirens, a hundred cable channels of chaos. He could hear distinct chewing, bone-cracking sounds.

'Maybe a dozen, max,' he said. 'Could be a scouting party. If they stick to form, there'll be more of them soon.'

'A dozen's bad enough,' Heath said, pausing to talk into his mike.

The Cobras passed over their position. Captain Heath signed off his comm net. 'We've got eyes on targets north of Magnolia, but they're already inside the residential blocks. Between that and the civilian aircraft overhead, the gunships can't get a clean shot.'

Overhead, a pair of louder Ospreys roared through the darkness on their way north. One of the aircraft veered suddenly to get out of the bright white cone thrown down by the searchlight of a news helicopter above it.

Allen and a couple of the cops swore loudly.

'Ostermann?' Heath said, calm if somewhat exasperated. 'Seriously?'

The SWAT boss scrunched his flushed, sweating face into a furious mask before snarling into his headset.

'I don't care if you have to shoot them down; get those news choppers out of there. Now!'

As Dave tried to ignore screams and worse, he looked up

into the cloudy night sky, where civilian helicopters duelled with the military and the police for airspace. A soft rain began to fall. He thought about saying something to Heath about loitering on open ground. About having so few men with him. The Hunn and Fangr would charge them if they encountered the group. They'd leap right over the snarl of cars blocking the intersection of Magnolia and Washington, picking up speed across open ground.

But it was the searchlights that brought him up short.

'Captain?'

'Yes, Dave?' Heath said, exasperated. 'Let's move out,' he ordered everyone.

'They don't dig the light,' Dave said. 'Those spotlights will be freaking them out.'

'Noted.'

Another body lay in the street ahead, this one undoubtedly a victim of the creatures. They stepped around entrails crawling with ants and flies. A black man's unseeing face looked up at Dave, the throat ripped open. The sickly sweet stench of drying blood, shit, and urine filled his sinuses. He swore, blew his nose, and cleared his throat loudly.

The SEALs stopped and looked back at him. Again he was sure he felt Lucille trying to speak to him, to admonish him in some ultra-low-frequency hum that he felt in his hands as an unpleasant, almost electric sensation. It was nuts, but this stupid fucking sledgehammer was nagging him somehow. His body ached from the effort of carrying it. The discomfort reminded him of how his back used to hurt from carrying his boys around as toddlers. They got heavy quick. He realised he'd been cursing loudly only when Heath hissed at him.

'Dave!'

'I know, sorry, my bad,' Contrite Dave stage-whispered back. 'Be wery quiet. Hunting wabbits. I know. I'm on it.'

'You okay?' Allen asked, concerned.

Dave shook his head. 'I'm not sure. Let's just get on with this.'

Moving down both sides of the street, the shooters kept their weapons at the ready, searching the rooflines, the alleyways, and the deserted lots. The SEALs, he noted, kept their weapons trained on the few civilians who passed by. The SWAT guys lifted their barrels up, allowing them safe passage. Different strokes. Dave carried Lucille in both hands, ready to swing. Trash, discarded clothes, and occasional bodies slowed their movement, but only slightly, as they picked a path around the obstacles in the dark.

'You boys headed to the lot?'

The SEALs turned as one, muzzles zeroing in on a greying African-American man who stood in the doorway of Jazz's Po'boys. He held a shotgun much the same way a hunter might, pointed toward the street, not quite away from them but not quite toward them, either.

'What have you seen, sir?' Allen asked quietly.

'The End of Days,' the old man said. 'You boys army?'

'Navy,' Allen said.

'Huh, go figure. Long ways from the beach here, Popeye. Name's Ferguson,' the man said. 'If you head down on that street toward the builders' lot, you'll find all the trouble you're lookin' for.'

Allen moved quietly toward the shopkeep. 'The builders' lot?'

Ferguson pondered the team for a moment as a Cobra flew low over the building, toward the lot, Dave assumed. 'Over on Washington,' the old man said when the roar died down. 'Big new development. For folks with money. Or was. Have to drop the asking price now, I reckon.'

Heath introduced himself. He was sheened with sweat, and his face was tight. 'Sir, we could use a secure place to base from. Your establishment is definitely better than the location I had in mind.'

'And what location was that?'

'There's a mosque –'

'Oh, hell, no.' Ferguson laughed, a rattling wheeze, as he pointed at a careworn shack behind them. It looked like a tumbledown garage to Dave, but Ferguson assured them this was the local mosque. 'That ain't one of them Ay-rab mosques with gun turrets and shit. That's an American mosque, Navy. Bigfoots'll run right through that.'

'Bigfoots?' Allen asked.

'Or whatever,' Ferguson conceded. 'Figured them for indigenous monsters. Saw a show on the History Channel about them once. The Bigfoots. Figured they'd come back to take what we took off of them.'

Lieutenant Ostermann, delayed by dealing with the helicopter issue, at last caught up with the SEALs.

'Those boys with you?' Ferguson jerked his thumb at the SWAT contingent.

Heath nodded. 'They are. I need every gun. Will that be a problem, sir?'

'I ain't broke no laws since I got an Article 15 in Oakdale after I got back from the Nam,' Ferguson said. 'I got me no business with the po-lice. And they got them none with me. Go on, Navy; get yourself set the fuck up. But you break something, you bought it.'

A news chopper, one Dave hadn't seen before, swooped low over the roof. Heath and the rest of the party looked up in annoyance that soon translated into incomprehension. Dave followed their gaze. It was his new eagle eyes that caught the problem.

A long arrow – a Sliveen war shot, arrakh-du for sure – had punched through the pilot's window, pinning the dead man to his seat. The news chopper spun around and around in a tightening gyre, losing altitude fast. The nose dipped lower, and as the cabin tilted over crazily, a body dropped from the rear compartment. Dave grimaced as he watched the man plummet, flailing through the night air. He recalled how much he'd wanted to toss Compton out of the chopper on the way in.

Not my finest moment, he thought. *But I didn't actually do it. So that's one to my credit.*

The Bell helicopter dropped just beyond the roofline, hitting the earth with a crunching explosion that shook the ground and threw a great gout of fire into the air. Dave reckoned it had crashed somewhere between the marines and the Horde.

Igor stepped up, hefting a long-barrelled weapon with a scope, which he handled with ease. He nodded at Ferguson and then turned to Chief Allen. 'Anyone started a tab yet? I could murder a po'boy.'

25

Urspite Scaroth Ur Hunn found his vanguard, or at least part of it.

One of the Hunn dominants had lost the leash of control over his Fangr acolyte. They were busy ripping a pile of calflings apart as Scaroth emerged at the head of the Queen's Vengeance, the thresh a few quick strides behind him. In the village to the east the growls of another Fangr acolyte could be heard along with the screams of its victims being eaten alive. This realm smelled wrong. As it had before. The thresh had wondered last time what it was, and now, upon returning, the answer came to it in a burst of quickthinkings.

This world smelled like a giant foundry.

An entire realm of forged metal and bellows fire.

'Hold!' Scaroth roared, ignoring the hammering wings above him. The thresh cringed as it looked up toward the creatures in the air, wondering what they were, even as Urspite ignored them. The gaze of a great single eye blazing with a terrible fire traversed the field, passing over them, but without burning anyone. Urspite's anger with his Hunn dominant kept him in place as the others cowered away.

The blood madness was on the Hunn and his leash. A

terrible second of disbelief followed for all who beheld the scene. It had been many eons since the Hunn had established their domination of the Fangr, and in all that time none of the inferior daemonum had ever disobeyed a direct command. It was not in their meat to do so. But so, too, in all that time, the thresh knew, none of the inferior daemonum had ever tasted the scent of the old prey in their nostrils, either. The thresh had just enough time to wonder what Scaroth might do before the BattleMaster had already done it. Reaching into the long quiver slung over his enormous shoulders, he withdrew a pilum with deliberate slowness, and not even bothering to line up the throw, he unleashed the shaft in one fluid movement. It streaked through the night and impaled one of the Hunn's Fangr with a dull, wet crunch, affixing it to the ground, where it squealed once before shivering and going limp.

'Attend me, Hunn!' Scaroth barked to the errant daemon's master.

The Fangr may have been lost to the killing frenzy, but the guilty Hunn had presence of mind enough to pull away from the bestial scene. It helped that one of the strange flying creatures turned its burning eye on the warrior and its leash, driving them away from the slaughtered prey. The daemon shrieked and snarled and leaped out of the circle of light. It stood dumbly for a moment, long ropy strands of skin and meat hanging from its jaws, and seemed caught between horror, humiliation, and giving in to the siren song of the bloodwine.

Humiliation won out. And fear of the inexplicable Drakon-like creature that hovered above them. The thresh could feel the Fangr's distress as a hot, empathic prickling under its own hide. Most compelling of all, though, was the force of displeasure emanating from Urspite Scaroth Ur

Hunn in malignant waves. The BattleMaster's dark rage and disapproval was so intense that it caused the thresh to moan softly. It tried to shield its smaller, weaker mind from the fearful thinkings of Urspite Scaroth Ur Hunn, but it was as pointless as a grosswyrm trying to outrun a magma flow.

The massive shoulders of the disgraced Hunn warrior slumped, and it hung its great gnarled head in shame, approaching the BattleMaster slowly, with its surviving Fangr acolytes attending it in a series of small looping circles, as though torn between the need to approach and the desire to avoid the will of Scaroth.

The BattleMaster did not even deign to speak to the failed Hunn. To lose the leash over one's charges was unforgivable. The Hunn dropped to its knees before him. Turning to the remaining members of its leash, it demanded that they bare their throats to the blade, which they duly did, becoming mostly still but keening a wretched death song. Three quick slashes and hot ichor spilled onto cold mud. The Hunn turned back and presented the blade to Scaroth, but even that mercy was not due him because of his failure.

When the BattleMaster refused to release him from dishonour, the Hunn plunged the tip of the long curved blade into his abdomen and ripped out his own innards.

He died hissing. In shame.

The thresh sniffed at the stink of it. Around the lesser daemon, its superiors did the same.

The scent of prey was much stronger this time with fresh blood in the air. There were many of them nearby. Some even crawling away from the bloodied pile of prey that had tempted the Hunn and its leash into ruin. Their screams and high keening wails were a delight to the senses, but there was no time to indulge. The rest of the vanguard came pouring up out of the tunnels and into the night Above, fiercely scarred Hunn and their leashed Fangr claiming the clawhold in the realm of *dar ienamic*.

The thresh was confused by the thought. It had been taught to think of men only as meat for the blood pot, and that only as a legend. When had it formed the idea that the calflings were anything as notable as *ienamicae*? The thresh worried that some madness had claimed its mind to dignify the creatures with the ancient and noble crown of *dar ienamic*. But then, the powerful magicks it had encountered on its last visit here were . . . powerful.

It recognised the field into which it had emerged, an open wasteland on the edge of the village in which small fires and candle lamps burned. There was no sign of the minion in the ruins to the left, but the source of the heady aroma of man meat was immediately obvious. A small clutch of the creatures stood around their strange beastless chariots where the thresh had fallen upon the filthy minion just before its nest mate had been slain by some trickster's wizardry. The thresh stuck close to Urspite Scaroth as much for protection as anything. The Queen's Vengeance, cloaked in sweet darkness, arrayed themselves in a loose scythe formation. Fangr acolytes leashed to their Hunn dominants growled and snarled, eager to get to the kill. The Hunn growled in turn, quieting their inferiors but eyeing the cyclopean Drakon suspiciously, sniffing the air, and detecting the scent of sweet, sweet meat.

The thresh could not long gaze in the direction of the foe.

Its thoughts were confusing. Were they foe now? Not food? Its waving forest of eyestalks cringed away. There burned a great number of lights in that direction, as though the men had established a large war camp in the red-roofed building with all of the fires. As eager as Fangr and Hunn were to have at them, all shied away from the light and the promise of fire and pain that came with it. Lieutenants Grymm stomped and stalked, exchanging quiet thinkings on how best to put out the lights. Reaching a talon up, the thresh attempted to gain the attention of the BattleMaster by tugging at its armour.

'What?' growled Urspite Scaroth Ur Hunn, busy attempting to brute his forces into a formation resembling something from the war scrolls.

'The light, sir. The eyestalks water and squint from it, but it does not burn. Not if it is as it was before.'

Urspite Scaroth Ur Hunn reached down and picked the tiny daemon up by its throat, all but choking it.

'Shall I throw you into the fire light and test that thinking, thresh?'

Struggling to choke out an apology for bothering the BattleMaster, the thresh begged not to be sacrificed so. It had much to offer in the way of thinkings. Urspite Scaroth opened his massive claws and dropped the thresh into the mud. It was thankful for the mud. The soft ooze broke its fall from such a prodigious height.

'If . . . if . . . I might . . . my lord. Your host is not yet used to the thinkings I have thought here about the harmless nature of such lights. And not having my lord's vast intelligence or fortitude, they might yet be misled by poor thinkings. Perhaps if we were to head into the darkness of the village, where just a few fires burn?'

Scaroth appeared to consider the advice. There was a reason he was one of Her Majesty's Chosen. Not simply a great unthinking mass of talon and fang, he obviously had the gift of slower thinking than one normally found in a feeding frenzy. He barked and snarled directions to the Hunn beneath him to dress the scythe moonward.

The amulets of the men flashed with some inexplicable magick, as if pleased by the spectacle.

The thresh had to concede that the sacrifice had been well made. It did return a good measure of discipline to the thrall. Thresh blinked into the terrible light where individual calflings appeared to be pointing toward them. It was difficult to make out what lay beyond the great river of coloured lights in which the men appeared to bathe without a thought. Chariots and covered wagons without beasts to draw them raced back and forth along the shining way, some of them even screeching to a halt. Thresh tried to identify the source of that loud, piercing screech, thinking that it must be the hidden beast that drew along the chariots, but nothing could it discern. And how did these wagons move about, lacking a visible beast to pull them? Well, that had to be the most arcane of magicks and so far beyond its meagre thinkings that nothing was to be gained by pondering the matter.

Urspite Scaroth Ur Hunn was glad that the weak link in the chains binding his host had been broken so quickly. It served his purposes to lay a hard example upon the assembled warriors before they met the . . .

Enemy?

He still had difficulties accepting the idea of mere men as a foe. As a meal, certainly. But certainly not anything as storied and worthy of respect as *ienamic*. And yet . . . Her Majesty had been quite specific about the dangers of sorcery he might encounter Above. She still wondered at the role of magick in her long banishment beneath the capstone that had been sealed atop the UnderRealms.

'The Sky Lords surely sealed us beneath our rightful place, Hunn,' she had said to him in the privacy of her chambers. 'But how did the Sky Lords come to intervene? Were they summoned by sorcery? Have men been perfecting this sorcery while we have remained trapped beneath their feet? This truth you shall seek out for me.'

Standing in the realm of the Above, reining in his unruly thoughts at the unexpected sights and smells, Scaroth knew it would not be as simple a task as raiding some piss puddle of a village and slowly eating the inhabitants' smallest nestlings until they gave up the secret. As entertaining as that would be. He kept his eyes on the war party for the most part, beasting them into submission, but when he turned toward the lights where ever more men were gathered he could not help wondering what had happened up here in the long eons since the banishment of his kind, of all daemonum. Nothing of this place recalled the teachings of the scrolls. Why did the men not flee?

'What are those things, thresh?' he demanded to know, raising one massive arm and pointing at the bobbing points of light that seemed to attend each and every one of the calflings. 'Are they the amulets of power? The ones of which you spoke? Are they all wizards in this village?'

The thresh poked its head around the giant trunk of Scaroth's haunches. Grudgingly, the BattleMaster had to admit that the tiny thresh, nowhere near full grown, did not shrink away from the light as some of his warriors did. (He noted which ones; have no fear of that. They would thicken up the regimental blood pots if they proved themselves cowards on this quest.)

'I think so, my lord,' it confessed. 'But again, I do not know that we must fear this light. Surely if so many talismans were invoked against us and were to have any power, we should have felt that power by now.'

Scaroth growled. It was a fair point for one so small and feeble.

The Vengeance now was fully deployed in a double scythe formation, oriented for the most part toward the dark lines of the village rather than the river of light and its immediate promise of slaughter (although the promise of immolation in human fire probably had something to do with that, too, he thought darkly). The Queen's Vengeance, a dread company of two reinforced Talon of Hunn and their leashes of Fangr, and of course the Lieutenants Grymm – there was no avoiding the arrogant scum – shifted and growled. The gutted carcass of the disgraced Hunn still had them in its power, but Scaroth knew he must act now: either attack the village as planned or make an opportunistic lunge at these curious calfling wizards with the glowing amulets. He would never admit it, for to do so was a terrible weakness, but part of him wished to consult with the thresh and even the Grymm to seek their counsel. The daemon inferiorae was the only one of his host with any experience in this realm, and the Grymm, he could not deny, were learned in the sacred war scrolls.

But a BattleMaster of the Grande Horde did not keep his chariot with counsel. He maintained his grip on the reins by riding down on his enemies and driving them before him.

And Scaroth had enemies at hand.

'Turn dagger-wise,' he roared, and the war party wheeled

in the direction of the light, finishing the manoeuvre with a great single stomp and a clattering clash of blades on shields.

'HUNN UR HORDE,' they roared in unison, even the Fangr and Grymm.

That evoked a response in the calflings at last. Some even jumped in fear. Excellent. Others began to back away. This was how it should be. Things were finally making sense.

It was a gamble, but he could scent the musky fever of his dominants to be among the meat and blood, and for the moment that meant over there. In the light.

He bent down to hiss softly at the thresh.

'You are certain this unnatural bright glow is harmless, thresh?'

'Yes, my lord,' it replied, although it didn't seem all that certain.

'That is good. You shall lead us into it.'

At that moment, one of the Drakon dropped out of the sky. It smashed against the ground, flailing and shattering its wings, the bones of which flew into the assembled ranks of the Queen's Vengeance, cutting down Hunn and Fangr and even a Lieutenant Grymm. The thresh cringed behind its BattleMaster, but even as it soiled itself with its own pastes, its quickthinkings admonished it.

It had been wrong.

The flying creatures were not creatures at all.

The thresh turned its eyestalks on the fallen Drakon, and the thinking came upon it that . . . that what had dropped from Above was not beast but . . . but chariot.

Some form of chariot, the thresh was certain, and from

which even now an injured and bloodied calfling crawled.

Around it, the revengers' thrall strained and thrashed on the very edge of disintegration. The discipline of the war party was near breaking point and might have failed if Urspite Scaroth had not whipped out his great blade and decapitated another of his less reliable Hunn as a lesson.

'HOLD!' he roared. 'The Hunn ur Horde will HOLD!'

'Hunn,' a few of the warriors barked with unthinking obedience. 'Hunn . . . Hunn . . .'

'*Hunn ur Horde*,' roared the surviving Lieutenants Grymm, which was very generous of them, and soon enough the entirety of the Dread Company had taken up the chant, calming themselves with it.

The BattleMaster turned his baleful glare on the thresh.

'Did you witness these before?' Scaroth demanded to know in a low rumbling growl.

'No, my lord,' the thresh replied, shouting over the death screams of the chariot beast. Inside the thing, yet another rider struggled to free itself.

'Then pray the Sky Lords send no more down upon us, thresh. Now. Move.'

The thresh stumbled forward. It could not untangle its many thinkings and feelings.

It knew the fear of the unknown, of the uncertainty about the bright, hot light into which it would take the revengers. It knew pride that one so inferior might lead such a mighty force into battle. The thresh also knew that the war party was actually quite tiny by the standards of the Horde, especially the Grande Horde, but it had rarely seen the Hunn clan assembled in greater numbers than this, and never with the intent to have at a foe. It felt anxiety that it might falter and bring shame upon its nest like the Hunn that had lost control of its leash. And as it slowly began to lope toward the light, stretching out its gait, accelerating toward the enemy lines, there was the savage exultation of which it had dreamed so many times. The blood frenzy was rising.

The muddy ground, broken and uneven, dried out and became flat, slipping away beneath the thresh in a blur. The men, its prey, reacted to the charge, some fleeing, some climbing aboard their chariots, others holding the glowing amulets to their faces as if to hide behind the strange candle. As it closed with the calflings, the thresh heard more screeching as human riders reined in their chariots. It smelled a strange, alien miasma of scents, most of them completely unidentifiable. And it heard the most confounding sound.

A deep, thudding roar that filled the skies.

It searched in the direction of the sound.

Skyward. And what it saw froze the ichor in its carcass.

There was more than one skyborne chariot.

26

An NOPD command unit rolled up while Heath and his men were rushing to establish some sort of forward post in the po'boy shop. Dave wasn't entirely sure what they were doing there. Building a little fort? Constructing a blind, like hunters, from which to observe the Hunn? Maybe just setting up a bolt-hole into which they could flee if necessary. The shop was a solid brick structure that offered more cover than the shacks and shanties around it, but that didn't fill him with confidence.

They weren't facing a human enemy. The Horde wouldn't stand off and throw stones or even spears at this place. They'd swarm it.

He already felt as though he was just baggage to these guys, and apart from telling them which orc was which, he didn't seem much good for anything besides getting in the way. He stepped out of the store just as the NOPD truck arrived. It looked like a mobile home to Dave, and he found it all too easy to imagine a couple of Hunn carving it up with cleavers and war axes. Professor Ashbury, wearing police body armour she had picked up somewhere, jumped down out of the rear cabin door before the vehicle stopped moving. Heath managed to look both pissed and relieved at their arrival.

'I hope this is not precipitate, Emmeline,' he said. 'I do hope I have an OP to fall back to.'

'Your guys took over the café at the hospital,' she said. 'It's defensible. Compton even offered to stay and defend it –' She smirked, all ham and wry. '– but they didn't need his help.'

Dave could pick out the sallow face, fiery neckbeard and bald head of the anthropologist in the rear of the command unit. He was fiddling around with a bank of screens while taking notes on a stack of tablets and a block of paper. Jostled by the police and ignored by the SEALs, he looked like he'd rather be anywhere else on earth. When he wasn't busy, he looked at his cell phone as if expecting it to ring.

His problem is he never gets laid, Dave thought.

Ashbury's eyes met Dave's. Was there something there? Dave thought there might be something there. And he wasn't even drunk.

'Hello, Hooper. I see you're still hanging around like a fart in a telephone booth.'

Okay, maybe not.

'For now,' he said. 'What's on TV?'

He nodded at the banks of monitors inside the big van.

Heath didn't wait for an answer, climbing the two small metal steps into the cabin. Ashbury followed him back inside, and Dave followed her, still carrying Marty Grbac's splitting maul. There were half a dozen men and women seated at consoles in the command unit, all of them uniformed officers of the New Orleans Police Department. Compton and Ashbury were the only civilians besides Dave. For the first time in what felt like a long while, nobody paid him any attention. They were all transfixed by the scenes playing out on the two largest wide-screen displays. Both ran monochrome low-light vision from news choppers.

Dave could see the leader of the war party on at least two monitors. There was no missing the ugly prick. The Hunn was noticeably larger than any other creature in its . . . in its *thrall*, he thought. *A war party assigned to a Master of Hunn is known as a thrall*, a word from the Olde Scrolls that could mean everything from a small raiding party of half a dozen Hunn and their leash of Fangr up to a Grande Horde. This thrall ran to roughly a couple of hundred strong and faced the marines, who were taking up position in and around an abandoned McDonald's. On another screen, an injured reporter screamed and pleaded for someone to come and save him. One of the uniforms turned down the volume on that.

For a moment Dave found himself searching for signs of a physical leash, a chain or a long thick rope of treated hide that could bind a Fangr to its master, but that was his rational twenty-first-century mind attempting to impose a preferred meaning on a much older form of understanding. The leash was not physical. It was like . . . the authority of a squad leader, he thought, satisfied with that. The BattleMaster held all in his thrall. A Hunn dominant merely controlled a leash of Fangr.

Chief Allen appeared at the door of the truck.

'All set up inside, Captain,' he reported to Heath before following Dave's gaze. The Hunn leader was festooned with fangs, scalps, and skulls with a headdress of Drakon scales forming a sort of Mohawk on his boiled leather helmet.

'Nasty,' said the CPO.

'Yeah. That ugly-ass monster could really use some wardrobe advice,' Igor said from the door.

'A little Queer Eye for the Straight Orc?' smirked Allen.

'Just sayin'.'

Dave's skin itched with the need to get moving, as though something inside him wanted to burst out and fly to the scene of the battle. A dumbass move for sure. No way was he leaving the protective circle of these heavily armed professional killers. Even the lady professor was probably better suited to this than he was. She had her Asperger's thing to make her a little scary. She was rocking it. He was a freak with a magic hammer, so far out of his depth that just remembering to draw breath was an effort.

So Dave Hooper just stared at the screens. There were banks of them up and down the interior of the command unit. The SEALs and NOPD had pulled in a lot of coverage. Or rather, Ashbury had. A lot of the video was from the news channels, but at least half came from feeds he didn't recognise. Drones, maybe? Or even satellites. Perhaps the CIA was stealing the video from the phones of those idiots who hadn't run away yet. There were plenty of them still hanging around. Compton pushed the occasional button or stroked a touch pad to pull in close on an image, but to Dave he looked about as useless . . . well, as Dave felt.

'There's hundreds of those things out there,' said Allen.

'Yeah. Better to just take off and nuke them from orbit,' Dave said.

'Only way to be sure.' Igor grinned.

Allen measured Dave with a look that clearly implied that he thought it could be a live option.

As much as his rational self knew not to be a damn fool, there was a damn fool part of Dave that wanted nothing more than to raise Lucille on high and charge into the Horde, swinging left and right. It was a hunger as needful as any he'd known since waking up in the hospital. Something inside

Dave, deep in his blood, sang to him of the righteous urgency of closing with *dar ienamic* and destroying them. That was how part of him thought of the Horde now. Not as monsters but as an enemy. As *ienamicae* in the Olde Tongue. He shifted Lucille carefully from one shoulder to the other. The heavy maul had grown even more uncomfortable to hold while he watched the drama on the command van monitors. Dave felt like she was humming with a resonance below human perception and the only way to silence her was to give voice to that song. A hymn to murder.

When he could stand it no longer, he turned to exit the van, needing to move, to do something, if only to get away, but he found Heath in the doorway blocking his path.

'I need that air support, and I need it now,' Heath said urgently, holding down the push-to-talk button of his headset. The navy man listened to a response that Dave could not hear, shook his head, and cursed softly.

'Problemo?' Dave asked.

Heath stared mutely at Dave for a moment, perhaps wondering whether to let him in on the conversation. After a glance at the screens, where more and more of the Hunn appeared to be spewing up out of the earth, he made his decision.

'We're trying to get some A-10s up, but the nearest units are in Georgia,' Heath said.

'And what? They're on vacation? Or just sitting at home watching *Cake Boss*?' Dave asked.

'No,' Heath said, almost offended. 'These are experienced combat aviators. But contrary to what Hollywood would have you believe, we generally keep the munitions separate from the weapons systems themselves.'

'Why?'

'So they don't blow up,' Heath said flatly. 'Anyway, this sort of thing takes a bit of time.'

'What about your other choppers?' Dave asked, shifting Lucille over to his other shoulder. The heavy maul started humming to him again. Nobody else could hear it, of that he was sure. 'They've got those big-ass guns.'

'If I need to, I'll put them in, but I'd rather not risk the Cobras after what I've seen with the news chopper,' Heath said. 'All I need now is a couple of choppers getting shot down and dropping through the roof of a mall. We have blocking forces in place, we have the initiative, and we have the advantage. I'll wager where these things come from they don't do close air support.'

'Not that I know of . . .' Dave thought for a moment, but nothing came to him. Flying creatures were not unknown to the Hunn, especially dangerous ones like Drakonen. Urgon, for his part, didn't have anything helpful to offer, 'Pretty sure they don't, anyway.'

Heath's eyes lost their focus as he pressed one finger to his earpiece and took in some new development.

'Acknowledged. I'll have my second platoon of marines attack from their position,' he said. 'They can still flank them.'

Allen was at the door again. 'Sir, we can get there faster. Second Platoon simply isn't going to make it.'

'Well, they'll have to,' Heath said calmly, as if he were a commentator for a golf match. 'Or we will. Air support is taking too long.'

'Too late,' Dave said. On the two big screens beside him, the Hunn had finally turned themselves to face the downed helicopter and the marines of First Platoon. With a loud, ground-splitting bellow that he could hear inside the command vehicle, the Horde charged forward.

Heath bounced out of the vehicle, grimacing as he landed badly on his artificial leg and hobbling to run in front of Dave. 'You stay here. This is our job.'

'I'm cool with that,' he said.

But something wasn't cool.

Outside on the street he found the SEALs ready to roll, but the SWAT team stood at the edge of things, arguing among themselves. Igor the giant jerked his thumb at the cops. 'Sure glad we brought those guys along.'

Heath waved a warning finger at Dave – *stay put* – and limped quickly over to Lieutenant Ostermann. 'What is the problem?'

The senior police officer looked pained as he pointed at his own headset.

'I've got the mayor arguing with the chief, and I can't get clear orders,' Ostermann said. 'Mayor wants us back at the hospital. Right now. Chief says we've been detached to you. Mayor says you're not paying the bills. Chief –'

To his eternal credit, Captain Heath did not shout or curse or grab the SWAT officer by his collar and beat him to death. Dave watched the man grit his teeth and take one step forward into Ostermann's space. He spoke in a calm, quiet, reasonable tone, low enough that even with his newly enhanced hearing, Dave could not tell quite what he said.

Ashbury stuck her head out of the command vehicle. 'Second Platoon is jammed up with refugees and tourists. They can't get to First Platoon.'

'Ostermann?' Heath said, with more volume.

'Yes,' the now-compliant SWAT officer said.

'Please get *your* Second Tactical Platoon to assist our marines on Claiborne at McDonald's. The ones who are dying for this city right now.'

Ostermann reached up to his throat mike for his radio, presumably to call his fellow platoon commander. Dave ignored him, staring down the long road toward the waste ground where the Hunn had emerged. He could see nothing of them beyond a thickening crowd of refugees. Two cars had crashed at the intersection a block down, creating a dam in the flow of terrified civilians.

'First Platoon is breaking cover and advancing toward the downed chopper,' Ashbury said. 'They say there are survivors. The hostiles are charging them.'

Shit was getting out of hand. Dave didn't need to waste four years in ROTC to know that. Didn't even need his limited chops in *Call of Duty*. Heath had a team of disparate groups not used to working with one another dealing with something they'd never seen before. They weren't in some shitty neighbourhood in Baghdad or the mountains of the Hindu fucking Kush. They couldn't just switch to full auto and open fire, and hose down the problem. Even a dude like Heath could do only so much with limited resources and unlimited constraints. But he had to do something, and quickly. Dave could clearly hear the massed gunfire and the rumble of the Hunn stampede. It reminded him of being trackside at the Kentucky Derby.

He thought about putting his head back into the van to check on what was happening, but as soon as the thought occurred to him, he staggered, almost dropping Lucille, stunned by a low-grade electrical charge that ran through the handle, into his arms, and up through his skull. Or something that felt like an electrical charge.

'Prof, what's happening over there?' he asked, almost gagging. 'With the marines.'

She didn't bother to look away from the displays, answering him by raising her voice.

'The Hunn are charging them. Getting shot down. Charging again. It's keeping them out of the residential streets for now. Shouldn't you be leaping tall buildings or swinging your mighty tool or something?'

Dave spun around, not really sure why but aware that he'd just heard something that sounded like a hissing whip crack.

A strangled cry and the sound of a man falling to the hard road surface drew his eye to one of the SEALs. Impaled by a four-foot war shaft. The arrow of a Sliveen scout. Blood boiled up out of the victim's mouth as his body spasmed in shock, and everyone dived for cover.

'What the fuck?' gasped Ashbury.

Compton went rigid with fright, then launched into a tangle of uncoordinated action, diving for the command unit's door and trying to slam it shut.

'Sniper!' Allen yelled.

'*Sliveen arrakh,*' Dave corrected him at high volume without thinking, without even knowing what he'd just said until he actually thought about it. 'Arrows,' he cried out then. 'It's arrows.'

SWAT started shooting. The SEALs dashed for cover. Chief Allen, Igor the giant, and a cop grabbed the body of the man who'd been struck and dragged it out of the middle of the road. They hadn't moved more than a few steps when another police officer screamed and fell, run through by a shaft that pierced the back of his body armour.

Dave already was turning toward the source of the danger

when he saw the second arrow fly, a dark blur in the night. Not waiting for permission, not bothering to ask or consult with Heath, he exploded from a standing start, moving in the direction of the Sliveen. Everything seemed to slow down around him.

No, that was wrong. Time didn't *seem* to slow down; some monstrous force actually did apply the brakes to the flow of reality as he suddenly accelerated into motion. Part of his mind, detached and curious, noted how slowly Heath was dropping through the air as he leaped toward the command truck for cover. Ashbury cried out, but not in fear. She raged at Compton, wrestling for the door handle with him. Her infuriated screams reached him as a weird, elongated sound effect, as though he was watching the scene in super slo-mo. His own mind was unaffected. Dave was able to calculate the flight path of the second arrow as he found himself again calling on equations and math solutions. The deadly path of the war shaft led from the slowly crumpling body of the SWAT officer back into the night air at an angle of thirty-two degrees between the point of release and impact. In his mind's eye he saw the passage of the arrakh-du as a dark red trace image, a slight parabolic curve accounting for gravity's downward pull on the shaft. He could, if he chose to, examine gently floating clouds of calculations that would lead him to understand the speed of the projectile, the pounds per square inch of pressure it had delivered to the spinal column upon impact, the draw strength needed to use a conventional Sliveen war bow, the time to . . .

But he chose none of these things, ignoring them in favour of calculating a path to the place where the daemon scout stood atop the bell tower of a red-brick church one and a half blocks up Fourth Street. It looked like about . . . No, it *was* a distance of 169 yards. Or 169 yards and nineteen inches from where Dave was launching himself toward the ancient *ienamic* to where the Sliveen, which looked like a much thinner, darker, more insectile version of a warrior Hunn, was slowly, slowly, slowly reaching back over its shoulder into a giant quiver for another war shaft. The Sliveen, he was pleased to note, moved no more quickly than Heath or Ashbury or any of its targets. So pleased was he to note this interesting fact that a wolfish grin spread over his face, giving him a fierce canine aspect.

Lucille was singing to him again, but a soft and soothing love song this time. A gentle melody that paradoxically urged him toward violence at even greater speed.

The path to the daemon opened up before them, an imagined trail that ran straight and true for half the distance to the monster, jagging left around a pick-up that was slowly, slowly, slowly rounding the next corner, up on two wheels, impossibly balanced between tipping over and making the radical turn. Then it veered to the right to avoid a clutch of a dozen or so fleeing residents, all of them bunched tightly together, none moving at anything faster than a fraction of a fraction of half speed, with one in mid-turn, pointing back and upward, quite possibly at the dark shadow of the UnderRealm scout. A leap onto a Ford F-150 emerging from the parking lot of the church would help launch Dave onto the steeply sloped roof of the nave.

He remembered the term 'nave' from a long-ago lesson in a compulsory first-year civil engineering class. EGR 151: 'A History of the Built Environment'. He knew, without bothering to test the knowledge, that he could recall every detail of that class now if he so chose. A wonder, given how close he'd come to failing it the first time around. He'd bothered turning up only because there was a particular hottie who was enrolled that semester and . . .

The leap onto the nave would present him with an interesting physics problem, he realised, consciously putting aside his memories of the hottie, which was a non-trivial effort. She'd banged like an outhouse door in a high wind when he'd finally nailed her, and he could remember every tactile detail of that encounter, too, now. But he would, if not careful, punch right through the tiles and into the attic or even the main body of the church where the congregation would be seated of a Sunday on the pews.

Where some worshippers undoubtedly were seated or kneeling right now, he thought, praying by candlelight for deliverance.

Better to just get the fucking job done, Dave. Monster first. Hotties later.

He saw that he would have to hit the steep tiled roof at a shallow angle, bleeding off the energy of his touchdown by running away from the Sliveen for . . . eight and a half yards . . . before performing a tight, looping turn and coming back at his foe from what would then be his right flank. What the Hunn called shield-wise when they deigned to pay their enemies the honour of carrying a shield into battle.

The Sliveen bore no such protection.

Dave performed the calculations required to map out his route between his first step and his second. Those two steps carried him more than twenty feet, so great was the explosive power of each stride. He passed through the floating world like a thought through a line of dead text and experienced a moment of cognitive dissonance that was rooted in the realisation of just how quickly he was moving. The air itself cleaved apart at his progress, roaring in his ears as a gale force wind. Some part of him felt as though everything should have blurred around him, becoming an indecipherable smear of colour and movement. But the world was slow and everything within it impossibly unhurried and deliberate. Suspended.

He was the blur, flashing past the fleeing terrified residents at such a speed that he was long gone before the most alert of them had turned even partway in his direction. He slapped his palm lightly into the side of the pick-up, imparting just enough of a hit to tip it back toward safety as it curved ever so slowly around the corner.

As he leaped onto the hood and then the cabin roof of the F-150, he felt the metal crumple under the enormous pressure of his lift-off. But his calculations were good, and as the windshield exploded outward, Dave launched himself toward the roofline. As he sailed up and up, his boyhood self called him back toward memories of that summer when he and his cousin Darryl had imagined something just like this and pushed the trampoline up against the back fence and . . . But he closed off that remembrance, too, for it served no purpose now as he touched down on the grey roof tiles lightly enough that only a couple cracked under the soles of his boots. More shattered as he decelerated, channelling the enormous velocities he'd generated into the structure of the building. One foot slipped as he reached the apogee of his own particular flight path and turned toward the Sliveen.

It had sensed the shocking swiftness of his approach and was turning much more rapidly now as Dave lost his footing on the disintegrating tile. The long, sinewy arm had drawn out the length of the arrakh-du war shot and in a heartbeat would have it notched and aimed. But Dave Hooper, the defender of this realm, moved within the space between heartbeats. Feeling his feet lose traction, he allowed the stumble to become a controlled drop, dipping his shoulder toward the peak and allowing the muscle memory of a judo roll he had performed only a few times as a child in a free class, and with no real grace or skill, to well up from within.

He hadn't even wanted to go to judo. It was a stupid martial art. Not like fucking karate, which kicked ass. But his mother said judo was good for his brother's asthma. So they went to a few classes, decades ago. Dave executed the roll over the handle of Lucille and up the incline of the steeply pitched church roof perfectly, as though he'd never stepped off the *tatami*.

The Sliveen had the arrow notched and half drawn as Dave powered toward the creature. It almost certainly knew in its cold reptilian way that it could not afford to indulge in a full draw of the bowstring, which would deliver enough energy to punch the shaft through the human's torso with momentum enough to fly on for hundreds of yards beyond it. Dave Hooper doubted he'd recover from a wound like that as easily as he'd healed from the cut in the hospital.

Knowing it had to act quickly, the Sliveen scout loosed the shot as Dave closed the gap between them to talon range.

Too slow. Too late. Too poorly aimed.

Dave saw the long, spidery fingers of the scout let go of their grip on the taut wulfin-hide bowstring. He had time enough to watch the arrowhead of sharpened Drakon-glass begin its short journey away from the recurve bow. Time enough to shift his weight and bring Lucille up, one hand gripping her base and the other wrapped around the throat of the splitting maul just below the heavy steel head. He was certain she was singing. A light, skipping child song, almost laughing the melody.

He pivoted and swept the air in front of him, tilting his head, watching curiously as the dark hickory knocked the arrow off course, sending it flying high, soaring at a greater angle of elevation, to land safely, he hoped, in the waste ground of the new housing development or even, should he be exceptionally lucky, in among the ranks of the raiding party. That, he thought, would be sweet. A Master of Hunn shot in the ass by one of his own thrall's arrows.

They'd be yucking it up about that one around the ol' blood pots for a dark age.

Momentum carried him on toward the scout, whose savage features were only now beginning to contort in rage and dawning confusion. Dave's thoughts were running at such an accelerated pace that his head felt warm, even fevered. He turned his next step into a driving kick that caught the shocked Sliveen amidships. Although smaller than even a simple warrior Hunn, the stealth fighter still enjoyed a considerable advantage in height and weight over any but the largest human opponents. Even Sergeant Swindt would have to give away a few pounds and a good half foot in height to this bad boy. The kick landed square and true. Dave felt some of the force of the blow travel back up his leg and into his hips.

Most of the power, however, was transferred from his body into the daemon. It began to fly.

Talons screeched on tiles as the creature scrabbled for purchase. Dave took another step toward his now airborne opponent, swinging Lucille like a baseball bat, swinging for the parking lot. The twelve-pound head caught the beast in mid-thorax. Dave had not thought to check his grip on the weapon. If he had, he would have made sure to attack with the cutting edge of the axe lest he strike any sort of armour. But it was the dark metal fist of the sledgehammer that struck the Sliveen.

The daemon exploded, flying apart with a dull, wet roar of detonation. Viscera, bone shards, purple-black ichor, and flesh all expanded outward in a foul blast of organic chemistry. So great was the force of the blow that it spun Dave around, turning him away from the sight of the carcass, which was trailing long strands and loops of offal. He turned back in time to see most of the corpse land in the middle of the crossroads.

As if released from suspension, fleeing residents suddenly sped up. The tyres of the pick-up screeched as they bounced down and the rubber bit into the tarmac again. The odd, distant damping effect on Dave's hearing cleared, and he could hear screaming and sirens and gunfire. A shaky breath leaked out between his trembling lips.

Turning slowly around, taking everything in, he observed the scene back at the po'boy shop, with medics running to attend to the wounded and the dead and the SWAT and SEAL teams still hunkered down around the command unit for whatever cover they could find. He saw Ashbury punch Compton on the nose, and he actually laughed as another quarter turn found him facing west, where the beleaguered marines were bunkered down at the abandoned McDonald's on Claiborne.

The laughter died at the back of his throat.

Dave hurtled toward the marines without thought or intent or any notion about what he might do when he landed. The muddy, weed-choked lot in which the helicopter had crashed was a good half mile away, but he covered at least a third of that distance with one convulsive leap. He did not hit fast-forward this time. The world did not slow to a crawl around him.

For a moment he was able to watch Heath and Allen and Ostermann whipping their men into action, and then his forward flight carried him away from them and into the airspace occupied by five helicopters. Two were civilian, carrying news crews, and the crash of their colleagues in the Bell had induced at least some caution in those pilots. They stood off a ways, circling the burning wreckage, their spotlights picking out the charge of the Horde across the wasteland toward the downed aircraft and the small contingent of marines who now defended it.

He landed on the road surface, which buckled slightly under the impact. Two more strides and he leaped for the stars again, taking care this time, as he had not before, to note the short looping flight paths of the military helicopters that swarmed and swooped and raked at the thrall with their guns.

Wouldn't do to jump into a rotor blade.

Dave wondered why the choppers didn't just unleash seven kinds of hell on the orc swarm, hosing them down with everything they had, but it was no mystery. The thrall was so close to the marines and the survivors of the chopper crash that letting fly meant killing any number of people, too.

And so he sailed on, not quite sure what the fuck he was doing but carried forward as much by Lucille's sweet song, which now sounded undeniably real and human inside his head, as he was by the power of his leap. That power was even more unexpected and frightening to him than it had been when he had intercepted the flying barbell back at Camp Mysteryland.

It felt as though there were no limits to what he might

do. Jump hard enough and perhaps he'd find himself in the vacuum of space after a few minutes. A ridiculous thought, but how much more ridiculous than whatever he was doing right at that moment?

What am I doing? he thought.

So did the pilot of the Cobra gunship as Dave flew past him, winking and cocking a thumb and finger play gun at the guy, whose mouth hung open in abject confusion.

'Yeah. Be cool. Super Dave's got this,' he said.

Ahead and below, the double scythe formation of the Horde swept around the downed helicopter. For a moment the flames and the coordinated fire of the marines held them back. Dave could easily imagine, or even remember, the stinging sensation as the heat and light tightened the creatures' hides. It might have been enough to protect and shield the survivors and the handful of uniformed men and women – yes, that was definitely a woman in full battle kit down there – if a couple of Grymm had not targeted them with . . . what was that?

Dave dropped down closer and closer to the encounter and strained to make out what sort of weapons the elite warriors used. Crossbows, it looked like. Whatever, they worked. He saw a couple of blurred streaks shoot out from their hands before two of the marines spun into the dirt, their own weapons spraying ribbons of tracer fire into the sky. The Grymm worked furiously at their tiny handheld weapons, loading and cocking them, but to no purpose this time.

A Sliveen warrior loped up out of the half-light and put three war bolts into the remaining survivors before the Grymm could fire again.

Gravity steadily took hold, and Dave Hooper began to descend again, dropping below the nearest news chopper, moving down toward the marines of First Platoon, who were precisely thirty-six strong. They had been forty-one before the squad was cut down around the flaming wreckage of the WVUE helicopter.

'Oh, hell, no,' he barely breathed when he realised that the better part of the platoon had broken from cover and the relative safety of the McDonald's and was advancing in stages, fire and movement, toward the main body of the thrall. He dropped rapidly through the night, preparing to land. The thunder of the thrall's charge was loud under the dull thudding of the helicopters, the industrial jackhammer of heavy weapons, and the percussive thump and crunch of grenades. A last quick glance back over his shoulder showed the SEALs and New Orleans SWAT racing toward the thrall on foot. He could see Heath falling behind the more able-bodied men and struggling to stay in contact with them.

Hundreds of civilians, maybe a thousand of them, in front of the strip mall across the main road had scattered when the Horde had bellowed its battle roar. Some were so freaked, they had run toward the engagement, and the others were spreading out through the nearby streets, making the job of herding them to safety all but impossible.

Dave was almost down, but ready with the perfect comic book hero landing this time. Then he had trouble focusing. A fast-growing headache tried to drill through the bone between his eyes.

Lucille chose that moment to become impossibly heavy.

If the splitting maul could speak, Dave, who felt a powerful wave of nausea sweep over him, imagined she would be telling him the same thing his wife frequently told him all the way down the broken road that was their marriage.

I tried to warn you.

The ground rushed up with impossible speed. Tucking in his shoulder, Dave ploughed into the dirt as he attempted to roll off some of the momentum and energy he had built up. Lucille fell from his grip and landed next to a startled marine who looked all of nineteen. Dave probably had ass pimples older than this kid, who was sporting an impressive spray of his own acne. He looked only slightly more freaked out by the man who'd fallen from the heavens than he did by the rapidly approaching wave of slavering monster flesh.

All this Dave took in as a strobing, washed-out colour wheel of imagery while he rolled over and over, not stopping until he hit the remnants of a chain link fence, bending a thick steel pole.

'Ouch,' he said.

'Corpsman!'

Dave stood up and shook himself off.

The world responded by suddenly tilting, spinning, and dropping him back on his ass again. A giant iron vice snapped around his head and squeezed like a bastard.

'Dude, are you all right?' a soldier asked. Or maybe a marine. Or even something else. Possibly just some helpful asshole who had wandered out of a Cheaper Than Dirt gun barn loaded for orc. Dave couldn't make him out through the migraine aura blooming across his visual field. Not that he could really tell any of these characters apart, except for the SWAT guys in their natty black outfits. 'Mr Hooper? You jump out of a chopper or something? Did you break anything?'

This guy knew him?

He tried squinting through the distortion that lay over everything now.

'Feel . . .' Dave grunted, '. . . sick.' He rolled over onto his side, curled into a foetal position and vomited.

'I got Hooper here. He says he's sick,' the man shouted into a helmet mike.

Dave rolled over. 'The Hunn . . .'

'We got them,' the marine said without sounding for a moment like he believed it. Hooper struggled up onto one elbow and tried not to retch again. His vision cleared slightly, and he realised he knew the marine. It was . . .

Everly? Enderson?

Everding!

His name tag read EVERDING. The guy from the Longreach. The big private who hadn't been able to lift Lucille more than an inch or so off the deck.

'Hey. I know you. Do you know a guy called Swindt?' Dave asked groggily, feeling as if he'd just had a hit off a nitrous tank. 'Likes to work out?'

'Who?'

He squinted at their surroundings. He was at the edge of the worst of the fighting now, stuck out on the end of the marine line, as best he could tell. The platoon had moved forward, taking what cover it could, denying it to the enemy, which was caught on open ground. A great tactic against a human foe, but against a daemon thrall intent on overrunning you no matter the cost? Not so much.

They had forced the Hunn, their leashes of Fangr, and a few sundry daemonum back from the downed chopper, where four marines frantically worked on one of their comrades who was showing signs of life. Dave squinted and turned his head over on its side, lining up an unaffected area of his eyesight on the scene. It was the woman Dave had spied a few moments earlier. The long shaft of a Sliveen arrow had entered her body at the hip and emerged from the opposite shoulder, but she was screaming, which meant there was breath in her body. Muzzle flashes from her comrades lit up the night. Gunfire raged in a storm of superheated steel. Tracers whipped from dozens of glowing, smoking muzzles, lashing at the thrall, cutting some down and knocking others back. Every now and then a bright yellow strand of tracer fire as thick as a fire hose and as bright as Vegas would light up a daemon. Like, for real. Causing it to burst into flames and scattering the monsters around it. In this way the marines broke three daemon charges that Dave witnessed up close through the shifting veil of pain and distortion that had fallen over him. The Horde shivered under the firepower of the marines. Fangr and Hunn alike went to ground, diving into shallow holes and behind whatever meagre cover offered itself, only to be thrashed, kicked, and manhandled back up onto their haunches by the tallest and largest of their number, a creature that made Urgon look small.

The BattleMaster, Dave thought, without being able to do a damn thing about it.

He had a bad hurting on him, way more serious than the worst hangover or fever he'd ever known. This felt like a sickness of the fucking soul as much as the body. A medic dashed over to them, yelling questions at Everding and then yelling more at Dave. But he had trouble understanding the corpsman.

That was what Everding called him: 'Corpsman'.

The marines threw grenades like confetti and swapped

out magazines constantly as they tried to wear down their foe. Bursts of pepper-black explosions bit into the front ranks of the Horde. Fire teams darted from cover, pushing forward through the spotlights of police and news choppers. Dave could smell the alkaline tang of the human warriors' fear and something more. Something seemingly at odds with the terror. Their killing joy. They reeked of it, the madness and glory of it.

The thrall leader pointed his cleaver at the marines, who had formed a firing line to the left and right of the downed news chopper. As bullets sparked and flashed off his chain mail and plated armour, and dug bloody chunks where they struck thick hide, the giant Hunn opened his broken-fanged mouth and a deep-throated heavy bass growl reverberated through the ground, bouncing off brick and wood, asphalt and concrete. It rattled the back of Dave's wisdom teeth, drowning out every other sound except his own weak, thready heartbeat. Which sounded like a tom-tom inside his head. The BattleMaster's war shout – his *shkriia* – made the previous call to slaughter sound like a feeble cough.

Everding cursed, eyes going as big and round as dinner plates.

'Uh oh,' the corpsman muttered. 'This cain't be no good.'

The great mass of surviving Hunn and leashed Fangr suddenly rose up from where they had cowered and burrowed into whatever cover they could find in the rubbish-strewn lot. They stepped into the incredible volume of fire, ignoring the loss of an acolyte next to them, a warrior in front.

And then they surged forward, looking like a landslide of bristling muscle and tusk and hard-armoured, tattooed flesh.

'HUNN UR HORDE!'

Slowly at first but soon gathering speed, the Horde moved en masse toward the marines, the front ranks absorbing the bullet storm, warriors falling, Fangr shrieking and tumbling in broken tangles.

'HUNN UR HORDE!'

But never stopping, never faltering, just coming on with the mindless fury of beasts. Dave struggled to raise himself, but his limbs were weighed down by some impossible burden. He was not paralysed. He could feel and move his fingers, but he could no more push himself up off the ground than Everding had been able to lift Lucille off the deck back on the Longreach.

'HUNN!'

'HUNN!'

'HUNN UR HORDE!'

The first marine fell, cleaved asunder by one great swing of a blade that looked half axe and half machete. His dying shriek as the top of his body separated from the lower limbs cut through Dave's miasma as cleanly as the edged weapon had passed through the man. Dave's vision cleared, but not the crippling inability to move. He saw the firing line overrun. Hunn and Fangr and one lone, loping Sliveen vaulted over their own dead and wounded, knocking aside guns, ignoring ineffectual bayonet thrusts. Fangr fell on marines in threes and fours, pulling them apart with fiendish and violent glee. The awful sound of limbs torn from sockets with a sucking, popping sound would stay in Dave's memory for the remainder of his days.

In less than a minute, the firing line disintegrated and the vanguard of the rampaging thrall broke out into clear ground, running straight toward the hundreds of civilians who had not fled quickly enough. The great mass of daemons was heedless of Dave and his two companions hunkered down in the shadows on the far left flank. But not all of them.

'Behind you,' Dave grunted.

The corpsman stood up with his weapon held low at the hip. Some sort of assault rifle. Normally it would have intimidated the hell out of someone like Dave, who had never had a thing for guns, a distaste that was only confirmed by his brother's death. But in the hands of the corpsman, spraying fire at a charging rhino-sized Hunn dominant, it looked utterly ridiculous. A toy. The corpsman emptied the full magazine into the Hunn, ignoring the smaller, more agile Fangr that bounded along beside it. Tracer rounds flashed and flared off the creature's armour. Armour-piercing ammunition punched through boiled leather and dull grey metal plate, but to no avail. The killing frenzy had come over this one, too. Raked by deep gouges and bloody welts, the Hunn roared in pain and outrage, swatted the rifle away with the point of its cleaver, and kicked the corpsman in the chest. The giant horned claws impaled the screaming man, and the Hunn shook off the carcass the way Dave might try to shake off a piece of paper stuck to his boot by dog shit.

Still Dave could not move. Still he lay helpless in the dirt as Everding shouted useless obscenities and unloaded a full mag of tracer and penetrator rounds at the Fangr leash. The 5.56-millimetre ammo scythed into the three daemon slaves, cutting two of them down with extravagant sprays of blood and gore. The third beast jagged to the left and sustained only a few grazing shots.

'Run, Hooper! GO!' the marine yelled at him. But Dave could not. He couldn't run. He couldn't even crawl to where

Lucille lay a few feet away. All he could do was lie there and wait to die.

Some fucking big league superhero he'd turned out to be.

Wounded, coughing dust and pink foam, Everding tried to draw his knife before the Fangr reached him, but it was moving with animal swiftness, and then it was airborne, jaws clamping shut around Everding's neck before he could even raise the tiny-looking blade. Man and daemon tumbled over together, fetching up in a writhing, caterwauling tangle on top of Dave, who could not even squirm out from underneath them. Everding lashed out weakly with his bayonet before the Fangr tore out his throat.

Hot blood poured out of the terrible wound, blinding Dave, getting into his nostrils, flooding his mouth with the coppery sweet taste of violation and death. The great dead weight of the marine who'd sacrificed himself in vain suddenly lifted clear of his chest.

The Fangr loomed over him, a snarling, stooping vision of horror painted in human blood, jaws festooned with man meat. Dave's heart was beating like a hammer just inside his rib cage.

Beside the leashed killer the Hunn stood bleeding and panting and regarded him with slow deliberation. Dave could feel the will of the dominant creature, the physical force of it restraining the leashed inferior. The battle or its aftermath raged on elsewhere, but the world, which he was about to depart, contracted down to the small dark circle in which the three of them eyed one another.

'You have shortened my leash,' the Hunn said in clear English.

Then Dave realised it hadn't used English at all. It had

spoken in the Olde Tongue, but he had understood it as clearly as he would understand Brian Williams reading a headline.

'Go fuck yourself,' Dave spat back at him, but it came out as a choking gargle, and he swallowed half a mouthful of Everding's lifeblood before gagging and vomiting again.

The Hunn understood well enough what he meant, though, and roared like a wounded bear. It stomped on Everding's head, crushing helmet and bone alike with a sick crunching pop. The Fangr snarled and strained at its invisible leash, which Dave could actually feel, the same way you feel the vibrations of a church bell inside you if you stand close enough when it strikes the hour.

The dead and the dying were all around. Screams and groans mingled with cries of fear as some of the laggard daemonum stopped and feasted on the fallen men. Sporadic gunfire cracked through the humid air, adding the slightest tincture of more hot copper and spent powder to the night scent of blood and iron. Tyres squealed and sirens wailed. Above them somewhere gunships pounded away, their rotors counting a drumbeat cadence to measure the pace of the massacre he, David Hooper, had spectacularly failed to prevent. In the distance, almost drowned out by the uproar, he could pick out the bass thump from someone's overpriced car audio system. Pink. Telling Dave to keep his drink and just give her the money.

He felt tired beyond endurance, wanting to just lay his head down and wait for the end. The zoo sounds of the Hunn and Fangr seemed to fade away. Everything faded away.

He thought at first he was losing consciousness. The nausea, the deep-body aches and burning pain, so many aches and pains that it was impossible to distinguish one hurt from another, the sense of futility and sorrow – they all faded as dark flowers bloomed in front of his eyes. He blinked, the eyelids sticking together with Everding's blood. And then he blinked again at the statue of the Hunn and its evil butt monkey.

They roared no longer. They moved not at all.

Nothing moved, and no sound came to him except for one sweet high note of song. An old battle hymn. Old before men had the language to sing hymns.

Lucille.

The pain vanished, washed away on her song. His strength and all his energy came surging back, carried in on the same channel. When he moved to stand up, the world did not spin around to plant his ass in the dirt again. His arms and legs were no longer immobile and leaden. He was able to spring up onto the balls of his feet and perform a playful roll to gather up the splitting maul, which honest to God *sighed* as his hands closed around her.

'Marty Grbac says hi,' he snarled, and with one overhead blow collapsed the Hunn from head to foot into a shower of broken bone, torn flesh, and blood. Still nothing moved. Not any speed that a hyperaccelerated Dave Hooper could perceive as movement, anyway. He stepped toward the frozen Fangr and swung Lucille at its head like Barry Bonds aiming for the cheap seats. He imagined knocking the thing's skull into orbit, but it merely disintegrated in a disgusting explosion of gore. A slow, strange geyser of thick daemonic ichor erupted from the creature's neck, the physics all wrong, and time slowed down again.

Until a sudden jump cut fast-forwarded the world back into sync with Dave.

He spun around with the force of the blow to find a few

dozen members of the thrall stopped in their tracks, distracted by their appetites. They hunkered down over human remains, tearing into the corpses and occasionally one another as they fought over the choice pieces. Many of the Hunn staggered about, snorting in a way that Dave recognised as laughter. Urgon had snorted at him in just the same fashion. They were drunk on the freshly decanted bloodwine of the First Platoon.

He found himself caught between the urge to charge in and start laying about him with Lucille and the more rational response of getting the hell out of Dodge. Running back to Heath and letting him figure out what to do.

After all, Dave had proved pretty conclusively that he wasn't Marvel material. He'd jumped in here, hadn't he, and look at the results of that. Thirty plus men and women dead a minute later. Hundreds more dying now as the main body of the thrall ran them down and tore them apart.

He started to back away from the creatures, mopping Everding's tacky drying blood from his eyes, ignoring Lucille, who seemed to be humming sweetly that she thought having at the thrall would be a fine and manly course of action.

The squeal of tyres caught his attention. A deep bass thrumming rolled across the killing field from Claiborne. Tupac declaring his intent to ride on the enemy. Doors popped open and slammed shut as men and women, all of them black and gunned up, emerged from behind the Pizza Hut, walking down on the Horde with an arms bazaar of weaponry: everything from comically small pistols to AKs and one belt-fed monster that reminded Dave of the old Rambo posters.

T-Qube, Dave thought.

The first rounds cracked out, targeted on the monsters feasting before him.

Not wanting to find out if he was bulletproof now, Dave did the only sensible thing.

He hit the dirt.

'Light them niggaz up!'

A wall of sound rolled over the battleground. The discrete pops and bangs of single-shot pistols, the hammering crack of a full auto, and the heavy pounding of what had to be the big belt-fed gun.

27

Dave looked up from the dirt with some dismay as the daemon war party turned away from the new threat and toward the crowded residential area south of the main road. The gangbangers pursued them, ignoring Dave lying prostrate on the ground but stopping to check on the marines. A few took what weapons they could scavenge from the dead. A young boy, too young for this sort of thing, Dave thought, went for a pair of dog tags, and another backhanded him.

'Show some respect,' he said. 'My brother's in the Marine Corps. Your cousin Tyrell, too, you little asshole.'

Dave couldn't say exactly how many people lay immediately in front of the daemon stampede, but it had to be hundreds, perhaps even a thousand or more. Many of the blocks were dark except for candlelight or torches, and here and there a burning oil drum. Some of the residents were on the streets, attempting to flee on foot. Some just milled about, talking to one another, checking their phones, attempting to find out what was happening. Others rode in vehicles that weren't moving much more quickly than the people on foot. But many were obviously staying put, unaware of the danger, not believing it, or perhaps simply possessed of a contrary frame of mind that was about to get them killed.

Once the gangsters were away, Dave took a couple of steps and leaped out into clear air and landed with a grunt in the parking lot of a church. He was moving at normal speed now, as were the congregation spilling out onto the front steps and the residents he'd passed earlier at warp speed walking down the middle of the road. Dave accelerated again, covering the distance back toward the command van in a dark glimmer. He found the SEALs a block down from the truck, running toward the battle.

'Whoa, what the hell, man!'

Allen jumped back a step as Dave materialised in front of him with a whoosh and a soft pop of displaced air.

Dave tried to get around Allen, but the SEAL stepped in front of him. 'What happened over there? One minute you're down and the next minute you're up?'

Captain Heath limped over. 'Forty-three marines are down.'

Dave hung his head low, nodding. 'I know. There's no time to explain. If you don't get on top of this, there'll be a heap more folks joining them.'

He could see medics worked frantically on the fallen SWAT trooper and the navy SEAL back by the truck, but Dave could tell by looking at them that they were gone.

'I took care of that, by the way,' he said. 'Sliveen scout. He's gone now, but there's probably a couple more around. That T-Qube guy and his crew are chasing the thrall straight into the neighbourhood. I thought I might be able to help the marines, but something went wrong. I couldn't . . .'

Heath looked at him as though he were mad, although that could have been because he was covered in gore and dripping ichor. SWAT officers and SEALs moved past the group, setting up to flank the Horde. Dave wiped some of the Horde off the hammer's head. Lucille, for her part, seemed satisfied with him. She sighed like a just-fucked prom queen.

A line of SEALs and SWAT officers opened fire from their improvised positions, enfilading the Horde, wearing down its right flank. Just as before with T-Qube's people, the combined firepower of the SEALs and SWAT whittled away at the weaker members of the Horde. Any other fighting force might have stopped to deal with the problem. The Horde instead sped toward the houses, leaving their fallen comrades behind. The gunfire was having the effect of herding them in the wrong direction.

'I need that gun run,' Heath said into his headset, ignoring Dave. 'How much longer?'

'Heath, you gotta stop shooting,' Dave said.

No one listened to him. The noise was too loud.

'STOP SHOOTING,' he shouted again. 'CEASE FIRE.'

'Who the fuck are you?' a SWAT officer shouted back.

'You're pushing them into the houses, asshole,' Dave said.

Heath ran over. 'Do as he says. Cease fire.'

The firing came to a halt. The Horde slowed for a moment to ponder the brief silence before another ragged volley from the gangbangers prodded them forward again.

'Look,' Dave said, feeling as though his head might twist right off the top of his body in frustration. He wanted to be able to move as quickly as he had when attacking the Sliveen. Everyone else's reactions and thoughts seemed to be dragging along at a glacial pace.

'We've got about a minute before they break into the streets at the edge of the field just south of Claiborne,' he warned. 'There's hundreds of people in those two or three blocks alone.

They are all going to die unless you can head off the attack.'

Allen appeared beside them. 'We gotta go, Captain,' he said. 'We have to move now if we're going to get there and set up any kind of blocking force. Second Platoon is still jammed up with refugee traffic. If they get free, they can reinforce us and we can limit the damage.'

Heath glanced briefly overhead, looking for deliverance, but it was hopeless. The sky was still full of news helicopters adding to the confusion, drawing onlookers to the area, and scaring the shit out of the residents. But even if the Cobras had a clear shot at the daemons, they were about to lose that advantage when the Horde got in among the residential streets. The one free gun run Dave had witnessed had seemed heavily constrained by the proximity of all the civilians who had gathered outside the strip mall on Claiborne to watch the show. He was no soldier, but it looked to him as though the choppers had held back.

'We don't have time,' he insisted. 'We don't have time for any of this crap. I can hold these guys. I can hold them off on my own for a few minutes, guaranteed, if you can get yourselves set up around the intersection two blocks north of here.'

'Why?' Heath asked. Allen also looked as though he'd appreciate an explanation. Dave had to shout over the uproar of orbiting helicopters, the crackle of gunfire, and the growing screams and cries of alarm to the north.

'There's some sort of school up there,' he said. 'Flood-damaged, I think. A lot of open ground out the front or maybe the back. Whatever. Two blocks north of here and then another block back east.' He pointed up the street along which he'd warped to take out the Sliveen. 'If I can get them in there, packed in tight, and you can keep the ground clear of civilians, does it give you enough space to use the gunships?'

Ashbury ran up, handing over the ruggedised tablet she was carrying. Heath had a quick look at the map onscreen and passed the device to Allen, who examined it and nodded.

'What are you going to do?' she asked. 'This isn't contained at all, Michael.'

'I'm going to make them an offer they can't refuse,' Dave answered. 'Literally.'

The two navy men and Ashbury exchanged a couple of brief, largely incomprehensible sentences in the jargon of their trade before Allen turned on his boot heel and began barking orders at both his men and Ostermann's. The SWAT commander, who had been tending to the body of his slain comrade, looked worried.

'We moving?'

Heath handed him the tablet, pointing out the intersection where they needed to concentrate their forces.

'We need to get as many civilians away from the blocks around that intersection as possible,' Heath said. 'Civilian non-combatants,' he added. 'Your man T-Qube and his crew just saved our asses up at the McDonald's. If they're willing, we can always use the extra firepower.'

'Oh, I don't think there's any question the Qube's boys are willing,' Ostermann said. 'Probably best if the request comes from one of your guys rather than mine, though.'

Dave cocked an ear to the north, where he was certain he could hear things getting worse. More gunfire. More screaming. Screeching tyres and the crash of metal on metal.

'Clock's tickin',' he said.

'I know,' Heath snapped. 'Dumb it down for me. What are you going to do? And what do you need?'

* * *

The thresh felt better in both its thinkings and its feelings as soon as they charged into the outskirts of the village. Although, it told itself, it really had to stop thinking of this place as a village. Nothing it had ever been told of men had prepared it for the grandeur and scale of this settlement. Straight lines and hard angles ran off toward a vanishing point. It was possible that some of these streets ran true for a bow shot or more. Grand structures, some of them towering more than two or three times the height of the BattleMaster himself, loomed over them. It was almost, though not quite, like running into a canyon.

And dark, so blessedly dark when the accursed flying beasts suddenly left off the chase. The thresh searched its thinkings for some clue why, having wounded their party so grievously, the ferocious insectivores would simply disappear like that. But as its eyestalks scanned the Above, it realised that not all of the wretched creatures had departed. Some of the larger, heavier beasts still circled high above, their eyes flashing red and, it suddenly realised, with men hanging suspended from the bellies of the beasts. Under the wings or . . .

Around it the earth thundered with the charge of the Vengeance. It was a charge, the thresh told itself. Not an ignominious retreat and headlong flight into the relative safety of the human village. Shaking its head at the confused and contrary thinkings, the thresh gave up on trying to understand what was happening. How could this strange species of Drakon ally itself with these animals? How was it that men rode in the belly of these Drakon? Where the thresh could see them standing, waving and gesturing with the staffs and wands it now recognised as the source of their killing magick. So many confused thinkings. So few satisfying answers. It was all so very different from how the thresh had imagined this might turn out.

They had meant to storm into the village in the first place. To kill the elders, eat a few nestlings and spread an exemplary terror among the calflings. As the dirt and sharp stinging stones kicked up around its pounding claws and the air about its head cracked and buzzed with the magick fires of the human wizards, the thresh kept telling itself that this would all end well. It had to.

Urspite Scaroth Ur Hunn was vexed. As the remnants of his force stampeded toward the human village, which he now conceded appeared to be somewhat larger and more impressive than any human settlement he had ever read of in the scrolls, the BattleMaster was uncertain whether he should be leading the charge from the fore or from somewhere in the rear ranks, driving it on as though it were a chariot so that he might best wield the whip of command and direct his thrall in such a way as to recover this situation.

Not that there was much chance of recovery, he thought bitterly. The surviving Grymm sprinted along on either side of him, bellowing orders – Orders! The hide of them! – that they storm into the village square and laager up, forming a defensive perimeter to hold off the attacks of the wizards while a messenger returned to the UnderRealms to bring back reinforcements. A full legion should be enough, they agreed.

A third Lieutenant Grymm had been adding his snarls and barks to the argument when the bizarre human lightning that flew as straight and true as a war shaft struck him at the base of his neck, causing his head to fly off. The corpse kept running for a few steps before collapsing and almost tripping a leash of Fangr coming up on the Grymm's tail. It was heresy, but the BattleMaster sent a silent prayer of thanks to whichever human wizard had been responsible for the favour. The other two lieutenants, however, redoubled their efforts.

If Scaroth had not been short of breath already, he would have laughed in their snouts. Bad enough that he should have come here with a Dread Company only to have it mangled by wizard men who not only refused to flee (the fools!) but who hid behind whatever cover the battlefield might provide (the cowards!) and then continued to fight from that same hiding place. With vile magicks (the fiends!). His enthralled war band was broken. His Sliveen scouts were lost somewhere beyond trumpet call. And for all these losses he had not one shred of man meat on his fangs to show in mitigation. It was a disaster. There was no chance of quitting this accursed realm unless he would be able to place before Her Majesty such tribute as would erase the shame to be forever attached to his name upon the scrolls.

As they entered the boundaries of the village, however, Urspite Scaroth Ur Hunn was faced with another conundrum. His thrall maintained something that might pass as good order and discipline while hemmed in on either side by the surprisingly large shelters and temples of the settlement. But that cohesion was already fraying as Fangr and Hunn on the flanks of the sortie scented fresh man meat and heard the screams and cries of the villagers. Defenceless villagers. With their wizard mercenaries falling behind, even as the dangerous magicks continued to lash at his rear, the village lay open before them.

But just as he had been vexed by the question of whether to lead from the fore or the rear, the BattleMaster now found himself roaring over the heads of the Grymm to impose some form of discipline on his host, which was disintegrating as the bloodlust took hold of it. Entering the village would not be the deliverance they sought if the war party fell to pieces in an orgy of singular slaughter and mayhem. Two Fangr and one Hunn fell to his slashing blade, and he was forced to race to the head of the column, cutting the legs out from under another Fangr before the great heaving, panting mass of daemonum slowed and eventually stopped.

'You will hold,' he roared. 'We will reduce this village when the time for its reduction has come. But now you will hold and –'

But they were not attending to him. All of them – Hunn, Fangr, thresh, and even the Lieutenants Grymm – stood staring past him, over his head. Their jaws were agape, their features mute with confusion and stupidity. Urspite Scaroth Ur Hunn tightened his grip on FoeSunder and turned slowly in place, wondering what fresh hell could possibly await him.

When he saw the lights of the city – it could only be a city – his jaw dropped, too. He realised that they stood not in some small, isolated village but on the very edges of a great metropolis. A human metropolis. How was such a thing even possible?

A quick glance at the thresh confirmed that it, too, had come to the same conclusion and was as stunned and defanged by the revelation as he.

They were going to need more than a company, more than a legion. Something terrible had happened in the Above. Man had been allowed to rise far beyond his natural station. The vast wall of light on the horizon, a towering gap-toothed edifice that soared as tall as a mountain range, was greater – heresy to say it, but it was true – in size and scale (and possibly even power, he whispered in his silent places) than all but the mightiest of Her Majesty's strongholds.

Urspite Scaroth Ur Hunn let FoeSunder drop to the guard position, the point of his great blade striking the ground in a shower of sparks.

'Unholy minion shit,' he grunted just before a titanic war drum boomed a challenge not two strides from where he stood.

28

Dave Hooper flew, and the city passed beneath him. Failed husband, absent father, wastrel, and asshole, he flew through the night air holding Lucille to his chest, knees bent and eyes slitted against the wind of his passage. Beneath his boots slipped the rusted roofs of shotgun shacks and cinder block apartments, some of them slumped and all but tumbled down, others maintained with the best of intentions in the face of the crushing, relentless weight that bore down every day on those people, those countless millions, who lived at the bottom of the heap. Dave Hooper flew over them all. Over stunted, leafless trees, rubbish-strewn vacant lots, lovingly maintained church gardens, darkened homes, and great fires ablaze where vehicles had collided and exploded, where flames consumed houses that lay cheek by jowl, and where some idiot was having a barbecue on his back porch. He was watching the Apocalypse engulf his neighbourhood on a small portable television he had carried out onto a card table and plugged into an extension cord. Dave soared over it all. A quick turn of the head, as though he were driving his car and checking the side mirror, and he could see Heath leading his men and Ostermann's away from the Horde. So quickly was Dave moving that they appeared as tiny, static figurines arranged by a model maker.

Turning his attention to *dar ienamic*, he measured his progress toward the pack of slavering man-eaters and was content with his calculations. He would land exactly where he had intended: two strides from the figure that stood noticeably separate from the mass of daemons. He would land in the tray of a pick-up abandoned in the street by an owner who had tried to flee on foot and who now lay in pieces by the front wheel. Maybe the car had stalled. Maybe the driver had panicked. It didn't matter. Dave flew toward his intended destination, powered in his flight by one great leap of such prodigious motive force that his rational human mind had doubted his ability to make it in spite of all that had happened.

His rational human mind was wrong, and Dave flew. He flew down upon them like an avenging eagle, talons out, ready to rip and tear and rend limb from limb. As he flew from the flat-topped roof of the Advance Auto Parts depot, he measured his foe. There stood the BattleMaster at the head of his fighting column, the tip of his sword resting on the surface of the road as though he were lost and pondering his next move.

'Should have checked Google Maps, dickhead,' Dave muttered.

Like gargoyles, two Grymm lieutenants stood shield- and dagger-wise to the Master of Hunn. Dave contemplated the representatives of the ancient warrior order, as much priests as they were soldiers. The BattleMaster towered over them, naturally, and even the rank and file of the Hunn had the advantage of them in size and reach. All of which meant nothing, he knew. The Grymm lieutenants were combat-adept, as were all the members of that clan and order. He searched for a word from his human vocabulary that would do them justice. A couple suggested themselves: 'fanatics', 'jihadi'.

They would do nicely.

As he began his descent toward the BattleMaster's thrall, Dave took the measure of their power. There were still over 200 daemonum afoot down there, frozen in tableau by the hyper-accelerated speed of his approach. But from their posture, from the way they appeared to be standing rather than leaping and running at the nearest prey, he was reasonably sure that they had ceased their charge into the housing projects while the BattleMaster issued his orders. Dave guesstimated there to be a reduced Talon of Hunn and their leashed Fangr. The Hunn were down to half of their original number. As he dropped through the night toward the tray of the pick-up, he noted the distance between the rearguard of the BattleMaster's thrall and the lead elements of the pursuing marines and gangsters. He hoped that Heath would get word through to the pursuers to disengage before they made contact again.

He needed the Horde to focus. Not on the marines, the SEALs, or the gangbangers, and certainly not on the hundred or more terrified residents he could see within a few lazy strides of some of the outermost members of the daemon pack.

He needed the Horde to focus on him.

Dave flew down upon his prey, swinging Lucille in a great circular arc like a cathedral bell ringer or that guy who used to swing the big puffy mallet to make the gong go *boom* at the start of the old movies.

He landed, boots crashing into the open tray of the pick-up, the twelve-pound steel head of Marty Grbac's enchanted splitting maul slamming down on the roof of the empty driver's cabin with an explosive, head-splitting detonation that blew out not just the windows of the truck but all the windows up and down the street. As he decelerated, the world around him sped up, with thousands of tiny twinkling shards of automotive glass spraying outward, and some of the closest daemons flinching away from the fearsome noise; even the BattleMaster of the Hunn took one involuntary step backward. Car alarms blared up and down the street. Gunfire fell silent, then roared up again out of nowhere. People screamed, and dogs barked with such abandon that they sounded authentically mad.

'Hi,' said Dave. 'My name's Dave. And I hear someone sent out for an ass kicking.'

The thresh flinched from the enormous, volcanic noise, but it did not retreat. It was proud of that depth of self-possession, for even the BattleMaster could not help taking one unthinking step back from *dar ienamic*. That was hardly the fault of Urspite Scaroth Ur Hunn.

This human had allowed his fellow warriors to sacrifice themselves in battle; a brutal, noble act. A sacrifice that the scrolls had explicitly described. The thresh realised that they were dealing with something far more dangerous than human warriors or skyborne riders in the night's clouds. They were dealing with the supreme human champion – for that was what he had to be, their ur-Champion. Nothing else could explain the calamity that had befallen the Dread Company.

The ur-Champion had come out of nowhere. Or rather, appeared to. But the thresh had seen it coming. This was not to boast of its superior thinkings and attention to the battlefield minutiae; rather, it had been a stroke of luck. The human form, impossibly suspended high in the air, silhouetted against the bright background of the mysterious city in the distance, just happened to be exactly where the thresh was looking when this warrior, the ur Dave as it called itself, appeared.

It was just for the briefest of moments, a fraction of a fraction of the tiny space between one beating of the hearts and the next. Indeed, when the thresh turned over its thinkings and feelings on the matter later, it decided that it had not in fact seen the Dave but rather a shadow, a ghost image of this Dave as it passed in front of an opportune light source at just the right moment. The Dave simply moved too quickly to keep one's eyestalks on it.

'What?' Urspite Scaroth Ur Hunn roared in confusion. 'Seize him!'

But the Dave seemed unperturbed. As one of the Hunn set two Fangr on the solitary man, the thresh scuttled forward to advise caution.

'He knows the Olde Tongue, my lord,' the thresh hissed. 'He comes upon us like a great boulder, afire and falling from the sky. We should –'

The world turned upside down as the BattleMaster cuffed the lesser daemon across the head, knocking it end over end. When the thresh came to rest at the foot of one of the Lieutenants Grymm, it saw what was happening to the acolytes as they tried to carry out their orders. The Dave did not so much as twitch when they approached. Not until they passed within reach of its lower limbs, which suddenly struck out with such speed that none could see them move, certainly not the hapless Fangr. Each squealed when struck, but the shriek of pain and shock was cut off by whatever damage the blow did, and they fell broken and dead to the ground many strides away.

'What's your name, big fella?' the Dave said, speaking directly to the BattleMaster in the Olde Tongue with the slightly guttural, snouty tone of a Hunn from the Fourth Legion. The daemonum of the war party remained as still as bedrock. Only the Lieutenants Grymm moved, and only to lean toward one another and whisper in the secret voices of their clan.

Urspite Scaroth Ur Hunn was at a loss. His talons clenched and unclenched around the urmin-hide hilt of his long blade. He snarled and bared his fangs at the upstart human.

'Are you the champion of this village?' he demanded to know.

'A champion?' the Dave replied. 'Hell, no. I'm just a guy. So who are you again?'

The insolent creature rearranged its facial features in a way the thresh did not much care for. If it did not know better, it would have said the Dave was mocking them. Both Lieutenants Grymm tried to speak with the BattleMaster, but he pushed them away as they approached. One even stumbled and fell on its tail, sending a jolt through the assembled host.

'Pity I don't have my phone,' said the Dave. 'That would've made a great BuzzFeed GIF. So, really, who are you assholes?'

The shock that ran through every sinew in the BattleMaster's body could have been no greater if the queen herself had inserted a white-hot branding iron into his cloaca.

'I am the BattleMaster of this thrall,' roared Urspite Scaroth Ur Hunn. He drew his sword, the point screeching across the hard black surface of the street, a shower of sparks pouring from the tip. 'This is my great blade, FoeSunder. With it I have slain *ienamicae* without number –'

'Wait a minute, hold on,' the Dave interrupted, holding

up one of its small pink hands. 'Did you say your gay blade? I mean, not that's there's anything wrong with that, but I noticed that none of you are, like, wearing pants, and if I've ruined a special moment here . . .'

The BattleMaster drew himself up to his full height, standing at least again as tall as the human champion, although they did stare level into each other's eyes because the Dave still stood atop the beastless chariot onto which he had jumped with such a great booming report to announce his arrival.

'I am Urspite Scaroth Ur Hunn,' bellowed the commander of Her Majesty's Vengeance.

Again the Dave did that strange unpleasant thing with its face that made the thresh feel it was being mocked.

'Seriously?' he said. 'Well, same as before, I'm Dave.' He spread his hands wide. 'And these are all the fucks I don't really give about who you are.'

The thresh twitched its ears in the direction of a new sound, a high-pitched keening that reminded it of claws scraping on a rock. The sound was growing. It risked taking a few of its eyestalks off the human champion for just a moment, and what it found was even more disturbing. Villagers were gathering at the edge of the confrontation, pointing and staring and – it was sure of this – *mocking* them. The screeching and squealing it could hear was the sound of human mockery. It chanced a furtive look at the Lieutenants Grymm who had also noticed the change while most of Scaroth's thrall remained mesmerised by the confrontation between their master and this arrogant calfling.

Arrogant with reason, thought the thresh.

The BattleMaster let loose such a roar that his thrall

retreated from him. The sound of human screechings and mockery ended abruptly, replaced by a few satisfying cries of alarm. But not from the Dave. It merely quirked the edges of its mouth in a gentle way that suggested it was not much concerned by anything. Certainly not by Scaroth.

The BattleMaster raised FoeSunder on high, making ready to cleave the Dave in two, but even then the curious expression on the human's face did not change. It did deign to speak, however, before the BattleMaster could bring the giant blade down upon its head.

'I challenge you, Urspite Scaroth Ur Hunn, leader of this feeble pack,' the Dave cried out, stunning the assembled host. 'I challenge you according to the lore of the ancient scrolls and by virtue and warrant of my worth to make this challenge. You shall answer it or your name shall be etched into the scrolls forevermore as a byword for shame and cowardice and failure. I challenge you, Urspite Scaroth Ur Hunn, and you shall answer this challenge in front of your thrall.'

The proper and prescribed form of the old words hung like a blade over Scaroth's neck. They stayed his weapon from the downward strike against the Dave. The BattleMaster's shock, his indignation, and his disbelief rippled out across the entire thrall, transmitted from Hunn to Fangr to Grymm and even down to the lowly thresh.

The BattleMaster's blade, dark with ichor and gore and bloodwine, did not waver at the apogee of its killing stroke. Scaroth drew the great sword down slowly but deliberately, as though he could not believe this was happening and so was forced to handle his blade with added caution lest in the madness of the situation it turn on him, too.

'You dare not do this,' Scaroth hissed at the human.

'Oh, you'd be surprised how often I hear that,' the Dave replied. 'My wife, the IRS, Urgon Htoth Ur Hunn.'

Hackles suddenly flared up all along the back of the thresh. The Lieutenants Grymm, too, it noticed, suddenly fell into a huddle of silent quickthinkings. Scaroth had the sense to look, if not troubled, then at least intrigued.

'What news have you of our brother Urgon?' Scaroth asked quietly.

The Dave twisted his face again into that annoying challenge that made his eyes squint and bared what few and tiny fangs he had.

'I kicked his ass. And I intend to kick yours in a few minutes, but by the lore of the scrolls we must settle on terms. And my terms are pretty simple. I'll kick your ass, and you'll get the fuck out of here while the getting is good. Once your ass has been kicked, I promise to let all of your friends here leave without kicking theirs, too. But you will agree to withdraw from this realm without harming one more of these villagers. And you will not return. These are the terms of my challenge, now laid before you in the presence of your thrall. Disgrace your nest if you have not the stomachs for this fight.'

The entire thrall was focused on the confrontation between the BattleMaster and the human champion now. None could imagine how it had come to know the ancient forms of address and challenge. But it did, and the BattleMaster was bound by honour to respond. The thresh, being concerned with actual thinkings and feelings rather than with the baser pursuits of mere slaughter, was free to let its considerable mind wander, however. The Lieutenants Grymm, too, of course, were known to be wise in the thinking of things, although they seemed to have fallen into a dispute over whether Scaroth should accept the challenge. The thresh was more concerned, even disturbed, by the change that had come over the villagers. There were at least a company's worth of them now, edging up through the shadows to watch their champion. Some had even begun a war chant.

'USA. USA. USA.'

The thresh was at a loss to understand the meaning of the chant, but he did not like the way it seemed to embolden the cattle.

'By what right do you claim the worth of challenge?' asked one of the lieutenants without seeking the permission of Scaroth to speak. A fact that for the thresh was telling.

'Dispute my right, then, if you have the talons for it,' replied the Dave, as though he did not care whether the Grymm answered him. The lieutenants reared back as if struck. Scaroth seemed almost amused by their umbrage.

'Yes, why don't we test the worth of its challenge? And of your craft at arms, my Lieutenants Grymm? Before I would lower myself or befoul my blade with the ichor of this creature, I would first know that it is worth raising my sword arm against him.'

The BattleMaster turned back to the human and seemed almost in good humour.

'You know your scroll lore, calfling,' it said. 'Our brother Urgon has taught you well. So you would know that I might test the virtue of your claim by right of proxy.'

The Dave lifted its shoulders as if this was no concern to it.

'Whatever. An ass kicking delayed is still an ass kicking, and you got one coming, buddy.'

'Indeed,' said Urspite Scaroth Ur Hunn.

* * *

It was working, Dave thought as he saw black-clad SWATs and uniformed patrolmen insinuating themselves into the narrow spaces between the houses, pulling residents away, forcing them to go at gunpoint if necessary. The volume of fire from the marines and T-Qube's crew had died away, too. They were hunkered down behind whatever cover they could find, about fifty yards behind the last of the daemon pack. The air still thudded and hummed with the rotor blades of a dozen choppers. He dared not look back over his shoulder to check on Heath's progress toward the ambush spot. He needed to keep the Horde focused on him.

The ritual of challenge by right of worth seemed to be doing that.

Fuck knew where that had come from.

Perhaps this Scarface dude was right and he did owe Urgon a solid. He'd wondered back at the command vehicle how best to confront the orcs and instantly knew without having to search for the knowledge that a challenge offered to the BattleMaster in the proper form could not be brushed off. It was an offer he couldn't refuse.

Not so long as Dave proved his worth, and these monster Nazis in the char-grilled bone armour were about to do that for him.

The Grymm.

Sort of like the SS of the six clans.

Old Scarface certainly seemed happy enough to throw them under a bus, but from what Dave knew of relations between the Grymm and the other clans, that wasn't surprising. These guys would be hurrying back to the palace first chance they had to badmouth the BattleMaster no matter how well the raid had gone.

And it hadn't gone well at all, had it?

So Urspite Scaroth Ur Hunn would be scoping hard for some way to cover himself in glory. The chance to meet and defeat a human champion, perhaps one who could explain why the Horde had taken such a bloody snout here – that was a redemption shot worth taking. Especially if it meant seeing off a couple of Grymm as well.

Dave felt a slight hunger pang.

He waited for the crippling wave of pain and nausea that had taken him down earlier. The shame of that failure, his own failure, pushed Dave to find a way to redeem himself. If even just a little.

Lucille sent him reassuring vibes.

Be cool, Dave, he told himself. *Time to get this party started.*

'So, Scarface,' he said directly to the BattleMaster. 'This all you got? These two cockchafers? Because you know what they say about the Grymm, don't you? The only real fighting they do is over which one of them gets to ass-kiss the Low Queen in the parts the other Grymm can't reach. Maybe you want to throw in a couple of Hunn as well? Some real fighters. I got plenty of whup-ass to spare.'

The effect on Scaroth's thrall was interesting. Many of the Hunn dominants snorted appreciatively at the insult done to the Grymm clan, but their amusement turned to dangerous offence when he offered to take on a couple of them, too.

Another hunger pang.

He casually fished a chocolate bar from one of the breast pockets of his shirt. Not making a big deal of it. He was just a casual chocolate-lovin' motherfucker, was all. Lookin' to kick him some ass and maybe eat him some Hershey Bars while he was waiting.

The hunger pangs dialled back a little as he chewed and swallowed.

A disagreement flared into an argument among what he took to be the leadership group of the raiding party: Scaroth, the Grymm, a couple of Hunn dominants, and a smaller critter.

A baby Threshrend, he thought idly. Thinky little fuckers.

The daemon inferiorae tried to offer its two cents worth, but a Hunn kicked it away. It yelped and slunk back to the rear ranks of the company. The daemons, he was glad to see, were tightly bunched now, many of them jockeying for a clear view of the challenge.

Dave took the opportunity to uncap an energy gel.

He drained that one as casually as could be, trying to look bored, all the while looking around, checking on progress. They played a lot of poker on the rig. Not everyone could get on the Xbox at the same time, after all. And though he wasn't the coolest hand at the card table, he liked to think he had more game than these ass biters.

'So,' he said, deciding to push things along, 'what happened to you guys? You used to be cool. And now a dude throws down a challenge and you gotta get into a full circle jerk to figure out who's gonna get their asses kicked by him. Scaroth, man. That's lame.'

'Enough,' Scaroth snarled, sheathing FoeSunder. With a flick of his wrists, he motioned forward two of the largest Hunn. They grinned hungrily at Dave, moving left and right, dagger- and shield-wise, to outflank him. The Grymm meanwhile drew their own blades and began to advance on him as the daemon war band took up their own chant.

'Hunn ur Horde. Hunn ur Horde. HUNN UR HOR–'

Dave Hooper didn't let them finish. He tossed aside the

gel pack and hopped down from the rear tray of the totalled pick-up. As soon as his boots touched the ground, he stomped on the accelerator.

Again he was thrown by expecting the world to become a blur, when of course he was the blur within it. The Horde, the anxious human onlookers, the long swaying stalks of grass in the wasteland across the street, the outlines of the helicopters circling above them – all these things grew not just clearer to him but more vital, as though they somehow pressed themselves into the fabric of reality with much greater force.

He didn't bother with theatrics for the Hunn, jagging shield- and dagger-wise, using the axe head of the maul for the first time to decapitate the two dominants before turning on the Lieutenants Grymm in the blink of an eye. He swung Marty's heavy-hitting sledge down low, breaking the knees of his first target, sweeping the slow-moving feet out from beneath it. The momentum of the swing carried him across to the other unholy warrior, whose skull he split with the axe head before spinning in place to finish off the first lieutenant, who was busy crashing to the ground.

He had time to eat another chocolate bar before the carcass thudded down on the tarmac, but as soon as it did, Dave brought the hammer down on its head with such force that the explosion of bone shards, broken teeth, and brain flecks painted everyone within three strides.

He decelerated back toward the truck as the first racking gut cramp hit him.

He was hungry. He'd burned through all of his stored energy, and now his white-hot metabolism was eating him from within. Taking a pull from the CamelBak Chief Allen had rigged up flooded Dave's system with Gatorade. The cramps subsided again while he threw in a couple of CLIF bars, chocolate-chip cookie-dough flavoured, to power the internal turbine that was throttled up to full capacity.

'Damn if kickin' so much ass don't give a man a powerful appetite.'

He kept a cheesy grin plastered on his face, but it was hard. Sweat began to bead his forehead.

'So, worthy enough for you?' he asked the BattleMaster, who stood with jaws agape and dawning horror filling its black sharklike eyes.

'We can just leave it at that if you want,' Dave said, all but grimacing with the need to bend himself double around the terrible pains shooting though his guts. 'Dead Grymm won't tell no tales. How about we call it done and you just fuck off back where you came from?'

Urspite Scaroth Ur Hunn let go with an animal roar of enraged hatred just as Dave got his second wind. The BattleMaster strode toward him, each foot tread punching a two-inch depression into the road surface. With slow, casual relish, Scaroth unsheathed FoeSunder from his silver-trimmed scabbard, twirling the great blade. Glints of dark iron flickered in the night, giving Dave a glimpse of the spike that extended from the pommel. It was all too easy to imagine that nasty fucking thing driving through the top of his skull.

'Trifle with the Horde?' Scaroth growled. 'Think that treacherous Urgon has taught you everything? You have the strength of a score of your kind because you took all that Urgon had.'

Dave could see flashes of Urgon's life. Long hours of training, rites of initiation, battles and campaigns fought with rival clans. The sacrifice and ritual required before each battle to sustain one's strength. He could sense how Urgon might deal with Scaroth if he relaxed and let the knowledge flow to him.

'Hear that, Urgon? You Dave's bitch now.' Dave shifted his grip on Lucille. Tried not to hold her too stiffly. 'Make me a sandwich for ol' Scaroth here.'

He could have sworn the splitting maul purred in his hands.

'Just as you stole all that Brother Urgon had,' Scaroth said, 'I will take all that you have. But I will take it with honour. By killing you here.'

Scaroth brought FoeSunder up and flowed into a killing stance. The point of the blade glinted high above Dave's head before rushing down with terrible speed.

Dave dropped to his right knee with Lucille above his head, blocking the first blow, half expecting Scaroth's blade to slice straight through the wooden handle. But the enchanted hardwood held, the blow landing with a giant clang. Holding the Hunn's blade, he pushed up with his right hand, using the maul's head to drive the blade off to his left. Coiled tightly, Dave's legs launched him into Scaroth's midsection, knocking the BattleMaster off his feet. Hooper rolled over the snapping fangs and hot froth to land on his feet a couple of yards away.

They circled each other one step at a time, shield-wise. Helicopters, hammering overhead, focused their searchlights on the action, driving the remnants of the Horde away from the two combatants.

'I will feast on you this day,' Scaroth said, lunging toward Dave. 'The little champion's blood will make a fine aperitif before I feed on your nestlings.'

'They have aperitifs in Monsterland? Man, you guys have changed. It used to be all about the skulls full of bloodwine.'

Dave parried down with Lucille, a great clash of sparks bursting where the two weapons made contact. He whipped back and swung in an upward arc from the parry for Scaroth's wrists, but the BattleMaster merely caught the splitting maul and with a twist of his wrists sent it flying through the air.

Shit, Dave thought, scrabbling across the ground.

'A charmed weapon?' Scaroth asked. 'Is that all you have, Champion? Pathetic.'

Scaroth kicked Dave, launching him skidding across the street. When he stood up, Scaroth was already there with a backhand that knocked him down. The BattleMaster raised his foot to crush Dave's skull.

Hooper rolled across broken glass, avoiding the foot stomp that punched up a cloud of pulverised asphalt. His lungs burned, and his mouth was full of cotton-thick spit that made it hard to breathe. Every muscle ached from the exertion of defending himself. With his last reserves, Dave backed up to the shattered truck, where the tailgate hung by a single hinge. He grabbed the F-150's tailgate and tore it off.

Scaroth kicked the improvised shield dead centre as Dave brought it down to protect himself. It folded like tinfoil around the Hunn's foot, launching Dave across the street and through the front porch of a vacated home. He heard old dry wooden slats crack and explode, tasted dust, and felt broken bones knitting back together. His strength ebbed away ever more rapidly, and he wondered if he could even get back on his feet, when Chief Allen emerged from cover to kneel beside him. Scaroth approached slowly and surely, carrying his great war cleaver as though it weighed nothing.

'Dave, let Igor take the shot,' Allen said. 'You are getting murdered out there, buddy.'

Dave rolled to his feet, sucking down most of the remaining Gatorade in one long draw. 'Zach, I gotta do this.'

'Why?'

'Reasons.'

They made eye contact not as civilian and soldier but as men, allies in a common cause. Chief Petty Officer Zach Allen drew his Gerber Mark II fighting knife. He handed it to Dave.

'Take this at least.'

'Thanks. A Snickers would have been better, but . . . no matter what happens,' Dave said, taking the knife, 'if I kill Scaroth, you have to let the rest go. It's a deal. They'll honour it. That's why I have to kill him, not Igor.'

'I'll let Heath know,' Allen said. 'And Dave?'

'Yeah?'

Allen extended his hand. 'Good luck, man. Fight dirty.'

Dave took the blade. 'It's all I got. And beers later. Lots of beers.'

Scaroth casually swung FoeSunder through the picket fence, atomising it, and stepped over the wreckage. 'Champion? Why do you hide from me? Do you wish dishonour to your realm? Come and let us finish this bargain of ours. Perhaps if you die well, I will spare a few of your kind from this realm. Her Majesty could keep them as pets.'

Dave got to his feet and stepped onto the front porch. In the distance, he could see Lucille lying in the middle of the street, calling dolefully to him. He wondered if he could just wish her into his hand. Like Thor's hammer.

Tried.

Failed.

'So that's a bust,' he muttered.

The Gerber, the small black fighting knife, seemed

pathetically inadequate for the job of carving up Satan's own rhino. He might as well have at him with a plastic coffee spoon. Nonetheless, he concealed the blade behind his forearm, gripped in the palm of his right hand, and closed with the giant Hunn. Knees bent, empty hand forward, just as his stomach cramped painfully and his vision greyed out at the edges.

'I can make this painless for you if you hold fast and bare your neck to the mercy stroke,' Scaroth said in what passed for a whisper. 'I would do you that honour, for you have rid me of those inconvenient Grymm.'

They circled each other in front of the shack. Dave was vaguely aware of onlookers nearby. Not just the SEALs watching from cover but local people huddled fearfully in the shadows, peeking out from behind curtains as if thin doors and glass might protect them.

'Scaroth?' Dave sighed. 'You talk too much.'

Dave hit the accelerator and with a flick of his wrist threw the Gerber straight into Scaroth's right eye, where it buried itself up to the hilt. The Hunn screeched in pain and fury as Dave tried to run for Lucille, dizzy with hunger. The giant daemon lashed out with one foot, extending a talon that tripped Dave as he tried to slip past.

Scaroth howled, bringing his blade down again. With only one eye his aim was off, and Dave rolled away from each strike until he could scramble to his feet. He ducked a slashing attempt to behead him and drove a solid right hook into the BattleMaster's naked crotch. Cock-punching an enormous monster penis was among the most unpleasant things he'd ever had to do in his life. A bellow erupted from within the creature's chest as he sailed backward.

'You know . . .' Dave gasped for air as he staggered over to collect Lucille. 'For once I'm actually grateful someone has balls bigger than mine.'

He made it to the splitting maul and felt a measure of his strength return as his hands closed around her. Scaroth gathered himself, still unsteady from the low blow, facing Dave, both hands on the hilt of FoeSunder, claws out. Blood ran down his face from the Gerber that was still embedded in his right eye.

'Trickery,' he grunted. 'Feeble trickery is all you offer.'

'And a prize-winning cock punch. Gotta give me credit for that.'

'There will be much pain for that!'

Dave was at the point of collapse. The members of the thrall were piled up across the roadway, straining against their bloodlust, wanting to charge him but mindful of the grave dishonour they would bring to their clans and nest if they intervened. Allen had disappeared back into the darkness, and those residents who had foolishly gathered or stopped in their flight to watch his challenge were all slipping away as quietly as they could. Time to roll a hard six. Summoning the last of his energy, drawing what he could from Lucille and not really understanding how that was even possible, Dave launched himself into the air, bringing the hammer up behind his back. Scaroth turned to carve him in half, but Dave was moving too fast, bringing Lucille down with the last of his rapidly failing might. The splitting maul shattered the forged metal of FoeSunder and bit into Scaroth's right shoulder. Dave roared his own *shkriaa* as the great wedge of American steel sliced through the BattleMaster's armour, hide, sinew, and bone, bisecting him diagonally from shoulder to hip in a geyser of blood and horror. The two halves fell to the ground with a wet, spurting plop.

The Horde stood silent as the choppers circled overhead and sirens wailed in the background. Another Hunn stepped forth to look at the body of the slain BattleMaster. With a couple of kicks to the shoulder, the daemon grunted, nodding to itself.

'We shall withdraw from your realm, ur Dave,' the beast said, its voice thick with contempt and shame.

Dave, hyperventilating now and swaying on his feet, took a gulp of air and nodded. 'Well . . . bye, then. Don't let the door hit you in the ass on the way out.'

The Horde turned as one and began to retrace their steps. And that was it. They were done. None broke ranks to feed on the calflings of New Orleans or even to gather the bodies of their fallen. With heads low, they trudged back to the construction site where the portal grew wider with each passing minute.

Dave leaned on Lucille, feeling a wave of fatigue and nausea building, threatening to sweep him away. Casting a glance at Scaroth's corpse, he searched for some feeling but came up empty.

Chief Allen and the SEALs emerged cautiously from cover, tracking the monsters with their weapons. Dave knelt down to pluck the Gerber from Scaroth's sightless eye socket, and his knees gave way, spilling him onto the ground next to the thing he had killed. Igor, towering over the pair, took a long look at the BattleMaster's carcass before giving a nod of approval.

'You need training,' Igor said. 'You fight like an idiot.'

Dave shook his head. 'Nah, I don't think so. We're done here.

Next time we see these cocksuckers, it'll be at the multiplex.'

'I'll bet they won't show their junk,' said Igor. 'Not if they want an M rating.'

Marine Corps helicopters roared overhead as he spoke. A mechanical ripping sound, perhaps the longest fart Dave had ever heard in his life, tore through the darkness. Long streams of tracer fire arced away over the roofline, and a shower of brass casings rained down on the street, a line of tinkling metal charms that raced away in the wake of the gun run. Dave spun around. He could see Heath looking at him, as shocked as he. He hadn't ordered the attack.

The war party scattered under the onslaught of the helicopter's nose-mounted machine guns, but the surviving leaders of the thrall were there in the chaos and madness, organising their forces back into a rough line of battle facing to the east, toward the tightly packed grid of slum housing in which hundreds, maybe a thousand people still cowered.

'Betrayers!' a Hunn commandant shrieked. 'Kill them all!'

'Zach, get him to stop,' Dave gasped. 'We're breaking the deal. We had a deal.'

Chief Allen shook his head, dragging Dave out of the fire zone. 'Dude, I'm sorry. I dunno what –'

Tracer fire and rockets reached out from the sky, lightning bolts of technology breaking monster bodies apart, splitting muscle and bone, spilling the blood of the Horde into the soil. Dave took a step to intervene, to stop the Cobras himself if needs must.

Heath half ran, half hobbled over to where Allen and Dave had taken shelter on the porch of a small home. He was holding one finger to his ear as he ran with an increasingly debilitating limp, screaming into the headset that connected him back to the command truck and presumably up the chain of command. With his other hand he fired short bursts at any of the thrall that made to charge at him.

The screaming started again, the sounds of slaughter as dozens of Hunn and Fangr that had escaped the conflagration of high explosives and flying metal burst into the surrounding streets and fell upon the fleeing populace.

'What the fuck did you do?' Dave shouted as his head swam and his muscles cramped. Allen tried to feed him a drink tube from his own CamelBak, and Dave knocked it away at first before angrily grabbing the nozzle and sucking for all he was worth.

'Well, tell him to shut it the fuck down,' Heath yelled into the tiny microphone of his headset, ignoring Dave. He looked truly out of control for the first time since Dave had met him.

'We just avoided a war, and that fucking idiot starts another one.'

The SEAL officer almost ripped the comm equipment off, but training and discipline got the better of him and he repeated himself in a calmer voice. He was still quivering with anger and stopped to fire two more bursts from his assault rifle but was no longer yelling.

'What happened, Heath?' Dave asked when the officer signed off.

Heath let go one long, bitter exhalation of breath.

'Compton,' he said. 'Compton did an end run around us. Plugged himself right into the command authority and got the green light for the gun run.'

Heath took up a firing position on the porch, sweeping the street with his rifle, taking head shots when he could. Beside him, Allen did the same thing after emptying his pockets of energy bars for Dave.

The whole street blazed and crackled with gunfire that was cutting into the surviving warriors of Urspite Scaroth's broken thrall and probably killing dozens of innocent civilians as the high-powered rounds passed through flimsy walls and open windows.

'Compton?' Dave asked dumbly. 'He can do that?'

Heath waved a hand despairingly at the street as if that answered the question.

'But I thought you were in charge here.'

Heath cracked off another double shot, knocking over an unleashed Fangr that was dashing to and fro like a rabid dog.

'I've never been in charge of anything but a couple of men on the ground, Dave. I don't make the big calls.'

'And that fucking moron does?' Dave exclaimed.

'No,' said Heath, 'but he's got the number of the morons who do.'

The gunships opened up again a couple of hundred yards away, lighting up the vacant lot through which the Horde had emerged into the world.

Three Cobras were working the kill zone now. Miniguns, rockets, and door gunners were churning up the field.

Heath listened to something over his headset again, acknowledged the transmission, and climbed slowly and painfully to his feet.

No. To his one good foot, Hooper thought.

'Chief, round up your squad and Ostermann's if you can. The hostiles have mostly broken and run for it. Back to the . . . the . . . what did they even come through, Dave? How did they get here?'

'No idea,' he said without emotion. 'Neither do they. But I

guess there's some sort of portal thing in that lot. And under the Longreach. And on the highway up to Area 51. And who the fuck knows where else now?'

Heath and Allen both stared at him.

'Chief,' the officer finally said, 'priority one right now is protecting the civilians. Sweep and clear the AO. Establish a perimeter with NOPD, then sweep and clear again. Casevac will need protecting when they roll in. There's sure to be stragglers here and there. And find me Ostermann. He's gonna have to run this. I need to get on the line and let the bosses know we're at war.'

Dave tried to stand up, but the world tilted on its axis and tipped him off into darkness.

The thresh did not think.

The thresh did not look back.

The thresh ran like a hunted urmin.

It ran through fire and steel, past warriors who did not know what to do. It sent out quickthinkings for them to follow, but their minds were shocked and unmoored by the fire of the men's captive metal Drakons.

It found the entrance to the UnderRealms and picked up the tempo, matching the speed of a Sliveen scout headed in the same direction. The thresh took some solace from that. The scout bore many scars and inked markings of skirmishes and battles below. None could doubt its proven courage, yet it outpaced the thresh on the race to escape this accursed realm.

The Sliveen's head exploded just as it raced past.

Quick panicked glances dagger- and shield-wise finally revealed black-clad human warriors wielding magick staffs.

They sent dark enchantments in the thresh's direction, condensed bolts of searing sunlight that crashed like thunder as they whipped past the thresh, impossibly faster than the swiftest arrowhead. Bodies and pieces of bodies were blown through the air every time the bolts touched the thrall.

Puffs of dirt and stone erupted around the thresh as it redoubled its gallop for the portal, churning up the filthy maelstrom of mud and ichor that had turned the small field where they entered this realm into a quagmire.

The thresh stumbled, and a young Hunn warrior changed course to offer help, only to be blown apart a few feet away. Gore splashed over the thresh just before another explosion covered it in soil. This whole world was an insane mandala of explosive violence in which the lives of individual nestlings and even grand storied BattleMasters were meaningless.

A cloud of smoke puffed from the ruined buildings on the thresh's shield flank as a single Fangr disintegrated in a ball of flame.

Thresh could hear its own voice wailing wild thinkings inside its head, shaken and terrified and somewhat disgusted with itself as it recalled the words of Her Majesty.

'This shall not stand. We shall not be mocked thus. Not by the likes of men.'

A Hunn zigzagging in front of the thresh lost his head to a long ropy ribbon of bolt fire licking out from the dark, foreboding tangle of the human village. The thresh was so close to the portal now. But even there the path was not clear as a solid crush of broken, terrified thrall-mates attempted to climb over one another to get away from the dire magicks of mankind.

Torn and blasted bodies of clan warriors and human

fighters lay entwined together in death. Almost promiscuously, until one could see that the nest lovers had bitten one another's throats out, torn their bellies, raked one another to offal.

The thresh slowed as it approached, not sure how to proceed. It could not scramble over the frenzied press of bodies at the portal mouth. It could not even crawl under them. But neither could it stand and wait while sun bolts and Drakon fire rained down.

It could only . . .

Some human wizard riding a metal Drakon solved the puzzle by throwing down one of the hissing, shrieking war bolts that exploded like small fire mountains, utterly destroying the crush of Hunn and Fangr at the portal mouth.

Seeing its chance, perhaps the only one it would get, the thresh raced forward, ignoring the smoking remains of the slain and the cries of its thrall-mates.

Once within, the thresh raced down into the passages, past the straggling survivors of the once proud Vengeance. It waited a few moments for others to come through after it. There surely had to be more. But reaching out for the thoughts of those still on the surface, the thresh found only silence.

No more were coming, the thresh realised.

Not a one of them.

Turning its back on the Above, the thresh began the journey back to Her Majesty to tell of the Dave, of his inexplicable familiarity with the lore of the Horde and his betrayal of that lore.

There could be only one answer to this, the thresh knew.

War.

EPILOGUE

She emerged through the mud and silt, past the breach in the barrier holding the UnderRealms apart from the Above. With powerful strokes she pushed and shoved and wriggled through rock and stone, holding her breath until she punched through into water. With emerald eyes open she saw the faintest hint of starlight above, filling her with a fervent hope that after ages of privation, she might have found her way back.

With the same powerful strokes she beat the water into a flurry, swimming up to the surface past startled fish and other creatures too small to feed on. She emerged in the steady current of a river and took a deep breath. Scents both wondrous and sublime tickled her memories of when she and her kind had soared above the mountains, above plains and forests. Memories of creatures from this realm came to her. The calflings and their feedstock.

From time to time in the past, they had been scarce and she had known hunger. Yet now her nostrils flared. It was as though they smelled the whole world. The air itself was a banquet of possibilities. She hammered at water and air, expanding her gas bladders, clawing her way up with puffs and snorts of fire jetting from her snout.

She broke the surface. Catching a thermal, the ancient Drakon lifted herself into the sky, giddy with the thrill of flight after so long in slumber beneath the crushing rock and the unmovable capstone. She climbed higher and higher, revelling in the freedom of unrestrained flight for the first time in unknowable ages. A few powerful beats of her stiff, aching wings and she was powering through the clouds, swooping and twirling, basking in the remembered joy of her hatchling time, when she had first learned to fly. Clouds and stars above rolled with her in a tumbling twirl.

She paused in her reveries.

Something was wrong.

Very wrong.

For night-time it was far too bright, she realised. Where was the heavy cloak of darkness that covered her approach to the fields and tiny homesteads of the prey?

There were strange sounds in the air. The growling of metal on metal and the mating call of untold numbers of creatures rang in her ears. An oily, nasty odour overlaid the sweet delicate scent of what lay beneath her wings.

Gliding in the direction of the coast, *dar Drakon* saw that the land beneath her was awash in light far more powerful than mere candles and burning torches. It was as though the land itself were burning. What wizardry was this?

Surveying the land below her with sharp emerald eyes, the dragon saw a brightly lit clearing of stonework.

Strange, but perhaps there would be answers, she decided.

She spied a creature she had never seen before. Some winged beast of magnificent ivory, silver, and blue glided across the masonry work, attended to by smaller grey hatchlings.

Their wings did not flap. They did not seem to exert

themselves in the slightest as they glided along.

A roar of unearthly power reached her ears.

A challenge! This strange Drakon must be the dominant of this region.

She had never abjured a challenge, not across the eons, and what tales would be told if she could best the new, strange creature.

She slipped into a power dive and launched herself at the creature's nest from out of the clouds, narrowing her wings and letting out as much of her gas as she dared. Soaring over treetops and fields, she could feel her speed increasing as the great white creature howled and began to climb into the air, attended by her hatchlings.

Stupid, *dar Drakon* thought, waiting for the blue-headed thing to turn its gaze toward the challenger. Such contempt and surety was unknown among even the most hardened of her kind. She would teach this creature a hard lesson about impudence.

Shiggurath Ur Drakon clicked her jaws together twice to ignite her remaining gas reserves and let the creature feel the heat of her challenge. Squirting a tight stream of fire through the night, she caught one of the hatchlings. The tiny thing's gas bladders exploded, singeing her scaly hide so badly that it alarmed her. Bits of bone pierced her wings, but she kept on until she caught the larger creature's head in her claws. She had timed her attack perfectly and sat astride the creature, as Gulyok Ur Drakon had mounted her to plant his seed in her belly so long ago.

The triumph was marred by Shiggurath's complete incomprehension about what to do next, however. Her claws dug into and punctured the skin of this beast, but it did not yield as flesh might. She raked at the exposed neck, just behind the animal's bulbous head. But the head never moved, and she gained no purchase on the vulnerable meat. It was passing strange. Indeed, the only thing to which she might compare the experience was a vague recollection of biting down on an armoured calfling in the far distant past.

The creature's attendant nestlings, unsurprisingly, were deeply disturbed by the attack and swooped around her, coming so close that the roar of their gas bladders all but deafened Shiggurath. They did not mount her as she mounted their mother, however, and tiring of trying to unravel the mystery, she opened her jaws wide and bit through the armoured hide of this odd, stiff Drakon.

Wind erupted from within the beast, carrying with it the dimly remembered scent of calfling meat. Cooking calfling meat.

Flames licked the wings of the Drakon foe and ran down its spine.

Shiggurath tore free a large strip of the creature's hide and tossed it back at one of the hatchlings that was flying behind her, possibly hoping to creep up and mount the old, wily Drakon when she was not paying it due heed.

But Shiggurath did not get to be an old and wily Drakon by falling for that sort of Fangr guano. The massive chunk of stiffened hide slammed into the pursuing nestling. To her surprise it exploded, as though all of its bladders had ruptured at once.

Decapitated and burning, the mother's death scream was short-lived as it plummeted back into the masonry work.

Shiggurath flipped in midair, landing on the masonry work with a cracking thud.

At the last possible instant before impact she had seen something.

A man. She was sure.

Inside the belly of this beast. It made no sense to her at all.

She rolled back onto her hind claws and examined herself. All around, the air was filled with strange howls and screams. Chariots rushed out in livery of yellow and red toward the slain creature, torchlights blinking and flickering in their mad dash across the stonework field. Shiggurath searched for a shank of meat or perhaps a wing that might have come from the collision, sniffed for the scent of rich blood.

The hide she found, jagged and sharp, was charred with flame. She picked it up, examined it, and tossed it aside.

Just armour. No meat at all, at least nothing worthy of the name.

High overhead the creature's remaining hatchlings screamed. She could see them fleeing through the clouds, off into the stars. Maybe they would go find her a worthy foe with some meat to its bones instead of the thin, curved armour shell that now lay burning in the wreckage. Confused and not a little frustrated, *dar Drakon* returned to tending her wounds, plucking bits of metal armour from her hide, gently playing the sting of her own fire to cauterise flesh and stop the bleeding.

Across the field, a line of chariots charged toward her.

The Hunn can't be here, she thought. Nor the Djinn or Morphum. She had surely found the break in the capstone first.

The chariots came on nonetheless, bouncing over grass and mud, gaining purchase on the stonework before plunging into the grass again. And then another shock. Men drove these beastless chariots, she saw now. Her stomach growled.

Dar Drakon leaped back into the air, mindless of her

wounds and hurts. She was not afeared of the little men, of course, but she preferred to come at them from above with fire. Climbing through the billowing smoke of her slain foe, she thrust her wings up and down again and again, building power, clawing up into the clouds, away from the lights of the strange stone field. Strange thoughts piled up in her mind, demanding her attention. Each memory was a gem, and a fastidious Drakon would sort them all into neat, orderly little piles, with the emeralds in one place, rubies in the next, silver ingots on the third level of the lair, while the gold, the sweet, soft, luxurious gold, always went to the bottom of the trove.

The creature she had slain was no animal of flesh and blood as she knew it. It seemed entirely crafted from metal and fabric and powered by magicks. She turned in mid-flight to find the two surviving hatchlings roaring up from behind, spitting fire at her. Her surprised offence soon turned to shock and even fear as a thousand burning stones tore through her wings, prompting her to loose her own fire too soon in a roar of pain. Balling up to evade the hatchlings, she dived through the clouds, looking to gain an advantage. An old master at the game of cloud cover, she was confident that the young hatchlings would grow bored and give up.

Such thoughts were proved for a falsehood when a large iron spike flared through the clouds. Her temper in check, she took a deep breath and blew her own fury back at the spike.

That should . . .

Dar Drakon fell through the night sky.

She fell down through the clouds, chased by a glowing hail of red-orange lightning.

She felt the cool air slip over her grievously wounded body, the cauldron within extinguished. Idly, without feeling as though it had anything to do with her, Shiggurath watched her own severed wing falling alongside her. Her belly ripped asunder, she could feel the black bile of her insides running out.

She was numb from snout to tail spikes. It was as though the hot rocks the nestlings had spat at her had severed her from all her feelings. Or maybe she was just stunned by the blow of the flying iron spike.

It had exploded right next to her.

Shiggurath had not expected that at all.

She felt lightheaded and, when she thought about it as she fell, a little melancholy. Songs would be sung of this day when *dar Drakonen* returned to the Above. Her name should be in those songs, but as she fell, such hopes dwindled with her slowing heartsbeat.

The hatchlings were near her now, circling in her death spiral. She caught sight of one of them.

Such power for creatures so small.

She chuckled darkly as the river below raced up to meet her.

Slain by such a tiny thing, she thought. Who would have thought it possible?

ACKNOWLEDGEMENTS

Who to thank first? *Dr Who*, I think. It drove me nuts as a kid that guns seemed to have no effect at all on monsters. Like, why did Brigadier Lethbridge-Stewart and UNIT even bother? The Dave Hooper series is an attempt, in part, to rectify that.

I'd also like to thank the producers of *Reign of Fire*, who annoyed me greatly with movie posters promising all sorts of dragon vs helicopter gunship awesomeness. And failed to deliver.

Less flippantly I have to thank my ur Champion publishers Cate Paterson, Tricia Narwani, Haylee Nash and the incomparable Alex Lloyd who all took up sword and shield with me on this long, strange quest.

To my wizardly agent, Russ ur Galen dar SGG, I offer tribute from the highest blood pot.

And for my armsman, SF Murphy, acknowledgement of his skill with blades and fire staff. His gurikh is second to none.

Finally, for my nestlings, Jane, Anna and Thomas . . . You are my Realm.

ABOUT THE AUTHOR

John Birmingham is the author of the cult classic *He Died With a Falafel in His Hand*; the award-winning history *Leviathan*; the Axis of Time series: *Weapons of Choice, Designated Targets* and *Final Impact*, and the *Stalin's Hammer: Rome* ebook; and the Disappearance trilogy: *Without Warning, After America* and *Angels of Vengeance*.

Between writing books he contributes to a wide range of newspapers and magazines on topics as diverse as the future of media and national security. Before becoming a writer he began his working life as a research officer with the Defence Department's Office of Special Clearances and Records.

You can find John at his blog, http://cheeseburgergothic. com and on Twitter @johnbirmingham. You can also buy his books at johnbirmingham.net.

Want to save the world? Join the conversation on Twitter at #TheDave.

DAVE vs. THE MONSTERS
ASCENDANCE

BY JOHN BIRMINGHAM

As a hardworking monster-slayer, Dave Hooper tries not to bring his work home with him. But nowadays it's hard to keep them separate. Email, cellphones, empath daemons, they never let a guy rest.

The Horde has been raising hell and leveling cities from New York to Los Angeles, keeping Dave and his fellow monster-killer, Russian spy Karin Varatschevsky, very busy. But when the legions of hell invade the small seaside town his boys call home, Dave has to make a call. Save the world? Or save his family?

Not as easy a choice as you'd think, since Dave's ex-wife expects to be saved too. And there's no convincing her that the supersexy Russian spy isn't his girlfriend. She's just his sidekick—and an assassin.

WITHOUT WARNING

BY JOHN BIRMINGHAM

March 14, 2003. In Kuwait, American forces are locked and loaded for the invasion of Iraq. In Paris, a covert agent is close to cracking a terrorist cell. And just north of the equator, a sailboat manned by a drug runner and a pirate is witness to the unspeakable.

In one instant, all around the world, everything will change. A wave of inexplicable energy slams into the continental United States. America as we know it vanishes. As certain corners of the globe erupt in celebration, others descend into chaos, and a new, soul-shattering reality is born.

AFTER AMERICA

BY JOHN BIRMINGHAM

On March 14, 2003, the world changed forever. A wave of energy slammed into North America and devastated the continent. The U.S. military, poised to invade Baghdad, was left without a commander in chief. Global order spiralled into chaos.

Now, while a skeleton U.S. government tries to reconstruct the nation, swarms of pirates and foreign militias plunder the lawless wasteland of the East Coast, where even the president is fair prey. With New York clutched in the grip of thousands of heavily armed predators, is an all-out attack on the city the only way to save it?

ANGELS OF VENGEANCE

BY JOHN BIRMINGHAM

When an inexplicable wave of energy slammed into North America, millions died. Around the globe, wars erupted, borders vanished and a new reality was born.

From shattered streets to gleaming new cities, three women are fighting wars of their own—for survival, justice and revenge. In South America, a special agent trails a ruthless terrorist, in Texas, a teenager vows to avenge a brutal murder and in Australia, a smuggler is hunted by unknown assassins. As a conflicted U.S. president struggles to make momentous decisions in the face of rebellion, the final battle for America and the new world begins.

For more fantastic fiction, author events, exclusive excerpts, competitions, limited editions and more:

VISIT OUR WEBSITE
titanbooks.com

LIKE US ON FACEBOOK
facebook.com/titanbooks

FOLLOW US ON TWITTER
@TitanBooks

EMAIL US
readerfeedback@titanemail.com